Celestine

"*Celestine* by Kevin St. Jarre is an emotional exploration of the passing of time, the impact of loss, and ultimately what matters most in a changing world."

—SHANA YOUNGDAHL,
author of *As Many Nows As I Can Get*

"Futuristic and yet incredibly relatable, Celestine's loneliness and confusion becomes what we connect with the most. St. Jarre's gripping writing and witty humour captures a sense of alienation that is familiar to any reader, no matter if they're an interstellar voyager or teenage girl in her senior year. *Celestine* turns the old and ordinary into the strange and unknown, invoking fresh starts and nostalgic curiosity within everyone."

—BRUNA GOMES,
author of *How to Disappear*

Celestine

KEVIN ST. JARRE

Encircle Publications
Farmington, Maine, U.S.A.

Book design and cover design by Deirdre Wait
Cover photographs © Getty Images

Published by:

Encircle Publications
PO Box 187
Farmington, ME 04938

http://encirclepub.com
info@encirclepub.com

Printed in U.S.A.

For my daughter, Sophia Dale.

I love you, Peanut.

Prologue

BY THE TIME WE RETURNED, the bodies of my parents had spent nearly a year in the storage compartment. They were next to the meat, and bagged like leftovers.

On the day we landed, the ship rose and fell with the waves. Designed for either solid ground or a liquid sea, we hadn't been entirely sure which would be the case. What we had been sure of was that we would never return home. We were wrong.

We few survivors didn't rush for the doors. We didn't scramble off. In fact, when our rescuers boarded, we were all sitting or lying on the deck. A nurse lay flat on her back and was screaming at the top of her lungs. I felt dazed. The surviving pilot sat on the floor, rocking. I was nearest the hatch, the one I had passed through only once, two years before. Smelling the salty sea air, I wondered, after the hell we'd been through, if we had made it back to Earth only to sink and drown in whatever ocean was out there.

When the door opened, I looked up and saw the first man, concealed in a white hazmat suit, with a gun in his hand. Our rescuers came prepared to defend themselves from us. He stopped and looked down at me; I saw his shoulders fall. He holstered his weapon and asked, "Can you confirm that this is the *Phaeacia*?"

Was he fucking serious? I stared up at him and nodded.

"So, you're confirming that we are aboard the *Phaeacia*?" he asked.

I glanced around. It was shadowy, the nurse's screaming

echoed off the hard surfaces, there were people scattered about in little mounds, and lights on panels glowed. In between the screams, when she took a breath, I could hear the hiss of an unseen radio. I held up my hand, and said, "This is the *Phaeacia*."

He stepped past me, and a second man, dressed like the first but without the gun and holster, came to me. He looked down, began to kneel but then stood again before his knee could touch the floor. "Can you walk?" he asked.

I just wanted out. We'd been trapped aboard for years, trapped with an unseen killer. It was swift, invisible, still unidentified, and merciless. Entire families had disappeared into body bags. People had died horribly, some with grace, but most without. Imprisoned with fewer and fewer survivors, we had little hope, as we hurtled back toward Earth.

"Can you hear me?" he asked.

I looked past him, out the door, and up at the sky. It was so incredibly blue. I hadn't seen a clear blue sky in so long. My mom wouldn't get to see it. I looked back toward the infirmary, and then toward the galley, where my parents were in the refrigerated compartment.

The man bent over, his head quite close to mine. I could see his glasses inside his hazmat hood.

Was all this happening? Did we actually land? Were my parents truly dead? Was I really alive? Looking up at the man, I wondered if he were real. Falling forward, I slapped the hard, cool floor. I pounded on it and then sat up. The nurse screamed again. I bit my wrist, hard, as she kept screaming. Putting my forehead to the floor, I pulled my own hair.

"Can you walk?" he asked again. "Are you sick? Who are you? Are you Celestine Tolland?"

1

I WAS CELESTINE TOLLAND. I *AM* Celestine Tolland, I thought. Nauseated, both from the motion of the sea and from the enormity of what was happening, I looked over at the nurse as she continued to scream. A man in a white hazmat suit stood over her, shouting questions at her each time she drew a breath.

My own voice came first as a whimper, with no tears, just a strange sound from deep in my throat. More and more people were coming in—each dressed as the first man was. Those in protective clothing were moving around and shouting the same questions. I began rocking in time with the pilot, trembling all over, and I softly echoed the nurse's screams, moaning in harmony with her. My cry didn't only grow stronger and louder, but it was as if it were increasing in physical size, like a kernel of sound had expanded into a fist of pain in my throat. The moan became a wail, and then a cry of rage and agony so fierce that the closest rescuer backed away. I raised my fists toward the blue sky and screamed out the door, with no words, but with everything I had to say, until my lungs were completely emptied.

The ship felt charged with sorrow and fear, and I wanted to be full of hope like we were on launch day. When we first took off from Earth, we were filled with a sense of destiny. Nervous, yes, but we felt chosen, as if we were meant for great things.

In addition to my parents and me, there were twenty other people aboard when we lifted off, although, as we left the surface I could only see my parents and, off to my left, the feet of Barbara Stenhouse, the wife of the mission leader. As we roared into space, my body weighed three times what it normally weighs. My legs weighed seventy-five pounds each, and my head weighed thirty-five pounds. In a few seconds I had gone from my normal weight to 450 pounds. I screamed then too, but I couldn't hear my own voice inside my helmet. The engines shook the entire ship, and we were thrown skyward. I thought, in that moment, that it would be the most helpless I would ever feel. It wouldn't be long before I realized that wasn't true.

A few months into our flight, the first of us to get sick were two strong men. The illness killed so quickly, we felt like the first victims were gone before we even considered that they might die. By the time we decided to abort the mission, there were sixteen of us left. After making the necessary calculations and getting the ship turned back for home, it took nearly three days just to reverse course, there were only eleven of us. No one laughed any more, because it seemed so gross and out of place. After the dying started, the only laughter I had heard was when a technician learned he was going to die and join his dead wife. It'd been like a madman cackling in a creepy movie.

Other than that, there was no laughing, and my tears dried up too. They seemed locked away, as if one more tear would kill me. My mother used to hold me when I cried, even when I was a teenager, and crying felt like a cleansing thing. Without her, tears felt like the ice that I'd slide on, into a deep, dark hole.

Only six of us lived long enough to land. I glanced around at the other five. The nurse who had tried to save so many, who treated the sick as if they were family, was still unloading all the horror she had bottled up, screaming, when two men pulled her to a seated position.

They carried me out of the ship on a stretcher, and that first breath outside I took was like being newly inflated. The ship had taken air we'd breathed time and time again, scrubbed it clean, and given it back to us; it seemed to exhale on us from the scrubber-vents. Early on, I believed in the filters, and thought the air was as good as new. As people got sick and died, we became more and more paranoid and didn't trust anything. We suspected the first victims had been exposed to something, and we searched for it. Then, when more and more people became sick, we thought maybe it was the food, or maybe the water. We next thought the bathing facilities were contaminated, and then the air filtration system. I think we would've been worried about the air system earlier if we'd known a way to do without it, or even some way to change it. You really don't want to think that your only source of air is killing you. When an engineer's wife, afraid of the air, donned a full spacesuit breathing only air from tanks that had never been filtered, we watched and waited. When she became sick inside the suit, we couldn't convince her to remove the helmet and she died weeping, still wearing it.

Although the medical personnel on board assured us it was viral, we began to fear all chemicals. As a group we believed that anything that smelled like glue or cleaner or fuel was deadly and terrifying.

Finally, we began to suspect someone aboard was secretly killing us—a theory we didn't give up on until we had a series of suspects who became sick and died themselves. The fear only faded after the hope did. Courage is made of hope, but fear can't exist without it either. When the last of our hope had gone, and we had all accepted that we were probably going to die, the constant dread became more like an ache rather than a sharp pain.

We stopped thinking, we stopped hoping, and we sat in our fear and breathed the filtered breath of others, including so many last breaths. We stayed like that until we landed.

When I had come through the hatch and into the sunlight, I was completely enveloped by the blueness of the cloudless sky. I suddenly realized that I was being separated not just from the ship, but also from the other survivors and the bodies of my parents.

"Wait!" I said.

No one listened. The men holding the ends of my stretcher didn't even look down at me. We moved off the gangway and onto a small boat, and they lay me on the deck. In the distance,

I could see a much larger ship, like from the navy or something. There was nothing comforting or familiar about it. I looked back at the *Phaeacia*. Her outer hull wasn't shiny like it was when I first saw her, but instead she was scorched, with streaks of blue and yellow. For all the horror, she looked safe to me. I knew the faces inside, and the confined space. Thrown suddenly into the vastness of the outdoors on a shoreless ocean, I felt like I was in danger of falling upwards.

Watching and waiting, I hoped to see another survivor come out, but I didn't. The small launch I was on motored away and headed for the ship. Trying to crane my head back enough to see someone come out, I saw no one, and I panicked. I was sure they were going to sink the *Phaeacia* with everyone, and my parents, aboard.

"Stop! Don't let them do it! Get them off!" I said.

A woman in a uniform with huge eyes knelt beside me and said, "Be quiet now." She patted my chest.

I said, "No!"

"We're almost to the ship. You can get a hot shower, some food, and sleep in a nice clean rack," she said.

I pushed her hand away.

She dropped on me, pinning me down, and looked at someone and nodded. He walked over, knelt, and without saying a word, injected something into my hip. As I flinched, he withdrew the needle and nodded at the woman. She turned to me and said, "There, you rest now. Just rest."

The injection worked quickly and my body grew heavier. My face felt slack. I didn't fall asleep, but my limbs became impossible to move.

The next images were of bright lights and doctors, first in their own hazmat suits, and then in simple surgical masks. Their voices were metallic, as if speaking inside soda cans, and I could understand less and less. They poked me with fingers and needles, turning and lifting me, scanning me with eyes and machinery. I was terrified, but couldn't resist. Instead, I retreated into myself and hid.

I felt myself pulling away from everything that was happening to my body and creating a new safe space. Finite and solid, I was in a new capsule. My legs retracted into my new internal sanctuary like pulling them out of a pair of pants, and my arms came out of the sleeves of reality. I turned myself into a hardened ball inside the cocoon of my own head.

2

ON THE DAY OF MY first clear memory of being in the hospital, the morning began with the sensation that I was completely disconnected from my body and watching the world swirl around me. Not questioning where I was, who these people were, or what was coming next, I was profoundly confused and wondered if I were dead.

Did I have to breathe consciously and why couldn't I tell where my fingers ended? My heart pounded in my ears and was taking too long to fall silent. The bed sheets were heavy. The whole hospital seemed to be sliding downhill, slowly, to my right, giving the sensation of free-falling into a strange place. Terrified, I held onto the bed, with that feeling a passenger has when they're in an out-of-control car waiting for the big crash, but it didn't come, and my anxiety only got worse.

The room smelled like cleanser and week-old bedding. My mouth was pasty and tasted like plastic. Looking straight up, I noticed the ceiling was only a bit whiter than the wall behind me. A whiteboard was covered in multicolored marker, written over older writing hastily erased, but I couldn't decipher any of it. Was it all about me? Feeling like the room was constructed of frightening secrets, I couldn't put it all together. There was a privacy curtain around my bed, but it was pulled wide open.

Gripping the cool metal railings, I watched a woman come in and speak to me, her words incomprehensible. Her face seemed cruel, her mouth was hidden by her mask, and her eyes looked wild. Repeating herself, louder this time, she touched the sheet. I kicked her hand.

As she extended both arms toward me, her voice was low as if casting a spell. Kicking both of my feet now, I couldn't reach her. She called back over her shoulder and it was only then that I realized the entire wall between my room and the hallway was made of glass, as if I were in a terrarium.

Showing me her palms and growling, the woman's head rocked up and down as she stepped closer. Scanning the room, I saw nothing to defend myself with. When she came too close I slapped at her face, but hit her shoulder. Lunging at me and pressing my shoulders into the bed, she felt like she weighed 500 pounds. Convinced she wanted to kill me, I shrieked and kicked, but just couldn't budge her. Howling over her shoulder she looked like a demon, and then there were shadows moving beyond the glass.

When her forearm brushed my chin, I bit into it as hard as I could. Roaring at me, she let my shoulders go. I could taste her blood. She screamed in pain as she slapped me with her free hand. She smacked me repeatedly until I finally released her, but I instantly felt a new wave of fear and snatched two fistfuls of her hair. I pulled down on her head as hard as I could, her whole body followed, and I was suddenly pinned to the bed beneath all of her.

With my fingers still locked in her hair, she turned her face up to mine; it was twisted with rage, or fear, maybe both. I wanted her to be afraid. Watching the sickness aboard the *Phaeacia* stalk and kill us, sometimes taking two at a time, we felt so helpless because there was no shape to see, and no form to fight back against. It had been an invisible monster moving through the ship.

However, my struggle with the nurse was with a flesh-and-blood opponent. She was yelling and punching, but I wasn't powerless this time, and yanked her hair and head from side-to-side with all the strength I could muster.

With her weight on me, it was hard to breathe and I was tiring, but I was still winning until a large man in pink scrubs, but no mask, appeared. There was nothing about him that looked afraid as he grabbed my wrists in his rock-hard grip; he squeezed so hard that my hands popped open and the nurse climbed off me. Kicking both legs at the man, my knee hit his ribs with all the force I had left, but it had no effect.

Feeling powerful went away, and my strength left with it. Helpless again, I was at the mercy of someone or something else. Losing the sense that at least the space I occupied was my own left me devastated. Worse than never having felt it, was having that feeling of control, briefly, only to lose it again. Overwhelming sadness came rushing back.

The man in pink didn't make a sound and held my wrists until the nurse stuck a needle into my hip. Feeling feeble and so alone, I wanted to be with the other survivors and, most of all, my parents.

I wished things could be as they were when my parents handled the toughest decisions and when responsibility for my safety was mostly theirs; I missed them so much. I wanted to be a little girl again and to have my mom tuck me in to bed, and to feel like I did when she wrapped a big, fluffy towel around me after a bath, or when my dad lifted me off the ice when I fell skating. I wanted to feel like I did when I could go to sleep while someone who loved me would be awake and watching over me.

Instead, I was losing consciousness against my will, while my enemies stood over me; the nurse, rubbing her head, scowled at me. The man in pink was still holding my wrists as I succumbed to the drugs, and the last thing I saw was his face, with no trace of kindness or even interest. His expression didn't contain the slightest sign of compassion or contempt, and instead he only stood there, holding my wrists as I slipped into what felt like nothingness.

3

WAKING UP BOUND TO THE bed, with soft but secure loops around my wrists and ankles, I saw that the whiteboard read, "March 11," but there was no year. With a sheet pulled nearly to my chin, an IV tube snaked down into my arm. Deep sadness and fear gripped me; having not spent any time alone in so long, the isolation was overwhelming. Pulling hard at the restraints, I couldn't budge them. With my arms held at my sides and my legs held slightly spread open, I felt extremely vulnerable; a layer of thin cotton was my only protection. For all those terrifying months on the ship, I would curl up into a ball and try to hide inside my head, but now I couldn't. Tugging and then thrashing at the restraints, I wasn't able to loosen them at all and I screamed.

Outside my glass wall, people appeared, and then rushed into my room. One woman grabbed my IV stand, and the others put their hands all over me. Bucking my hips upwards again and again, I couldn't get loose. They all stayed out of reach of my teeth.

"Stop!" I said.

Avoiding eye contact, none of them addressed me directly. One nurse said, "Is her catheter still in?"

The sheet was ripped away, and my gown was pulled up, exposing me to all of them. Shrieking, I was terrified.

Another nurse said, "Let's sedate her first. We can't do anything with her like this."

One of them injected something into my IV, and the effect

was nearly immediate. I wanted to keep fighting but my body wouldn't respond. Still, even through the fog of the drug I was aware that I was still exposed, and unable to resist. It seemed like forever before one of them pulled my gown down again, and the sheet came back up.

"I don't know how many times we'll have to sedate this kid," one said.

I felt myself drifting and losing consciousness again.

4

THE DATE ON THE WHITEBOARD was March 13. When the nurse came into my room, she did not hurry, and I did not fight the restraints that still held me tight. Quietly, while there were no tears, I whimpered, faint sounds of grief, fear, and frustration.

She said, "Celestine, everything is going to be alright." She attempted to move hair from my face, but I turned my head away from her. She reached farther, and brushed my hair back. She placed a cool damp cloth on my face, and then gently rubbed it across my forehead, back across my hairline.

I paused for a moment, breathing heavy, comforted a bit in spite of myself.

"That's it. It's going to be fine. We'll help you," she said.

My eyes closed. In that moment, I was so scared and exhausted that I almost surrendered to her, to them. Maybe I could just turn it all over, let other people worry about everything. I could feel myself ready to let it all slide, but then, as if waking just in time, my protective walls went flying back up. I didn't want her help; I only wanted out. She dabbed the cool cloth on my cheek and I recoiled away from it, as far as the restraints would allow. She tried again, and I whined, and pulled at the restraints.

"Doesn't it feel good?" she asked.

"No," I said, my eyes shut tight.

"You sure?" she said, pulling the cloth away.

I nodded, and froze.

"Okay. I'll let you sleep some more," she said, rising, and she left.

5

WHEN I WOKE, I WAS still in the restraints, and the date was March 14. Looking out through the glass wall, there was a woman in the distance.

"Nurse," I called. My throat was so dry, and my lips cracked.

She lifted her head and looked my way. Nodding, she spoke to someone I couldn't see. The man in the pink scrubs appeared, and the two of them came into my room. Neither were wearing masks, and I couldn't remember when they had stopped doing that.

"Water?" I asked.

"Of course," she said. Her nametag read, "Gemma R."

I had so many questions. *Where were the other survivors? Where was I?*

She raised the bed so that I was sitting nearly upright, and adjusted the sheet over me. She retrieved a pitcher and a cup, and poured me some water.

As I was drinking, she said, "Go slow."

Pulling my mouth from the cup, I lay my head back against the pillow. *Are the other survivors in this hospital too?* I'd have felt so much less lonely if I had known even one of them was in the same building, but I couldn't make myself ask. I didn't want to engage with anyone outside of my internal cocoon of safety. She and the pink man checked my restraints.

"My parents?" I asked.

The pink man said, "They didn't make it."

The nurse, Gemma, froze and stared at him.

"I know they didn't make it, asshole, I was there," I said. "Where are they now?"

The pink man didn't say anything else and left the room. The nurse said, "Sweetie, I honestly don't know where they are right now."

"Who would know?" I asked. "Can't I even know where my parents are?"

"You need to rest," she said, lowering the bed once more.

I moaned, a soft and sad sound. She put her hand on mine, just below the restraint, and said, "We're trying to make you better, and we don't want to rush things. You've been through so much. Just trust us."

She turned and left me alone, heartbroken, and frustrated. There was a small crack in the ceiling near the wall, and I could see the brushstrokes in the paint. Staring, I remembered the survivors, and my fear lay like a pillow over my face. Trying to breath through it, fighting panic, I had so many questions. *Was I sick and they were hiding it? Were they trying to heal me, or was I a lab rat?* One thing I was sure of was, if they untied me, I'd get the hell out of there.

· · ·

March 15. Jerking at my wrists, I couldn't get loose.

"Maybe those can come off today. It's up to the doctor," the nurse said. "Do you remember why you've been in restraints?"

"Fighting," I said. I looked at the pink man; he neither said anything nor even nodded.

"That's right, so we want to make sure it's safe for us and you. We've been giving you medication to help steady you, to help you through your adjustment. It's part of a longer process of dialing in the correct dosages, which could take months," she said.

I won't be in here for months, will I? Feeling despair, I pulled at the restraints.

"The doctor will be here within the hour," she said.

"Could I get drink, please?" I asked.

She poured and lifted the cup to my mouth, and I drank more of the plastic-scented water.

"There you go," she said. She pulled the corner of the sheet, revealing my left arm and the IV line. She placed a call button in my hand and said, "If you need anything, just ring." She glanced at the pink man, and they both left.

Strapped to the bed, I could do nothing but obsess about being tied down, or worse—think. Trying my best to piece together my memories since the *Phaeacia* landed, they were muddled and jumbled. Through the glass wall, I could see busy adults, all strangers, walking back and forth, or typing at monitors.

There was natural light coming in from behind me, but I couldn't look out. There was little in my room other than some towels, sheets, and tissues. With no way to see what was in the drawers and cabinets, I couldn't locate a single object that was loose, hard, and heavy.

Pulling at the restraints again, I was careful not to make any noise. Still just as impatient to be free, I tried to appear calm. The minutes ticked by much too slowly. Those people didn't understand that while waiting, I was trapped not only in my bed, but also in my head. I was caught in memories of losing my parents and the others, how each person's death scene had been unique, and how they had been less individuals in their living than they had been in their dying.

The pilot, Greg McCormack, had died praying. He had only paused long enough to tell his co-pilot wife that he loved her, and he was convinced that she would survive. I wondered if she, too, were bound to a hospital bed somewhere, but I bet she was a lot tougher to tie down than I had been.

When the doctor finally came in, I could barely contain myself. He was tall and thin, with short hair. He said, "Hi Celestine, I'm Dr. Schilz."

Nodding, I immediately asked, "Can we take these off?"

"How are you feeling?" Dr. Schilz asked.

"I feel good," I said. "Calm." My insides were churning.

He sat on the edge of the bed, and I pulled away a bit. He asked, "Physically? No pain? Dizziness? Nausea?"

I shook my head.

"And emotionally?" he asked.

"Good," I said. *Actually, I'm so confused. No one's even told me what year this is.*

"Do you have feelings of anger or rage at all?" he asked.

"No," I asked.

"We are putting a support plan in place for you which will include someone to talk to, but for now, we are treating your body mostly. We promise to do our best to help you make sense of, or at least achieve some sort peace with, everything you've been through and adjusting to your new life. Information such as what year it is, news of the outside world, new technology… we're going to have to manage that information as we feel you're ready for it. Believe me, we're not withholding anything just to mess with you. There's a plan in place, and a phased approach to this. We're doing our best to take care of you," he said. He shined a light in first my right eye, and then my left. He placed a stethoscope on my upper chest, moved it, listened again, and then smiled. He said, "You can talk to us, you know. You can share how you're feeling."

I nodded, trying to appear peaceful. I'm sure he heard my heart racing, but I didn't have any tension on the restraints at all, and it took all the patience and strength I had to stay so still.

He seemed to pause a moment before saying, "If you promise to behave, we can try taking these off."

"Yes," I said, trying to smile.

Nodding, he said, "I'll send Ruthie in."

"Okay," I said.

Dr. Schilz left without another word and soon, the giant man in pink arrived and began undoing my restraints.

I asked, "You're Ruthie?"

"Yeah, what of it?"

"Nothing," I said.

Once my wrists and ankles were free, he left without looking back. As he walked away, I rubbed my wrists. I glanced through the glass wall and shifted my weight; my ass was sore from lying in the same position for so long.

Looking under the sheet, I pulled my gown up a bit. There was a clear, plastic tube running right into my groin. It was light yellow—filled with pee. Checking again, I could see one nurse typing something at the counter, but no one else.

Wrapping my fingers around the tube and clenching my teeth, I gave it a tug and was relieved that it came out painlessly, although I did get some pee on the bed and me.

Peeling back the tape on my arm, I yanked the IV out, and that did hurt a bit. My arm was bruised, as were the backs of my hands. Scanning through the glass, nothing had changed, except that I was free.

Despite the adrenaline rushing through me, I lay there a moment. Although I had no idea what floor I was on, I had heard the elevator many times. My only plan was to find that elevator.

Watching the nurse at the counter, I eased my feet toward the floor. My back and legs were stiff, and the tiles were cool under my toes. As I slowly got out of bed, my gown flapped open in the back, but I really didn't give a shit. If I could get out of this hospital, I'd be just fine with running bare-assed down the road. Slowly making my way to the door of my room, the nurse looked up and saw me just as I got there.

"Hey!" she yelled.

Taking off down the hallway as fast as my stiff legs would carry me, I passed a patient walking with an IV pole.

"Stop!" the nurse called behind me.

Finding the elevators, I hit the "down" button. The nurse was coming. *C'mon, c'mon!* Pressing a couple more times, I glimpsed the door to the stairs, but then the elevator opened. Jumping in, I selected the ground floor and then repeatedly tried to close the doors. Just as they began to move, the nurse's arm came into the elevator, and the doors immediately re-opened.

Screaming, I pushed her hard. She staggered back a bit, but grabbed hold of my gown as she went. The strings at the middle of my back let go, but at my neck they held fast and burned me. Completely exposed to people in the hallway, and caught around the neck, I fought to pull the gown loose from her grip.

The man in pink then suddenly appeared, and wrapped his arms around me, lifting me off the floor and pinning my arms at my sides. Kicking, I tried to fight back, but couldn't. Wanting to resist but unable, I fell limp. No sedative this time; I just had nothing left and my spirit was crushed. I was so sad, so alone, and the little spark of hope I'd had was gone. He carried me back to my room, where the doctor was waiting.

Dr. Schilz said, "Place her on the bed."

"Want the restraints again?" a nurse asked.

Softly, I said, "Please no."

Dr. Schilz looked at me. With my hands on my chest, I lay frozen in place.

"You know, you could've really hurt yourself, running like that," Dr. Schilz said.

"Restraints?" the nurse asked again.

Dr. Schilz nodded, and when they moved to tie me down, he didn't help them.

"No," I said again, but with no fight left in me and too many of them anyway, and I was soon secured to the bed.

Dr. Schilz said, "I'll come see you tomorrow, and we'll have a talk."

Looking at him, I asked, "What do you want from me?"

"We'll talk about that tomorrow," he said.

I hesitated, but then asked, "Where are the other survivors?"

He stepped a bit closer, as the others stepped away. He said, "You are all being cared for in major medical centers around the country."

"Why are we separated?" I asked.

"Nothing insidious. We've tried to locate you in the regions of the country you each called home, with the hope that the transitions would be easier, there might be potential family in the area, and any post-release outpatient care wouldn't require air travel. I haven't spoken directly with any of their physicians, but I am told you are all doing fairly well in light of your ordeal," he said.

"Am I in Maine then?" I asked.

"Not too far, but Celestine, that's enough for one day, don't you think?" he asked. "Get some rest, and we'll talk tomorrow."

Turning to leave, he let everyone exit before he did. On the other side of the glass wall, he spoke to the nurse, who peered back in at me and nodded. When Dr. Schilz left, she came and reinserted my IV.

"Just ring for me and I'll help you with the bedpan," she said. Returning to her seat at the counter, she looked in at me every few minutes.

• • •

The next day, Dr. Schilz came in by himself. He said, "Good morning. How are we today?"

"Good," I said. I pulled a bit at the restraint around my left ankle.

Sitting on the edge of the bed, he folded his hands in his lap. "Yesterday, you made a mistake. We're really here to help you."

I nodded.

He paused, looked up at the whiteboard. He said, "Let's try it again, but Celestine, don't even go to the toilet without ringing for assistance, okay? If you get up again without asking for help, I will order the restraints be reapplied."

I tried to smile, and said, "Okay."

"Alright," he said, and brushed some hair from my face. He paused, and then said, "Celestine, we need your help," he said.

"What do you mean?" I asked.

"We need you to help us understand what happened aboard the *Phaeacia*. So, we've set up a schedule of meetings, called debriefings, after which we'll begin a plan of evaluation and treatment that will eventually lead to you going home," he said.

Going home. There was really no home to go to. My home had been two people I'd last seen in body bags, and no one would tell me where they were.

"So, I have to talk about what happened?" I hated the idea. It was a terrible idea. They wanted me to relive the time I spent on the *Phaeacia*? Were they crazy? "I want to forget."

"We need to know what happened, and how best to help you

survivors. All of the others have agreed already," he said.

"I don't want to do this," I said.

"I thought we were getting along now," he said. His face wasn't quite as friendly, and I understood that he was going to leave me restrained if I said I wouldn't cooperate. He was trying to make me feel like I owed him. I pulled at the restraint on my left wrist.

"Don't get excited. Stay calm," he said. "You have to stay calm."

That was a threat. All he had to do was say I was out of control or even too excited and I'd be stuck in these restraints for another day or more. Taking a deep breath, I pulled myself together, and asked, "When would this start?"

Smiling, he stood and unfastened the restraints. The nurse on the other side of the glass wall stood up and watched. He said, "In the next day or two. Until then, try and rest."

Lying there, my mind raced, but I couldn't come up with a way out. Maybe I could have lied to them and pretended I didn't remember anything, but the problem was I did. When they asked me questions and I recalled what had happened, I was sure it would be written all over my face.

6

ON MARCH 15, THE NURSE named Gemma came into my room carrying a tray. Having just finished lunch, I was curious. When she set it down, I saw there was a single bowl of chocolate ice cream on it.

"I thought you might like a treat," she said, smiling. "It's really pretty good," she said, raising my bed. "Now that your hands are free, and you can feed yourself."

What are you up to? I looked at the ice cream. *They don't need to poison my dessert; they could inject anything they wanted into my IV drip. Why the babying? Am I dying?*

"Go ahead and try it," she said.

Lifting the spoon, I took a bite. It was incredibly sweet, but good.

"How is it?" she asked, smiling.

I shrugged, and slowly took another bite.

Pulling a brush from her pocket, she asked, "Want me to work on your hair a bit?"

I shrugged again. She moved behind me and began pulling the brush through my hair, working it straight back while I ate ice cream, and it felt really good.

"Someday soon, you'll be out of here, you can have your hair done by a professional, put on something cute," the nurse said. "You're really pretty."

I hadn't felt pretty in a long time.

Emptying the dish of ice cream at about the same time she finished brushing my hair, I watched her walk over to a shelf, return with a small mirror, and hold it up for me to see. My hair was brushed out, but a bit oily, and in serious need of a cut.

"What do you think?" she asked.

Nodding, I said, "Thanks."

"Okay, good, let me get that tray. I'll see you later," she said, seeming happy with herself, and she left. That was nice, but after she left, I was still in a strange hospital with more questions than answers. I wanted to go home and hear birds, smell the ocean, and feel snow or rain falling onto my face.

7

REMEMBERING MY DAD WAS DIFFERENT than remembering my mom. I was closer to my mom, and I could tell her anything. Even though we had argued more in the years before the flight, especially as I got into middle school, I still thought she was cool. We would go shopping, or to see a movie. My mom was the one who would take me to the doctor, or for a haircut. We would talk about deep things, too, and she was starting to seem like a real person to me. My mom had even let slip once that she wished she'd had one more child, maybe a boy.

Remembering my dad was not the same. It was just as warm, but instead of many little memories, like my mom and I teasing each other about what food we liked, I seemed to associate my dad with larger events like going to a museum, dancing at a cousin's wedding, or camping at the lake. Somehow, I still had him on a pedestal, like a hero, but the truth was, I had no sense of who he really was. Not even watching him die had revealed that. Instead of the intimate friend my mom was becoming, my dad, although I loved him very much, was more like a tour guide for major life events. Knowing that I'd never know him the way I knew my mom, and missing them both, left me heartbroken. It made me horribly depressed.

A young man came into my room then, and walked past my bed without saying a word. Not recognizing him, I asked, "Nurse?"

Without answering, he walked out, and returned with a

cart of spray bottles and paper towels. He stepped into my bathroom, and I could hear him spraying and wiping.

What a jerk. Maybe he hates his job; it can't be fun. Still, he didn't have to be rude.

He came out, and placed the spray bottle back on the cart, dropped the used paper towels in a can, and then emptied the wastepaper basket in that can as well.

"Thanks," I said.

Nothing.

"Hey!" I said. *What the hell? Is this guy deaf?*

He suddenly looked my way, and saw me staring at him with my hands up in frustration. He stood straight, smiled, and hurried over to me. There was something pinned to his shirt, and he thrust it forward. It read, "I'm hard of hearing. Place face me when speaking."

I really am an asshole. "You read lips?" I asked.

Nodding, he signed something. I said, "I don't understand."

Pulling a pad of paper and the stub of a pencil from his pocket, he wrote, "Do you need anything?" and then watched my mouth.

"No, thanks," I said. "Sorry, I thought you could hear me."

He wrote, "No problem. Happens all the time."

"Tough job, housekeeping," I said.

He wrote, "I'm in environmental services." His face was stern.

Agh, I screwed up again. I suck.

Then he smiled suddenly, and quietly laughed.

I smiled. "You got me."

"Nice smile," he wrote.

I nodded a thank you, and then both of our smiles faded.

He wrote, "Have a nice day."

"Thanks," I said, but it made me instantly sad again. *I won't have a nice day. I'm trapped, and I'm dreading talking about everything that happened. I miss my parents. I have no one, and no real hope.*

He put the pad away, waved, sort of bowed slightly, and left with his cart. I watched for him after that, but never saw him again. When I asked about him, no one seemed to know who he was.

It scared me that I might have imagined him. The only thing I had left was the "me" inside my head, and I thought I might be losing that too. *I mean, what's the point anyway? Why am I even here?*

8

MARCH 17 AND THE MEETINGS had not yet begun. In anticipation, I spent all my time thinking about what I didn't want to remember. The sounds of grief, the smell of vomit, and the images of clear plastic sheets that the dying pressed their hands up against, hoping to feel some sort of human contact pushing back. Visions of parents preventing medical specialists from taking their kids to the infirmary, as if going with the medical crew was what was killing people.

Getting up, I glanced out through my glass wall and saw the nurse was watching me, but she didn't say anything, or motion for me to return to bed. Out my window, there was a brick wall that rose high, and far off to both sides. Unable to see around it, there was a bit of blue sky visible above, and many stories below sat a white van.

The ledge outside my window didn't lead anywhere, but I thought it might serve if a person wanted only to go down. Convinced they were never going to let me out of there, and rather than relive the time on the *Phaeacia* point by point, why not just let myself drop? My tummy fluttered as I imagined being in complete control of my fate again. The window had a little lock and when I flipped it, the nurse didn't notice.

Thinking that in one fluid motion I could throw the window open, jump out, and that would be that, I yanked upward. It moved, but only by two inches. Pulling hard, I couldn't lift it any higher. At the top of the window, there was a bar bolted into place, limiting how high the window might open.

"What are you doing?"

I turned around and the nurse was in my room.

Looking up at that bar again, I said, "Just trying to get a little fresh air in here."

Chuckling, she said, "It won't be that fresh. The loading dock is down there," and she turned and walked out.

Pushing the window closed, I watched a man cross the space below and realized how close I had come. Staring for a moment, I felt a surge of shame, but I was also grateful that the window hadn't opened wider. So many aboard the *Phaeacia* had died, while I lived, and my survivor's guilt was now much worse. Lying down in my bed, I pulled the pillow over my head, and tried to push some of the faces out of my mind for a while.

· · ·

The next morning, for the first time since returning, I had pancakes, with real syrup, from real maple trees. I decided that if I ever got out of the hospital, I would go hug a maple tree.

A nurse with a nametag that read "Meghan A" came into my room to get my syrupy plate and tray.

"You have to go to your meeting today," she said.

"Today?" A knot formed in my stomach.

"Some people want to talk to you," she said.

"Dr. Schilz?" I asked. I hadn't seen him in a couple days.

"Not sure. I suppose part of your recovery plan," she said.

Knowing it was the debriefings, and that they would drag me through my memories of the ship, I asked, "Why do I have to go to them, instead of them coming to my room?"

"Why didn't you eat your Cream of Wheat?" she asked.

"Because they still haven't found a way to make it taste good," I said. As nonchalantly as I could, trying to hide my anxiety, I asked, "Okay, honestly, what year is this again?"

"Uh uh, you won't trick me, missy. You know we're not allowed to discuss time or dates or space with you," she said, with a bit of a smile.

Not liking that she had called me "missy," since I had turned seventeen a couple weeks before, I was still painfully aware that I was the only "child" aboard the *Phaeacia* to survive. The sadness-wave washed through me again, and joined with the worry. Always hurting, the anguish rose and fell to and from the front of my consciousness, and I was desperate for distractions. I looked up to where my television should have been, but instead there was only an empty mount.

A lot of years had gone by since we left, but we had no way of calculating exactly how many. During the two years on board the *Phaeacia*, because we traveled at nearly the speed of light, time on Earth had passed much more quickly than it had on the ship. MCGS we called it, which stood for "moving clocks go slower." That always made more sense to me than time dilation or whatever. We were able to estimate that somewhere between 20 and 45 years might have passed, but none of the physicists had survived. The pilot, the biologist, and the nurse had done their best with the math, but variables kept changing as well, and the reversal of our course had been a lot like drifting in a car, trying to do a U-turn on an icy road. When we finally were heading home, we weren't precisely sure of our exact location. All these things together made it impossible to nail down the Earth year of our return. Learning what year it actually was had become more important to me than the information was really worth, as if just getting her to tell me would be a small victory. It would be the first crack in a wall of secrets that was the foundation of my paranoia, and I hated that everyone knew something that I didn't know.

She smiled more broadly. "Ask at your meeting; I think that's the sort of thing it's for."

• • •

Not allowed to walk to the debriefing, although I'm sure I could have, Meghan A. pushed me in a wheelchair through three sets of powered double-doors before we entered an elevator. With a terrible sense of dread, I felt like a little kid being lured into the forest, expecting to be abandoned there. I tried to memorize every detail, as if I'd have to find my way back and my life depended on it.

Megan A. didn't turn me around in the elevator; she left me with my back to the door. Unable to see which button she pushed, or to see which floor we went to, made me even more paranoid. I was almost certain that the elevator went upwards, but that's all I knew.

She pulled me backward off the elevator, and there was no sign indicating what floor we were on. The room numbers were "A32, A31, A30" and so on.

"I'm on the A-floor?" I asked. The walls were two-tone, with the bottom half a flat brown and the top a creamy white. There were many doors and several people milling around. No one seemed to be in a rush; there seemed to be no sense of urgency. They all walked with purpose, but without hurrying. No one smiled or laughed, nor did anyone frown. They could've been working in an office building or a meatpacking plant. I was frightened and there was nothing comforting there. Two people speaking at a counter stopped talking and turned their heads to watch me go by.

Meghan A. didn't say anything, she only pushed me through another set of double-doors when, without a word between them, a large man wearing a white jacket and powder-blue pants took over driving my wheelchair, and she left the way we had come.

Who is he? Why the switch? I watched Meghan leave, and then looked up.

"I'm Jamie," he said. The stubble on his face was salt-and-pepper, like his hair.

Looking in every direction, I searched faces. *Are any of the other survivors here?*

"I'm only your chauffeur," he said and smiled warmly.

It made me feel a bit better. "Why is the floor a secret?"

"It's a secure floor. Sometimes government witnesses or VIPs are treated here, and we don't want every Tom, Dick, and Harry knowing which floor it is," Jamie said.

"Why can't I know?" I asked.

"That's because, Celestine, we're hoping that within a few weeks, you'll be just some other Tom, Dick, or Harry," he said.

Although Jamie's voice was reassuring, and no one seemed tense in the hallway, I was being pushed toward re-experiencing a nightmare that lasted for months, killed my friends and parents, and nearly killed me. A friendly tone wasn't going to help me that much.

He wheeled me into a room with a table and plastic chairs all around it. There were large, synthetic plants in the corners and a giant framed poster of a city skyline at night. At the bottom-center, in block letters, it read, "BOSTON." There was no one else in the room.

"Am I in Boston?" I asked.

"You didn't know?" he asked.

I didn't answer.

"Okay, you're in Massachusetts General Hospital, in Boston," he said.

"Close to home," I said softly.

"Not far," he said.

The desire to go, to run from Boston, was suddenly overwhelming. Maine was so close a person could easily hitchhike, which should've been comforting to know, but instead it made things worse. There was no way to avoid what was coming; there was no escape, no matter how near home was.

Right about then, I saw him for the first time when he walked in with two other men, all three in white coats, dress pants, and ties. They carried what I thought were clipboards, but they turned out to be a laptop and two tablet computers, things I'd never seen before.

As they sat across the table from me, Jamie left with a pat on my shoulder.

"Hi Celestine, my name is Dr. Richard Caledon. This is Dr. Alexei Tupov and Dr. Arun Sood."

Nodding, I asked, "Where is Dr. Schilz?"

Dr. Sood asked, "Who?"

"Celestine, we want you to take as much time as you need,

but we'd like you to tell us, in your own words, in your own way, what happened aboard the *Phaeacia*," Dr. Caledon said.

"Don't you know?" I asked. My knee started bouncing involuntarily. I rubbed my face; it was cool and clammy.

"We know what we think we know, but you were there. You lived it. We'd like your perspective, please," Dr. Sood said.

"I don't want to talk about it," I said.

"We understand that this may be painful," Dr. Caledon said.

Both knees were bouncing now, and I was picking at my fingernails.

They looked at each other, and then Dr. Tupov said, "Please tell us the story as you remember it."

"Where do I start?" I asked.

Dr. Caledon said, "We know about your preparation and the launch. We're interested in what happened after the launch, after you were underway. Tell us whatever you can remember."

Lifting my gaze to the ceiling, I said, "I don't want to."

Dr. Tupov said, without a moment's hesitation, "It would be a great help to us."

"The other survivors would know more," I said.

They all looked at each other once more. I wondered if it was because they hadn't been told much by the others, or maybe they agreed that I couldn't add much.

"Please," Dr. Caledon said.

Hating them for making me think about it, and resenting the forced politeness of Dr. Caledon, I was beginning to not only feel sad and trapped, but angry. "I'll trade you," I said, and my knees stopped bouncing.

"What?" Dr. Caledon said.

"Tell me the date," I said. Not nearly as tough as I was trying to sound, with my voice breaking a bit. I was still terrified.

"This is important work we are doing," Dr. Sood said.

I only stared at him.

"It is March 20, 2022," Dr. Calendon said.

"2022?" I asked.

"That's right. Now, tell us a little of your story," Dr. Caledon said.

Taking a deep breath and slowly exhaling, I tried to stay steady. *Holy shit. 2022. It was like being in* Back to the Future, *but not funny.* Suddenly dizzy, I was trying to grasp that almost forty years had actually passed.

"Are you okay?" Dr. Caledon asked.

"I was born in 1968," I said. *So, how old am I? No, I'm the same age.*

"We know," Dr. Tupov said, as if I had been talking to him.

"Water, please?" I asked.

"Sure," Dr. Caledon said. He never moved, but within a minute, Jamie came in with a glass of water and left without saying a word.

I took a small sip. *Warm and stale.*

"Can you tell us a little about your time on the *Phaeacia*?" asked Dr. Tupov.

After another sip, I said, "Only six left."

"We know that," Dr. Sood said.

What do you want to know? In 1984, I was a high school freshman, and then the next year, I was an astronaut pioneer. When the ship returned, I was one of six survivors. I was never a scientist or a mission specialist or anything. My mom was a psychologist and my dad was a meteorologist. I went along because my parents were selected for their expertise, not because I'm some sort of science nerd. *I'm normal. Well, I used to be.* I asked, "What?"

"What about the sickness?" Dr. Caledon asked.

The sickness. The first to get sick were members of the extravehicular team, so we wondered if they had somehow caught something outside. Dr. Stenhouse told us that was impossible, but they were the first ones affected, so his insisting it was not possible only made some people distrust him. I said, "EVA team were first, then the rest."

"And the symptoms were all the same?" Dr. Sood asked.

"Fever, bruises," I said, and I began trembling.

"How long did the subjects last, once afflicted?" Dr. Tupov said.

"The subjects?" I asked. The tremors in my hands were visible now.

Dr. Caledon said, "Sorry, Celestine. The victims—how long were they sick before they passed away?"

Searching them for signs of sympathy or compassion, there might have been some in Dr. Caledon, but I didn't know if it was genuine. All I saw in their faces was curiosity, like people examining something they'd found in the sink drain.

Closing my eyes, I said, "About a week. My dad got sick, and then my mom a couple days later, but they both were gone in the same week."

"Interesting that they marked time in Earth weeks," said Dr. Tupov.

Dr. Sood asked, "Do you remember what the medical staff did in the attempts to save them?"

Hesitating and sitting on my hands, I felt sweat on my neck.

Dr. Caledon said, "I know this is hard, but talking about it will help you process it all."

I said, "They gave Mom some of my blood."

"Did they say why?" Dr. Sood asked.

I said, "No." The medical staff had said they were not sure, but that I wasn't sick, so maybe there was something about my blood… I had the antibodies, they said, so they knew I'd been exposed, but I didn't get sick… they hoped my blood would somehow help my mom. Remembering how I wanted to dump all my blood into my mom brought on a wave of nausea.

"But it didn't save her," Dr. Tupov said.

Turning to Dr. Tupov, I said, "She died." She got a bit more energy that day, so I hoped, but no. She had died gasping like a fish lying on a dock; they had not bothered to intubate her because they knew there was no chance and instead, they gave her a heavy dose of morphine. After she was gone, they zipped her up in a bag and took her to lie beside my dad.

He didn't hesitate and asked, "Who was the last of the children alive, aside from you?"

Sick to my stomach, I reached for my water. Bringing the glass to my mouth, my hand trembled enough that Dr. Caledon looked at Dr. Tupov and said, "Maybe we should take a break."

"We've just started," Dr. Sood said.

The water went down my throat, hit bottom, and bounced back up like a rubber ball, bringing the contents of my stomach up with it. Throwing up on myself, into my glass, and onto the table, I wanted to cry right then. My face sort of did, it contorted, but still no tears. I just hung my head. None of the three doctors said anything, but Dr. Sood stood. Jamie quickly reappeared with a towel, wiped my face, and took me back to my room.

9

MEMORIES OF THE FOLLOWING FEW days were blurred, but I know I next saw that doctor when he came to my room on March 24.

"How are you doing, Celestine?" he asked.

"I'm fine," I said, but I struggled to focus my thoughts.

"How's the anxiety?" he asked.

"I don't want to go back," I said.

"You won't have to. The decision has been made that we've gotten enough from the others. Obviously, that was very traumatic for you. I have to apologize; sometimes scientists don't make for the most compassionate people," he said.

I asked, "What's your name again?"

"I'm Dr. Caledon. I am a psychiatrist and the team leader in charge of the re-assimilation effort to support the reintegration of you and the other survivors into society," he said.

"A team?" I said.

Dr. Caledon paused, and then said, "The medication seems to be clouding things for you a bit. Indulge me for a moment—Do you remember where you are?"

"Boston?" I asked.

"What is the name of your hometown?" he asked.

Thinking for a moment, I found it and said, "Goodwin."

He looked at me, squinted, and then wrote something down. He said, "Celestine, it's clear that you'll all need help getting through this transition. We've put together a support group for you and for the other survivors of the *Phaeacia*. You'll meet once a week, maybe every two weeks, for a while at least."

"But I want to go home," I said, with my eyelids feeling heavy.

"You will. We'll meet virtually. We'll see each other through the computer screens from your homes. You won't need to travel. I'll be online with you all, facilitating those sessions. You'll live in Goodwin," he said.

"With my aunt?" I asked.

"May I sit?" he asked, and then he did before I could respond.

"Can I?" I asked.

"She's not against it, but Celestine, your aunt Rena is seventy-six years old and lives in a small apartment now," he said.

"Oh my God, she's seventy-six?" I asked.

"I have some good news though. Her daughter, your cousin Deborah, has agreed to take you in," he said.

"Deb? She's six months younger than I am," I said.

"She's almost fifty-two years old," he said.

"Rena is fifty-two?" I asked.

"Your cousin, Deborah, is fifty-two," he said. "I think we'll take down your meds a bit."

"Does she live alone?" I asked.

"She's married to a man named Raymond Hoyle. They have a son, but he's grown, married, and living in North Carolina," Dr. Caledon said.

"Debbie had a kid?" I asked.

"You'll also have a personal therapist to talk to, face to face. Her name is Muriel Berber, and she's supposed to be very good," he said.

Reentry into society was like being dropped out of a moving car, as if the Earth and I were at different speeds, and I had to painfully adjust. *Group therapy, personal therapy, Debbie has a kid, and Aunt Rena is old.* "I just want school. Like, a normal life, you know?" I asked.

"After consulting with your cousin, and the therapist, we all agree that you should wait for the fall, and return to high school in the 12th grade. There are only a few months left in this school year. Let's get your feet under you first," he said.

"But therapy?" I asked. Sure that therapy would be as bad

as the debriefing meeting I had attended, I pictured myself vomiting at every session. Digging into the memories that I had secreted away still seemed horrific.

"I think it's a good idea, don't you?" he asked. "Besides, it's a condition of your release. They secured a court order mandating, for your own good, that you six attend these therapy sessions for a while to maximize your chances of success."

"Who are 'they'?" I asked.

"NASA," he said.

"But NASA…"

He said, "Celestine, you have so much to work on, for yourself. Don't take on fights you don't need. Just work on making yourself whole again."

I asked, "NASA wasn't part of it, so why are they involved now?"

"The world has changed. When you left, you were part of a secret—and illegal, I might add—collaboration between a private foundation and the Soviet government. Of course, governments around the world knew that a large rocket had launched from Kazakhstan, but I honestly do not know what they knew of your mission at the time. That is still classified. I have searched, and there was very little mention in the media about one more launch into space from that region," he said.

"So, what changed?" I asked.

"The Soviet Union is gone now, Celestine," he said.

"Nuclear war?" I asked.

"There was no war. It collapsed politically and economically, and after that happened, many things once kept secret were shared. So, in the 1990s, western governments learned the true nature of your mission, but all agreed it should remain classified, and the crew aboard would simply remain missing," he said. "As one of the world's leading space agencies, and since many of the crew members were and are Americans, NASA naturally became involved—along with help from the CDC—and has taken the lead in ensuring your care and assimilation, including therapy."

Pausing, I asked, "Not that I want to, but is there anything

I'm not supposed to talk about? Like, I should keep it secret?"

"Feel free to talk to anyone about any of it; it may even help you come to terms with your experiences," he said.

Nodding, I asked, "When can I leave?"

He said, "Your cousin will be coming down to collect you on Thursday."

"Thursday?" I asked.

"Is that alright?" he asked.

"What day is it today?" I asked.

"Friday," he said.

Suddenly nervous, but unsure why, I said, "Okay."

"Alright then," he said, and stood.

"Can I get a TV?" I asked.

"Celestine, I wouldn't want you to watch contemporary television as a window on society. These reality shows are really quite awful," he said. "The Internet would likely be worse. Let's work up to a TV."

"Inter-what?" I asked.

He paused. "How about a few newspapers?"

Ugh, man, newspapers. "Can I get one from Maine?"

"Fine, let's start with that," he said. "Anything else?"

Coming in just then, a nurse with a nametag that read, "Nancy L," said, "Pardon me, I just need to get in here."

"I'd like some modern music," I said.

"I'm afraid I can't help you there," he said.

"I have my own cassette player, somewhere," I said.

The nurse stopped and looked at Dr. Caledon, and then at me. She said, "How about I bring her a radio?"

Dr. Caledon said, "An actual radio, yes. Don't bring her a smartphone with music."

"Smart phone?" I asked.

The nurse said, "Girl, you have no idea. Smartphones and all the apps. You'll have every song and video at your fingertips, you can find restaurants, call an Uber to get you, GPS. You'll love it."

Dr. Caledon said, "Keep it simple for now."

The nurse pouted her lip at me, and shrugged. "But a radio for now."

Talking to each other, they left. Feeling exhausted, I tried to get comfortable. Later that afternoon, I woke from my nap to soft music playing and a newspaper on my food tray. Out of my reach, near the sink, was a brown radio and when the next song began, I wrinkled my nose. Somewhere in my clothes, I still had my "Disco is Dead" shirt, but listening to the radio I wondered if it might have been reborn.

Picking up the paper, I scanned the headlines. The drug fog had cleared a bit and, better able to focus, it was still mindboggling how much had changed. There was a lot of talk about terrorists, the new president seemed to be cleaning up the mess of the previous one, and there was reference to a president who had been black. That was pretty cool, I thought. In the thirty years I'd missed, we'd probably had several black presidents and, of course, female presidents. My mom always said, "If the leaders of all the countries around the world were women, there would be world peace in our lifetime," but then we left the world, so I don't think she was very optimistic after all.

When I came to the third page, I noticed the bottom half was filled with a story and photograph about protestors who were upset that we survivors had returned and were scattered around the country. Our exact locations were confidential, but there were reports of two survivors in Boston-area hospitals. While wondering who was in Boston with me, I read about unrest outside hospitals in Dallas, Denver, and New York.

As scary as that was, there were also many disturbing quotes saying that none of us would be released until it was clear that there was no danger. However, the director of the Center for Disease Control had already announced that we survivors were not a threat to public health, and that only out of an abundance of caution had we been quarantined. He explained that while the survivors carried the antibodies, meaning we had been exposed, the actual virus itself could no longer be detected in our blood. They said it meant we couldn't be contagious. He said their fears were understandable considering the pandemic the world had recently suffered through, but he assured them all that we survivors did not have that virus. Additionally, he said that there was a protocol in place in case anything came up, but he never explained it. I didn't ask for details on that, I had other questions such as: were they going to keep us locked up or not?

· · ·

My cousin Debbie walked into my room on March 30. Recognizing her immediately, I squealed with joy.

"Cel, oh my word!" she said.

It was amazing to have her arms around me. For the first time since returning, I felt I might actually get to go home. Hugging, then clutching her hand, and even grabbing a fistful of her sweater, I stayed right at her side. Debbie was the first person I had recognized; she meant possible rescue from this place, and from the nightmare of having been in space. My fear was that if I didn't hold onto her, she might leave forever without me.

"This is so wild," she said. "You've barely changed. It's one thing to look at old pictures, but in person, it's so freaky." Her voice was as I remembered it, her hair was a different shade of brown, and her face was simultaneously fleshier and more angular. There was more of her, but it was definitely her. She was wearing jeans and an oversized cardigan.

"You look good," I said, smiling.

"Liar," she said, smiling back. "Did they tell you I'm married?"

"With a kid!" I said.

"Well, he's not a kid anymore. He lives in Raleigh with his wife."

"That's so rad," I said.

She giggled. "Rad? We have to update your vocab. All of your clothes and your other things have already been delivered to my place," she said. "The town has changed a bit, but I'm sure you'll still know your way around."

"I can't wait," I said.

The nurse, Meghan A., was back, and with a wheelchair. "Sorry, it's the rules. I have to give you a ride to the front doors."

"I'll walk," I said.

"I'm sorry, regulations," the nurse said.

Debbie stepped between the wheelchair and me and said, "She's walking."

There was a tense moment, and then the nurse turned and left without saying anything more. Deb started giggling again.

"You're still a badass," I said.

"Nah, I'm all soft and mushy now," she said. "You hungry?"

"I only want to go home," I said.

We went down to the parking lot, she pushed a button, and there was a beep from her vehicle.

"A button to help you find your car?" I asked.

"I was unlocking it," she said.

Driving back to Goodwin from Boston, we just listened to the radio. I had the window down, despite the cold, and the noise made talking tough. The air was rich with all kinds of things I hadn't smelled in a long time, and I grinned at each new scent. There were no flowers yet, but the melting snow made mud, and it smelled like life waiting to happen. A large truck passed us, and the diesel exhaust was wonderful.

As we made our way into Maine on I-95, I looked out at the pine trees and white birches, and was dazzled by how beautiful it all was. Struggling with processing everything, I had to consciously tell myself it was all real, and that I was really back. My senses were completely overwhelmed; I was over-stimulated and I tumbled through the relief of being home combined with the grief of knowing my parents wouldn't be sleeping in Maine tonight.

As we came into town, the smell of Koch's Burger Stand blew in and my mouth watered to the point that I thought I might drool. Passing the park where my dad would take me to swing, and the hair salon where my mom used to go, I realized that Goodwin would be just one reminder after another of my parents, and that coming back wasn't going to be an escape from everything that happened. Driving by the road that led down to the high school, I got only a glimpse of the redbrick building, and understood that like the hospital, it would be full of strangers.

We pulled up to the house; it was mint green clapboard, with a purple door, and tan shingles on the roof. It was a little cape, with two dormers and there were rhododendrons out front.

"Cute," I said. "Yours?"

"No, Cel, I just pull up and stay wherever I want," she said, smiling.

Inside, it was nice, with a simple kitchen, a modest living room, and a neat bathroom. She showed me her bedroom and then her son's.

"You'll be staying here. This is your room now. You can put his stuff away and hang yours," she said, pointing toward plastic totes on the floor.

The room was decorated in teenage-boy style, including a poster of someone named Lucia Dvorská in a bathing suit. Turning to Deb, I said, "Thanks."

Grasping my arm, she said, "I love you, Cel. I thought I'd never see you again. You can stay here as long as you like. It's your home." She had a few tears but my tears, locked away on the *Phaeacia*, still wouldn't come and it was a bit embarrassing, because I knew she expected me to cry, so it felt awkward not to.

"I'll leave you to this. If you need something, just holler," she said. "I'll make some sandwiches in a bit."

When she left, I went right to work taking down the posters and putting away the trophies, trying to make it my own space.

By opening the totes, I revealed my clothes and all the stuff I'd brought along on the *Phaeacia*. The odor of the ship was not present. Sniffing my clothes, they smelled fresh and clean.

Placing my boom box on a shelf, I deposited the plastic case of cassette tapes beside it. Next to that, I set my Cabbage Patch Kid. Playing with dolls had been far behind me even at the time, and maybe I was too old for the gift, but it was something my dad had given me the Christmas before we left. He had joked that he had to beat up an old lady in K-Mart to get it.

In the tote, I found a sweatshirt that had been my mother's. It was pink, with white stripes down the sleeves, and a huge Adidas logo on the chest. It smelled just as fresh and clean as all the other stuff; I wished they hadn't washed my mother out of her sweatshirt. Carefully, I placed it in a drawer of its own.

Debbie called from downstairs. "Sandwiches!"

Putting the last shirts away, I pushed the drawer closed, and carried the empty tote downstairs.

"Want something to drink?" she asked. Placing two paper plates down on the table, each with a sandwich and some potato chips, she sat.

Joining her, I finished my sandwich before she was halfway done.

"What are you going to do next?" she asked.

Having no idea what my options were, I shrugged.

"You could watch a movie, or read a book, or even go for a walk," she said.

I shrugged again. *I'm not bored. I just got here.*

She stopped chewing for a minute, and then said, "You know, Cel, if you ever want to just talk about stuff."

I really didn't want to talk about anything important. It was the unimportant stuff I was dying to talk about, like a twenty-minute conversation about nail polish or shoes would be great.

"Really, Cel," she said, and placed her hand on mine.

Reflexively, I pulled my hand away. There was an awkward pause, and then I said, "Thanks."

I threw away my plate, went back to the bedroom, and I sat on the floor with nothing else to put away. Slowly falling over on the carpet, the pile against my cheek, I fell asleep.

In my dream, my mother was still alive, wearing the pink Adidas sweatshirt. She was cooking and as I tried to peek into the pot, she covered it. Smiling, she didn't say anything, but looked over her glasses at me.

"What're you cooking?" I asked.

She still didn't say anything, but instead she lifted the cover just high enough to get a spoon inside and stir. When I tried to look inside, she quickly withdrew the spoon and sealed the lid.

"Let me see!" I said.

Shaking her head, she never stopped smiling. Frustrated, I tried to push past her, but she was strangely solid and I couldn't get by. Turning to face me, her face fell, and I felt a sudden dread. Stepping away as she spread her arms wide, she seemed to be inviting me to look.

"I don't care what's in the pot anymore," I said.

Tears started streaming down her cheeks. Her arms grew longer and longer.

I said, "I don't care what's in the pot! I don't care! I don't care!" and then I woke up.

My door opened, and Debbie rushed over to me. "My God, Cel, did you fall down?" she asked.

Looking around, I said, "Sleeping." *A nightmare.*

"I heard you screaming," she said. "Are you okay? Want to get into bed?"

"No," I said.

"Want to come to the living room with me?" she asked.

When I didn't respond immediately, she said, "I bet you'll need a lot of time to yourself to sort stuff out. Don't worry, we won't be insulted. Take the time you need."

Used to being surrounded by people, I said, "Not really." *I don't really want to be alone.* When isolated, the silence was oppressive. Pulling me to my feet, Deb put her arm around me and we went downstairs. Once we got to the sofa, she held my hand and looked at me. It felt really awkward.

"Want to watch TV?" I asked.

Reaching for the remotes, she said, "So this one is for the television. This one is for the cable box."

I nodded. "Can you get a single remote to control both?"

She said, "There's a way to make it do that, but I can't figure it out, and if I ask Ray to set it up, we'd probably have no TV for a week while he tears the thing apart trying to make it work. But normally, once the TV is on, you only need the remote for the cable box."

Looking at it, I really had no idea what she meant, and it must've shown on my face.

She chuckled and I cringed. Every time she laughed, it took me back to the maniacal cackle of the heartbroken technician on the *Phaeacia*. So, whenever people even giggled, it made me squirm a bit. It had become so inappropriate on the *Phaeacia*, in light of all the suffering, that no one did it. It was more a trigger of emotions than something I longed for.

"So, you point the remote at the cable box and then you can change channels with this button. But there are so many now, you'll probably want the guide," she said.

Looking around, I asked, "Where is it?"

"What?" she asked.

"The *TV Guide*," I said.

"You mean, like the little magazine?" she asked.

I nodded.

Pointing at another button on the remote, labeled "GUIDE," she said, "Press that one."

When I did, the screen became a list. "Whoa."

"That's what's on," she said. "Push the arrow buttons and you can scroll up or down through the listings."

I asked, "How about Internet?"

"Why not get the hang of cable TV first? Maybe this weekend we can set you loose on the World Wide Web."

"The what? I'd rather go on the Internet," I said.

She said, "This weekend we will."

Looking back at the TV, I jumped up. "'Scooby-Doo!'"

She laughed, and I flinched again. "You know, Cel, you can probably spend all day watching stuff even you've already seen on that thing," she said.

"Cool," I said.

Shaking her head and grinning, she walked away. Watching the caveman episode of "Scooby-Doo" took back me to a time before the trip, back when I had my mom and dad. Simultaneously happy and so desperately sad, I watched the entire episode. When it was over, I turned off the TV, but I had no idea what the cable box thing was doing.

That weekend, I did go onto the Internet, with her supervision. Saying the laptop was going to be mine, Debbie insisted we ease into things. We set up my email, Instagram, and Facebook. My first email was from her, while we sat face to face.

"Why email me?" I asked.

"Yeah, I know we're right here, but you could email anyone in the world. And on Facebook you can find people and keep up on that person's life," she said.

"Creepy," I said.

"What do you mean?" she asked.

"People watch you?" I asked.

"I have about 400 Facebook friends," she said.

"I don't know twenty people," I said.

"I don't know most of them either," she said.

"So, strangers?" I asked. *They read about your life, and see pictures of you, but you don't really know them?*

"You make it sound bad," she said.

"I'm not sure I want this," I said, looking at my Facebook page.

"Relax, you don't have to accept any Facebook friends that you don't want. They will ask for your permission first," she said.

"Have you ever said 'no' on Facebook to a new friend?" I asked.

"Once, but I think he was like a Michigan militia recruiter or something," she said.

"What's that?"

Closing the laptop, Debbie said, "Why don't we put this away for a bit? Do you want anything at the store?"

"What store?" I asked.

"Supermarket," she said.

"Can I come?" I asked.

"Of course. If it's overwhelming or whatever, just tell me," Debbie said.

"Why would I be overwhelmed in a supermarket?" I asked.

Deb shrugged and said, "Okay, cool, let's go."

Walking into the Hannaford's, I was initially relieved that it just looked like a grocery store. No floating carts, no robots shopping or cashing people out.

I'd be totally stoked if we could buy some Smurf Berry Crunch. "Cereal?" I asked.

Debbie's eyebrows shot straight up. "I don't know if you'll recognize any of it."

Bummer. Corn Flakes is probably still around.

When we stepped into the cereal aisle, I was overwhelmed by the number of choices and the wall of colors and cartoon characters. I recognized a box with a cartoon frog on it. Picking it up, I asked, "Smacks?"

"They used to be called Sugar Smacks, and then Honey Smacks for a while, but now they're just Smacks," Deb said.

"Why change?" I asked.

"Because sugar became evil," she said, chuckling.

They took all the sugar out of the cereal? I turned the box around and found the ingredients, and I read aloud, "Sugar."

"No, sweetie, they took 'sugar' out of the name, not the product," she said.

I don't get it. Did that fool people? I put the box back and, selecting based only on the image of the cereal itself, I chose SpongeBob's Square Pants cereal. *What the hell is a SpongeBob?*

As we continued shopping, I noticed more and more differences. Organic, gluten-free, GMO. I had no idea what any of it meant. Every once in a while, I spotted something wonderfully familiar like a frozen Hungry Man Turkey Dinner, Underwood Chicken Spread, B&M Baked Beans, or a simple can of Campbell's Chicken Noodle. Still, the sheer size of the store and the endless variety were wearing me down. I was tired. The space was cavernous, but simultaneously seeming to close in. Bright lights, flashy colors, movements in every direction, and I had nowhere to hide.

As my anxiety built, and my energy faded, I then noticed that people were staring, and some were whispering.

"There's that girl, one of the survivors from TV," one said.

"She's not contagious," another whispered.

"You trust the government? You remember COVID?" still another asked.

Soon, the stares and whispers were all I could focus on.

"You okay?" Debbie asked.

"No," I said.

"Okay, okay, let's get you out of here," Debbie said, and she abandoned the cart and put her arm around me. Which of course drew more stares, as if I was collapsing from my terribly contagious illness.

"No, Deb, buy the stuff," I said.

"We can just go, hon, if you need to. I can come back," she

said.

"No, buy it," I said. Not wanting to hurt her feelings, I didn't shrug her arm off of me, but was relieved when she let me go. She grabbed the cart, and took off for the lines of cashiers.

Hustling to catch up, I only attracted yet more attention. The whole thing was turning into a nightmare. While in line, the people around me kept trying to look at me without being noticed. The cashier, with her purple hair, was less subtle and was openly staring, and then Debbie asked the worst thing she could've asked.

"Are you sure you're not feeling sick?" she asked.

Everyone turned and looked right at me, all of them waiting for my answer. A woman carrying a basket in one hand and holding a baby with the other left our line and went three registers down.

I said, "I am NOT sick."

Debbie looked around and said, "Oh God, Cel, I'm sorry."

"Yeah," I said, staring at the floor.

"She's not sick," Deb said to everyone.

I winced, and said, "Stop."

A few people took out face masks and put them on. *Why were people carrying face masks?*

Deb said nothing else and we paid for our groceries. Walking out to the car, she said, "Cel, I'm so sorry. I was focused on you, and that one lady looking at you, I thought she was just concerned too, and I didn't even think that they…"

"Forget it," I said.

Loading the few bags into the car, Debbie said, "It just didn't occur to me that they would be scared of you, instead of for you. After the pandemic… I'm sorry."

I nodded, sat in the car, and asked, "What pandemic?"

"While you were gone, we had a terrible virus. All over the Earth, but we had it worst here in the United States. We tried to fight it but we blew it, and we had a lot of people get sick, and many died. So, people are really sensitive about getting sick. It was awful. Everyone wore masks just to go into the store. Many businesses closed, and a lot of those never reopened," Debbie

said.

"Is the virus still around?" I asked.

"They say it'll never really be gone, but we have a vaccine now. You got the shot, too, they told me, while you were in the hospital," she said. "You'll need your booster next month."

I sat and stared back at the doors of the supermarket. They had been afraid of a disease that had killed a lot of people. I could relate to that.

10

RAY CAME INTO THE LIVING room the next day, and plopped down on the other end of the couch from me. It seemed like he only started working out what he wanted to say after he sat. Finally, he said, "Celestine, I think you should let people here in Goodwin get used to you being around. I think that way, what happened at the supermarket would eventually stop. You know, after they all adjust, and you become just another face people see around."

Remembering the store, and those people staring at me, my anxiety level instantly jumped. "It was, like, freaky. Creepy."

Ray listened, and paused, before he said, "I hear ya, but what if you just walked through the downtown every afternoon. I'll even go with you when I can, if you want."

Picturing the two of us walking in downtown Goodwin, I couldn't imagine something that would look less normal or cool.

"Nah, it's okay," I said.

"Well, give it try. Become another face in the crowd," Ray said.

Nodding, but not saying anything, I really thought it was a terrible idea. He stood, put his hand on my head, and said, "Okay, kiddo. Let me know how it goes."

Ray walked away, pulling his Dad-jeans up as he went. Ugh, but I smiled. He wasn't my cousin, he wasn't a step-dad, and I didn't really know him but I could sense something good about him, something Deb must've seen long ago. He gave off like this sense of calm. It was pretty cool.

11

WHILE I SAT LISTENING TO music in bed, Deb came in. She sat slowly near my feet, and I took my earbuds out.

"Cel, I wanted to talk," she said.

I nodded.

"You haven't really said much. I'm a little worried. You aren't sharing much," she said.

"So?" I asked, and then winced.

"I don't think it's good for you. I know they are setting up therapy for you, and you could probably open up then, or with the others you already know, but I remember you back when we were kids, and you always talked a lot," she said.

"About kid stuff," I said.

"I'm not suggesting you talk about the hard things. I just mean, you always had so much to say about everything. And you were funny," Deb said.

"Sorry. I'm not feeling funny," I said.

"No, I don't want you to be sorry. I'm only trying to say, if you want to, you can open up a bit more," she said.

"Okay," I said, and nodded, but I was getting really annoyed.

"Cel, c'mon, it's me. It's me, Deb. You can just come out of your shell a bit," she said.

"How can I? You've climbed right into my shell with me," I said, but then felt bad for it. Softening my voice, I asked, "If I feel like sharing, I'll talk, but right now, I don't really want to, okay?"

Deb looked hurt. I hadn't wanted to be mean. She stood up, and quietly walked to the door.

"I'm sorry," I said.

She paused, and then said, "Dinner will be late tonight. We have to wait for Ray to get home."

"Okay," I said, and she left. *Oh my God. I've come back to Earth to be an asshole.* Falling back on my bed, I stared at the ceiling, and decided to try Ray's advice. I'd attempt to go out.

•   •   •

The next day, only wanting to become another face in the crowd, I soon learned that it's difficult to blend in with people who are scared of you. Even with all the assurances I'd had about not being contagious, I still had some lingering anxiety myself. Who wouldn't? I could logically suppress it, but my emotional side would win now and then.

Just about everyone I cared about had died from the illness. My friend, a pretty girl named Josée who lived in Quebec before the flight, was the first of us kids to get sick. She just lay there crying. Visiting her, I watched her through the sheet of clear plastic, but she wouldn't talk. She only wept. Never saying she was afraid or even that she was in pain, she soon lost consciousness, and later that day died without a word. I haven't had a close friend since.

Five days after the trip to the supermarket, walking downtown near where the J.J. Newberry's store used to be, I looked up and saw three girls about my age walking toward me. Trying to think of some way to talk to them without sounding like a total dweeb, I was running out of time as the distance between us quickly shrank. Maybe I could ask where I could get a good burrito or decent shoes, I thought, and maybe that would turn into an invitation to join them.

Chickening out and deciding I'd just say, "Hi," and walk on past as if I wasn't desperate and lonely, I looked up and saw that they had stopped, and were staring at me and whispering to each other. Then they crossed the street, obviously avoiding me. As I watched them pause on the sidewalk on the other side and look back, I felt something snap inside. Frustrated, and maybe trying to chase my own lingering fears away, words erupted from my mouth and I shouted at them before I could stop myself.

"I'm not sick! You didn't have to cross the street! You won't catch anything from me!" I said.

They looked shocked at first, and then they began to laugh. They were still giggling and bumping into each other as they walked away. Certain they were mocking me, I was furious.

Angrier this time, I shouted, "Hey you skanks! I'm not sick, bitches! You get that?"

They never looked back; they just kept walking. However, all around, people had noticed. A woman with a stroller, an old man getting into his pickup truck, two guys standing by the gas pumps, and a man wearing sandals with black socks were all staring at me. Wanting to yell at them too, I fought the impulse, and instead went on my way.

My anger quickly burned off, and in its place, I felt lonely. Looking in through the windows of a sandwich shop, I saw small tables encircled by people engaged in conversation. There was a lot of laughter. Unable to just walk in and sit down, I was so separate, so apart from everyone.

Sitting instead on the curb with my feet in the street, I hugged my knees to my chest. Plenty of adults walked by, but no one said anything to me. They obviously knew I was there, but they pretended not to notice, while walking a wide route around me. Having no more shouting in me, I decided to just go back to Deb's, and curl up in bed.

The whole thing made me think about all those who were sick and were hiding their illness so they wouldn't be shut out like this, keeping it secret because they dreaded the fear of others. I had seen that dread on the *Phaeacia*. The medical staff kept the dying separated behind clear plastic. Some would have held their loved ones through their last breaths had they been allowed but others couldn't get past the horror. Like the technician, Will Klempner, who stood in the doorway, far from his wife's deathbed, not going any closer. She pressed her hand against the inside of the clear poly sheeting, reaching for him, and all he could say was that he was sorry. He died a week after she did, and I remember he said that he was glad to.

Looking once more at the girls who had crossed the street, they were a couple blocks away by then. In that moment, I worried I may never have friends. It would've been nice just to have some distant someone to write letters to, and I considered doing that for an invented pen pal, just for the exercise and the feeling of connection to anyone; I could've written letters to a fictitious person who would be waiting on news of how I was doing.

·   ·   ·

Doubting even a made-up friend would care, I didn't write those letters, but I did meet someone real. It had been two years since I'd been to an optometrist—or maybe thirty, depending on how the years were tabulated—and it was time for me to have my eyesight examined. Deb dropped me off and said she'd run an errand and be back in thirty minutes or so. As I waited for my appointment, I saw a girl trying on different frames. Slipping on a pair that was sort of shaped like a cat's eyes, she looked into the small mirror. The glasses were dark, and against her tanned skin and extremely blonde hair, they really stood out.

Deciding to take a chance, I said, "Cute."

She looked up and smiled. "You think?"

A smile was a good sign. "Really," I said.

"You don't think they're too big?" she asked.

"No," I said.

She smiled and put them back. "Thanks."

There was a pause, and then I said, "I'm Celestine."

"Cool name. Oh, wait, right, are you that girl, the space thing?"

Was she asking if I were a space thing? Scared she'd run away just as those girls had, I said only, "Just moved back to Goodwin."

"That's so weird! I'm Alicia."

Excited, I asked, "So what are you doing?"

"Just an eye appointment," she said.

I was already kind of committed, and taking the risk to talk to her in the first place had worked, so I took a deep breath and took another chance. "I mean after this. Want to go get a coffee or something?" I asked.

Still smiling, Alicia's face froze, and then she glanced at my shoes, before saying, "Yeah, that'd be cool, but I can't." Pulling out her phone, she tapped and looked at it. Her tone was suddenly different, and she seemed uncomfortable.

Thinking she wanted my number, I said, "I don't have a phone yet. Deb says we'll get one soon though."

She looked up, apparently a bit confused, and said, "I was just checking the time." She put the phone away, and said, "So, I gotta go."

"Okay. Nice meeting you," I said. My heart sank, and I wondered what had happened.

"Yup," she said. Once she had left and the door closed behind her, I felt like such a loser. Knowing how desperate I would look if I did, I fought the urge to follow her.

"Celestine?"

Looking back, I saw the receptionist was standing in the doorway with a professional smile. She led me into the back room; the walls were covered in paneling that had probably been there since I boarded the *Phaeacia*. Pointing to a chair, she said, "Have a seat and Dr. Ochi will be right with you."

When he walked in, I was surprised at how young he was, and how skinny.

"How are we today?" he asked, and then before I could answer he said, "I'm Dr. Ochi. I see it's been quite some time since your last exam."

"A couple years," I said.

He paused, and then said, "Well let's see where we're up to."

Why did he keep saying we? He pointed to a chart on the wall and said, "Let's read the third line from the top."

"Read it together?" I asked.

He paused again, and said, "Go ahead and read it."

Reading it easily, I figured I could speed things up and looked three lines below and offered, "I can see all the lines clearly down to the line that goes E-G-B-something. That's the first one that's hard to see."

He cautiously stepped a bit closer, and lowered the large hanging device with all the different lenses in front of my face.

"What's this thing called, anyway?" I asked.

"A phoropter," he said.

It was a couple inches too far from me, so I reached up to move it. When I did, Dr. Ochi yanked his hand away. His movement startled me, and I jumped back in the seat.

"What's the matter?" I asked.

"Nothing," he said. "Let's just leave our hands down. The equipment is pretty sensitive."

"You didn't move the equipment away from me. You pulled your hand back," I said. I reached toward him and he quickly stepped away.

"Celestine, we should just sit still," he said.

"You're afraid of me," I said.

"Nonsense," he said.

Standing, I walked toward him, and he scrambled backward. Between Alicia's rejection and now this, I could feel my sadness shifting to anger again.

"Why did you agree to see me today if you're scared?" I asked.

He said, "I didn't take the appointment. Laurie did."

"Aren't you worried I'm contaminating the entire office? Your chair? Your phoropter?" I asked. My voice was rising, and as I strode toward him, he walked away and into the waiting room.

"Celestine, I appreciate how hard the experience must have been for you, but we've just been through a pretty scary time ourselves. This office has barely recovered financially from the last virus. Perhaps you should just go," he said. He passed the receptionist's desk, and the two of them stood behind it.

"What's happening?" she asked.

Walking to the desk, I said, "I'm not sick. I'm not contagious. You get that?"

They both nodded. Placing my hands on the desk, I leaned forward and they shifted backward a bit. My face was red hot. Trembling, I said, "I'm not sick." They both nodded again. There was nothing else to say or do. Heading for the door, I felt a wave of nausea wash over me. Gagging, I made it outside, quickly stepped into the alley where the trashcans were, and threw up on the ground beside them.

"My God, Cel, what's going on?"

Glancing up, I saw Deb walking toward me, hands outstretched.

"Please just get me back to the house," I said, wiping my mouth.

"Did you have your appointment?" she asked.

Noticing a man staring at us, I said, "Please just get me out of here."

Deb looked up at him and then back at me. She said, "Yeah, okay, the car is just up the street. Should I go get it?"

"I'll walk. Let's just go," I said.

She wrapped an arm around me as we walked. Once in the car, she asked, "What happened?"

"He was scared that I was sick," I said.

"So, he wouldn't examine you?" she asked.

"He was so afraid that he ran away from me," I said.

As we pulled into traffic, she said, "Cel, I'm so sorry. You just don't know…"

"Yeah, I get it, you had an epidemic. Try having that in a tin can, with recirculating air, and your parents, half the pilots, and the entire medical staff except one nurse is dead, while you're hurtling through space and back to Earth," I said.

"Cel, hundreds of thousands…" she started, but then said, "I'm really sorry."

"I just want to go to bed," I said. Dejected and angry, all I wanted was to be alone. I watched people walking on the sidewalks smiling at each other, and some stopped to talk as we drove by. I thought I'd never have that again, that I would always feel like an alien, and then I saw an older woman, sitting alone at the bus stop. She had a purse in her hands, and she was wearing a cloth mask over her mouth and nose.

12

WAKING UP IN THE MIDDLE of the night, I was sure I could smell my mom's hair. It was her conditioner, with a melon scent, as if she were right there in the room with me. The odor made me feel warm and comforted. Sitting up, I looked around the room, and whispered, "Mom?" My skin was tingling. Climbing out of bed, I walked into each corner as if expecting to bump into her with every step, but I found nothing and the smell was gone.

Missing her so much, and falling back onto the bed, I ached all over with sadness and want, but I still couldn't cry. Wracked with guilt about it, I tried to. It wasn't that I wanted, like, a huge release of feelings or anything; I wasn't attempting to have a big emotional breakdown like on the Donahue show. Instead, I was trying because if I couldn't cry, I thought I must be really screwed up. I'd stopped while still aboard the *Phaeacia*, so it wasn't my new meds. Besides they told me I'd continue to feel emotions while on those pills, but that the swings up and down would be more manageable. Lying in the dark, staring up at the ceiling, the only light was a clock-radio which read 2:04 a.m. Picturing my mom—her smile, her eyes, her neck—I thought back to lying on the couch with my head in her lap while she rubbed my back, but still nothing. My lips curled as if I would cry, I scrunched up my face, but no. Heartsick, and sure there must be something wrong with me, I wondered, "Who the hell can't cry for their dead mom?"

Intense pain but no tears. People have no idea what it

feels like to lose a parent until it happens. It's more than just missing an important person, or even two of them. I felt like the connection to everyone who came before me was gone and my primary safety net had disappeared. It was the loss of support I couldn't remember gaining, and energy I'd never been without. It was a feeling of being thrown alone into the unknown, the limit of my second chances, and the absence of unconditional love. It was the vanishing of permanence.

When they died, I couldn't curl up in my room with my stuffed animals and have a good cry, because I was still stuck aboard the *Phaeacia* with more dead bodies than live ones, including theirs. My parents had kept the monsters away, until they couldn't. In the end, as they lay dying, they were more sad for me than for themselves.

One of the last things my mom said to me was, "Celestine, no one your age is ready to lose her parents. It's not fair and I'm sorry. Remember the good times and talk to people about us. Don't cry alone." She started to cry, and we pressed our hands together, with the plastic sheeting between.

The loss was immeasurable, and remembering it made me choke on the grief, gulping, but still no tears. She told me not to cry alone, but I wasn't sure I would cry at all, ever again. The house was silent, and I heard a car drive by outside. Feeling so isolated, my sorrow was unbearable, but my eyes did not well up, and when I eventually fell back asleep, I didn't even dream I was crying.

● ● ●

As I came into the living room the next morning, Debbie was there watching television. She immediately switched it off and dropped the remote on the coffee table. I stopped, looked at the remote and the TV, and asked, "What's up?"

"Nothing," she said. "Just sick of the news."

Walking over, I picked up the remote, and turned the television back on. There was footage of a crowd in front of a multi-storied government building, the façade was concave and glass. People were clearly upset about something, waving signs and shouting.

The television caption read, "Protesters voice concern over *Phaeacia* survivors."

"What the hell?" I asked.

Appearing in the shot, a reporter with a microphone in hand, said, "Here at the Arlen Specter Headquarters Building of the Centers for Disease Control and Prevention in Atlanta, perhaps as many as five hundred people have come together to share their fears about the survivors of the *Phaeacia*. They say that not enough information has been released to the public concerning the nature of the illness that killed so many aboard, nor about how it was determined that the survivors pose no health threat to the general public. The CDC, for their part, has promised to release any new information as it develops."

"Is this for real?" I asked.

"Looks like it," Debbie said.

The reporter pulled a man into the frame. Short, he was bald except for a bit of grey hair above each ear, wearing a white polo shirt with navy, horizontal pinstripes. The reporter said, "So here I have Denny McKone…"

"Danny," the man said.

"Sorry, Danny, and sir, can you explain why you're all here this morning?"

"Well, you know, we think the government needs to come clean about the *Phaeacia*. If they've got nothing to hide, why not just give us the information?" he said.

"What information are you looking for? The CDC has said that the survivors are not a health threat to the public," the reporter said.

"Let us decide for ourselves. We don't even know where these people are. You could be in the IHOP, eating next to one of them and you wouldn't even know it. And we won't know until so many of us are sick that they can't cover it up," he said, and his face reddened a bit.

"You want the CDC to make their addresses public?" the reporter asked.

"Of course. They say they're not living secret lives, and that they're living openly, but we've been trying and we've only been able to track down two of the six. Where are they? It's not acceptable that we, the people of this country, have these probably sick individuals that are living right in our neighborhoods, near our kids, and they could have some space disease that could turn into the next pooponic plague, you know? The Black Death, like what killed all those people in England, a hundred years ago. Do we need to wait until that happens?" he said.

"What do you propose? If the CDC releases their addresses, what then?" the reporter asked.

"You know, either release their addresses or better yet, lock them up. In a quarantine place. That's what I say, anyway," he said.

"Alright, sir, thank you for speaking with us today," the reporter said.

"You bet," he said.

The camera shifted, so that the reporter was the center of the shot, but the protester's right ear and shoulder were still visible. The camera zoomed in on the reporter's face. He said, "There you have it. Protesters in front of CDC headquarters calling for the *Phaeacia* survivors to be quarantined, or else their addresses revealed. Thomas?"

The screen was suddenly filled with a man wearing a tie and jacket, sitting in a studio, who said, "Thank you, Miguel Sigala, from Atlanta. In other news…"

I turned off the TV, and asked, "Are they going to tell people where we live?"

Debbie sighed, stood, and walked over to me. She said, "They told us from the beginning that we weren't going to be in some sort of witness protection program type of thing, and that if we wanted to get unlisted numbers, we could."

Imagining a mob in Goodwin was terrifying. The man said they wanted us to be locked up in quarantine; it had been one of our fears on the *Phaeacia* as we returned. There was no way of knowing if the people we found on Earth would kill us on arrival, lock us up, or do medical experiments on us. The reality turned out better than our worst nightmares, at least.

But on the television, the protestor sounded like a glimpse into our greatest fears. I said, "He compared us to the Black Death."

Deb said, "The government also said that they wouldn't release the addresses of the survivors, and my understanding was that you were a bit better off, since you're a minor living in the home of people with different last names."

"But everyone knows that I was from Goodwin, Maine. It wouldn't be hard to find me," I said. "I mean, it's bad enough I'm so lonely; now I have to be afraid too?" I could feel the panic rising.

Debbie hugged me, and said, "Cel, there's nothing to stop the protesters from finding any of you. We knew this might be an issue, and we agreed to give you a place to live anyway. We'll deal with it one day at a time. It seems most people either believe the government, or they don't really care. Look, there are like 325 million Americans, and only about a thousand cared enough to protest in Atlanta. By those numbers, there would be like three people in Maine who would bother."

My nerves calmed a bit, and I asked, "You figured that out in advance?"

She looked down at me, beaming, and she said, "What? No! How could I? I'm smarter than I look, you know."

"Nuh uh," I said, and smirked.

"I'm fat, not dumb," she said.

Hugging her, I said, "Thanks, Deb."

"I've got your back, yo," she said.

"No. Don't try that hard to be cool," I said.

She laughed and I smiled, but there was still a lump of fear in my stomach. Looking up at her, I asked, "But Deb, what if they're right?"

"About what?" she asked. "About you being sick?"

Nodding, I asked, "They said they were still working on figuring it all out, so how could they be sure we're okay?"

Taking my face in both her hands, she said, "They were trying to figure out what happened on the ship, not whether or not you're contagious. They said they had that part figured out. Cel, you're alright. I don't need a doctor to tell me that. I can just tell that you're going to be fine. You'll live to be an old lady sitting on her front porch swing, mumbling at the cars as they drive by."

Deb's attempt to be funny and reassuring was sweet, but I could tell she was worried too. Letting my face go, she rubbed my shoulder. Between the idea of protestors showing up in front of the house and my possibly being sick—and contagious—anyone in their right mind would be scared. Looking out into the front yard and picturing angry people with signs, shouting that I should be locked up, was horrifying.

"Want some breakfast or something?" she asked.

"What does Ray say?" I asked.

She looked puzzled, but then asked, "About you being sick or protestors or what?"

"Me being sick," I said.

"He doesn't believe it. He thinks you're fine," she said.

"He does?"

"Well, he worries that maybe you spend too much time in your own head, but he believes them when they say that you're not contagious," she said.

"Do I spend too much time in my own head?" I asked.

"Yes. Just like every other teenager I ever heard of," she said.

I asked, "What about the protestors? Is he worried about them?"

"Ray? Nah. I doubt it's even occurred to him, and if it has, I bet he'd love to do the 'get off my lawn' bit," she said. She smiled again, but it was wearier this time; the effort to cheer me up was draining her. Deciding to let her off the hook, I smiled back, and said, "Yeah, I bet he'd like that."

We went to the kitchen with brave faces, but I knew that we were both still afraid.

13

THE NEXT DAY, I MET with Muriel Berber, the personal therapist that Dr. Caledon had mentioned. She looked like she might be seventy years old, although I'm sure she was younger.

"Let's just get to know each other a bit," she said, with a smile, but it was sort of upside-down, in the shape of a frown, and didn't seem genuine. Muriel didn't appear to be afraid of me like the optometrist was. Her facial expressions looked fake, and the mood was uneasy. From the start, I didn't trust her, and didn't feel safe. Even the plants around us looked plastic.

Besides, it's not like I asked to be there; they were forcing me to come, and what were they expecting? Honestly, how could anyone have understood what I'd been through?

Pointing at my folder, I said, "You probably know all about me already." It sucked that yet another person knew more about me than I knew about her.

"Let's get acquainted," she said.

It was overwhelming that so many people knew my face or name, while at the same time, I had no friends. I could use someone to talk to. My initial gut feeling on Muriel was to be careful, though. I still wanted to withdraw, go back to bed, and hide in a cocoon of blankets. I asked, "What should I know?"

Licking her lips, she blinked, and then said, "I realize you've been through a lot, and I want you to feel this is a secure place. A place where you can say anything."

There really was something off about her. It was as if she were part lizard; her eyes were all analysis, with little compassion. She seemed uncomfortable in her skin, constantly fidgeting and shifting her weight in her seat. I said, "Thank you."

"I'm very pleased to be working with you," she said. Her tone was wrong; it sounded rehearsed, without true empathy. Her body language was stiff, and I didn't know what to say except, "Me too." I felt vulnerable.

"How are things going at…" she checked her clipboard, "Deborah and Raymond's?"

"Fine," I said. "Really, it's going good."

She just stared at me for a moment and then, jotting something down, she hummed. Even the tone of the hum was disturbing; there was a critical aspect to it, as if she didn't believe me. Then it got too quiet, so I asked, "Have you always wanted to be a therapist?"

She said, "I have always wanted to help people who want to help themselves."

There was another awkward pause. Looking around the office, I asked, "Did you read all of these books?"

She sat back, as if confronted, and said, "I don't have a color-by-numbers painting in here."

Completely confused, I asked, "What do you mean?" I thought maybe she was the one who was nuts.

She seemed to relax a bit, as if my not getting the painting reference was a bit of a surprise for her. She asked, "Do you like books?"

"I do," I said. "Especially the ones that don't treat teenagers like babies or idiots."

"For example?" she asked.

I asked, "You mean titles of books or, like, scenes?"

"How can an author treat a teen like an idiot?" she asked.

Not realizing the visit would turn into a book report, I thought for a moment, and then said, "Female characters who are rescued by falling in love with the right boy. The skinny kid who finally stands up to the large bully and beats him in a fight. The stepparent who is a monster. Sudden conversions of mean girls at the ends of books. A school where every single character in the book, except for one, hates the new girl."

"Is that what you're actually worried about?" she asked.

"Huh?"

"That everyone at school will hate you?" she asked.

"No, I'm saying in a book, it's insultingly unrealistic when every single person at a school immediately hates the new kid," I said.

"You said 'girl.'"

"It doesn't matter. I meant student," I said.

"Then why do you think you said 'girl'?"

"I don't know. I really was just talking about books. You asked me what it is about certain books that insults teenage readers, and I told you."

"Celestine, I think if we're going to make progress, we'll have to seize these moments when you've revealed something that your subconscious really wants to deal with. You weren't really looking to engage on the topics of books; you simply used it as a vehicle to divulge what was actually worrying you—that the kids at school might not like you," she said. She smiled a self-congratulatory grin, placed her pencil across her notes, and sat back.

Unsure of how therapy was supposed to go, I didn't say anything in response, but I knew I didn't like this. It felt as though a trap had been set, I'd walked into it, and I doubted even more that I'd ever trust her.

"If you say so," I said.

"You said so," she said, still looking smug.

She began talking about how I would have to take rejoining society slowly, without unrealistic expectations. She said, "Maybe you could invite someone your age out to get a coffee or something."

Wincing, I said nothing else and decided therapy was terrible. Having shared something as simple as my feelings about books, I'd been tricked into giving her what it was she wanted to talk about.

How was I supposed to talk to this person about the *Phaeacia*, about what it's like to wake up every morning and immediately check yourself for symptoms of the illness that killed your parents, about sitting on the floor silently staring at the handful of others still alive and wondering who was next, or if you even cared anymore?

After telling her a few thoughts on books, and she twisted it into me being afraid of not being popular in high school, how could I tell her that for the last twenty sleep sessions on board, I dozed off while pondering suicide?

Muriel didn't even notice I wasn't paying attention. She went on and on until we ran out of time and the first session ended.

14

TWO DAYS LATER, I WENT downtown again. My last experience had been awful, and I was uneasy. I was scared not only of running into more girls like those who had crossed the street, or of people like the optometrist, but also of my own reactions. Even if people began to accept that I wasn't contagious, if I kept acting like I had been, screaming and yelling down Main Street, I was sure they would come to believe there was something seriously wrong with me.

I stopped into a small coffee shop. Cup in hand, I turned to find a table, and spotted Alicia sitting in a corner, intently focused on her phone. Taking a deep breath, I walked over, my stomach flopping as I approached her.

"Hey, how's it going?" I asked.

Alicia looked up; there was a slight eye roll, and then she went back to her phone again before she said, "Hey."

Noticing her backpack, and the books peeking out of the top, I tried again. "How's school?"

"Sucks," she said, shrugged, and asked, "So, how come you're not in school?"

"Debbie and I thought we should wait for senior year in the fall," I said.

"Ah, so you're in my graduating class."

"Radical," I said.

She frowned and looked up. "What?"

Feeling about as uncool as I could imagine, I said, "It means 'good' like 'a really good thing.'"

"Oh," she said, and then sort of smiled. "Who's Debbie?"

"She's my cousin and I'm staying with her," I said.

"Oh, right," she said. "Love your retro look." She actually did smile then.

"My clothes," I said, looking down.

"I was looking at a shirt like that online and it was really expensive," she said. "Where did you find it?"

"Not sure," I said, thinking I got the shirt at Banana Republic the summer we left; it had been looser and longer then. When Alicia's phone vibrated and she quickly tapped the screen, I sat down with her.

"My mom's coming in," she said. "Oh, she saw you on TV and said she knows you, or knew you, or whatever."

"Cool," I said.

Just then, a woman in her forties walked into the coffee shop. Dressed like girls our age, she waved at Alicia and headed toward us. When she saw me, she slowed.

"Celestine?" she asked.

"You recognize her?" Alicia asked me.

"I know you," I said.

"Thea. It's me, Thea Rand," she said.

"I've been talking to your daughter! Freaky!" I said.

"I know, right?" Thea said.

"So, like, how does that work anyway, that you knew each other, but my mother got old," Alicia said.

Thea looked at Alicia for a split second, but then went back to studying my face. "That's really wild," Thea said.

"Hello? Explain?" Alicia said.

"Well, when you travel near the speed of light, in space, time slows down. So, time passed here on Earth like normal, but it slowed way down for me," I said.

Alicia's eyes narrowed. "Weird."

Thea said, "Yeah, Celestine and I were born the same year. We used to be in the same graduating class. We were in English class together in 9th grade, but then she left and went into space." Thea chuckled and added, "She didn't age, but I sure did."

I said, "It's good to see you." Standing up to hug her, I reached out with both arms, but she held out a hand for a handshake that felt more like keeping me at a distance than a welcome home.

"You too," Thea said.

There was suddenly a thick tension, despite Thea's smile, and Alicia was obviously beginning to pick up on it. Sitting back down, I didn't know what would happen next, but I did feel that sense of isolation. It was the sense of being contaminated, unclean, and disgusting. I wondered how much courage it took on Thea's part to even shake my hand.

"So, did the government ever figure out what happened?" Thea asked.

"Us getting sick, you mean?" I asked.

"Do they know what it was?" she asked.

"It was a virus. We figured that out before we got back. I don't know how much more they've learned, except that they say we're safe. We're not contagious," I said.

"Yeah, I saw that on the news," she said.

We both nodded, but I was sure Thea thought I was a walking disease.

"Yeah," she added, and nothing more. She stood there looking down on me like I was oozing germs onto everything I touched.

"Get a chai, Mom," Alicia said.

"No, hon, we have to go," Thea said.

"What? Why?" Alicia asked.

"I have something I have to take care of," Thea said.

"Wait, what? Why are you being weird?" Alicia asked.

"Come on, I have an appointment," Thea said, her smile beginning to fade.

"So go," Alicia said, and rolled her eyes.

"You're coming with me," Thea said.

Looking at my cup, I shifted in my seat. Even when I found ways to reach out, there was always that fear. The frustration and anxiety on Thea's face were clear. Feeling more like the disease itself than a person, even though I wasn't sick, I thought I'd never be able to connect with people.

"Why would I have to come? I'll just hang out in town instead. I was waiting for Sarah," Alicia said.

"No. You need to come with me," Thea said.

"You better go," I said. If they would just get out of there, at least I could start dealing with the loneliness, which would be better than suffering through the spectacle of their leaving. Other customers were glancing over.

"I have my car with me," Alicia said. "Do you want me to follow you or something?"

"Just come now, I'm going to be late," Thea said. She grabbed Alicia's wrist and pulled her to her feet.

"Ow! Fuck, Mom!" Alicia said.

"Watch your mouth in public!" Thea said.

Alicia yanked her wrist loose. "Get off me," she said.

"It was nice to meet you, or actually… to see you again," Thea said.

"Nice to see you too," I said, nauseated.

Thea waited, and after a few huge eye rolls, Alicia took the lead and the two of them left. Alone again, my stomach was so upset, I couldn't drink my coffee. Alicia might have become a friend eventually, but it was clear her mother was one of those who were sure I was sick. Picturing them in the car, I could imagine Thea telling Alicia all about the illness, the *Phaeacia*, and why I must be avoided at all costs. Leaving my coffee on the table, I walked out. The loneliness was horrendous.

15

THE NEXT DAY, STILL IN my PJs, I was headed to the kitchen when I saw Debbie sitting on the couch, reading a book. Something ran through me, like the saddest, most needy feeling, and I was pulled toward her. Without saying a word, I climbed onto the couch on all fours.

"Oh, hey, morning," she said. "Hungry?"

I moved to her, lying down on the couch, and I put my head on her lap. Her hands hung in the air above my head until she put the book down, and began stroking my hair.

"You okay?" she asked.

Reaching, I draped my right arm over her knees, and held on. I just wanted to stick to her; this was my first human contact like this in years. My feelings were a mess. Relief and sadness at the same time. I could also sense that there was like an emotional cliff I didn't want to fall over, like if I hugged too hard, I'd lose my grip.

"It's okay, Cel. It's all going to work out," she said.

I nodded, and she just kept stroking my hair. It felt good. It made me miss my mother, but it was also comforting. It was just what I needed.

"Is there anything more we can do? I'll do whatever I can," she said.

"No," I said.

She stopped stroking my hair, leaving her hand still on my head. I gently nudged her hand, and she started again. She stroked my hair and face for a long time, and neither of us spoke again, until Deb cleared her throat and said, "I got you something."

She shifted, and I lifted my head out of the way, as she stood and went into the other room. I felt better than before, but would've let her stroke my hair all day. I don't know how much affection would have been enough. Returning less than a minute later, she placed a white box on the coffee table, and knelt beside the couch. She stroked my hair once more, and said, "I got you an iPhone. Unlimited calls, unlimited texting, and thirty gigs of data."

"I don't know what all that means," I said.

"You will, just play with the thing. It's the best way to learn," she said.

Sitting up, I took the phone out of the box, and asked, "Okay, can you first tell me how to turn it on?"

She laughed, and then taught me a few basics.

"Thanks, Deb," I said, and gave her a little hug. She hugged back, hard, and kissed the side of my head.

"I love you, Cel," she said.

Nodding again, I said, "Me too."

16

LATER THAT DAY, I WAS in the kitchen, and Deb walked in. I smiled her way, thinking of the time on the couch, but I saw that she seemed nervous.

I asked, "What's wrong?"

She sighed. "So," she said, "someone's coming over. Her name is Lauren Silva. She's your age and, well, sort of your age, or your age now."

"I actually am seventeen, you know. I'm not like forty-six, and trapped in a younger body. I've only been alive for seventeen years," I said.

Debbie said, "Right, you're right. Sorry. It's just, it's almost as if I'm talking to you, but then I feel like I'm talking to your daughter or something. I don't know, it's hard to explain."

There was a quiet pause, and then I asked, "So, who is Lauren?"

"She lives up the street, and I talked to her mom. She's coming over to meet you and hang out."

"Oh my God, gag me with a spoon," I said. "You made me a play date?"

Debbie stepped out of the kitchen, but kept talking to me from around the corner. "I didn't make you a play date. When her mom told her about you living here, Lauren got curious. She thinks of you as a time traveler or something."

"She saw me on the news?" I asked, wanting to die. Either I was a nerd she felt bad for, or a circus freak or something from *Star Wars*. The whole thing with Alicia and Thea was bad enough, and now Debbie was fixing me up with people who saw me as a curiosity or a charity case. Would Lauren run away once she decided I was contagious?

"Sort of… the video of you, like news footage of when you got back, went viral," Debbie said.

"Viral?" *As in, virus? Seriously?*

"Oh, I'm sorry. It just means a video that was shared again and again on the Internet."

I loved surfing online, and was learning fast, but for everyone else it had gradually developed and expanded. When I left there was no such thing; my old high school had just purchased its first computer, and that was in the office. It was huge, the monitor was deeper than it was high and wide, and the keyboard was stuck to the front of it. The first time I saw it, two secretaries were carrying it the way movers would carry an armchair, and when they laid it on a desk, it came down on Mrs. Hachey's hand. She yelped and danced away. It was silver, hummed when powered on, produced more heat than a car engine, and the screen contained only green text on a black background.

By the time I returned to Earth, people were sending messages on handheld computers as they walked down the street, watching feature films on the bus, and could take a selfie of themselves on the toilet and post it before they were finished.

And it turns out that I had gone viral before I knew what that meant. In the movies I'd seen, the creature from outer space was always more technologically advanced than the Earthlings. In my case, I was some sort of caveman-spaceman. Honestly, who could've predicted someone would invent a world-wide system of linked computers so children could watch porn, adults could flirt with strangers, people could shop at two o'clock in the morning for stuff they didn't need, and so that an entire subculture could be created that shared cute photos of their cats?

•   •   •

When Lauren arrived, Deb introduced us, and we retreated straight to my room, which was awkward but I didn't know what else to do. She was wearing a grey hooded sweatshirt and leggings, but the hoodie wasn't covering her ass at all. I wasn't sure I'd be able to get myself to wear that to school.

"I like that, but I'd feel self-conscious. We used to wear a long shirt or sweater with stirrup pants or leggings or whatever," I said.

"Everyone wears them like this. Or yoga pants," she said.

"My mom was way into yoga. She wore heavy, loose cotton pants that looked more like judogi pants," I said.

"Judogi?" Lauren asked.

"You know, pants for judo?"

I could tell from Lauren's face that she had no idea, and we were silent for minute. Back in the 1980s, I never had to work hard at making friends, but in my room with Lauren I felt like a total misfit. Clearing my throat, I took a breath to say something, anything, but she spoke first.

"Whatever. People wear this now."

"I need to go shopping," I said.

"Let me see what you have," Lauren said.

A new wave of anxiety. What would she think of my clothes? Pulling open the closet, there was a mix of the old stuff that still fit me and new things Debbie had picked up. Lauren began to look through it.

I pulled out a light blue blouse with a plunging V-neck and sleeves that went almost to the elbows, with the ends rolled up a bit and buttoned in place. The skirt I pulled out was navy blue and went down to mid-calf, kind of a wrap-around.

"How about this?" I asked.

Lauren looked horrified. "Let's not." She took the clothes from me and hung them back up. Embarrassed, I wanted to shut the closet, but she pulled out a simple pair of jeans and a black hoodie, stuff Debbie had bought.

"I haven't even tried those on yet," I said.

"Do it," she said.

Without a second thought, I pulled off the clothes I was wearing and stood braless in a pair of bikini underwear.

"Not very shy, huh?" Lauren asked.

Looking down at my body, I lifted the hoodie. "Sorry, I haven't had a lot of privacy and sort of got over it."

"I'm good," Lauren said. "You look good. I mean, not to be awk, or whatever."

"Awk?" I asked, pulling the sweatshirt over my head.

"You just let the girls swing," she said.

"I hate bras," I said.

"Who doesn't?"

I hesitated. "Should I always wear one? Does everyone wear one all the time?"

"Do whatever you want," she said. "I was just sayin'."

I had only spent a few minutes with Lauren and that old feeling was back. She was so cool and pretty. Maybe all teen girls felt it? Like a mix of admiration and jealousy. That cute and relaxed friend we had, who seemed so with it while we felt like toads and lizards following along, hoping to warm up in the sun.

When I lifted the jeans, they didn't look like they would fit. "I don't think I'll be able to cram my fat ass into these."

"They stretch," Lauren said. "Try it."

She was right. They were snug, but not uncomfortable. I did get an immediate wedgie, though, and tried to pick it free.

Just then, Debbie poked her head into my room. She had a huge grin and asked, "How's it going?"

Rolling my eyes, I walked to the door and closed her out. "Fine," I said, and Lauren giggled.

"So, you're going to school in the fall?" Lauren asked.

"They want me to get settled first," I said.

"Lucky, I wish I could take the rest of the school year off. Chemistry sucks," Lauren said.

"Are you flunking?"

"Totally, I have like an 88 in that class," she said.

I was confused. "Isn't that like a 'B' or something like that?"

"I know, right? Awful."

I said, "I used to be pretty happy with a 'B' in math classes."

"Nobody gets lower than an 'A' anymore. I mean, nowadays, anything less than a 95 or whatever is, like, bad. For honors students anyway, if you want to go to a good college."

"Everyone is smarter?" My anxiety about school was high

enough already; things would be a lot worse if all these people of the future were geniuses.

She shrugged. "My mom says they grade easier now," Lauren said. "But you know, they always say they had it tougher than we do, about everything."

I was relieved. "But you take school seriously?"

"I just want good enough grades to go to the school I want to go to," she said.

"Which school do you want to go to?" I asked.

"I dunno." She shrugged.

It got quiet for a moment, and I was worried things would get tense again, but then she saw my boom box. "No way, you have one of those?"

"I have an iPhone, too," I said sheepishly. "And Deb says it can play music."

"Play something on it," Lauren said, grinning and pointing at the cassette player. "It's like wicked old, right?"

"Actually, it's only about three years old," I said.

Lauren laughed and said, "Right, right. That's weird. Play something."

Selecting a tape, I dropped it in. I hit "play" and Journey's "Send Her My Love" filled the room, but the song was halfway through.

"Dude, that's so retro. I mean, we have an old cassette player thing in the basement, but it's not like this," Lauren said. "Play the song from the beginning."

I hit rewind, and then play. It still wasn't the beginning of the song, so I rewound it some more, and then pressed play again. It still wasn't the beginning of the song.

"What are you doing?" Lauren asked. "Just play it from the beginning."

Smiling nervously, and feeling like a dork, I said, "I'm trying to find the beginning." Trying once more, when I hit play, the last bit of "Separate Ways" was playing.

"That's a different song," Lauren said.

"I know, relax, it's the end of the song before, give it a sec," I said.

"Okay, I'm chill," she said. We sat, tense and quietly waiting. It seemed to take forever, and then finally the song ended and the next began. Grinning with relief, we listened to it quietly for a minute and then Lauren said, "It must be cool. To suddenly have, like, an iPod, a phone, and stuff."

"It's a lot to get used to," I said. "You've always had it?"

"Yeah, I can't remember a time before the Internet," she said.

"Why do people use so many different things on there? Why Facebook and Twitter and Instagram and SnapChat? Is it just that something is cool for awhile and then it isn't?" I asked.

"That's it," she said. "They're always coming up with the latest."

She lay back on her elbows. Her smile was so reassuring that I just blurted out, "So, you're not scared of me being contagious?"

"I dunno. Older people were always more afraid of coronavirus," she said.

"Kids weren't afraid?" I asked.

"Not like them. Maybe because it hit older people harder. I mean, at first we were, like, all careful and stuff, but we got over it. Pretty much the whole time, we were in cars with our friends without masks, or we went to parties in people's homes, or we played sports," she said.

"And you didn't get sick?"

"I didn't, no, and I know some people that did, but no one my age that got super sick," she said, and then she changed the subject, "So what's it like in space?"

"What do you mean?" I asked.

"If you don't want to talk about it, like, I get it," she said.

"If you mean like weightlessness and stuff, we weren't weightless all that long before the spin got up to speed."

"My nan says that she didn't even know you all had gone to space until the news broke in 1991. She said the space shuttles were flying then and she remembers one blowing up in the 1980s, but she didn't know anything about your ship," Lauren said.

"The *Phaeacia* was a secret," I said. "I spent a year keeping it secret from my friends, and telling them instead that I was moving to Alaska."

"Alaska?" she asked. "How is saying you've moved to Alaska going to hide that you're in space. I mean, wouldn't they just message you and email or whatever?"

I waited a moment, and then she answered her own question, "Ah, right. You could actually disappear back then."

"It's impossible now, huh?" I asked. "To disappear, I mean."

"Well, I don't know anyone that would honestly want to, even though people say they do. But yeah, getting off the grid is pretty much impossible. Even the people that think they have, really haven't," she said.

"What if someone went into the woods and built a cabin, with no electricity or whatever? Couldn't they disappear like that?" I asked.

"Yeah, but then you're like that bomber-dude my history teacher was talking about last year, writing like a manifesto against technology and stuff, and sending bombs to people," she said.

Not having the first clue what she meant, I got the impression she barely knew what she was talking about. I said, "Right, I get it."

"No, you don't," she said, and grinned.

Smiling back, I said, "No I don't."

She laughed loudly and said, "You're awesome."

I was awesome! I smiled so broadly, my face hurt. My nerves about her coming over, and it being a social nightmare, were slowly shifting to anxiety about me screwing up a meeting that had gone well.

Her smile fell a bit and she asked, "But like I was saying, why did you have to keep your time in space a secret?"

"They told us that if word got out that we were going to set up a colony, there would be a lot of fear that the Earth was going to blow up or something. People would panic to be onboard, like watching the last lifeboat leave," I said. "We were told that if we were successful, others might follow, but I never understood that part. I mean a radio signal would've taken years to get back here, and we would've been sending a message to strangers."

"So, you were never coming back?" Lauren said.

"To what? I mean, we weren't even halfway there when we

turned back, and returned to an Earth where forty years had passed. If we'd gone all the way, and then come back, it would've been more like 100 years. We wouldn't have known anyone back here; there would've been no one to come back to," I said.

"Weird," Lauren said. "Wait, are you even allowed to tell me all this? Like the government won't come get me now or something?"

"Yeah, it's okay, they told me I can talk about all of it," I said. I worried for a moment that the good time was over, but she smiled again.

Smiling back, I said, "So, anyway, the friends I had back then, like even Debbie, had no idea."

"Why did you go? Like, all of you, why did you go? What made you all think you should go start a new colony on another planet?" she asked.

"For me, it was not about the mission. It was about being with my family. But there were some that felt it was just human destiny to seek out new places, and back then it seemed like the world was on track to destroy itself anyway, like in a nuclear holocaust. Which I found strange, because we only got to go because the Soviets helped us, and we launched from Kazakhstan. But there was no plan to ever come back. Like when Cortes burned his ships when he arrived in Mexico," I said.

Lauren blinked, and then said, "I have no idea what you're talking about right now."

Feeling like a total nerd, I said, "It doesn't really matter. The true believers thought that the mission was a fresh start for humanity."

"Wow. You all must've been really sad when things didn't work out, huh?" she asked.

"Like I said, I went for my family, so when they died, all my reasons for going were gone," I said.

"Right, sorry," Lauren said.

"No, it's okay, thanks," I said.

We both sort of stared at the floor for a moment, and then I said, "The others had all lost family too, and we were all afraid of dying ourselves. So, to us, by the time we got back here to Earth, it'd been more than a year since we gave up on the mission, on the idea of a colony. Our new mission was just to get back here," I said. "Some of us made it."

"But where exactly were you going? Like another planet, right, but which one?"

"We didn't know. Dr. Stenhouse was predicting there must be an Earth-like planet in orbit around Alpha Centuri B," I said.

"That's another sun?" Lauren asked.

"A star, yeah, a sun. So, we were betting on it," I said.

"But you didn't know for sure?"

"My father seemed pretty sure. He trusted Dr. Stenhouse," I said.

"What if it hadn't been there?"

"What if Columbus hadn't found land?" I asked.

Lauren's face became serious and she said, "Columbus was a monster who brought slavery and disease."

Shocked at how negative she was about Columbus, I asked, "He still has a holiday, right?"

"Yeah, but, I think it's just an excuse for a day off now," she said. "Some states have changed it to 'Indigenous People's Day' or something like that. I think Washington was first."

"Washington D.C.?" I asked.

"The state," she said.

"Why not just call it 'Indian Day'?" I asked.

"Dude, no, no one says that. Besides, Columbus was wrong when he called them Indians. This isn't India, you know?" she said.

"He wasn't trying to reach India," I said.

"Well, whatever, no one calls them 'Indians' anymore," she said.

"Isn't there a baseball team called the Indians, like from Chicago or something?" I asked.

"They're changing the names of sports teams too, and there are protests. I guess one of the worst was the 'Redskins,' the football team from Washington; they dropped that name, too," she said.

"Washington state?" I asked.

"Washington D.C.," she said.

"Ah," I said, and nodded. We were quiet for a moment, looking at each other and then at the room. Desperately wanting to get back to something fun, I asked, "So do you have a boyfriend?"

Lauren's face lit up, and she said, "His name is Cole. He's so cute. I mean, he's a guy, so he can be a dick sometimes, but he's pretty cool."

Smiling, I asked, "Does he go to school in Goodwin?"

"Yeah, he plays football and lacrosse," she said. I could tell by the way she spoke about him that she was really into the guy.

"We'll have to find you one," she said, and then she giggled again, as if hatching a secret plot.

"I don't know," I said.

"Oh, if you don't go that way, we can find you a cute chica. It's cool," she said, still smiling.

"Wait, a girl?" I asked. "No, no, I like guys."

"Honestly, it's okay," she said.

"Seriously, I go for boys," I said.

She rubbed my hand. "Are you sure?" she asked. She was so pretty, with a sly grin, that she made me wonder for a moment, and then I jumped when she laughed loudly, pulled her hand back, and said, "You were thinking about it!"

I said, "No I wasn't!" *Was I?* It was confusing.

Still laughing, she threw her arms around me and said, "Aw, it's okay!"

Hugging her back, I didn't know what to say. Her phone vibrated, and we let each other go.

"I gotta go. His highness beckons," Lauren said, rolling her eyes.

"You're leaving?" I said, and then realized how desperate I sounded. It was just that I definitely felt something click with her, and I hadn't felt that in so long.

"Yeah, I've got to, but we'll do something," she said. "Give me your number."

Not knowing it yet, I pulled out my phone, and we found it together. She entered my number in her phone, and then put hers in my contact list.

"Cool," she said. Her phone buzzed again. Reading it, she sighed and said, "He's here. Gotta go. I'll see ya." We hugged briefly, and she headed for the door.

"Okay, thanks for coming over," I said, and then felt like a dork again.

She looked back, beamed, and said, "No problem. See you soon."

Once she was gone, I fell back on my bed. It was as if in trying to find my way out of a dark cave, I had turned a corner and spotted a brightly lit passage out.

17

MAKING MYSELF A BOWL OF the Sponge Bob cereal, I took my breakfast to my room, and sat on the bed. My pajama pants were new and covered in yellow cartoon characters from a film called *Despicable Me 3*. Having not seen any of the movies, I wasn't quite sure what a minion was or did.

Flipping the laptop open and waiting for it to wake, I ate a spoonful of the cereal. It was time for another group session, virtually meeting with the other survivors and Dr. Caledon. This would be our third one and, even though we'd only had two before, I already didn't like these computer-screen gatherings. I wanted to look ahead, not back, and it was as if something were clawing at my leg as I tried to walk forward. With a bowl of cereal, wearing cartoon PJs, and having finally made a friend, I felt like I was making steps towards a normal life. However, during these sessions, I was forced to see the sad and empty faces, and remember.

To be honest, it seemed like I was doing better than they were, maybe because I was younger. I mean, I loved my parents a lot, they were great, and I was heartbroken at losing them, but I wasn't spending all my time depressed. I had the feeling sometimes that the group wanted to see me cry, maybe they even needed me to, but I hadn't, and I really didn't want to.

The laptop screen was soon populated with eight panels, and beneath each there was a name. The only one with a face in it for the moment was mine. One of them had no name listed, so I knew we'd have only one facilitator this session, and his was the next face to appear.

"Hi, Celestine," he said.

"Hi, Dr. Caledon," I said.

"Is everyone late this morning?" he asked, but then faces began popping up around the screen. Dr. Leon Stenhouse, an astrobiologist, had been the team leader, whose wife, Barbara, had been one of the first ones to die. Dr. Glenna Kendall, the xeno-horticulturist, had lost a daughter named Caroline who had been a couple years younger than me. LTC Dana McCormack had been one of the pilots of the *Phaeacia*, and had lost her husband Greg, the other pilot aboard. Sovanara Norris was a nurse and the only surviving member of the medical team. She first lost her husband, and then her twin sons. Ian Mokone was a mechanical engineer who had been in charge of the shelter modules, and he had lost his wife. Before she got sick, I remember being jealous of her, because I had such an enormous crush on Ian. His skin had been beautiful, dark, and shiny. Now, all you could really see in his face was his grief.

"Good morning, everyone," Dr. Caledon said.

There were a few mumbled "good mornings" in response. It wasn't like a happy reunion. We had seen each other at our worst, and we'd said and done things we wouldn't have under different circumstances. When your heart has been ripped out by loss, and you live in fear of being next, and all this while trapped in an aluminum tube streaking through space trying to get home, your moral compass and your filter get a bit out of whack. What had gone unspoken, also, was the fear of being the last one left alive aboard the *Phaeacia*.

Still, despite the horror—or maybe because of it—we also saw examples of the best in us. When a mission specialist named Lucy Gendille lost her son, she blamed the nurse, Sovanara Norris, who had actually cared for the boy day and night. It was nasty, and the two women couldn't be in the same part of the ship. Shortly thereafter, the nurse's own twin sons fell ill and died in each other's arms. Lucy Gendille herself got sick next, and it was Sovanara Norris who cared for her. Nothing negative was said between them; they were simply two grief-stricken mothers, one a patient and the other a nurse. A few hours before her own death, Lucy promised, "I'll take care of the boys."

Sovanara Norris said only, "I know," and, as her friend and nurse, held her hand until she was gone.

During the online sessions, Dr. Glenna Kendall was always asking about my life, and this particular Saturday morning was no different. "Hi Celestine, big plans for the weekend?" she asked. Her face was happy, but by her voice I knew she was still devastated.

"Nothing too major," I said. "I made a friend, I think."

"That's nice," Dr. Kendall said, but her smile was a sad one.

"Let's get started." It was the voice of Ian Mokone, the shelter engineer. Glancing to that corner of the screen, I saw him rub his face with both hands. Perhaps hating these sessions more than the rest of us, he seemed to see getting started as the best way to get to the ending.

In addition to what Dr. Caledon had told me at Mass General, it was hinted in the previous sessions that not participating may be taken as an indicator to someone important that we were not dealing with our return well and that we might need in-patient care.

My iPhone vibrated on the desk behind me. Picking it up, I read the message. It was from Lauren.

It read, "*Sup?*"

"Whose phone was that?" Dr. Caledon asked.

"I'm sorry, that was me," I said.

"No, that's great," Dr. Kendall said. "You're really assimilating, aren't you?"

Feeling like an invading alien, I said, "I guess."

"Perhaps you could turn off the phone during the session," Dr. Caledon said.

"No! They never do that!" Dr. Kendall said.

"It's not an issue," I said, and turned off the phone.

"If it isn't too much trouble," said Ian Mokone; his tone was sarcastic.

Dr. Caledon cleared his throat and then asked, "So, how is everyone feeling?"

This was a really heavy question. It had been a daily one, asked every morning aboard the *Phaeacia*. At first, if someone admitted they had become ill, everyone was sad, but after a while it had become almost mechanical. Those who were still well learned to remain quiet while those who were symptomatic spoke up. With Dr. Caledon's question at the beginning of these sessions, everyone fell silent.

"Fine," Dr. Caledon said. "Now, what are everyone's feelings today?"

The members of the group took turns trying to think of something basically meaningless to say in order to have their turn pass them by, and soon everyone had shared some boring thing from the past week. It was lame, but it was quickly over, and so was the session. To be honest, there never seemed to be much therapy going on, and it wasn't much more than checking in.

Dr. Caledon said, "Alright then, let's meet again two Saturdays from today. Everyone have a great week."

There were a few "good-byes" and the panels went blank once more. Closing the laptop, I picked up my phone. That one-word message from Lauren was all there was. As I contemplated what the appropriate response might be, Deb called up to my room.

I said, "Coming."

She was standing at the door, and said, "Cel, I'm going to Dunkin' Donuts. Come with me."

"Okay, cool," I said.

We drove over and, walking in, I could see there were many teenagers there, but apparently only two of them had bought anything. Everyone looked our way, and then most turned away again, but some continued to stare. I spotted Lauren sitting with a group on the far side, occupying a couple booths.

"Listen, Deb, don't take this the wrong way, but I'm going to hang out here," I said, glancing over toward Lauren.

Deb caught it, and looked that way too. "Oh sure, no problem."

"Thanks," I said.

"Need money?" she asked.

I really didn't want her digging in her purse and handing me money in front of everyone. "No, I'm all set, thanks though," I said.

"Have fun," she said, and turned to the counter.

Remembering the girls on the street, I was nervous, even though Lauren had been cool.

"Hey!" she said, with a grin.

I said, "Hey," and smiled back.

This was met by a chorus of "hey" from the teens sitting with Lauren.

"This is Celestine," Lauren said. "She's cool."

There was a second round of "hey," but there weren't that many smiles among the others.

"Hey everyone," I said. There was a moment when I thought I might remain standing while everyone else stared, until there was a sudden shifting and space for me appeared.

"So, what's up?" I asked.

"Just chillin'," one said.

There was a sudden roar of laughter and shouting from the other side of the room. I jumped, and we all looked.

"There he is, being hot shit again," one said.

There was a tall, beautiful guy. He was clearly the center of the fun, and was holding the attention of the teens sitting at four different tables.

"Who is he?" I asked.

"That's Ken Apocino," Lauren said. "He's a jerk."

More laughter. "What do you mean?" I asked.

"Total quarterback dick, stereotypical," said a thick-necked girl with heavy eye make-up.

"It's so cliché," another said, her hair streaked purple.

Everyone was laughing and cheering Ken on, except for one guy. Sitting in the popular circle, but with only a slightly amused smile, he occasionally shook his head. His hair was tousled, and auburn. He wore a jacket with "GHS football" on the front. He was examining the sides and bottom of a plastic saltshaker.

"He's not that bad," said the only boy at our table.

"Dylan crushing on Kenny," the purple-streaked girl said.

Looking at Dylan, I sensed something was different about

him. His hair was sandy, but his eyes were dark. He was lanky; his hands and grin were a size too large.

"Who is the guy with the red hair, sitting down, playing with the salt shaker?" I asked.

"Jackson?" the purple-streaked girl asked.

"That's my brother, Jackson," Lauren said. "He's a dweeb."

There was more laughter from Ken's audience. He was telling a story, over-acting the scenes, entertaining everyone around him except Jackson, who looked restless, until he stood. He put the saltshaker down, glanced around, made eye contact with me, and he paused. The audience cheered, and I lost him to Ken and the crowd again. Jackson had only paused a moment, but Lauren had seen it too.

"Ooh, he noticed you," Lauren said, laughing. "Don't do it. I'm warning you." She shoved my shoulder, and I remembered her hand on mine.

Smiling, I shrugged and forced myself to look away from him. I asked, "Don't you guys buy anything? Like a donut or anything?"

"So, your real name is, like, Celestine?" the girl with the purple streak asked.

"What's your name?" I asked.

She hesitated and then said, "Emily."

Lauren said, "Oh, right, this is Emily, and Dylan, and this is Heather."

The thick-neck girl immediately said, "Not Heather. Call me Arielle."

Emily giggled. "Like the mermaid."

"What mermaid?" I asked.

Emily shot a look at Lauren, who smirked and nodded.

Arielle said, "There was a movie called 'Little Mermaid' and her name was Ariel, but that's not where I got it from."

"Why did you choose it then?" I asked.

"Arielle Holmes," she said.

"Who?"

"She's a writer and an actress. She was, like, a junkie and homeless, and then she got discovered, and she kicks ass," she

said.

Dylan agreed. "And smokin' hot."

"You're gross," Arielle said. "There's more to women, you know?"

Dylan grinned. "No."

Arielle rolled her eyes. "Pig."

Smiling, I looked at Lauren, who was chuckling.

Arielle said, "Don't encourage him."

At first, I thought she was kidding, but she was glaring at us both. I asked her, "Is she good looking?"

"Well yeah," Arielle said. "But she's more than that."

"You don't think it's flattering if someone thinks you're good looking?" I asked.

"I think it's degrading," she said.

Confused, I said, "The world has definitely changed."

Dylan laughed, and said, "Why am I even sitting over here?"

"I wonder the same thing," Arielle said.

There was a pause, and then I asked, "What else do you do for fun?"

Lauren said, "We're going to hang out at Crescent Beach tomorrow. You should come."

I frowned. "It's April. Kinda cold for the beach," I said, not wanting to turn down the only social invitation I'd had since returning, but I was a little surprised.

"Don't wear a bikini or anything," Lauren said.

Dylan jumped in, "Yeah, don't wear anything." He was still grinning when Arielle backhanded his arm.

Shrugging again, I said, "I'll go." Turning to Emily and Arielle, I asked, "Are you guys going?"

"I don't do the beach," Arielle said.

Dylan said, "Yeah, you know, because it's degrading."

"But we won't be in bathing suits," I said.

Arielle ignored me and, to Dylan, said, "Shut up, dick."

"Are they always like this?" I asked.

Lauren chortled, and said, "It never stops. It's like they're married."

Arielle pushed Dylan, and said, "Eww, no."

Smiling, I looked back over at Jackson, and saw him punch another guy hard in the arm. The guy who was struck howled, and then walked away laughing, holding his shoulder. Jackson stood there, snickering. They were like cavemen. Shaking my head, I thought, even after all these years, boys were still so dumb.

18

AT THE BEACH, IT WAS a crisp spring day, maybe 50° F. Looking around, I was relieved to see that I had picked the right clothes. Wearing jeans, a long-sleeve shirt, and a barn vest, I'd even guessed right with the sneakers on my feet.

People sat around on blankets, and many had their hoodies pulled tight around their faces, but there were no masks in sight. We were beach kids over-eager for the summer to come, too impatient to wait, and no one seemed concerned about me being there. The waves rolled in, and seagulls pin-wheeled above waiting for the wayward Cheetos and Pringles to appear.

Even with the vest, I was a bit cold, although none of the other girls seemed bothered by it. Lauren and I arranged a blanket on the sand and we sat hugging our knees. As we watched a few of the boys play Frisbee, she moved closer to me, placed her head on my shoulder, and giggled. It felt amazing; I grinned and blushed. Unlike the others, these people seemed completely unconcerned about me possibly being sick, and it seemed that Lauren accepting me was enough for her friends. I was tempted to ask her why she wasn't afraid, but I decided to leave wonderful alone. Just to feel human contact, when others had run away, was brilliant.

Jackson was among the boys. They all had their jackets off, if they had brought any, and were running around, clearly putting on a show for us. Jackson made a throw, scanned the other boys, and then our eyes met. His smile broadened, and he waved. I felt my face flush again, and I waved back. He started toward me, and I whispered to Lauren, "Oh my God, he's coming."

"What?" she asked. She lifted her head from my shoulder, and I immediately missed it being there.

"'Bout time you got here," he said, still grinning.

Straightening my legs, my feet together, I smiled, and took a breath to reply, but just then, from behind me I heard, "I got here as fast as I could. Had to work."

Looking back, I saw another boy, carrying a cooler, was just arriving. He passed Lauren and me, walked down to Jackson, and the two of them carried the cooler the rest of the way.

Feeling like a total geek, I wanted to die.

"You thought he was talking to you?" Lauren asked, smiling.

Frowning, I asked, "You're asking *me*, right?"

Laughing, she said, "Of course I am. You're so weird sometimes, Cel. By the way, don't worry. He saw you. Try not to be so obvious." She lay down, and so did I. Still feeling like an ass, I closed my eyes. Even with the occasional cool breeze, I was dozing a bit when Lauren turned over.

"Sun's so warm this time of year," she said.

"Twenty-seven million degrees," I said.

"Okay, that was nerdy," she said.

Grinning, I tried to backhand her leg and hit her bum instead, and again, the rush from human contact. I just wanted to curl up against her. Not in a sexual way, at least I didn't think so, but more like someone hugging her pillow.

She giggled, but then in a more hushed tone, she asked, "What was it like? To see the sun again?"

Thinking for a moment, I said, "It was, like, a relief. I mean, I saw it from the ship first, before we landed, before we entered the atmosphere, and I couldn't believe it was our sun at first, you know? But then when I came out into the fresh air after we landed, it was just relief. Moist heat, but clean and fresh."

"Ew," she said.

"What?"

"Don't say the word 'moist,' it's disgusting," she said.

A shadow fell across us both, and I looked up. Jackson was standing there, with a couple other boys behind him. Suddenly feeling self-conscious, and despite wearing a vest, I covered my midsection with my hand.

"Get out of the sun, dick," Lauren said.

"You're the space girl, right?" Jackson asked.

"You're the dweeb, right?" I asked.

Lauren laughed.

His smile widened. "Yeah, well, you should stop listening to my sister."

I said, "She doesn't say stupid things like 'space girl.'"

"It's not like 'dweeb' was that clever," he said.

His face was warm, his eyes bright green, and his teeth were perfect. I couldn't help it—I liked him, but I could almost feel Lauren rolling her eyes next to me.

"So, what's up?" he asked.

"Just here, trying to get some rays," I said.

"Get some rays? With jeans and a vest?"

"What the hell do you want?" Lauren asked.

There was a bit of a pause, and one of the boys behind Jackson laughed.

"So, you want to hang out sometime?" he asked.

"Aren't we doing that now?" I asked.

"I mean like hang out, me and you," he asked.

I wasn't sure what someone said in response to such an invitation in 2022. I tried a bit of the vernacular I'd heard and hoped it was appropriate. "Sure, whatever."

The boys laughed, and Lauren snickered.

"Alright, whatever. I'll message you. Lauren has your number?"

"Yeah, she does," I said.

"Cool," he said.

"Cool," I said.

The boys walked away.

"I knew he noticed you last night," Lauren said.

"Whatever," I said again. It seemed like a really useful expression.

Lauren and I were quiet for a moment, and then I asked, "So, what's he like?"

Lauren groaned and said, "Oh my God, my life."

Grinning, I pretended to know what that meant. Glancing over at Jackson again, watching him play like a little kid roughhousing with his friends, I dropped my hand on the small of Lauren's back, and I was happy.

19

THE NEXT MORNING, I WAS sitting in the living room scrolling through my Instagram when Deb came in with a shoebox.

"What's that?" I asked.

"Pictures. Of you, me, your parents, stuff like that. From before you left," she said.

I froze. "Why didn't you show these to me earlier?"

"I didn't know if I should, but I think it's time," Deb said.

She handed me the box, and I cradled it in my lap.

"I don't have any photos of my parents. I got an email that said they were going to send them, but I haven't gotten the pics yet, and besides I think there were only a few," I said. This reminded me that they'd also written that they would be holding my parents' remains for a time longer, and that they would release them as soon as possible.

"You have these now," she said, smiled, and sat beside me. "You want to go through them together?"

Looking down at the box, I was almost scared to open it. It was heavy; there was a lot to look through. "You kept this all these years?"

"My mom kept them. Probably sat in the back of her closet. When you moved in with me, she gave me the box to pass along to you," she said.

Rubbing the lid, my anxiety was growing.

"Open it," she said.

Turning to her, I said, "Deb, would it be okay if I took this to my room and looked through it alone the first time?"

Her smile fell, and I could tell she was disappointed, but she said, "Sure. Oh sure. We can look at it together later."

"Thanks," I said.

She stood and said, "Let me know if there is someone you don't recognize or something," she said. She smiled again, but it seemed forced this time.

"Thanks," I said again.

As she walked away, I went to my bedroom. Climbing on the bed, I put the box between my legs, and tucked my hair behind my ears. Turning off my phone, I lifted the lid, and saw that the photos were not organized, but instead they lay loose in the box.

The image on top, in the center, was of Gram, my mom's mother. She was at the kitchen counter, hands out of frame, caught mid-sentence with her mouth open. It was probably a holiday candid shot. We used to go over there at Thanksgiving; it was my parents and I, and Deb, her brother, and her parents, and of course my grandparents. We didn't sit at TV trays while the adults ate in the dining room like some families did. There were six adults and three kids, and we all just sat around the long wooden table. I always sat next to Deb, and we giggled through the whole thing, except for when Gramp said grace. We laughed especially hard when Gram would chew on the turkey neck. The crunching was unbearably funny, and we just couldn't figure out how she managed it with her dentures.

Sighing at the memory, I missed lreally aughing. I mean, I figured I'd learn to laugh again, but it just hadn't come naturally. As I sat there with that photo of Gram, I forced a fake-laugh, and was immediately uncomfortable and a bit nauseated.

Looking at all the photos beneath, I realized this was going to take a long time and would be emotionally exhausting.

The next photo was of Deb's mom, my aunt Rita. I decided I should go visit her, I hadn't seen her since my return, but then I realized she was one of the first to know I was back and she hadn't come to see me either. Frowning, I put the photo down on my bed with the first.

Pulling the next photo from the box, my hand began to

tremble. It was my dad and I when I was maybe four years old. He was holding me and we were smiling, looking at the camera and probably my mom behind it. In the background was the big yellow car we owned for most of my childhood. The backseat had been bigger than a park bench, and in the days before much seatbelt use, I used to stretch out when we drove somewhere and watch out the window as clouds and telephone poles passed, and listen to my parents' small talk in the front seat.

Sitting on my bed, I looked out the window, and saw clouds there too. I missed my parents so much. There had been six survivors aboard the *Phaeacia*. Why couldn't there have been eight? Was it just bad luck or was it fate? Why us? Why did we six live to return, and all those others didn't? I mean, even if there could've been seven survivors, at least I wouldn't have lost them both, but then I immediately felt guilty for thinking one could die if I could keep the other.

My grief was compounded by guilt and loneliness. Lauren was cool but there's a loneliness that goes beyond simply being alone, or even being rejected. It comes from finding yourself without people who have the same background as you. There was no one my age on the planet that I had common experiences with.

It wasn't like making friends for normal people. Everyone who came into my life would need me to teach him or her everything about me. Normally, a huge chunk of who we are doesn't need to be explained because the people we are beginning relationships with have had many of the same experiences, but not for me. I really felt like an alien.

Looking into the box, I pushed aside photos of me and Deb, my aunt and uncle, Gramp, until I found one of my mom. She was alone in the photo and caught mid-laugh, with her head back. Taking that one, and the one of me and dad, I stood them in the shelf next to my boom box.

"I'll buy some frames," I told them. Putting the lid on the shoebox, I decided I'd have to go through the photos a little at a time. It was heavy and I didn't know how far down I could go before I got stuck in it. Still, even then, with my stomach in knots, I didn't cry. When I turned my phone back on, there were five messages from Lauren:

"Hey."

"U sleeping?"

"U there?"

"OMG. Ur so annoying."

"Msg me."

I sighed. You really had to be available to your friends around the clock; they seemed to freak out if they couldn't reach you, or they got insulted because you didn't immediately reply.

I wrote her back. *"What's up?"*

The response was almost instantaneous. *"Wanna go to the mall?"*

"Will you pick me up at Debbie's?" I asked.

"Be there in 5 minutes."

Lauren arrived in a car that looked like one my neighbors had when I was a kid in the 1970s, but much newer. She never got out; I climbed in.

"Is this a Volkswagen Beetle?" I asked.

"It's my buggy," Lauren said with a broad grin.

It had a red exterior, a tan interior. "They still make these?" I asked.

"I guess. This one is old. It's a 2000 or something."

I looked down at the shift. "It's an automatic!"

Lauren looked confused. "An automatic what?"

"I mean… it's not a standard. The shifter, you know, with a clutch," I said, pointing.

"Dude, I know what a stick-shift is, but this isn't like some old pickup truck," she said. She grinned and winked, and I couldn't help but smile back. "You're really weird, you know that?" she asked.

When we arrived at the mall, I was relieved to see it was just a mall. There were new stores, new brands, and large flat screen televisions everywhere, but it was basically the same old place.

We walked one loop around the section we entered, came back to the food court, and sat without food. There was a steady stream of shoppers who were there to actually buy things mixing with a current of teenagers who only walked slow loops, sort of looking through shop windows, but never really going inside.

Two girls walked up, and everyone said, "Hey" and "Sup."

Lauren said, "This is Lily and Erin. This is Celestine."

"Right, the girl from space, right?" Lily asked.

"Actually, I'm from here," I said, and grinned like I was kidding, and they laughed like they got the joke.

Lauren asked, "So what's up?"

"Nothing," Erin said.

"Bored," Lily said.

Silence fell for a couple seconds, and then Lauren said, "Yup," and all three laughed, but I didn't.

"So, I guess we'll go for a walk, check things out," Erin said.

"Right," Lauren said.

"Nice to meet you both," I said.

"You too," Lily said, and the two walked off.

I watched them go and then said, "Well, that was interesting."

"What's there to talk about?" Lauren asked, "We're in the same mall in the same town and you shut down the space thing."

I didn't say anything, and Lauren didn't either. We were caught by surprise when Jackson and a couple of his friends approached us from behind.

"Hey."

"What do you want?" Lauren asked.

Jackson asked, "You have money?"

"I'm not giving you any money," Lauren said.

"I'm saying, if you need money, I've got some. You and Celestine don't have any drinks or food or whatever. I wanted to make sure you could get something if you wanted." He pulled his wallet out.

Lauren's mouth hung open, but she said nothing.

I said, "That's really sweet. We're all set. Thanks." I think I even managed to smile. God, he was so cute.

"No problem," he said. "Are you going to be at the pit later?" He put his wallet away and ran a hand through his hair.

Lauren smacked my wrist. I had been twisting my fingers in my own hair without knowing it. "Maybe," I said.

"Alright, cool. If you go, I'll see you there," Jackson said.

"Cool," I said.

His smile grew even wider. "Cool."

The guys walked off in the same direction Lily and Erin had gone. Downstream.

Lauren hit me again, this time on the shoulder. "OMG. He's into you."

"He is?" I asked.

"I know my brother," Lauren said. "He can be a player, so watch out."

"A player? You said that on the beach; what is that?" I asked.

"Like, he's had quite a few girlfriends."

"Is he a bad guy?" I asked.

"He's not a bad person, but you know, he's a teenage boy. They all basically suck," Lauren said.

As I watched Jackson fade into the shoppers, he looked back once, and flashed that smile again. I felt it, like a warm breeze.

"Stop!" Lauren said.

It felt good. I asked, "You hungry? Want to get something?"

"I don't have any money," Lauren said, and laughed.

"It's on me," I said.

Splitting the fries, she buried her half in ketchup, and I didn't use any.

"Did you not have ketchup back in the '80s?" she asked.

"We had ketchup. I'm alright without it," I said.

She pinched three fries together and crammed them into her mouth.

"So, are you going to the party?" I asked.

"Stop. Shut up," Lauren said.

"What?" I smiled again.

"Just stop," Lauren said.

"I was just wondering," I said.

"We'll go to the party," Lauren said.

I stole a fry with ketchup from her side of the paper plate and said, "Good."

She smiled, and said, "You're so annoying."

Eating the fry, I realized that I still didn't really like ketchup.

•   •   •

We drove to the pit that evening, and there were already cars, SUVs, and pickup trucks parked haphazardly all around. In the center of the piles of gravel was a fire. It was larger than a campfire, but smaller than a decent bonfire. Around it stood teenagers, their facial features already smudged by the fade of daylight. The boys all stood with their weight evenly distributed, feet shoulder width apart, while the girls shifted their weight from one foot to the other every few minutes, hips thrusting with each transferal.

"Don't leave me," I said.

Lauren laughed. "You know Emily, Arielle, Lily, Erin, Dylan… you can do this."

I exhaled.

"And there's your crush right over there," Lauren said, pointing. I looked that way and there was Jackson standing in a circle of people, who were once again watching the Ken show, as if the Dunkin' Donuts act had been taken on the road. I couldn't imagine walking alone anywhere near them without looking like a total dweeb.

"I'll stick by you for a bit," I said.

We exited the car and went to the back. Lauren pulled out two Nalgene water bottles and handed one to me. It was ice cold, and seemed to be filled with something purple.

"Wow, thanks," I said. "Is it wine? Where'd you get these?"

"Wine?" Lauren said, laughing. "Nobody drinks, like, wine. Like that's so sophisticated or whatever."

Being laughed at stung a bit. "What is it?" I asked.

"Pinnacle and Gatorade," she said.

"What?" I had no idea what Pinnacle was.

"Vodka and something mixed with it to make it taste better," she said, grinning. "Taste it."

Popping the cap, I took a sip. It was awful. Sweet and terrible, burned my throat and nose, and made me want to gag. Exhaling, I said, "It's good."

She took a sip. "Liar," she said, "but it works."

"What do I owe you?" I asked.

"It's all good," Lauren said.

"Thanks. That's awesome," I said, glancing once more at the bottle.

"Where can we leave the bottles?" I asked.

"You mean when you're done?"

"I mean, just to put it down. Or do we have to carry them around all night?" I asked.

"You never put the bottle down. Don't let it out of your sight. That's, like, crazy. You'll be date-raped in about five minutes if you do," Lauren said. She moved ahead of me, and I followed right behind. We walked into the middle of the clique-groups around the fire. Dozens of people glanced our way briefly before returning to their own conversations. One of the smaller circles erupted into loud group laughter. Still not used to it, the sound startled me.

"Chill," Lauren said.

We joined one of the little rings of people. Lily and Erin were in this one, and the chorus of "hey" and "sup" happened again.

Lily asked, "Have you seen Cole?"

I wasn't sure who she was talking to until Lauren answered, "Is he already here?"

Someone I didn't know said, "I think he's over there with your brother."

Everyone in our circle simultaneously looked over at Ken's circle. He high-fived someone, and the ring of people laughed. Ken stepped out of the center, and slipped in beside Jackson. I wondered which one was Cole. Lauren was on her toes, trying to spot him. Music suddenly came from the back of an SUV with the tail end opened wide. Everyone looked, and then there was a noticeable sway in the circles as members moved to the beat. Not dancing with their feet, just an upper-body rocking in each group as they talked and laughed. I felt it too, and the vodka; I took another sip.

"C'mon," Lauren said, as she stepped past me.

"Where?" I asked.

There was some giggling in the circle we were leaving, as we walked toward the popular people, including Jackson.

"Oh, man, Lauren. I don't want to just go up to him," I said.

"Everything isn't about you," she said.

"Ouch, harsh," I said.

She glanced at me as we walked, smiled, and said, "Sorry. So, don't talk to him."

Walking with that relaxed sort of buzz you get, my feet were a little heavy, my head-turns felt dramatic, and there were fewer problems in the world. The cool circle opened much more readily than I expected; I thought we'd have to ask permission or say a secret code word to get in.

"Hey, this is Cel," Lauren said.

Half-waving, I nodded, and the circle said their "heys" and that was that.

"What's up?" someone to my left asked.

"Nothing," Lauren said.

It grew quiet for a minute; I drank, and then realized half the circle had watched me do it. A guy to my right said, "You were in space, right?"

The alcohol felt good. "Finally," I said, lowering the bottle. "Everyone always asks if I'm *from* space. That's awesome that you asked it that way. Yeah, I was *in* space."

There was a bit of laughter around the circle; it felt welcoming.

"What was that like?" a girl to the left asked.

"It's hard to explain," I said, hoping I wouldn't have to.

"Were you weightless?" the guy to the right asked.

"Jesus," Lauren said. "She was up there for years; she wouldn't be weightless the whole time."

There were a few more laughs. I smiled, appreciating that Lauren was helping me handle the questions. "We were weightless for a little while, but then we weren't for most of the time," I said.

"Still, it must have been cool, right?" another guy, almost directly across from me in the circle, asked.

"Dude," the girl next to him said and elbowed him.

"Seriously, I would love to go to space," another guy to the right said.

The more they talked about it, the more images and feelings from the *Phaeacia* came back. The gloom and the fear. My buzzed feeling was beginning to suck; combined with the memories, it was shifting from a fun sensation to a dizzying and dark one.

"Did you see anything like UFOs or whatever?" another voice asked. There was laughter.

"God, you're dumb," someone else said.

"How did you go to the bathroom? One of those vacuum things?" Yet another voice asked, and I couldn't tell where they were coming from. The drinking was messing with my ability to focus.

Lauren said, "Okay, enough."

"Were people hooking up?" someone else asked, and there was louder laughter. "You know, like on a cruise ship; everybody hookin' up on a cruise ship."

A cruise ship? A fucking cruise ship? I felt my focus suddenly sharpen, but before I could say anything, Jackson was standing beside me and he said, "Shut up, you guys."

I took hold of his sleeve in my fingers.

"What's your problem?" a voice asked.

"Yeah, man, lighten up," another said.

Flashing with anger, I said, "Yeah, it was like a *cruise* ship. One with only a couple windows. Dimly lit. You know, with people sick and dying. It was like a cruise you go on and you watch your parents die. And your friends. And the doctor who tried to save your mother. And one of the two pilots steering the ship."

The silence was so immediate that even surrounding circles who hadn't heard me went silent as well, and the hush spread outward, like anti-sound.

"It was like a cruise where you're racing to get back to a place you thought you'd never see again, not knowing if you'll live long enough to get there, and not knowing if they'll even let you land," I said.

Jackson turned, facing out of the circle, and put his hand on my shoulder urging me to follow. He said, "Let's take a walk." He took the bottle from my hand, and handed it to Lauren.

As I was turning with him, over my shoulder, I said, "It was *just* like a cruise." We walked away. The circle was quiet, and I only heard the music, which was completely unfamiliar.

Jackson's arm was firmly around my shoulders.

Then I heard Ken's voice say, "Weird bitch." Only a couple people laughed, and even those uncomfortably.

Going with Jackson, I could walk fine and without stumbling, but I was buzzing in spite of the bit of clarity that anger brings. Trying to hold on to the pissed-off feeling, I sensed that right around the emotional corner I could be sobbing in a ball on the ground, and I was slipping that way.

"Are you okay?" Jackson asked as we walked.

Am I okay? What does that even mean? "I'm fine," I said, shrugging his arm off my shoulder.

"Listen, none of us have any way of knowing what it's like in space, to be trapped that way," Jackson said. "You could explain it a thousand times, but it's just too much, you know?"

Stopping, I said, "I do know."

"But some of them do remember what it's like to have sick family, and all of us spent some time scared of a disease," he said.

"It's not the same," I said.

"I get it was different, and that part is impossible for us to truly understand. But getting sick, contagious people and all that, that's something everybody wants to leave in the past," he said.

"I just want to blend in," I said. "I don't want to be Space Girl."

"Right now, that's all anyone knows about you. Let us get to know the rest of you. And as much as this sucks, expecting teenagers to not say stupid things is probably unrealistic," he said, and then smiled with those green eyes and perfect teeth. I couldn't help but smile back a little.

"It's going to be okay," he said.

Looking back at the party, I could see people were talking again. "I can't go back there," I said.

"It's the best thing to do. If you stay away, you'll be the weird girl who tweaked at the party. If you go back and just say sorry, everything will be fine," he said.

"Sorry?" I asked, knowing I hadn't done anything wrong.

"I know you have nothing to be sorry about, but it's the best move," he said.

He was smarter and, like, much more perceptive than I thought he was going to be. I said, "But that's not honest. It's not the real thing."

"Look, you have your whole life to be lonely. Don't do it now. It's the worst time to be a loner," he said, and he passed his thumb over my right cheek as if wiping a tear that wasn't there.

Above the music, I heard a laugh, and looked over to see Lauren holding the two bottles and laughing with the circle. At a nearby group, a smaller one, several girls with straight blonde hair were glaring at me, and one of them was Alicia. I looked back at Lauren.

"I have to apologize, huh?" I asked.

"Just because you were right doesn't mean it wasn't the wrong way to deal," Jackson said.

Walking back with Jackson beside me, I wanted my bottle. The circle grew quiet as we entered it.

"Hey. I'm sorry. You guys couldn't know and you were just trying to be friendly, so I'm sorry for being like that," I said. I only half-meant it, but I thought Jackson was probably right. Besides, I was sure there would be plenty more opportunities to be judged once school started.

Around the circle, they were all saying things like, "It's all good," "It's cool," or "It's okay." Lauren handed me my bottle, and I took a drink. There were a few encouraging comments from the group. A new song came on, yet another I'd never heard before. Lauren read something in my face I suppose, because she suddenly strode over to the car, leaned into it, and the music stopped. A female voice from the blonde circle called out, "Aw, that was my jam!"

When the music came back on, it was a different song, and Lauren returned with a big grin while "When Doves Cry" by Prince played. She raised her bottle, and I clunked mine against hers.

"Thanks," I said, smiling.

"No problem," Lauren said.

"Was this popular before you flew?" Jackson asked.

"That summer," I said. "It came out the summer before we left. Debbie was crazy about it."

"Debbie?" Jackson asked.

"My cousin," I said. "I'm staying with her."

Jackson listened a bit. "Show me how to dance to this," he said.

Lauren rolled her eyes, and I took a long drink to freshen up my buzz. It still burned, but less so.

"Yeah, I'll show you," I said. Handing my bottle back to Lauren, and taking Jackson's hand, I led him toward the fire and stopped just outside of our circle. Letting his hand go, I began dancing.

"That's wild," he said. "You dance just like that red-headed girl in *Breakfast Club*."

"What's *Breakfast Club*?" I asked.

"Holy shit, you haven't seen it?" he asked as he danced. "You have to see it. It'll make even more sense to you than us, I bet."

"It's a movie?" I asked.

He smiled again and said, "Why don't you come over to my place sometime and we'll watch it? My dad has it on DVD."

"Cool," I said. "Where do you live?"

Laughing, he said, "In the same house as my sister." He looked back at Lauren. Even from there, I could see her rolling her eyes, shaking her head, and sipping from each bottle.

Feeling good in the glow of the buzz and the fire, and dancing with a nice guy to familiar music, I started to giggle.

"What is it?" Jackson asked, grinning.

It turned into a small chuckle, and then, I couldn't help it, I laughed. I laughed at Lauren two-fisting the drinks and at Jackson laughing at me laughing. For the first time in almost two years, I was really laughing, and it felt so good.

Jackson, smiling, put his hands on my shoulders and asked, "What the hell is so funny?"

Stepping forward, I kissed him, and he kissed me back. His mouth was wonderful. Pulling away, smiling and closing my eyes, I extended my arms and danced in great wheeling circles. I danced and I laughed. Others came from our circle, and the other circles, and joined us.

20

TWO DAYS AFTER THE PARTY, I had another therapy appointment with Muriel.

"Tell me more about apologizing," she said.

"Well, Jackson thought I should apologize to the group for being kind of bitchy, but they were asking about the flight and they seemed really dense. Asking if it was fun, stuff like that, but everyone has basically heard what happened, so it seemed insensitive to me. I know they forget, and most of the time I *want* people to forget, but I don't want people to compare the *Phaeacia* to a cruise ship. My parents died," I said.

"Tell me about the apology, though," she said.

"So, he told me I should say I was sorry, even though he knew I wasn't wrong, so that they could feel good about everything and I could be back in the group, and it worked, so he was right," I said.

"I hear you saying he was right, but how do you feel about apologizing when you had nothing to apologize for, just to get back in the group?"

"I don't know, I guess it doesn't really matter," I said.

"Do you think you went along to get back into that group, or because this boy told you to and you wanted to make him happy?" she asked.

"Both I guess. It's not like I have friends to throw away," I said.

"So you drank?" she asked.

"Some. I don't know what happened to the rest," I said.

"Did you do drugs too?" she asked.

"Nope, just drinking. And I danced," I said. "Jackson told me to dance like the 1980s and I showed him."

"What else happened?"

"I laughed," I said, grinning, like a person springing a fun secret on a friend.

"You laughed?" she said. "Like a real laugh?"

"Isn't that amazing?" I asked. "I finally laughed; it felt so good."

"Have you since?" she asked.

Pausing for a moment, I couldn't remember laughing since the party.

Muriel asked, "Do you think you can laugh sober? Or do you think you have to be under the influence of alcohol?"

Shit. Did I have to be drunk? "I'm not sure."

She said, "I'd hate to see you get to a space where you have to consume alcohol in order to have fun."

"Get to a space?" I asked.

"End up," she said.

I said, "I'll hold off on drinking and let you know if I laugh."

She asked, "How about sex? Did that make you laugh?"

Oh my God. "I didn't do that," I said.

"You didn't have sexual intercourse with Jackson?" she asked.

"I just kissed him. We danced. We didn't do anything like that. We haven't even been on a date," I said.

"Well, you drank, you kissed him, you danced when he told you to, you made a public apology when he told you to, even when you felt you hadn't done anything wrong. I just wondered what else he told you to do," Muriel said.

My face warmed. "He isn't like that. And neither am I."

"Are you sure about that?" she asked.

Searching her face, I wondered when someone had kissed her last, or when she had last danced. It was clear she could use a drink. She had taken my fun at the pit party and turned it into something that might have been bad or dirty, or like I had been drunk and out of control, and manipulated. Therapists were supposed to make you feel better about things, but she had done the opposite.

"I'm pretty sure," I said.

"Why do you think you laughed?" she asked.

"I was happy. Okay, maybe a little drunk too, but I was just happy," I said. "Is that wrong somehow?"

"I'm not here to judge," she said.

"It sounded like you were judging," I said. The knot in my stomach pulled tighter and tighter.

She paused, and then leaned back. "Do you often feel like people are judging you?"

"I'm a teenage girl," I said.

"More than that," she said.

She was starting to piss me off. "Do people judge me more than they do the average teenage girl from the past and outer space, you mean?" I asked.

"If you're not serious about this work…" she said.

I said, "Okay, I suppose I do feel like people judge me more than the average teen, yes."

"Do you think they gang up on you?" she asked.

"Actually, I was telling you about a fun time I had," I said.

"But you won't examine why you were laughing," she said.

"I think if people began really examining the reasons they laugh, there would be a lot less laughter in the world. It's, like, a spontaneous thing," I said.

"But focus on the party," she said. "Why were you laughing then?"

There was a fire, Jackson, music, and dancing, and I had felt happy and safe. I said, "Relief."

Muriel sat forward. "Go on, tell me about relief."

"The music was from the 1980s. The dancing was '80s style. The boy was cute. I had a buzz. Fire in 2022 looked just like fire from 1984," I said. "I think maybe it was sinking in."

"What was?" she asked.

"That I was home and that I had made it. That I had actually survived, and that I wasn't dreaming," I said. In spite of myself, just then, I giggled.

"No survivor's guilt then?" she asked.

What? Why ask that? All the joy in me crashed to the floor. "Of course I have survivor's guilt."

"Do you often feel guilty for surviving?" she asked.

"I try not to, like, spend too much time thinking about it. I have dreams," I said, wanting the happiness back.

"But maybe when you're drinking, you feel less guilty," she said.

"Why are you so focused on the drinking?" I asked. "I went to one party."

"Because chemical dependence is a slippery slope and we need to keep an eye on it," she said.

I sat back, feeling worse and worse. These sessions were not helping me. "You know, I thought these visits were supposed to make me feel better and help me deal with all this stuff."

"Well yes, but first, we have to do some self-examination and determine which tools would be the most helpful," she said.

"I thought laughter was the best medicine," I said.

A grim smile. "When coupled with alcohol, I'm not so sure," she said.

"You are judging me," I said.

"Are you judging you?" she asked.

"You know, I'm not going to sit here with you messing with my mind," I said. "I don't believe you're trying to help me right now. I don't really trust you, so, like, I'm going to go."

"Well, that's very assertive of you," she said.

I wanted her to be sorry or at least ask me not to go, but instead, she was mocking me.

"I'm done," I said, and I turned to leave.

"See you at the next appointment," Muriel said. Looking back at her, I saw that she was the one smiling now, which was really creepy because she was on some sort of head-game power trip, messing with me. She seemed to be enjoying the fact that I was upset.

I said, "I don't think so. I don't think you will see me at any more appointments."

Her smile fell. "Oh, I promise you will. I'm afraid we're stuck with each other until I decide you're healthy enough to stop coming, or that you need more help than outpatient care can provide."

"Are you threatening me?" I asked, as my knees weakened.

"See you at the next appointment," she said. "Close the door on the way out."

Turning slowly, I left through the waiting area. I realized that I had never seen anyone waiting there, neither before nor after my appointments with Muriel. I walked out the door, down the stairs to the street, and I headed toward the coffee shop where Debbie was waiting for me. Looking over my shoulder, I was afraid, and it was not of the typical anxiety of every new social situation. Muriel had basically just threatened to lock me up in a mental hospital unless… unless what? She hadn't said; she was just showing her power over me. I decided I wouldn't miss the next appointment, but I wouldn't voluntarily say much from now on.

21

HOLDING A LARGE BOWL OF popcorn, Deb was already on the couch when I walked into the living room.

"C'mon, sit down, watch this," she said, grinning.

Smiling, I joined her and asked, "What is it?"

"This show is great," she said.

"It's already started," I said.

"Doesn't matter."

"What's it about?"

"Okay, there's this family—like her, and her sisters—and they live with their mom," Deb said, pointing.

There were four beautiful women on the screen, one clearly older than the others but she was still attractive. Two of the four had bleached their hair almost white, but by their skin tones and eyebrows, I thought they might be Greek. Leaning forward, I asked, "Is that their house? So, they're rich?"

"Yeah, her husband made a lot of money, but he's dead now," she said.

"Is it a show about them learning to deal with their loss?" I asked. I could certainly sympathize with that.

"Nah, he died more than ten years ago," she said.

The show jumped back and forth between scenes of the women interacting and individual interviews. I asked, "They all live there?"

"One of them—her, that one—she's married," Deb said. "But they hang out together a lot."

"But what's the show about?" I asked.

"There isn't really a story. They just do their thing," she said.

Confused, I asked, "How can that be a series?"

Deb paused, turned to me, and said, "Oh, hon, there's no plot or whatever. This isn't fake. It's reality TV."

"What do you mean?" I really didn't get it.

"This isn't acting. They live together, there's drama, and we watch," she said.

"It's their real lives? Like looking in through their windows?" I asked.

Deb nodded emphatically and her smile returned. "It's fun. Check this out... she is so pissed."

I watched as one of the women came in from another room and repeatedly attempted to strike her sister with a large purse, but she couldn't really manage the weight of it. They spoke over each other and used the word "rude" a lot. They separated, there was shouting, one taunted the other for crying, and the scene ended. It had been meaningless, tense, childish, and sad.

"Deb, what the hell?"

"What?"

"Why would you watch this?" I asked.

"I know, I know, it's dumb, but I can't stop!" she said, laughing. "I've even seen this one before."

"It's horrible. Who are they? Are they famous?" I asked.

"They're famous, but only because of this show," she said.

"Wait, that's chicken and the egg. If they only became famous because they were put on TV, why were they put on in the first place?" I asked, frustrated. Deb was smarter than this.

She stopped giggling but was still smiling. "I don't know. I guess they thought people would find it interesting," she said.

"Who are 'they'?" I asked, confused.

Deb's smile fell, she sighed, and her shoulders fell a bit. "The TV executives who decide what's going to be on."

"Why do they get to decide? And why would they pick this?" I asked.

"Look, Cel, they must know what they're doing. The ratings on this show are, like, crazy. Everybody watches it. The people in the show... they're household names now," she said.

I realized she was right. Blaming the networks was wrong, because everyone voted with his or her remote control. We got more of whatever had the highest ratings, and less of what didn't. The shows we got, the news we got… it was all just a reflection of us, of who we were and what we wanted. A viewer blaming television for what's on is like a man blaming the mirror for his ugliness. That only made it worse, though, because now instead of being irritated with Deb, or frustrated with TV execs, I had this sudden and overwhelming sense of hopelessness about humanity in general.

On the TV, the woman who had mocked her sister's crying said, "*BEEP* her. I'm sick of her *BEEP*."

My stomach knotted up and my heart raced. "That family is in trouble. I don't understand why anyone would want to watch this. It's like human wreckage," I said.

"Okay, okay, then don't watch it," she said. She looked disappointed, but I felt like she still wasn't getting it.

This wasn't about me; this was a huge issue. It was like returning home to find everyone brainwashed. I said, "No, like, it's wrong. Nobody should be watching it."

"Calm down, it's just TV," she said.

Calm down? That made me angry, because that was exactly the problem. Everyone was too calm about this stuff. "No, I won't! People are starving in the world, and we sit here with more food than we can eat, we're fat, watching shit like that!" I said, rising to my feet.

"You don't have to call me names," she said.

"Not you, I just mean, Deb, people… there are real problems around the world and people are wasting time watching these women act like middle-school girls? And you say it's a popular show," I said. My face was hot and my hands were balled into fists.

"Cel, you have to take it easy," she said, standing, and holding her hands out.

"No, Deb, fuck that! There are wars! People are dying from diseases! Like, diseases people can't figure out, parents are dying… watching their kids die… and we're sitting here in this country peeping in on these people who have no idea how stupid they look, in their rich house, acting like idiots? People are dying, Deb!"

Her face softened, and she walked slowly toward me, hands still outstretched. She said, "Cel, I'm really sorry for what you've been through. I can't even imagine."

"What does that have to do with anything?" I shouted.

"But, hon, we had no way of reaching you. We had no way of helping all of you aboard the ship," she said. Putting her hands on my uppers arms, she rubbed up and down.

Looking into her eyes, I could see them welling up with tears. Was I actually freaking out about the disease on the *Phaeacia*? Yeah, I decided, that was definitely part of it.

I said, "Maybe you couldn't help, but while we were up there, while my parents died, while we struggled to get back… people were watching this garbage."

"Cel, we couldn't do anything but wait for you," Deb said. "We didn't even know you were coming until last summer."

"To us, that was the last three weeks of the trip," I said. "Humanity had all this time while we were gone. All this time, and this is what you came up with? Reality TV?"

"Celestine," she said.

"All those people starving in Ethiopia, Russians in Afghanistan, smog, and… whatever… and you had all this time to make the world better, and this is what you did with it," I said.

"To be fair, Cel, I was here doing my best to be a wife and mom," Deb said, letting my arms go. "No one asked me to get the Soviets out of Afghanistan."

"What's that supposed to mean?" I asked.

"It means I did the best I could, and I still am," she said. "Besides, maybe we watch shows like this because we want to escape all the horrible stuff we can't do anything about."

Looking at the television and then back at Deb, I suddenly felt completely deflated. The rage went out of me; it released like a flash of steam. She had tried to share something she liked with me, and in return I'd tried to make her feel bad and stupid for it. It was all so overwhelming, and I just wanted to be a kid again.

These ups and downs, the way my feelings suddenly went out of control sometimes was really scary. It wasn't just rage issues; it was all the emotions. Having gone from happy to confused to furious, and then finally sad, I thought I must really seem crazy to other people. It definitely made me worry that I might be losing my mind.

Hugging her, I said, "I'm sorry, Deb."

Hugging me back, she said, "Me too."

I asked, "Am I nuts? I mean, I just went off. What's wrong with me?"

Without letting me go, she said, "You've got a lot on your plate, that's all. Too much."

But isn't that what crazy is? Having more on your plate than you can handle? Still holding Deb, I said, "Again, I'm really sorry."

She pulled away, smiled, and asked, "Wanna watch the rest?"

"No!"

She laughed, and said, "I know, just kidding."

I nodded.

"You going to be okay?" she asked.

"I'm okay," I said.

Deb sat back down, and picked up the popcorn.

Still sad, I forced a smile, and went to my room.

22

THE NIGHT WE WATCHED *THE Breakfast Club* was more than a week later. I hadn't seen Jackson at all, and I'd only run into Lauren once, picking through the clothing racks at Goodwill. Inviting me to her place to watch the movie, she said that Cole and Jackson would be there.

When I asked if she often double-dated with her brother, she answered, "Ew. No. Don't say it like that." She said that we'd be watching the movie, and not "making out '80s-style." Having no idea what that meant, I promised not to do it.

In Lauren's finished basement, there was a room clearly designed for adults to entertain guests, but there was no alcohol behind the dusty bar. Two of the lamps were missing bulbs, and the two that were on cast just enough light to see. There was a couch and two armchairs, and I took one of those, while Jackson grinned and jumped into the other. Cole and Lauren climbed onto the couch.

"Should we turn off more lights?" Cole asked, and Lauren hit him.

"I think it's good like this," I said.

Jackson sat forward and said, "Celly, you gotta brace yourself for the *Breakfast Club* experience."

"Celly?" Lauren asked.

"Does anyone call you that?" Jackson asked.

"Never," I said.

"Can I be the first?" Jackson asked, still smiling.

"You already are," I said, smiling back.

"Ugh, you're both so annoying," Lauren said.

There was something different about Cole. I'd only seen him at the pit party, but it seemed something had changed. I asked, "Did you cut your hair?"

Cole rubbed his head. "Yeah, I had the guy take it down to almost nothing. I thought about growing like a legit fro, like 1970s style, but I went with this instead. Think I should shave it clean?" His scalp was a warm brown with just a shadow of his black hair showing.

I said, "I don't think you should shave it to the skin; you'd look too old. It's cool like that."

"It's cool?" Cole asked. Smiling, he looked at Lauren, who smiled back and gave him a little shove.

She said, "You still have a big head."

Cole looked at me again and asked, "So you've never seen this?"

"Just don't talk through the whole thing. I hate it when you narrate a movie, especially when someone hasn't seen it," Lauren said.

"I'll shut up," Cole said.

"Start it," Jackson said.

Extending her arm, Lauren pressed a button on the remote. The screen read "DVD" but the movie didn't immediately start. Lauren began dramatically swinging her arm, like someone casting a fishing pole, pressing the play button with each try.

"Why isn't this working?" Lauren asked.

"Swing your arm harder," Jackson said.

Cole laughed, and I couldn't hide my smile. Lauren stopped and said, "The batteries are probably dead."

"Point the remote at the DVD and not the TV," Cole said.

Pausing for a moment, Lauren carefully aimed the remote at the DVD player and pressed a button, using what looked like enough force to break it. The screen changed immediately to the FBI warning against making illegal copies of the movie.

Jackson and Cole clapped at her success, and I giggled. Without a buzz, I was laughing.

"You guys all suck," Lauren said.

The movie began with a black screen and the words "…and these children that you spit on, as they try to change their worlds are immune to your consultations. They're quite aware of what they're going through… —David Bowie."

"Do you recognize that?" Lauren asked me.

"I recognize David Bowie. I like his song 'Let's Dance,' but I don't know that one," I said. The image of a large industrial-looking high school filled the screen next, and a lispy voice-over tipped off the audience that this was about students attending detention on, "Saturday… March 24, 1984."

"You were still on Earth then, right?" Cole asked.

"We didn't leave until that fall," I said.

"But you don't remember this?" he asked.

"Dude, it's like March 1984 in the story, but the movie came out in 1985," Jackson said.

"Oh right. Hey, look at the cars," Cole said.

"Don't start," Lauren said.

I hadn't really noticed the cars were any different than the ones today. To me, cars were just cars.

"Check out her clothes. Long skirt, leather jacket," Cole said, looking at me.

"Man, dude, enough," Jackson said.

Not wanting to have to comment on everything in the movie, as if I could vouch for the authenticity of everything in it, I was glad Jackson had told Cole to stop. People seemed to think that there was only one style of clothing or hair or music in the 1980s. Besides, I was only there for the first half of the decade.

"What did I say?" Cole asked.

"It's not what you're saying; it's how much," Lauren said.

Cole was suddenly excited, pointing at an 8x10 framed photo on the screen, "Cel, see that guy? 'Man of the Year'? Remember him, you'll see him again!"

"Stop it!" Lauren said.

"I didn't ruin anything! I didn't even tell her he's the janitor!" Cole said.

I laughed.

"You're so stupid," Lauren said.

Jackson was grinning and shaking his head.

In the movie, the students took turns arriving at the high school and then sitting, scattered, around the school library.

"This must be the whitest high school in Chicago," Cole said.

"Shit, Cole, shut the hell up, man," Jackson said.

Cole glanced at him, sank a bit, and said, "Racist."

Lauren chuckled and leaned against him, laying her head on his arm.

We watched the movie and I loved it all—the music and the story. I said, "That was so cool. The soundtrack was awesome."

Jackson said, "What's wild is all those songs are old to us, but they're brand new to you. It sort of dusts them off for me too, like, freshens them up somehow."

Cole snickered, and Lauren laughed too. Cole mockingly said, "You hearing them for the first time makes them new for me too. It's like Febreze for my iPod."

Jackson just smiled, and said, "Let's get out of here, and go for a walk or something."

"It's getting late," I said.

"I can walk you home," he said.

"I doubt you'll make it," Cole said, and they all laughed a bit, but I had a flash of anxiety. I don't know why.

I said, "I can find my way."

Jackson shrugged. "No problem."

I walked alone, and when I arrived at the house, Debbie was in the kitchen, popping microwave popcorn. Even having been in space, and traveled near the speed of light, I was still impressed by things like microwave popcorn. We had looked it up, and it had been invented before I left, but I had never heard of it.

"Hey, you want some?" Debbie asked.

"No thanks," I said. Maybe I should've let Jackson walk me home, I thought, and imagined kissing him goodnight on the porch.

"How was the movie?" she asked.

"Huh?" I asked.

"The movie?"

"Great, I loved it," I said.

"Want to watch with us?" Deb asked.

"What are you guys watching?"

"*Dancing with the Stars*," she said.

"I'm going to chill in my room," I said. I really wasn't in the mood for some science fiction movie; besides, the title sounded really corny, like it would be some cheesy romance in space.

"If you change your mind on popcorn, come make some," she said.

"What ever happened to them?" I asked.

"To who?" she asked.

"To the *Breakfast Club* people. Like, the actors and actresses," I said.

"They grew up."

"I know, but did they act in other stuff?" I asked.

She said, "They did, especially the nerdy one. But yeah, they all did a few more movies."

"Anything good like *Breakfast Club*?" I asked.

"Um, I don't know. I mean, the other movies aren't bad, but they aren't household words like *Breakfast Club*," she said. "Know what I mean?"

"Which one am I?" I asked.

"What do you mean?" she asked.

"Am I the basket case or the princess or what?"

She smiled. "I think you missed the point of the movie," she said.

"You've had a lot longer to think about it," I said, smiling back. I grabbed a glass and opened the fridge. "Why don't we have Coke or something normal? Why always this green tea or other weird stuff?"

Debbie ignored me and went into the other room. Pouring myself some lemon seltzer, which really didn't taste like lemon, I took it into my room and reached for my laptop. Googling the movie, I started following links on the actors. I was surprised to learn that one was from Maine. Just then, my phone vibrated, and there was a message from Jackson.

"*What's up?*"

I responded, "*nm, just chilling*"

"You left me here with these 2. Lauren is already sitting in Cole's lap. It's gross."

I giggled. *"That IS gross."*

"Let's do something just me and u."

I hesitated. Was he asking for suggestions? *"Like what?"*

"We could go to dinner or something. Or how about a hike?"

A hike? *"Like in the mountains?"*

"We could go anywhere you want."

I didn't feel especially athletic and he would probably be zipping through the woods. *"I'm not sure I could keep up."*

"It wouldn't be a race. Just a quiet walk in the woods. Up a mountain if you want. Whatever. Just an idea. Or we could go to dinner."

God, I was suddenly so nervous, in a good way. *"A hike would be cool."*

"Cool. I can pick you up. We'll go up to Bradbury Mountain. Do you remember where it is? Up by Freeport, Pownal, whatever."

I had never heard of it. It's not like hiking required formal trails in the 1980s. We just walked in the woods. *"Do I need to bring anything?"*

"Just dress comfortably and bring some water. Or we can get some. I'll pick you up around 10 in the morning?"

"Okay. See you at 10am."

He wasn't coming until the next morning, but I went to my closet and started looking for the right clothes. Beginning to panic, I went back to my phone and messaged Lauren.

"Help! I need to put together an outfit for hiking tomorrow."

The response came within minutes. *"Be right there."*

23

I DREAMT OF A BARRIER; IT was clear and thick. On the other side, there was a room with plain white walls and floor. The room had a simple door of knotty pine. Despite the bright light, I was unsure how the room was lit, because there were no visible fixtures.

While I stood there in a simple, white nightgown, the door opened and my parents entered, seeming a bit bewildered. Feeling such relief when my mom looked right at me, I waved, but she didn't wave back. Her facial expression did not change in the least. She couldn't see me.

Hitting the clear barrier between us, I tried to get her attention, but not only could she not see or hear me, even I couldn't hear the sound of my own pounding. Striking it with all my might, my hands hurt, and yet beating on it made no sound.

The door opened again and Lauren came into the room, and right behind her was Josée, my Quebecois friend from the *Phaeacia*. Next Nurse Norris's twin sons entered, and behind them, others I'd lost on the flight.

And then I noticed a fly. A housefly, fat and black and hairy, landed directly opposite my face on the other side of the clear barrier. Another fly flew through the room. Then, there were two more, and then their numbers doubled.

Feeling such dread, I knew something horrible was coming, but those in the room seemed only confused and mildly annoyed. Screaming and pounding at the barrier, I still couldn't make them hear me.

Into the room, through the pine door, came Jackson, running and swatting at flies as the room filled with them. The pine door slammed shut and the air was black with the flies. Swarming. Not hearing the insects or the people, even when my mom ran into the barrier between us, I soon could only make out occasional flashes of movement, until the cloud began to thin, and soon there was only Jackson. He stood, motionless in the center of the room, facing me. Only a handful of flies remained. There was no sign of the swarm. Not even the dead ones I expected to see on the floor. There was only Jackson, whose eyes were wide, as if looking right at me.

Shouting, I beat my hands on the barrier again and then pressed my forehead against it. I felt so helpless. Jackson did not move and still did not seem to hear me; he just looked incredibly sad. Opening his mouth, as if to say something, he was completely blocked from view when the entire swarm of flies suddenly flew from his throat and straight at me. They collided like a black, disgusting fountain against the barrier, right where my face had been. Seeing nothing but the flies, I screamed and backed away. When the flies cleared, the room beyond was empty.

Trembling all over, I covered my face with my hands, and then saw they were covered in dark bruises. Realizing they were spreading, I gasped, as they quickly ran up my forearms to my elbows, and then to my shoulders. Tearing off my nightgown, I watched as the color crept across my breasts and belly, and then down the fronts of my thighs.

"Oh my God, no. No, no, no. I'm sick," I said. Terror swept through me. Watching until the discoloration covered every inch of my body, I was then hit by waves of nausea and chills, just as Mom, Dad, and the rest had been. Walking backwards, I collided with someone. Screeching, I spun and was face to face with Ian Mokone, the engineer from the *Phaeacia*.

His face filled with rage, he said, "You cannot hide. It will get you too. It will get us all."

Terrified, I tried to cover myself with my hands, but he gripped my left wrist, stepped closer, and said, "It will get you too, Celestine."

Screaming, I yanked hard to be free of him and when I did, he exploded into a new cloud of flies.

Waking, I bolted straight up in bed then, soaked in sweat. I didn't sleep the rest of the night; I just lay there, scared, waiting for dawn, and watching the sky lighten.

24

JACKSON PICKED ME UP RIGHT on time. The doorbell was still echoing in the house when I opened the door. I stepped out and saw him look me up and down.

"What?" I asked.

"Nothing, it's cute. Let's go."

Stepping ahead of me, he opened the passenger door of his truck and I climbed in, placing my little pack at my feet. Closing the door behind me, he went around to his side, while I adjusted my leggings. They were just thick tights to me, sort of twisting under my skirt, so I kept tugging this way and that, hurrying before Jackson opened his door.

Also, I was unsure about navy leggings under a grey skirt, and small hiking boots. My hair was pulled back from my face by a wide headband, which was Lauren's, with my sunglasses across the headband. Wearing a cami, a T-shirt, and a black zippered hoodie, with a vest in my bag too, I felt prepared. It was May, and not cold, but I didn't know if it might be cooler up Bradbury Mountain, wherever that was.

The T-shirt was also Lauren's; it was a pale yellow and featured a band called, "Crywank," which I'd never heard of. A bit tight around my boobs, it was another piece of clothing to tug at. The whole outfit looked a bit odd to me, but Lauren assured me this was the cool "crunchy" uniform for free spirits going hiking.

When Jackson's door opened, I stopped adjusting tights and T-shirts. "Did you bring a pack?" I asked, as we pulled away.

"It's in the back," he said, thumb extended toward the bed of the pickup.

It was quiet for a bit and then he said, "Let's get the obvious out of the way."

"Okay," I said, not knowing what was obvious. He merged onto I-295 north.

"Do you want to talk about the trip in space?" he asked.

I said, "Oh, that. I mean, I'm not opposed to it. I probably won't start many conversations about it, but you can ask anything you want."

He said, "Well, I know it must have been horrible, so I didn't know if it was off-limits, but it just seems like the elephant in the room. Like we'd be avoiding the subject, so I just thought I'd bring it up. We totally don't need to talk about it, unless you want to."

"Honestly, as long as you don't say any of the stuff those hosers asked at the party, like comparing it to a pleasure cruise, I think we're good," I said.

"Hosers?" He grinned.

Suddenly self-conscious, I wondered if I'd sounded stupid. I asked, "Do you notice a big a difference in how I talk? I mean, compared to other people?"

"Not really, just sometimes you have an expression I haven't heard before, or I've heard it in a movie or something. Or my parents say it," he said.

"Can you think of an example?" I asked.

"I don't know. Maybe like 'eat my shorts,'" he said.

"I've never said that. Bender did, in the movie," I said.

"See what I mean?" he asked.

I didn't. "If I say something weird, point it out right away."

"I don't want you to change how you talk. I think it's cute," he said.

Smiling, I felt like a ditz getting silly-happy every time this guy complimented me. "How far is it?" I asked.

"About forty minutes," he said.

It was quiet again, and we just listened to the tires and the wind, until he asked, "Want some music?"

"What did you want to ask me about the space trip?" I asked.

He looked at me, and then back out at the road. "You sure?"

"Go ahead," I said, wanting to share with him, but still a bit nervous about what he might ask.

He looked out the side window, and then asked, "What were your parents like?"

A bit surprised, I thought he'd ask about the ship or space. "They were nice. Smart. My father was funny, and my mom was sweet," I said.

"You sure you're okay?" he asked.

"I'm okay," I said.

"I don't want to make you cry on our first time out, just us," he said.

"I haven't cried in a long time," I said and paused, unsure, but then I said, "You know, I hadn't laughed since being off the ship until you made me."

He looked at me. "Are you serious?" His mouth hung open.

Nodding, I smiled.

"That's wild," he said. "You have a great laugh."

He was still looking at me when I noticed we were about to run into the car ahead of us. "Look out!" I said, and we went around it. Giggling a bit from nerves, I fell back against the seat.

"See. A nice laugh," Jackson said.

He didn't ask me anything else about space during the drive; I'd proven it was okay to discuss the disaster on the *Phaeacia*, and the two of us put it behind us for the time being. We drove the rest of the way talking about music and movies and travel.

"Where have you been?" he asked.

"You mean, like on vacation?" I asked.

"Disney World? Paris?" he asked.

"We went to the White Mountains in New Hampshire. I've been to a lot of museums, like in Boston and New York," I said.

"But you were rich, right? Like astronauts make bank, right?"

"We didn't go anywhere fancy," I said. "Not like Paris or Rome or whatever."

He grunted.

"What?" I asked.

"You went into space, but you never made it past New York," he said.

"Well, we lifted off from Kazakhstan," I said. "Does that count?"

Smiling, he looked at me. "That counts."

"Watch the road," I said, and grinned.

When we arrived at the mountain, there were many other cars in the parking lot.

"A lot of people?" I asked.

"Oh yeah, we'll meet up with people going up and coming back."

I said, "I kinda thought we'd have the mountain to ourselves."

"Wow. That's sketchy," he said. "Were you planning to bury me up there?"

"What? No!"

"I'm just kidding," he said.

We laughed, slipped on our packs, walked past a small field, and headed into the trees where the trail rose before us. It was less than two minutes before we encountered the first couple we'd see that day, coming the other way. Soon breathing hard, I established a rhythm and was fine, and surprised that I could make the progress we were making.

"You're doing well, Celly," he said, looking back.

Ugh. It felt good that he said that, but I didn't want him cheering me on like a kid, either. I said, "So, tell me about school here."

"Like what?" he asked.

"Anything," I said. "I don't know a thing about GHS today."

"Well, I suppose it's pretty much like Goodwin High School when you went there," he said.

"What are the teachers like?" I asked.

"They're all pretty chill. Some are stricter," he said.

"Like they give a lot of detention?" I asked.

"Detention isn't really used," he said.

"What if you ditch?"

"Ditch? Like cut a class?" he asked.

"Yeah, if you don't go to class, you must get something, right?"

"They'll call you in and talk to you, and they will probably send an email to your... to Debbie, I guess," he said. "But you won't get detention."

"What happens if you don't do your homework?" I asked.

Jackson stopped climbing and turned back. "Are you planning a life of crime or something?" he asked.

Laughing, I said, "Just trying to figure out what school's going to be like now, that's all."

"The whole thing is laid back, really. You go to class, you do your work, you pass. No one really hassles you," he said.

I asked, "Are there a lot of fights?"

"In the school?" he asked. "I'm finishing my junior year there and I've seen only one fight in the hallways."

"That's incredible," I said.

He turned and began up the trail once more. "Was high school like the Wild West or something in the 1980s? I mean, don't get me wrong, I know there are still high schools today with metal detectors when you walk in, and gangs, fights, you know. But it's not like that at Goodwin."

I said, "We had a smoking section in the parking lot for students back then. I once saw a teacher keep other students from stopping a fight, so that they could 'get it out of their systems.'"

"That's pretty intense," he said. "What's your favorite class?"

I said, "Probably English. I like art classes too."

He said, "Like, Shakespeare and stuff?"

"That's okay, but I really like reading short stories, and I like to write too," I said.

He chuckled, "Nerd."

"Hey, just because I can read doesn't make me a nerd," I said, laughing. "You should try it sometime."

He stopped, stood straight, and turned with a smile. Walking back to me, he leaned forward like he was going to kiss me. Tilting my head back a bit, I began to slowly close my eyes, when he recited, "Love sought is good, but given unsought is better."

"What is that?" I asked.

He grinned. "*Twelfth Night*."

"Shakespeare?" I asked.

"What, surprised the dumb jock knows some shit?" he asked, laughing.

"I'm impressed," I said.

He bent forward to actually kiss me, but I turned away and I shoved him uphill with both hands to get him moving again.

We came to a sign that read "Summit" with an arrow. The trail turned sharply and then back on itself. Up ahead, I could see a break, and when we came out of the woods, we stepped out onto a massive expanse of grey rock polished smooth by wind and rain. There were two other couples up there, just standing and appreciating the view. We could see for miles and miles, overlooking a vast forest.

"Let's go to the edge," Jackson said. We walked forward until the rock platform began to descend, and sat. He pulled a bag of chips out of his pack, followed by two Cliff bars, two sandwiches, and finally a bottle of water.

"Did you bring water for yourself?" he asked.

"I did," I said, pulling a bottle from my pack.

"Cool. Here's your sandwich," he said.

We quietly ate and looked at the beautiful view. One of the couples left, and then the other, and we were alone on the edge of the mountain.

"Celly, what was the disease? On the ship?" he asked softly.

Reminded of Alicia and her mom's reaction to seeing me, and the girls that crossed the street, I froze.

He said, "On TV, they never really explained what it was. They only said it was a virus."

"We knew that much aboard the *Phaeacia*. If the government knows more now, they haven't told us. They've only assured us that we are safe and that we are not contagious," I said.

"They never learned where it came from or whatever?" he asked.

"They call it Phaeacia Syndrome. Not 'virus' but 'syndrome.' I think anytime they find something new, they call it a syndrome first," I said.

"Were you guys scared to bring it back to Earth?" he asked.

"A little, but when we got back, we learned you had a couple terrible virus outbreaks back here. At first, I really was confused, I thought what we had on *Phaeacia* was being called AIDS back here, and then I was confused about coronavirus. It took me weeks to realize that these were all different things. Our doctors did identify a virus associated with our outbreak, but they knew it wasn't the whole picture. It was a lot easier to catch than AIDS, it was more like coronavirus, and deadlier than both. If you developed symptoms, you were gone within ten days or so," I said.

"That's wicked scary," he said softly. "What were the first signs?"

"Bruising, fever, and sometimes stomach cramps," I said. "Then aches all over, and sensitivity to light."

He seemed to hesitate, but then asked, "How does it kill you?"

"Most of the time your kidneys shut down, but I remember it attacked the liver, and sometimes the lungs too," I said.

"Sounds terrible," he said.

"It was," I said. Many faces, my parents among them, were flashing through my memory; there were images of them both healthy and not.

He asked, "Did anyone who got sick recover?"

Starting to pack up the trash, I didn't say anything. Not angry or anything, I just started consolidating the sandwich bags, grape stems, and stuff.

"Cel?" he asked.

"No one," I said. "Every single person who showed symptoms died."

"And no one knows why some got sick and some did not?" he asked.

"Nobody's told me," I said.

"Don't you want to know?" he asked.

"I guess so," I said.

"If it were me, I'd call someone," he said.

If it were him? I asked, "Call who?"

"Someone in the government. They must know," he said.

"Just someone in the government?"

"Aren't you in touch with anyone?" he asked.

"I have group sessions," I said.

"Isn't someone in charge of those?"

"Dr. Caledon runs them," I said.

"Well, if I were you, I'd ask him," he said.

"Ask him what?"

"What the disease was. Why some people got sick and some didn't. Why the government hasn't released more information," he said.

"It's not really like that during group sessions," I said. "I mean, he's not really talking about that."

"I'd make him. I'd insist on some answers. You should, like, not take 'no' for an answer," he said.

Getting irritated, I felt like he wasn't really listening. "That wouldn't really work. I'm not sure he even knows anyway."

"Well, you could tell him you need to contact someone who knows," Jackson said.

"What?"

"If I were you, I would demand to talk to someone who could give me answers."

"You're not me," I said.

He looked a bit surprised. "What?"

"You're not me. You have no idea what it's like to be me," I said.

"I was just trying to help," he said.

"I don't need you to help. Just to listen," I said.

"I was listening," he said. "You said it was okay to talk about this."

"You're not listening, you're giving all this advice. You don't know Dr. Caledon, you don't know the situation, you don't even know me, but you're spouting off all this 'If it were me' horseshit. You can't macho your way through this stuff," I said.

"I didn't mean it that way," he said.

"God. I mean, you can't bully your way through everything. It's not like a football game," I said.

"Cel, I don't know why you're mad at me," he said. "I honestly didn't mean to piss you off. I was just trying to help."

"I don't need advice—just someone who will listen," I said.

"Well, why tell someone if you don't want feedback? Why not just tell a stuffy or a houseplant instead?" he asked.

What the hell was a stuffy? "You always think we want you to fix shit. Well, you can't fix this," I said. Angrier than I should have been, it just kept rising and I couldn't help it. No longer merely irritated, I was mad. "There's nothing you can come up with that I haven't already thought of. Just listen for a change; can't you just do that?"

Falling silent, he looked wounded. Feeling like I had ruined the day, I was mad at myself and disappointed, but I knew I was right. Without a word, we packed up, and started back down to the truck and he drove me home.

All the way there, I kept thinking I should apologize, but then I didn't want to. I swung back and forth between feeling sorry and thinking "fuck him." He took a deep breath twice, like he might speak, but then he didn't.

Opening the door when we pulled up in front of Debbie's house, I climbed out.

He said only, "See ya."

I said, "Yep," grabbed my pack, closed the door, and I walked up to the house. As he drove away, my anger shifted to sadness. Why didn't I just apologize? Everything I said was right and true, but maybe I was wrong in how I said it—again? Whatever. Maybe I just needed to be alone, I thought, and then I felt another wave of gloom.

Why did any of this teenage romance thing matter anyway—I'd been through way more important stuff. Wasn't I past this *ABC Afterschool Special* "he likes me" crap? I went into the house, and went straight to my bed.

25

SHOPPING ONLINE WAS ADDICTIVE. I'D look at Urban Outfitters; I liked all of it, but it was expensive. Lauren had mentioned something about finding what I liked on the expensive sites, and then looking for the same clothes on Amazon.com at cheaper prices, but I hadn't tried that yet.

It wasn't like I had a process, or a system or something; when I was shopping online it was almost as if I sort of zoned out—clicking on an interesting shirt, a cool pair of shorts, or whatever. Most of the time, I couldn't tell you what I had spent the last two hours looking at.

Spotting a really cute pair of sneakers, I paused. It was strangely reassuring that even though decades had passed, things like Vans were still around and still cool, or at least cool again. My last pair of Vans had been simple white canvas, low cut, with laces. It was my mom, a year before we flew, who had spotted them first.

She called me over and said, "These are nice."

"I like them," I said.

"They aren't leather high tops, but they seem comfortable," she said.

"All my sneakers don't need to be high tops," I said.

"Plus, if these got wet, I bet they'd dry fast. Might be nice for the beach," she said.

Picking up the shoe, I bent it, and loved how light and flexible it was.

She said, "I don't know how you wear those leather sneakers

to the beach."

"I don't. I wear sandals," I said.

"They're like boots, really. Your feet must get all sweaty," she said, reading the price tag on the Vans.

"Can I have these?" I asked.

"Well, we need to find your size," she said.

"I know. I didn't mean this exact pair in my hands," I said, rolling my eyes.

"I don't know, Celestine. I mean, $18 is a lot of money for a pair of sneakers," she said.

"They'd be good for the beach," I said, and grinned.

"You have sandals," she said, smiling back.

"Please?" I asked.

My mom turned, got the attention of an employee, and asked, "Can we see these in size seven, please?"

"Thanks," I said.

She bought me those sneakers that day, and I did wear them to the beach, and just about everywhere else that summer. Memories like that made me miss her so much. Some people get to have their mothers in their lives for sixty years or more. For me it was about fifteen years, and I could remember only eleven of those. It hardly seemed fair. I mean, there were people whose mothers were still alive, and they didn't even speak to each other. I would've done anything to talk to her just one more time.

When your mom dies, it's as if this pleasant hum that you've heard all your life goes silent, and the sudden quiet is staggering. At first, because of the grief and shock, you don't know how terrible the hush will be. You actually think the worst of it are those first few days after you lose her, but it gets harder. You wake up and lie there at three o'clock in the morning, wishing you could go climb into her bed, and she could tell you everything will be okay, but then you remember; it's a cruel and lonely sorrow.

Just to have her talk about the weather, give you advice about a date, or nag you about cleaning your room once more would be amazing.

Looking once more at the laptop, I wished I could have her opinion on the sneakers on the screen, although I'm sure she would've wondered how anyone could buy shoes without trying them on first. Clicking on the pair of Vans, I saw they wanted $55 for them. Smiling broadly, I imagined my mom's voice. "Good grief! For some canvas, rubber, and a couple laces?" Still smiling, my eyes went wet.

I wanted my mom back.

26

A FEW MORNINGS LATER, I LOGGED into my next group session. Six of the panels on the laptop screen were filled, and the other two were grey. There was only one facilitator again this session, and one survivor had not logged in.

"There you are," Dr. Caledon said.

"Here I am," I said. I scanned to see who was missing and realized it was Ian Mokone, the engineer. Remembering my nightmare, and his warning, "It will get you too, Celestine," I shuddered. Where was he? Anxiety swept through me; was he sick?

"Hi Celestine," Dr. Kendall said.

Startled, I tried to smile.

Dr. Caledon said, "Good morning, everyone."

No one responded this time—not even a mumble. There was an awkward moment and then it passed.

"How is everyone feeling?" Dr. Caledon asked.

"Not everyone," Dana McCormack, the *Phaeacia's* copilot muttered.

Dr. Caledon seemed to anticipate this and said, "Yes, Ian could not make it this morning and sends his apologies."

I asked, "He apologized?" Something was wrong; I could sense it. I'd never heard Ian Mokone apologize for anything.

Dr. Caledon said, "Well, after a fashion. Let's just say he seemed sorry. How do you all feel?" His tone was terse; there was strain in his voice.

"Fine," I said, although I wasn't.

Dana McCormack asked, "Where *is* Ian?"

"As I said, he could not make it today," Dr. Caledon said.

The tension grew worse.

"Is he sick?" Dr. Kendall asked. We were all thinking it, but to actually hear the words was awful. The silence that followed was so thick that I stood in spite of myself, and paced a few steps waiting for someone to answer.

"No one is sick," Dr. Caledon said softly.

"I was wondering why he isn't here, that's all," said Dana McCormack.

"It's of a personal nature. Surely we all respect Ian enough that we can let him have that bit of privacy," Dr. Caledon said.

Dr. Kendall asked, "Celestine, are you still there?"

Sitting back down, I said, "I'm here."

"How is everyone feeling?" Dr. Caledon asked again.

There was a different sort of tone in his question that time, and almost simultaneously, with much more clarity, all of us said, "Fine."

"And how is everyone doing? Does anyone have anything interesting to share?" Dr. Caledon asked.

Dr. Kendall asked, "Have you been making friends, Celestine?"

Thinking I heard someone groan, maybe Dana McCormack, I said, "I went hiking with a guy. It was fun." I left out the part about the fight.

"How nice," Dr. Kendall said. "Is he a nice boy?"

"He's nice and smart, good looking, and he plays football," I said, hoping that if I told the group all this, they would be satisfied and, with a little luck, bored, and move on.

"How nice," Dr. Kendall said again.

"Anyone else?" Dr. Caledon asked.

Sovanara Norris, the nurse, too quickly said, "If funding comes through, I may be participating in research into the nature of the illness aboard the *Phaeacia*."

The tension immediately returned. These sessions weren't therapeutic; I was always stressed out as the time approached to log in, and once in, there was one stressful moment after another. Personally, the nurse talking about research didn't freak me out as much as it did the others, but I hated how nerve-wracking it all was.

Dr. Caledon asked, "What sort of research?"

"Into the nature of the pathogen based upon antibodies which may or may not be still present in my system," Sovanara Norris said.

"We agreed we would not become lab rats," Dr. Stenhouse said. Until he spoke, I thought he might be dozing.

Dana McCormack said, "Yeah, you don't know where this might lead. I mean, right now it's voluntary but…"

Dr. Caledon interrupted, "Sovanara, just make sure you clear everything through NASA as well, and keep us updated." I didn't like it when Caledon included himself in the "us" because he hadn't been on the ship.

"I will," she said.

"I still don't like it," Dana McCormack said. "Any of this. She's going to be a lab rat now, and we're still putting on this sham. This so-called group therapy is only a way for the government to monitor us, to keep tabs on us."

No one spoke for a few minutes, and the tension built and built, until without really thinking about whether or not I should, I blurted out a question. "Dr. Caledon, does the government know more about the illness than they are telling us?"

Someone gasped, probably Dr. Kendall, and then there was silence once more. I asked, "I mean, you would tell us right? If you learned something?"

"Celestine, I have told you everything I know. I am also quite confident that I know as much as anyone. NASA and others are applying a great many resources to unlocking the mysteries of what happened aboard the *Phaeacia*, but I am certainly not withholding anything," he said.

"Sorry. I didn't mean it like that," I said.

"I caution all of you to keep a close grip on your paranoia about conspiracies and illness, et cetera. You are all very susceptible, given what you've been through. Please resist any thought of your government not being completely forthcoming. This is not a faceless bureaucracy working on this. These are dedicated men and women, good people, many of whom you've met," Dr. Caledon said.

"I don't know why I asked," I said.

Dr. Kendall spoke up. "Celestine, we're all scared. I'm glad you asked. It gave Dr. Caledon a chance to provide us with an answer we all needed to hear."

A couple of the other survivors nodded, and voiced their approval, but not Dana McCormack. Her face was stone.

After a pause, as a group we did what we always did in order to get the session to come to a conclusion. We each, in turn, shared something meaningless and then the session ended. We all said our goodbyes, and I logged out.

· · ·

The doorbell rang downstairs, and then Debbie called up, "Cel, it's for you."

Halfway down the stairs, I could see Jackson waiting on the rug by the door. My stomach filled with butterflies; I turned to go back up and run a brush across my head, but he spotted me.

"Hey, where you going?" he asked.

Stopping, I smiled but then decided to play it cool, and came down to meet him. I said, "I thought you'd send a message or something." I wanted to make it look like I didn't care if he just left, but I'm pretty sure he could tell how into him I was.

"I decided to try it '80s-style and just drop in," Jackson said. "You know, ring the bell and see if you were home."

"We really didn't do that a lot after age six or so," I said, smirking.

"Ah, I should've researched that better," he said and smiled back.

"So, what's up?" I asked, again trying to seem casual.

"Let's go do something," he said.

Shrugging, I asked, "Like what?"

"Do I have to convince you to come with me? Does where we're going have to be cool enough for you to come?" he said, chuckling.

I said, "Of course."

"Ice cream?" he asked.

"Nah," I said.

"The mall?" he asked.

"Promise to walk and look through store windows with me?" I asked.

"Can't I just walk beside you and not look through the windows?" he asked.

"Lazy," I said.

"Guilty," he said.

I sighed. "Okay."

The drive over was quiet at first until Jackson said, "Celly, I'm really sorry. You were right. You didn't ask for any advice."

"I don't know why I got that mad. Sometimes I just do; it's like I have anger issues now," I said.

"I wasn't trying to say you're stupid or whatever. I'm sure anything I'd suggest you've already thought of," he said.

"I shouldn't have treated you like that," I said. "I just need you to listen sometimes, you know, without trying to fix it?"

"Got it," he said.

The lots at the mall were packed, and parking was tough. Inside, it was shoulder-to-shoulder people. When we got to the food court, the only open table had a four-inch square of ketchup smeared in the middle of it and a French fry on a seat. Jackson grabbed a napkin and wiped the table. When he returned from the trashcan, I held up the fry and asked, "What did you do with my ketchup?"

"I can get it back," he said.

"Ugh, no," I said.

Dylan, Emily, and Arielle came by and waved without stopping, caught in the current of the passing crowd. Next to drift by was the pack of girls with straightened and fake blonde-yellow hair, led by Alicia. The little snot waved pointedly at Jackson, but not at me.

"Hey, what's up?" I asked them too loudly, and waved at her like a kid just home from summer camp. With one of the best displays of synchronized eye-rolling I'd ever seen, they tossed their hair and grunted, and kept on moving. Jackson laughed softly.

"I know Alicia. Who are the others?" I asked.

"Her followers," he said.

"They seem like such bitches."

"Typical mean girls. Peaking right now," he said.

"She was nice to you," I said. Imitating Alicia's smile and wave, I tried to appear as vapid and phony as possible, and we both laughed.

"They can act nice when they want to," he said, "but they can't keep it up for long."

"Yeah, I saw that for myself with Alicia when I first moved back to Goodwin," I said.

Jackson looked up and past me, and when I looked back, I saw Dylan approaching.

"Where'd the girls go?" I asked.

"They took off," Dylan said.

"Where to?" I asked.

"They went to vape," Dylan said.

"What's up?" Jackson asked.

"Not much, just hanging," Dylan said.

Jackson looked at me and asked, "You want some fresh fries?"

"With ketchup of my own?" I smiled.

"You bet," he said.

"Actually, I don't really like ketchup," I said.

"Hold the ketchup—got it," he said and went over to stand in a short line.

Dylan watched him go and then asked, "So, how are you?"

"Good," I said. "You?"

"What's up with you and Jackson?" he asked.

"What do you mean?" I asked.

"I mean, are you like boyfriend-girlfriend? Are you going out?" he asked.

Honestly, I didn't know. "We've just been on a couple dates. Went hiking."

"Hiking again," Dylan said and smiled.

"What do you mean?"

"He's taken more than a few girls hiking," he said. "Bradbury?

Up in Freeport?"

Not answering, I wondered why Dylan was doing this.

"I'm sorry," he said. "Just be careful. Like, guard your heart a bit."

Jackson returned. "I got a large so he could have a few."

Dylan laughed. "I'm all set, gotta go." Getting up to leave, he gave me an extra look, and jumped into the current once more.

"What's up with him?" Jackson asked.

"He's weird," I said. "Is he a fag?"

"Whoa! Shit, Cel, don't say that!" he said.

"What, why not?" I asked.

"Like, that's a really harsh word. People never use that word anymore, unless you know, they hate on other people," he said.

Hate them? I'd never really met any of them. It's not like they were common. I asked, "So, what do people call homos now?"

"Will you stop!" he said.

"Now what?" I asked.

"Do you have a problem with gay people or something?" he asked.

Afraid to say anything else, I said only, "I think I'm just having a language problem."

"I hope so," he said.

"So, you just call them 'gay people'?" I asked.

"Well, my friend Glenn is gay, so I typically call him 'Glenn'," he said.

Feeling like an ass, I said, "I'm sorry."

"You're not homophobic, right?" he asked.

"You can call them 'homos'?" I asked.

"I didn't call anyone anything. I asked if you have a problem with people who are gay," he said.

"I really don't. Honest," I said.

"Okay," Jackson said.

Trying to take it back to where we were, I asked, "So, is Dylan gay?"

Jackson took a deep breath, as if I'd finally gotten it right. "Not that I know of. He had a girlfriend once," he said. "Why?"

"I don't know. It's like he's *that* guy, you know? The one

guy who hangs with the artsy girls, gives advice, makes fun of people's clothes. Seems like those guys are always gay," I said.

"Did he make fun of my clothes?" Jackson asked with a grin.

Feeling relief, I smiled back. "He told me I'm one of the many you've dragged up Bradbury."

Not missing a beat, he said, "I like that place, and I like sharing it. I didn't even try to kiss you on that whole hike."

"Actually, you did. I had to push you away," I said, grinning.

"Oh, right. I was thinking of someone else," he said and laughed.

"You're a dick," I said and fed him a fry.

Hearing laughter, I looked back to see the mean girls passing, and shaking their heads, mockingly.

Jackson said, "Nobody likes them." This time, he fed me a fry.

Finishing the snack, we walked with the crowd. This part of the mall formed a long L shape, with a loop of human traffic moving around islands of wrought iron railings, benches, and golden pothos plants. I looked into store windows and Jackson did his best to appear somewhat interested. To be honest, I wasn't sure which stores were the cool ones. I mean, sometimes I could tell from the displays how hard they were trying to be cool, but I hadn't been plugged in long enough to know. What's in style and what's not is a constantly changing thing, and jumping into the cycle of in-and-out is tough. Every once in a while, we saw someone with a face mask, but mostly not.

Just then, to my surprise, Jackson dragged me into a store. Less surprising was that it was Spencer's. I thought he'd drag me right to the gross (and yes, funny) stuff in the back, but instead he stopped at a shelf in the middle of the store and took down a wood-framed panel covered in what looked like nails.

"It's called pin art," he said. "These existed in 1984, I'm sure."

"I'm sure they did. I didn't personally experience everything 1984 had to offer. There were a few things I missed," I said.

"Well, you put your hand in the back, and see?" Jackson pushed his hand against the back of the pin art, and on the other side, the pins came forward, making a 3D model of his hand.

"Cool, let me see it," I said. I let the pins fall back to flat, and then pushed my own hand against the back of the pins. Silver stems rose into a representation of my hand.

"Give it here," Jackson said. He lifted the pin art in front of his face, and I watched as first his nose, then his forehead, chin, and lips, and finally his eyes took shape. He slowly pulled it away and looked at himself.

"Wild," I said.

"It's so weird," he said. "You never see yourself as 3D and you usually see yourself as a mirror image. It's different, seeing yourself on the X, Y, and Z planes."

"Ooh, math!" I said.

He laughed. "Try it."

Taking the pin art, I tilted it until all of the pins fell back into a smooth surface, and pressed it against my face. The pins were cool, and smelled faintly of oil. Carefully turning the pin art, I saw Jackson was right. My nose was smaller than I thought, my lips bigger. My eyes were sightless, and my cheekbones high.

"Is that what I look like?" I asked.

"Not really," he said.

"What?" I asked.

He stepped close to me, put his hand on the side of my face, his fingers in my hair, and said, "You're much prettier." He kissed me. After, when I opened my eyes, he dropped his hand, but was still standing close.

"Do that again," I said.

While he kissed me, I tried to capture the moment by bringing the pin art to the sides of both our faces, but with my eyes closed, I only managed to hit Jackson with the wooden frame. The pins rattled.

"Ow, Jesus," he said, rubbing the side of his head. "Why ask me to kiss you again, and then brain me with a toy?"

Laughing too hard to explain, I was so embarrassed. He was smiling, and still rubbing.

"You're weird," he said. Taking the toy from me as if he was disarming a gunman, he placed it back on the shelf. I was still giggling when he put his arm around my shoulders, and said, "C'mon, let's go."

27

THE NEXT NIGHT, LAUREN SLEPT over and we watched movies. Throughout the films, I was messaging on my phone with Jackson. I added photos of Lauren and me in our PJs to my story on SnapChat, and uploaded pics to my Insta and Finsta.

Around midnight, Lauren received a message from Cole.

"Hanging at Hunter's. Come chill."

"At Cel's. It's late," Lauren wrote back.

"Come see us. Hunter's parents out of town. A lot of people still here."

Lauren asked, "What do you think?"

Laughing, I said, "We're in PJs."

"Let's go in PJs!" she said.

"Let's do it," I said.

Lauren messaged Cole, *"Be there in a bit."*

We went down the stairs, grabbed our jackets, and were almost through the dining room when Debbie stopped us.

"Where the hell are you girls going?" she asked.

"Oh hey, we're going out," I said.

"It's midnight. You're not going out. Especially in your PJs," Debbie said.

I was stunned. This was the first time Debbie had tried to exercise any kind of control over my life. I asked, "What are you doing?"

"It's midnight and two girls in their PJs don't need to be out in the streets," Debbie said.

Anger washed through me. Who did she think she was?

"Really? You're not serious, right?"

Ray walked into the room. He asked, "What's going on?"

"I am serious. It's stupid. You're not going out," Debbie said.

"Okay, it's seriously cliché and all that, but you're not my mother," I said.

"Hey!" Ray said.

"I know that. I knew your mother," Debbie said. "You think she'd want you going out at midnight in your pajamas?"

She wouldn't have, but she wasn't there, and I couldn't believe that Debbie had gone there. However, before I could answer, Lauren said, "Cel, it's no thing. Let's just go back to your room."

"No. Let's go out," I said.

"Celestine, listen to Deb," Ray said.

"You're not going," Debbie said.

"Seriously, Cel, let's just hang out here," Lauren said. She started walking and grabbed my arm, pulling me along. Moving past Ray, and not breaking eye contact with Debbie until I was past her, I followed Lauren back upstairs. Once we were back in my room, I said, "What a skag. She's not in charge of my life. We should've gone."

"It's cool. I mean, it couldn't have lasted more than a couple hours. By 2:00 a.m. everyone would've been sleeping or gone," Lauren said. "They can be annoying, I know. My own mother was all, like, weird today, about me coming here."

"What do you mean?" I asked.

She looked at me as if she wasn't sure she wanted to tell me, but then said, "My mom was asking all these questions."

"About coming here? About me?" I asked.

"About whether or not you're, you know, sick or contagious or whatever," she said.

A sinking feeling filled my chest. "What did you say?"

"I told her that you weren't sick, and that the government said you were safe," Lauren said.

"What'd she say?" I asked.

"She bitched about the government not knowing what it's doing, and that you can't trust them and stuff," she said.

"But she let you come over anyway," I said.

"Yeah, she didn't say I couldn't come hang out, she was just in a mood," she said.

Still, the idea of Lauren and Jackson's mom wondering if I was sick left a feeling of dread. We dropped the subject, but it hung on, nagging at me. We talked, while on our phones, about normal stuff. It was around 2:30 a.m. that we noticed the subtweeting.

"When a ho thinks that a football player loves her. #skank."

"Would Alicia tweet that about me?" I asked.

Lauren rolled her eyes. "She's a bitch."

"I'm going to write something," I said.

"Twitter fight!" Lauren said, smiling.

I typed, *"When a bottle-blonde bitch is so jealous and subtweets. #ratchet."*

I showed it to Lauren.

"Hey! Not bad! You've got this. 'Ratchet' is a bit old, but it fits," she said. We both laughed.

"Do I send it?" I asked. I was actually a bit nervous.

"Why not?" Lauren said. "I got your back." She grinned.

Clicking "Tweet," I posted the message. We waited for a response but none came.

"Wuss," I said.

Outside the window, we could see the stars, and Lauren said, "So weird that you were up there."

"It barely seems real to me anymore," I said. "Like I went to the movies with my parents and came home alone."

"Did you have a boyfriend before you went?" Lauren asked.

"Nothing real," I said. "Does Jackson ever talk about me?"

"Not really, but he's never talked about any girl with me," Lauren said.

"He's smarter and more interesting than I thought he was," I said.

"Yeah, he's actually a good guy. He has always had good grades and stuff. It's just not part of his image, so sometimes people don't know," Lauren said. "The teachers love him. It's really annoying."

"I think it'll be good to be back in school, in the fall I mean," I said.

"Are you nervous?" Lauren asked.

"A little. It's good that I'll already know a few people," I said.

"You'll be Jackson's girlfriend," Lauren said.

"I won't be the first," I said.

"Well, you've got Alicia jealous," Lauren said.

I asked, "Did Jackson and Alicia go out?"

"Not that I know of and I kinda doubt it. She's not Jackson's type," Lauren said.

"What is his type?" I asked.

"Someone like you," Lauren said, and smiled.

I really liked hearing that. We talked until the horizon began to lighten, and I think I fell asleep first, but I don't really remember.

. . .

It was still early May, and I went to the mall to get a new lightweight jacket, but I never made it to Ocston's. In the food court, Dylan was sitting with Emily and Arielle. He smiled and waved me over. Thinking I saw Arielle roll her eyes, I was not sure if I should join them. As I got to their table, I asked, "What's up, guys?"

"Guys? Do I look like a guy to you?" Arielle asked.

Frowning, I said, "I didn't mean 'guys' like men, I just meant it neutral, you know?"

"Don't worry about her. Sit down," Dylan said.

I hesitated, but Emily nodded, so I sat beside her.

"You come here alone?" Dylan asked.

"Yeah, I was just coming to get a jacket," I said.

"Ugh. Don't give your money to these corporate jackals. Go get one at Goodwill," Arielle said.

"For real, like, don't get ripped off," Emily said.

"What do you mean?" I asked.

"You know, it'll be way more money than it's worth. They gotta pay mall rent to be in here," Arielle said.

"And you know it cost them, like, fifty cents to make the jacket," Emily said.

"That's right, some eight-year-old kid named Akash sewed the jacket at, like, 1:00 a.m. in some Bangladeshi hellhole," Dylan said.

"Where did the jacket from Goodwill originally come from?" I asked.

Ariel's face darkened. "Aw, yeah, I know, but if we just reuse the stuff that's already here, the market for those sweatshops will dry up."

"But I thought even the stores were trying to find better sources for their merchandise," I said.

"Ha! You believe that?" Arielle said.

"Can you buy anything and feel good about it?" I asked.

"Maybe, like, vegetables at a local farmers market," Dylan said.

"Naw, the local farmers are trucking stuff in from more than 100 miles away and putting it out there like they grew it themselves. I mean, honestly, there was this guy selling tomatoes this past May. No way he grew those. And, like, he had potatoes in early June and wasn't telling anyone that they had to be last year's crop," Arielle said.

"Wouldn't people just know that potatoes in June must be from the previous year?" I asked.

"No way, people are stupid. They're all sheeple," Emily said.

"If people are stupid, but you know all this stuff, aren't you claiming you're smarter than everyone else?" I asked.

Arielle said, "Look, I just know the truth. I'm not saying I'm smarter; I'm just trying to spread the word. I'm just waiting for people to wake up."

I hesitated, and then asked, "So you really can't feel good about buying anything?"

"Not really. The world is a cesspool," Arielle said.

"There are so many amazing things though," I said.

"Like what?" Emily asked.

"I mean, we're lucky to live here. We have all the food we need, shelter, it's a relatively safe place. If you work hard, you can go far in life," I said.

"It's all rigged," Dylan said.

"What do you mean?"

"It's all a set up. The Man won't let you win," Emily said.

"Like, they track everything we do," Arielle said. "And they make sure they take care of the rich."

"Average people like us, we never have a shot," Dylan said.

I said, "But if you work hard and get good grades, you could go to Harvard or someplace like that, and make a lot of money after."

"No way," Emily said. "Getting into schools like that is all about who you know."

"Or who you blow," Arielle said.

Dylan laughed again and said, "And even if you get a degree from a fancy school, getting a job is all about connections. It's all rigged, I'm telling you."

Completely frustrated by this point, I said, "How can you go on living like this?"

"Are you suggesting suicide?" Dylan asked.

"I just mean, if you think the world is a cesspool without any real opportunities for happiness, how can you go on?" I asked.

"What, you believe there's hope?" Emily said. "You're so sickeningly positive."

Arielle said, "Was everyone deluded in the 1980s or something?"

I asked, "Do you think most people today think like you do?"

"Of course, except for the ones who have bought in to the corporate and governmental lies," Arielle said.

"Everyone who doesn't agree with you has been fooled?" I asked.

"You got it," Arielle said.

"There are so many examples of companies that have knowingly hurt people," Emily said.

"What percentage?" I asked.

"What do you mean?" Emily asked.

"I mean how many companies did something intentionally, knowing it would hurt people?" I asked.

"They all do. It's all about the dollar," Arielle said.

"Do we have proof?" I asked.

"Yeah, but not of all of it, because they're good at hiding it," Emily said.

"They're so good at hiding it that four teenagers in a mall in Maine know about it," I said.

"You know what? Go on living in your little happy world," Arielle said.

"Why do you insist on living in your screwed up one?" I asked.

"It's the only one I have," she said.

"Change it. We can change anything we put our minds to," I said. "And when we fail in life, we don't have to claim the whole thing was rigged and unfair from the start."

No one spoke for a moment, but then Emily said, looking suddenly bored with the whole discussion, "You win."

How did they get so jaded and cynical? Life used to be a hopeful thing. What had happened to make these people so negative, and to seek irony in everything? How could I ever fit in here? Saying nothing, I just stared right through Emily.

"You okay?" Dylan asked.

Not knowing what to say, I stayed quiet.

"Hey?" Dylan asked.

"She's zoning," Arielle said. "Is she high?"

"I'm good," I said, blinking.

"You sure?" Dylan said.

"You're not, like, epilepsic, or something right?" Emily asked.

"Epileptic," Arielle said, rolling her eyes.

"No, I'm good," I said. "But I have to go."

"You going to get that jacket?" Dylan asked.

Looking at them, I felt so detached, like I actually *was* from space. "I'm going to Deb's. See you guys later."

As I walked away, I heard Arielle whisper, "I think she's high."

28

THE NEXT DAY, LAUREN AND Cole came with Jackson and me to the lake. The boys brought hotdogs, which, of course, grossed me out, but I ate some chips and a pickle. Lauren ate the hotdog, making my mouth water in a bad way just watching her.

"Sure you don't want some?" she asked and laughed, and so did the boys.

"Ugh. It's like a tube of bologna," I said.

"You're weird," Lauren said.

"Celly, want me to go get you something?" Jackson asked. "There's a market a couple miles up the road."

"I'm good," I said. "Thanks though."

After we ate, we took two tandem kayaks to the water. Lauren and I climbed into the fronts of the boats, and the boys pushed us out and climbed in behind us. Smiling over at Lauren, I could see she was already complaining about something Cole had done.

"You okay?" Jackson asked behind me.

"This is cool," I said.

"You've never been in a kayak?" he asked.

"I've been in a canoe," I said.

"Another first for Celly," Jackson said. "Paddle on the left side for a while," Jackson said. We picked up speed, with Cole and Lauren pacing us to our left. Pulling harder, I could sense that Jackson had picked it up too, and we began to move ahead of the other kayak. When they realized, they chased, and soon both kayaks were zipping along, and I laughed out loud in spite of myself.

"I'm doing all the work!" Lauren called back to Cole.

Jackson laughed behind me. "My sister is such a ball-buster," he said.

In response, Cole was really digging in.

"Yeah, he's working hard," I said. I began to sing 1970s television-theme music as I paddled.

"What is that?" Jackson asked.

"*Hawaii Five-O.* It was this TV show when I was a kid," I said.

"I've heard of that. I think they made a new version," Jackson said.

Suddenly, the other kayak slowed. Lauren leaned back and said something to Cole we couldn't hear. He turned our way, and said, "Hey, we're going to put in over there."

Jackson said only, "Yep."

Cole and Lauren pulled away from us, and headed for a small wooded island.

Looking back, I asked, "Aren't we going with them?"

"I don't want to be anywhere near them for the next little bit," Jackson said, and he chuckled.

When I realized where they were going and why, I wondered if putting in on islands was the normal routine. Did these guys take girls out here and… I suddenly had a flush of butterflies. Excited and nervous, I smiled and asked, "Which island is ours?"

Hearing his paddling stop, I looked back over my shoulder and saw his facial expression betrayed genuine surprise.

He smiled. "Pick one," he said.

Chuckling, I saw a strip of beach and said, "How about there?"

"That's not an island, that's someone's private beach. Look." He pointed up at the cottage hidden in the trees.

"You pick one then," I said.

"Okay."

"Just…" I said.

"What?"

I said, "Pick one you've never been to with someone else."

He was quiet a minute and then said, "Celestine, you're not just the next girl I bring out on the lake. I've never taken a girl out to an island, and I didn't have a secret plan to get you out here alone."

His tone was different; it was softer. I said, "I'm sorry. Let's pick one together."

He said, "How about that one over there, with the pine tree laying in the water?"

It was another small wooded island. The beach was short, with a steep incline above it, covered in trees. Paddling, I said, "Looks perfect."

The kayak slid into the sand with a hiss under my feet, and Jackson was immediately out and pulling the boat ashore. Stepping out onto the beach, I took his hand and we walked into the woods without talking. We climbed the incline and the trees opened to a spot of sweet grass warming in the sun. We sat and kissed, and I felt so warm, happy, and simultaneously scared. I was nervous about pain, about how I looked, about getting pregnant. Wanting to get past the fears, I pulled his shirt off over his head and fell forward onto him as he lay back. The other pieces of clothing came off much more clumsily, and we giggled at a few of the struggles, but soon there was nothing left to take off. The long grasses brushed against our skin.

Jackson, the athlete and teenager, was actually tender and patient. He was generous and kind. I was cautious and shy, and he was gentle, and together we moved from careful to passionate.

After, I lay with my head on his chest, and looked up at the sky. Knowing that while everyone has a first time, I felt lucky to have this one to remember. We drifted off to sleep there in the sun and breeze, until I woke with Jackson brushing the hair from my face.

"We should go back soon," he said.

"How long was I sleeping?"

"Maybe an hour," he said, and kissed the top of my head.

Rolling over, I looked at him. His eyes were so green and bright. "I'm really happy," I said.

He smiled, and said, "I want you to be." Laying my cheek

against his chest, I sighed, and he resumed playing with my hair. We lay there for a few more minutes before dressing and then heading to the kayak. Paddling back, we saw Lauren and Cole sitting on the shore. Everything was already packed, and they were clearly waiting for us.

"Dude, what took so long?" Cole asked as we came ashore.

"Shut up," Jackson said.

"We've been waiting a long time," Cole said.

"You were done that fast, huh?" I asked, laughing.

"Ew. My brother, Cel. No details, please," Lauren said.

The kayaks loaded, we drove off. I had the sense that a huge weight had been lifted from me. The day was warm and perfect; the wind from the car windows blew my hair in every direction, with the sun shining on my thighs and face. I felt young, pretty, and content.

"Do you have a hair tie?" I asked Lauren. She reached forward with one and I tied my hair back in a ponytail. Jackson put his hand on my leg. I held it and breathed deep. I had come from the darkest moments on the *Phaeacia* to this. I thought of my mom and, perhaps in a sort of prayer to her, whispered, "Maybe, I'm really going to be okay."

29

THE NEXT TIME I SAT in Muriel's office, I decided she could conduct my therapy without me. During the previous visit, I'd felt bullied and alone, but at this meeting, I knew that I had friends and Jackson. Not only had I learned to laugh again, but I did it often. On firmer ground than I'd been since the *Phaeacia's* return, I decided that if Muriel wanted to mess with my head, it would be much harder for her this time and, in any event, I wasn't going to help her drive me nuts.

"So, Celestine, what is new with…" she checked her legal pad, "with Jackson?"

"Not much," I said. Thinking of the island and the grass brushing my skin, and his hands in my hair, I wished I were there instead.

"You haven't seen him?" she asked.

I shrugged, and thought of the way he smiled at me.

"Is that sad for you?" she asked.

She was completely off track now, and I loved it. I said, "Not really."

Muriel jotted something down and asked, "What about your friend Lauren?"

"Same," I said.

"You haven't seen her?" she asked.

"Oh, I have," I said.

"You two are still spending time together then?"

"Some," I said.

Muriel froze; she seemed to realize that I wasn't going to tell her anything. Bracing myself, I knew she'd try to push buttons now.

"What are you hiding?" she asked.

Ha! Was that all she had? *Lame.* "Nothing. Just nothing much to tell," I said.

"Did something happen between you and your friends?" she asked.

"No," I said. She was so annoying.

Muriel hesitated and then asked, "Did you sleep with Jackson?"

Whoa, too far. Wait, she's pushing buttons, don't fall for it. "Sleep with?"

"Did you two have sexual intercourse?" Muriel asked.

Gross. This perv had no boundaries. I asked, "Can you define that exactly?"

Sitting back a bit, her face darkened. She knew that I was messing with her. "I think you know what it is," she said.

"What if we define it differently?" I asked.

"What are you up to?" she asked.

"I mean, a lot has probably changed since your last time," I said.

Her face twisted; she was clearly angry. Headed down a one-way street, I knew there was no turning back, so I thought I might as well drive on.

"So, you have then. I mean, if we're comparing," she said.

"Just saying, you and I might have completely different ideas of what that is," I said.

She leaned farther back. "Do you have issues around sex, Celestine?"

Knowing she was just trying to take the initiative back from me, I said, "None. And, like, I'm flattered, but you're not my type. Plus, I'm pretty sure it would violate the doctor-patient relationship." I was so nervous, but I felt powerful too, and maybe a bit out of control.

"I'm not sure we've ever had a working doctor-patient relationship," she said.

"Yeah, me neither, and I don't want one. You're a bully and I have zero respect for anything you tell me. I know what you're going to say before you say it. While you're probably used to having patients who are smarter than you, I'd like to find a therapist that I can't think circles around," I said. Swallowing hard and hoping I sounded tough, I was actually pretty scared.

She stood up. "I'm afraid you've created a toxic therapeutic environment. We can't continue this way."

"I thought you said I was stuck with you. You even sort of threatened me," I said. At this point, it was almost an out-of-body experience. I could hear myself saying these things, but I couldn't believe they were coming out of my mouth.

"You don't want to work. You are exhibiting therapeutic interfering behavior, or even therapy-refusing behavior. I don't care what they say," she said, her face red.

"You mean NASA?" I asked.

"Good luck. I'm afraid we have to terminate therapy. You have baggage you haven't even begun to look into. And now you're questioning my intelligence," she said.

Standing, I said, "Oh, I have no question."

"Again with the toxicity," she said.

Turning, I left. My heart was racing, and I realized not only was I free, but it had been exciting. Not wanting to think about what might come next, in that moment, I felt clever and happy. I couldn't wait to tell Jackson.

Unfortunately, he wasn't the first person I got to talk to about it. By the time Debbie arrived to pick me up, she'd gotten a call from Muriel.

I climbed into the car and Debbie asked, "You're having sex already?"

"What?"

"I just spoke with your therapist. She says you're sleeping around," Debbie said. "That's not right. You are going to have a reputation before you even start school."

"Wait, this is none of your business, but I'm not hooking up with random guys all over town," I said. "And what about doctor-patient secrecy? Can't she get in trouble for even telling you?"

"None of my business?" Debbie asked. "I know I'm not your mom, but I'm responsible for you. You're a minor, and I'm your legal guardian, so I'm allowed to know all your medical stuff. We need to respect each other and ourselves here."

"You're giving me a place to live, Deb," I said. "I don't need any parenting. I've done enough growing up for a while. And I don't need to talk to that bitch therapist anymore. She's mean, she doesn't respect privacy, she's not even smart, and she hates me. She sucks."

"You kids today… anytime someone says something you don't like, you get all pissed off. She's a professional who is trying to help you, Cel," Debbie said.

"You're not in there. You don't see," I said, and then immediately regretted it.

"Do you want me to go in with you?" she asked.

Wincing, I said, "I'm all set with ever seeing her again."

"You have to. It's court-ordered, like the group therapy, you all have to. NASA went to court to make sure it would happen. It was a condition of your release," she said.

Release? "We were just in a medical hold to make sure none of us was sick," I said. "It's not like I'm out on parole."

Debbie didn't say anything. She seemed like she wanted to, but felt like she had already said too much.

"Look, I have friends and I'll be going back to school. My life is on track. I don't need a mommy, I don't need a therapist, I don't need meds, and I don't need group. I just need space. I've got a social safety net. I'm good. I mean, I'm grateful to you, I really am. I just need to do things my way," I said.

"Wait, you stopped taking your meds?" she asked.

"Just leave it alone. Just drop it. If I need help, I promise I'll ask for it," I said.

She looked at me, then at the road, and didn't seem convinced.

• • •

Sitting on my bed, I was messaging Lauren, but not really saying much. She sent me a selfie of her and her fish, and I sent a pic of my new tank top. Important stuff like that.

Outside my door, I heard Debbie and Ray quietly talking as they went to bed. They passed without stopping, and I couldn't quite make out anything they were saying except when Ray said, "Right. Right. Okay." Then, their door closed. It was almost midnight. Waiting for Lauren to write back, I checked BlemBam, a new app that allowed people to post anonymously, and one Bam jumped right out at me.

"I wanna know who you think you are. You show up and you're all like I'm Space Girl, like ur all that."

My face went hot. That was public for everyone in a twenty-mile radius to see. Hesitating, I wondered who had posted it, and I replied.

"I'm all set. I don't know who you are and I don't care."

Waiting for an answer, I received a message from Lauren.

"You still there?"

"Brb," I wrote.

"Ok."

The BlemBam anonymous response came.

"Guess what, Space Girl. He's just using you."

A cold wave washed over my scalp, and I wrote.

"Dylan?"

Nothing. I wrote to Lauren.

"Hey."

"Hey," she wrote back.

I wrote, *"Did you see BlemBam about me?"*

"Wait. Brb."

"It says I think I'm all that and that Jackson's just using me."

"Wtf?"

I wrote, *"I know, right? Like what have I done to anybody that someone would Bam drama like that?"*

"Just some troll. Don't worry about it."

I wrote, *"Lauren, you don't think he's just using me, do you?"*

"No, he's not usually like this. I think he's really into you."

I wrote, *"Ok, thanks. I should go to sleep. Ttyl."*

"Me too, night, love you."

I wrote, *"Me too. Night."*

Climbing into bed, I was thinking about the island and Jackson. His sister had just told me that she loved me, but he hadn't yet. Checking BlemBam again, I saw that there was more.

"You should be in a hospital, before you spread your shit all over."

My scalp tingled and my face flushed again.

I replied, *"I'm not sick."*

"Whatev. Your gonna get everyone sick with your virus or whatever. You shouldn't be walking around loose."

I wrote, *"Stop it. I'm not sick."*

"You probably already killed him, he's probably already sick, and his sister."

I wrote, *"Shut up! Nobody is sick!"*

"Serves him right, hooking up with a space skank, but now he's spreading it prolly."

So angry that my hands trembled, I messaged back.

"Tell me who you are! Don't hide behind this!"

"Ooh, are you threatening me?"

"Come over and find out!" I replied.

"Prolly just cough on me and kill me. Prolly what happened to your parents. No thanks."

"Who is this?"

"K bye, space skank."

"You're such a coward!" I wrote.

There was no reply, and I knew there wouldn't be. Putting the phone down on the nightstand, I could hear my heart in my ears. Thinking maybe Dylan at first, but not by the end. Alicia? Could she actually care enough to post stuff about me on BlemBam? Why not just leave me alone?

Lying awake for hours, angry and frustrated, I was more than a little scared. *What if they're right? What if I really* am *spreading the sickness and I don't even know it?*

30

WHEN I LOGGED INTO MY next group session, only five panels on the laptop screen were filled, while the other three were grey.

"Good morning, Celestine," Dr. Caledon said. The other facilitator panel was empty, as it had been for weeks.

Of the survivors this time, not only was Ian Mokone missing, but also Dana McCormack, the *Phaeacia's* copilot, was not logged in. Dr. Kendall was on the screen, but she did not greet me. In fact, she seemed to be staring at her own lap.

"What's going on?" I asked.

Dr. Kendall looked up, and put on a strained smile.

"What makes you think something is going on?" Dr. Caledon asked.

"Where is Colonel McCormack?" I asked.

Dr. Kendall's smile fell.

Dr. Caledon said, "Had you been on time, you would have heard the more complete explanation, but for now you'll have to just settle for knowing that she couldn't attend this time."

There was something about Dr. Kendall's facial expression that warned me not to ask anything more. There was a pause while the others were silent, as if to see if I'd continue. I didn't.

"Once again, good morning, all," Dr. Caledon said. "How is everyone feeling?"

"Fine. Fine. Good," came the responses.

"And *what are* everyone's feelings?" Dr. Caledon asked.

There were no answers. These sessions were only getting

worse. I didn't want to say anything. It had been empowering to choose how much to say, or not say, with Muriel. However, I wasn't surprised when it was the nurse, Sovanara Norris, who had the courage to say something.

She said, "I am experiencing some anxiety."

Dr. Caledon said, "Oh?"

"A third of the survivors are not online for this session," she said.

Silence.

"I know you've explained both absences, but it's still…" she said.

"I would have to agree," Dr. Stenhouse said.

Dr. Caledon asked, "You would have to agree with what?"

Silence again.

Nurse Norris said, "We have lived through something where, for almost two years, we watched our numbers dwindle."

"And now people are disappearing again," I said. It came out of my mouth before I could think about it. Dr. Kendall held one finger to her mouth with furrowed brow, as if I were a toddler interrupting the adult conversation. It made me want to say more but, at the same time, it seemed there was something else in her expression. Was it fear?

Another bit of silence. It was so tense.

Dr. Caledon cleared his throat and then slowly said, "I can understand how you feel, but these absences are nothing to cause concern."

Nurse Norris said, "Excuse me, but I don't think that's true."

My nose was only a couple inches from the screen, scanning the faces.

"I'm sorry?" Dr. Caledon asked.

Nurse Norris said, "I'm not sure you *can* understand how we feel. The reason we meet as a group is because we have a unique common experience. An experience you do not share. I'm not sure you can truly appreciate what it is like for us to watch fewer people show up, just as they did on the ship."

"Couldn't we persuade the others just to make a brief appearance next session? Just so we can see they are okay?" Dr. Kendall asked.

"Wait, you guys think they're sick?" I asked.

Dr. Caledon said, "No one is sick." His tone was more warning than comforting.

"But why would she ask if we can see they're okay then?" I asked. "Dr. Caledon, are they sick?"

"No one is sick," he said again.

"Would you tell us if they were?" Nurse Norris asked.

I held my breath for the answer. Just then my door opened behind me and Lauren walked into my room, smiling.

She said, "Whassup!"

"Shit," I said.

"What?" Lauren asked. She was scanning my screen. I could see her in my on-screen panel, which meant the others saw her as well.

"Who is there?" Dr. Caledon asked.

"A friend just came in," I said.

"Hi everyone," Lauren said, waving and leaning into me. When no one responded, Lauren's smile fell, and she backed away from me.

Dr. Caledon said, "Tell her to return later, after the session."

This made me angry. It was bad enough I had to log on to these, but now to have to chase my friends off?

"Oh, I'm sorry, I'll go. I shouldn't have let myself in," Lauren said.

"No, wait," I said to Lauren, and then to the group I said, "I'm leaving. I get more therapy hanging out for an hour with her than I do from all the group sessions combined. It's all bullshit anyway; we're just going through the motions, and fewer and fewer of us are even logging on. Count me out. I'm all set. See ya."

Dr. Caledon began to object, but I logged out. With a knot in my stomach, I wondered if I were more shaken by leaving the group, or by wondering if the missing people were sick.

"Cel, that was intense," Lauren said. "That was your support group?"

"Not much support there," I said.

"Those were the survivors of the *Phaeacia*?" she asked.

"Most of them. And this other guy," I said.

"Look, if you have to log back in, it's not a thing, I can come back later," she said.

"Nah. You coming in was like a rescue anyway," I said. "So, what's up?"

She sat on my bed. "What's it like?"

"What?" I asked.

"I mean, you don't have to talk about it but, like, I'm your friend, and you say that support group isn't helping, and I noticed you and Debbie don't talk much so, like, I want you to know that you can talk to me about any of it," Lauren said.

I said, "That's really cool, but I'm alright."

"Honestly, I'm not a shrink or whatever, but I'm a good listener. So, if you want, you can tell me what it's like for you. Is it really hard? I don't mean your parents because that's hard for everyone, but that's also different because there are so many people who actually know what that's like. But I mean, is it hard to adjust to a whole new thing?"

Falling silent, I thought for a moment. I mean, aside from losing my parents, was what I was going through any tougher than what any teenager goes through moving to a new town? New friends, new things to figure out about clothes, ways of talking, and the jealousy from the local girls when you're the new kid. Did my having been in space make that harder? Did the decades in between make things that strange? The technology had changed everything, and I missed being able to unplug sometimes from my peers; these guys never did. Around the clock, seven days a week, they felt they had to be available to their friends and to deal with drama.

Lauren said, "I'm sorry, maybe I shouldn't push. But I'm here."

"It's okay. I was thinking about how hard it is or isn't," I said.

"Well, I'm sure it's tough. I didn't mean to say it's not hard," she said.

"You know, aside from missing my mom and dad…" I said. "I haven't gone to school yet, and maybe that will have some really shitty surprises, but so far it really hasn't been that bad. In fact, most of my frustration comes from my old life, like therapy and group. My new life has been pretty cool. I've got you and Jackson, and you both rock."

She grinned, I smiled back, and we hugged.

"Well, I love ya, and I've got your back and even though it's weird that you're with my bro, it's all good," she said, laughing.

"I love you too. I love him more," I said and laughed.

"Ew, you're gross," she said.

She sat back and put her legs across mine. "So, what do you want to do?"

"What's Cole doing?" I asked.

"You mean, 'What's Jackson doing?'"

I smiled again, and she smiled back. "You're such a ho. Let's just hang out without boys for a while," she said.

"Here?" I asked. "In my room?"

"Yeah! Let's stay in here and play with Barbies or whatever you '80s chicks do!"

Our eyes locked for a minute and then we both laughed.

She said, "Nah, let's get out of here. We can go try on clothes we can't afford or something. Get some smoothies. Flirt with guys at the mall who aren't our boyfriends."

I asked, "Can't we flirt with girls?"

Our eyes met, and she said, "You're not pretty enough for me."

"That's it, I'm kicking your ass," I said. I jumped on her, and we wrestled. Childish play was better than any therapy. We stopped, laughing and gasping for breath, when Debbie came in.

Debbie asked, "What in the world are you two doing?"

"Dating," Lauren said.

"Pffft. I'm just using her," I said. We started laughing again.

"Whatever, just take it easy on my furniture," Debbie said, and left.

I rolled off of Lauren, and we lay there giggling for a bit.

"I'm so glad you were here," I said.

"Me too, kid," she said.

We stayed that way for a bit, and Lauren took my hand. Later, we did go to the mall, but what I remember best from that day were those five quiet minutes holding her hand.

• • •

The next day, while I was eating a bowl of cereal in the living room, Debbie and Ray passed through on their way to the kitchen. They were discussing the garden, when Debbie glanced my way.

"Wouldn't you rather eat that at the table?" she asked.

"I'd be at the table if that's what I wanted," I said.

Ray stepped past Debbie and said, "Hey, don't talk to her that way. It's not a lot to ask that you eat at the table. At least watch your manners just a bit."

Putting the bowl down on the sofa cushion, I stood, and said, "Listen, she and I go back a long time, but I have no idea who you are, so don't come in here thinking you can talk to me like that."

His facial expression hardened and he inhaled to reply, but Debbie stepped forward and between us, with one hand on his chest. She said, "Cel, we need you to eat at the table and not in here."

Looking at them both, thinking about bringing my bowl into the kitchen and finishing it there, I just stomped off to my bedroom and left the bowl on the sofa.

After I closed my door, I could hear their voices, but the only words I could make out were Debbie's. She was saying, "I know, Ray, I know. I know."

In a rage, I grabbed a pillow and threw it. Not satisfied, I pitched the clean and folded clothes from my bed. This, too, silently impacted the wall and fell. Picking up my wastebasket, I chucked that across the room. It gratifyingly crashed into the closet door. A book was next, and then another. These resulted in loud booms when they first hit the wall, and then the floor.

The door flew open, and Ray strode in, with Debbie right behind him. "Now what are you doing?" he demanded.

Glaring at him, and breathing hard, I said nothing.

"Knock it off!" he said.

I said nothing, and Deb pulled him back out of the room. Throwing myself on my bed, I was still fuming, but the feeling was slowly shifting to regret and sadness. I checked my phone. Nothing. Frustrated, I felt dejected, and guilty. In the moment, I'd felt totally righteous, but now I also felt bad about it. Why did I blow up like that? Why couldn't I control myself better than that?

I looked out at the sky, and then checked my phone again. Still nothing. I closed my eyes.

31

THERE WAS ANOTHER PIT PARTY. This time, I wasn't nervous because I had friends, a boyfriend, and more to drink. Even the strangers seemed to know who I was, but they were over it when it came to the space thing.

I hung out some with Jackson, but I wasn't glued to him. Just reassuring smiles for each other every once in a while, and we were good. Standing with Lauren and a couple other girls, I saw Dylan arrive, and I considered confronting him about BlemBam, but then was like "nah." Whatever. It was a party, I was buzzing, there was a big fire, and everyone was having fun.

Jackson, Cole, and Ken, standing in a wide triangle-shape, were throwing a football. It was dark, and they were playing by firelight, which made catching it tough. Whenever one of them dropped a pass, they would all laugh and complain about the dancing light. The music was good, I was watching Jackson, and didn't hear what Lauren said before she leaned heavily into me, laughing. I laughed too, as if I'd heard her.

"He's cute. You're lucky," a voice said.

Turning, I saw a pretty brunette standing close. She looked familiar, but I couldn't place her. She had an oval birthmark high on her left cheekbone, maybe the size of a nickel.

"Hey Sara," Lauren said.

"Hey Lauren," the brunette said.

"I'm Celestine," I said.

"I know, I remember you from the beach," Sara said. "You and Jackson, you guys going out?"

"Yeah, I guess so," I said.

"It's not official?" Sara asked.

"It's official," Lauren said.

"Cool," Sara said, and smiled.

I took a long drink. She seemed okay, and Lauren didn't sound hostile to her, so that was a plus. Jackson ran and leapt to catch the ball, missed it, twisted in the air, landed clumsily, and fell to the ground laughing. His laughter made me feel warm inside. Cole was laughing so hard that he sank to his knees. Jackson jumped to his feet and took a low bow before collecting the ball.

"Oh my God, he's actually hot, like, in that cute way," Sara said. "Lauren, do you have any other brothers?"

We all laughed.

"You guys get your class schedules yet?" Sara asked.

"I have calc with Huston," Lauren said, and Sara groaned in response.

"Is that bad?" I asked.

"Calc is bad enough, but Huston gives tons of work, lectures a lot, and gets all heated if you're, like, a minute late," Sara said.

"Yeah, she has no chill. Who do you have, Cel?" Lauren asked.

"For math? Someone named Bledden," I said.

"Lucky! I gotta go to guidance and see if I can get into your class," Lauren said. "What period?"

"Um, 4th I think?" I said, but I wasn't sure.

"Ugh. I have English that period," Lauren said.

"Me too," Sara said.

"Why am I in so many different classes from you?" I asked.

"Are you taking Honors English?" Sara asked.

"No, AP," I said.

"Ah, that's what it is, I'm not AP anything," Lauren said.

"So, you're like a brain, or whatever," Sara said.

"I just let them pick my classes. Is AP English hard?" I asked.

"Didn't you have to do some summer reading?" Lauren asked.

"They told me not to worry about it," I said.

Sara grunted and took another sip of her drink.

"I can't believe it's our senior year already," Lauren said.

"Me neither," Sara said. "The years flew by."

"Tell me about it," I said.

Sara laughed, and then Lauren did too. Cole stepped out of the football playing to get another beer, and Lauren wandered toward him without word to Sara or me, leaving us alone together. Jackson and Ken passed the ball between them.

"So, is it serious with Jackson?" Sara asked.

"Well, we're not seeing other people," I said.

"You guys in love?" she asked.

"I don't know," I said. "Maybe?" I was too buzzed for a meaningful discussion, especially with someone I just met.

"So, is it like just talking, hanging out?" she asked.

"It's more than talking," I said.

"But nothing serious. Just hooking up, no strings," Sara said.

"No, like, it's a legit relationship," I said. "Going out."

"So, you're, like, sleeping together?" she asked.

I just looked at her. This was too personal; she was reminding me of Muriel. Why did people want to know about such deeply personal stuff?

She said, "Sorry. I guess I was just trying to figure out how serious it was. Sorry."

"It's okay," I said, even though it really wasn't, and I drank some more.

"Cool," she said.

I said, "He's taken, like really taken."

"I get it," Sara said.

It got quiet for a bit. Jackson turned my way, made eye contact, and grinned. Smiling, I turned to Sara to see her facial expression, but she was walking away. Stepping into the circle of girls nearest the fire, Sara spoke to them. The girl to her left then looked back at me. It was Alicia. That's why Sara had seemed familiar; she was a bit-player in the bitch squad, and the token brunette. I wished immediately that I hadn't said a word to her. Alicia stared at me for a couple minutes more before turning back to her circle.

Jackson waved off another throw and walked over to me. He asked, "Hey, you okay?"

Glancing back at Alicia, I said, "I'm good."

"Good," Jackson said, putting his arm around me. He was sweaty and smelled so good.

"Want to walk a bit?" I asked.

"Let me get a beer," he said.

We walked away from the light and the music. He put his arm around my shoulder again, and I lay my arm around his waist.

"Do you think I'll fit in at school?" I asked.

"I think you'll be fine," he said.

"I don't think Alicia and her friends like me much."

"Ignore them," he said.

"They make me paranoid," I said. "Like they're plotting something."

"They live in a really political space. We've talked about them before," he said. "What brought this up tonight?"

"Sara was talking to me like we were friends, asking a lot about you, and I didn't know she was on Alicia's team or whatever," I said.

He asked, "Asking about me? Like what?"

"Like how serious we are," I said.

"Whatever, don't worry about them," he said.

"They're annoying," I said. "They make me crazy."

"Speaking of that, what's up with your group sessions?" he asked. "Lauren said that you quit?"

"Yeah, talk about making me paranoid," I said.

"What do you mean?"

"Well, there were two people missing and the rest of us… we can't help but think of when people were getting sick," I said, taking a drink.

"You think the disease or whatever is back?" he asked. "Like Alicia says people should avoid you. No chance she's right and you're sick, is there?"

"You talk to Alicia about me?" I asked.

"No, not directly. Alicia and some others are worried you're contagious and the government is covering it up. You know this," he said.

"What do you think?" I asked.

"I know you're not sick. I mean, it wouldn't matter if you were, I'd stay with you, but I think you're fine," he said. "So, what's up with the group sessions?"

"The guy who facilitates the sessions says no one's sick," I said. "I'm just saying that it freaks us out a bit, you know? And he was rude about Lauren walking in, so I'm done with them. Wasn't getting anything from that anyway."

Jackson sat on a grassy slope and pulled me down next to him. He asked, "Is there any way to contact the survivors who weren't coming anymore to find out what's up?"

"I don't know how," I said. "Our contact information wasn't shared, to give us space from each other outside of therapy, so we didn't band together instead of readjusting to today's society. We're only supposed to be in contact through group, but there's nothing to stop me from looking."

"Maybe the ones who are no longer attending have adjusted so well they don't want the group reminding them of their past lives," Jackson said.

"You make it sound like we were reincarnated," I said.

"You sort of were," he said.

We both drank, and then looked up at the night sky.

"So, which planet are you from again?" he asked, and laughed. I didn't laugh. "Sometimes, I have no idea."

He pulled me in close. "You'll be okay." He kissed the top of my head, and I believed. Leaning in, it was clear to me how much I needed him. Jackson, even more than Lauren, was the one I could talk to. He just got me, knowing what I wanted to say even when I couldn't find the exact words. He wasn't a lifeline or a safety net; he didn't complete me, or something corny like that. It was better. When I was hoping we'd make it back to Earth, without being able to picture it at the time, this was exactly what I was hoping for—to be clean, warm, silly, protected, loved, anchored, and free all at once. Looking up at him, I kissed his neck, nestled into his chest, and he pulled me in tighter.

• • •

Debbie came into my room the next morning and sat on the foot of the bed.

"We should talk," she said.

Rubbing my eyes, I looked at the clock, and pulled the pillow over my face.

"You were out late, drinking," she said.

"Oh my God, we're not doing this," I said.

"I'm responsible for you, I told you," she said.

"Jesus, Deb, the first time I got drunk—it was with you," I said.

"That was a long time ago. Maybe not for you, but I've grown up," she said.

"Let me grow up at my own pace," I said, pulling the pillow from my face. "I honestly appreciate everything you've done, but you're not my mom. You're not even your mom. I know you too well."

"You don't know me," she said.

"What?"

"The Debbie you know is back in 1984. I told you, I've grown up, and I learned a lot about life since then. I know I'm not your mother. But I am a parent, and I've got a lot more life experience than you do," she said.

I didn't answer. She was right, of course, but I resented her judging me about things like the party.

She took a deep breath and said, "And I think you need to go back to therapy."

"Not with that Muriel bitch," I said.

"In order for therapy to work, you have to hear stuff that you don't want to hear. You have to face what's your fault and learn to let go of what isn't in your control," she said.

"Oh God, you sound like a post on Instagram," I said.

"Celestine, you have to talk to someone. All that happened, that's inside you. It's bottled up and it's going to come out, and with a therapist's help, it can come out in a helpful way," she said.

"Muriel wasn't going to help me. She was a bully. She even sort of threatened me once," I said.

"See, that's what I mean. That kind of paranoia isn't healthy. People are not out to get you. Everyone is trying to help you," she said.

Sitting up, I said, "What if I don't want your help? What if I don't want to sit in a room or log in to some bullshit and, like, rip my own heart out for people? I just want to leave that shit in the past! I've got a nice life now, with a guy who treats me good and a best friend, and other friends. I think I've done pretty well so far. I don't want to think about the *Phaeacia* or my parents. All I did on that fucking ship for the last year was think about my parents and others who died. Every day, all day, thinking about them laying in storage. I even went in one time, sat in the cold, next to their body bags. I tried to unzip my mom's bag, but it wouldn't open. Like, is that what I have to talk about?"

I began to cry then. With tears, dammit. I hadn't cried, not even for my parents, before this moment, and now I was crying because of Debbie. Or at least in front of her. I hadn't been able to cry when I tried, and now that I didn't want to, I couldn't stop it. Maybe it was because I'd never said all that out loud? Maybe that's what therapy was supposed to do—make you so pissed that you shout your private shit, and then call it healing? All I knew was that being emotionally cut loose sucked.

"See this is what I mean," Debbie said, touching my shoulder.

I pulled away. "Mission accomplished, right?" I asked. "You got me to cry. Ripped open that horrible wound. Congrats— way to go." The tears fell, but they weren't cleansing or a relief; they only made me angrier.

Debbie pulled her hand back. "I'm not trying to hurt you. But this is why you need professional help."

Ray stepped into the room. "What's going on in here?"

I said, "Will you get out of here? This has nothing to do with you."

Ray stopped, stepped back, put both hands up, and walked out.

"You have no right to talk to him that way. He's giving you a place to live, too, you know," Debbie said.

"Just leave me alone. I can't even. Like, just go away and leave me alone," I said.

She hesitated, but then stood and left the room without another word. I lay down and cried a bit more, but pulled it together as quickly as I could. I wasn't going back to Muriel, and I wasn't going to talk about the ship anymore. That was going to be locked up forever, and instead I swore I'd focus on the present and the future.

32

WHILE WE WERE CHILLING AT Jackson's with a little Netflix, his mother kept coming into the living room. The first time, she asked if we wanted something to drink, and the second, she just walked through, stopped, said nothing and then kept walking.

"What's up with your mom?" I asked.

"She's weird," Jackson said.

She came back into the room, and this time Jackson asked, "What's up? What's the matter?"

She stopped and slowly sat. Looking right at me, she said, "Lauren and Jackson told me fewer people were logging in to group sessions."

"Mom, what are you doing?" Jackson asked.

Nodding, I said, "It's true, a third of us didn't show up last time, but I'm not doing those anymore."

"Doesn't that worry you? Perhaps the virus is back?" she asked.

"I've thought about it, but they tell us we're not sick," I said.

"But how do you know? How do they know? They were always changing the latest scientific thinking when it was the COVID," she asked.

"That's enough. Stop now," Jackson said.

"They just know I guess," I said.

"Did they even figure out what the virus or whatever was?" she asked.

"We knew onboard it was a virus," I said.

"How did it spread?" she asked.

"Mom, shut up!"

She recoiled. "Jackson… don't talk to me like that."

"What are you doing?" he asked again.

"I want to know about this, if it's around my family," she said.

"Cel isn't an 'it,'" he said.

"I mean the disease," she said.

I said, "It spread through physical contact with sick people. But I never got sick."

"They told you that you're clear?" she asked.

"They've told us that we're not sick," I said.

"But people are missing from your group session?" she asked.

Jackson said, "We covered that. Leave us alone, or we're leaving."

His mother looked like she was going to say something else, but instead only rose and left the room.

"You okay?" Jackson asked.

"I'm good," I said, but I was shaken. She and I had hardly ever spoken, and now she was treating me like this? It felt so gross, and this sense of dread began to build. I didn't feel welcome.

"You want to watch some more of the movie or go get a Blizzard or something?" Jackson asked.

"You know, I think I'm going to go," I said.

"Don't do that, Cel. It's okay. My mom's just a worrier," he said.

"I'm not mad or anything; I just want to chill a while," I said. "You know what I mean?"

He nodded. "You sure you don't want me to go with you?"

"I'll be okay. I'll see you tomorrow," I said.

"Kay." He walked me to the door, we kissed twice, and then I left. As soon as the door closed behind me, and before I could get off the steps, I heard him call loudly for his mom.

Walking back, I felt sick. I had been completely honest and open with everyone, and the authorities had made it clear that we weren't contagious.

Before pushing the door open, I took a deep breath, and then went into the house. I wondered why people were still scared. I felt healthy, and if I hadn't, if I had thought I was contagious,

I wouldn't have been walking around, kissing the person who meant the most to me in the whole world.

And, like, Jackson hadn't said much. I mean, I know he was stuck, and he even told his mom to shut up, but he was also the one who told her that fewer of the survivors were logging in to group. He could've said more to help convince her that I wasn't sick. Instantly feeling guilty for thinking that, as if I were being unfair to him, I regretted it. The whole thing sucked so much.

As I passed through the kitchen, I grabbed a cookie and my laptop. I decided to try to find the others. Not Dr. Kendall, though, because of the whole replacement-daughter thing.

When I Googled "Dana McCormack" I got a lot of hits, but not just about our Dana. As it turned out, there were a lot of Dana McCormacks in the world. There was also no contact information that I could find on the copilot of the *Phaeacia*. Learning that she grew up in Durango, Colorado, I checked for info there, but there was none. It was a dead end.

Deciding that there couldn't be that many people named Sovanara Norris, I Googled her and, again, there were news clips and many photos of her and us. Our faces when we first arrived, looking stunned and lost.

There was also a photo someone had snapped in a fast food restaurant and put up online with the caption, "Nurse from *Phaeacia*, Sovanara Norris, can't resist bacon double-cheeseburger." The post was tagged with "Burger King, Boston Common, Boston."

So, she was in Boston. At least she was a few days ago. I searched for "Sovanara Norris" in Boston. There were almost 100 people named Norris in the Boston area, but no one listed under "Sovanara." There were several registered nurses, but I didn't even know if she was still a nurse. She didn't have a Facebook page that I could find, or a Twitter account. Then, I noticed it. A "Lucy Norris" was a nurse working at a clinic in Boston. Lucy. It had been Lucy Gendille that she had nursed after being blamed for the death of Lucy's son. Was she using the name Lucy, at least on the website, as her public face? There was a work number, and I dialed it.

On the second ring, a voice answered. "Kenny-Kloepfer Clinic, this is Rachel speaking. How may help you?"

"Can I speak to Nurse Norris, please?" I asked.

There was a weighty pause. I might not have been the first to track her down, if it even were her.

"Can I ask who is calling?" Rachel asked.

My turn to pause. "This is Celestine Tolland."

"The little girl?"

I said, "I'm going to be a senior in high school."

"Please hold."

The music was acoustic guitar, and I waited with one knee bouncing.

The music stopped. "Celestine?"

"Nurse Norris? Is that you?" I asked.

"Celestine, this is Dr. Ayers. She isn't here."

"Where is she?" I asked.

"We're not sure. She has stopped coming to the clinic. Hasn't shown up this week. No notice, and then this morning we received word that she wouldn't be back for some time," Dr. Ayers said.

"Word from who?" I asked.

"It was a Dr. Caledon," she said.

My head began to spin. We were getting sick, and they were hiding it. Or wait, was she gone because she stood up to Dr. Caledon? Maybe she wasn't sick; maybe she was under, like, arrest or whatever. Each time, it had been a person who had attitude that went missing.

"Celestine? Do you need help?" Dr. Ayers asked.

"If she comes in can you have her call me?" I asked. "My number is…"

"We have your number," she said.

"How?" I asked. Paranoia. They knew me, and they had my number?

"Caller ID. We have it now," she said.

Oh, right. "Thank you," I said, and hung up.

I messaged Lauren.

"Three now. Three out of the six of us survivors are missing."

She messaged right back. *"What r u gonna do?"*
"I dunno. It's just so freaky."
"It really is."
"GTG"
"Ok"

I powered my phone off. Not silent, but instead, off. Heading downstairs, I put my phone on the fridge, and got a drink. Lemon seltzer, again, that didn't taste like lemon. Moving to the couch, I lay there, staring at the ceiling. I had no idea what to do next.

33

COULD HEAR THEM FIGHTING IN the other room. The argument was about me; they just kept repeating the same things over and over.

"She needs professional help, Ray," Debbie said.

"It doesn't work unless the patient wants to be there," Ray said.

"I know that, but she needs to see someone," Debbie said.

"She's told you she's not going back," Ray said.

"She claims that she was bullied," Debbie said.

"Maybe she was," Ray said.

"Stop! These are professionals who have dedicated their lives to helping people," Debbie said.

"What if this one *was* a bully?" Ray asked.

"We can try to find another one," Debbie said.

"Deb, we'll still have the same problem. She doesn't want to go," Ray said.

"She's supposed to be going to both individual and group therapy," Debbie said.

"We can't force her," Ray said.

Deb shouted, "What do you want to do then? Just let her lie around here? She needs help!"

Unable to take it anymore, I shouted so they would hear me. "Please! Please stop talking about me!"

Hearing nothing more, I expected one or both of them to suddenly appear in my room, but neither came. In the silence, I realized it was Ray who had been arguing more or less on my side. I was angry that they were discussing me *without* me, but having Ray fighting for me to not go back to Muriel made me feel bad for how shitty I had been to him. Then again, even Deb was fighting for me, even though I didn't want to see a therapist. She wasn't arguing with her husband over bills or some random thing; she was trying to get me the help she thought I needed.

In any case, though, this was my life they were discussing and it was frustrating that I wasn't included. My head hurt. I was caught spinning between being angry with them and feeling guilty about what I was costing them.

What was my being here doing to their relationship, to their home, and their lives? Deb was fighting with her husband because of me.

Not to mention Jackson and his mom, because I was sure that turned into a fight after I left. On my way out, when Jackson called for his mom, he used a tone I hadn't heard him use before. He sounded furious.

I wondered if I had survived only to come back to Goodwin, and cause problems for everyone I cared about. I felt bad. I mean, I had all this rage still, but I'd been venting it on the wrong people. Deb and Ray had opened their home to me, and I'd been shitty sometimes.

But, I mean, my mom and dad were dead, and I didn't need people trying to be my parents. I was old enough to watch out for myself, and being told that night with Lauren that we couldn't go out because it was midnight was bullshit. What was the worst that could've happened? I couldn't have ended up back in an aluminum tube with my dead parents and friends, sick people all around, and no real hope of getting home. So, being out at night in pajamas with a friend hardly seemed a problem. If everyone would've just left me alone, I felt we'd all have been better off.

Actually, that's not true, I thought. I would've been homeless, without friends, and without Jackson. Although, maybe that would've been better for everyone.

Suddenly standing, I shook it off, and softly said, "Enough feeling sorry for yourself." Pacing a bit, I tried to clear my head.

I stopped, picked up my phone, found some music, and paced some more.

I mean, it's not like I asked to be here, or to be this messed up. Nobody knew what it was like to be me. They all said they were sympathetic, but none of them really had any idea. Continuing to pace, I turned up the music until it washed my thoughts away.

34

THE NEXT MORNING, I WOKE to silence. There was still a bit of that negative energy that lingers in a house after an argument, the tension, but the quiet was nice, and it allowed me to think. Not just about immediate problems, but the bigger things, like about trippy stuff.

I wasn't a physicist, and despite getting decent grades in science, I never wanted to be one. You spend your whole life trying to solve some mystery about the universe and, best-case scenario, you find a solution. Next, everyone calls you a genius, while dozens of your smartest friends spend all their time testing to see if you're wrong, and eventually they decide you were, or only partially right.

But how could I know what was real, anyway? Not in a weird, like, abstract way or whatever. I mean, like, legit. How do we know we're not dreaming in any given moment? Lying there thinking, I wondered if I might actually be sleeping on the *Phaeacia*, and my parents getting sick might be part of a whole messed up nightmare.

Or maybe we never got on the ship. No one I'd told about the ship believed the technology to make such a trip existed in 1984. The space shuttle program used a lot of resources to barely claw their way into low-Earth orbit.

After we left, with the technology to colonize a planet in another star system, the space shuttle program back here on Earth suffered two tragedies. So, was it realistic to believe that we had traveled through space-time when the best and brightest at NASA were struggling to safely ferry a few satellites into orbit?

Was it actually 1984 and not 2022? What if I were dreaming upstairs in my corner bedroom, with windows looking down on Lynott and Michaud streets? What if it was actually a lazy Saturday morning and I were still asleep, with my mother downstairs, drinking her coffee, and reading a newspaper? What if my father were at the counter, with a cup of his own, balancing the checkbook like he did every Saturday morning?

Was there really any way to know if I had dreamt all those months of secretly preparing to go into space? We endured so much medical testing, which was ironic in hindsight. We ran every morning, lied to every friend about moving to Alaska, and shed so many tears. I had long talks with my parents, and with psychological evaluators. My parents explained to me, obviously excited, that I might be the first human to give birth on another planet, and it grossed me out.

Maybe I only dreamt that comment made me feel like livestock, like those horses that don't do anything but have babies. Maybe all those nights, when I lay there awake before we left, wondering about how I could be a mom on another planet, and how to explain to my kids why they were there, and not on Earth, were just bad dreams.

Maybe when we first got everyone together, those who would fly on the *Phaeacia*, it was only in a nightmare that I looked around wondering which of the boys would be the father of my children.

In that moment, I hoped I could wake up, go down and eat eggs and Sizzlean with my mom. Focusing really hard, I screamed inside my head to wake up. I pinched my arm and it hurt, but I thought that maybe I only dreamt that. I said aloud, "Please."

If I were still dreaming, if none of it were real, I really wanted to wake up just then—but I didn't.

Or had I been in a coma? My brain thought I was only seventeen, but what if my unconscious body was as old as Deb? Born in 1968, aging ever since, but unaware. It occurred to me that I was born before people walked on the moon, and that made me wonder what they had accomplished in space, while I was dreaming, or in a coma, or traveling on the *Phaeacia*, or whatever.

I decided I was awake. I chose to believe my memories were real, but that left the question about what people had done in space since we launched.

Grabbing my laptop, I Googled "NASA missions" and the site that came up had a long list. I was surprised and impressed. On the left side of the screen, I clicked on "Humans in Space" and the list got much shorter, with half of the remaining missions long past. All but the space shuttle launches were from my childhood, my first childhood, in the 1970s.

I clicked on "Future Exploration Plans" and under "Journey to Mars" there was an article about NASA experts discussing science fiction at some sort of comic book convention I'd never heard of. There was a link for robots on Mars, but I couldn't easily find plans for humans on Mars. Why were they so behind? I mean, when we were kids in the early 1980s, we were sure that by the year 2000 we'd have a base on Mars.

Instead, even though we had already done the space station thing before, and it came crashing down five years before we left in the *Phaeacia*, they put another one up there. And a telescope that needed corrective lenses?

It made me paranoid. Like, did they kill the scientists who'd designed and built the *Phaeacia*? Or were they locked up in a NASA prison or something? I'm surprised they didn't shoot us down as we reentered. There were still hearings in Congress about us, but I mean, who can watch those things? It seemed to me that the average IQ of politicians had gone down since we'd left. I watched a bit when they called Dr. Stenhouse to testify. They told him how they all should've been told about the *Phaeacia's* flight.

This congressman, who looked like most of the others— pudgy, really white, glasses—had asked, "Now Dr. Stenhouse, don't you think that as the branch of government holding the purse-strings that perhaps the entire Congress, and thereby the

American people, should have been informed of the investment in this mission to colonize another planet?"

Dr. Stenhouse cleared his throat, leaned forward, and said softly into the microphone, "Congressman, I believe at the time you were six years old."

"I don't mean me, personally, Dr. Stenhouse. I mean oversight budget members fiduciary responsibility to voters outrageous deficit budgetary funding..." or at least it sounded something like that. Whatever. It was mildly interesting, but I mostly felt detached from the politics of the launch.

Dr. Stenhouse then said, "A tiny percentage of the funding for our mission came from the U.S. government."

Debbie looked into my room and said, "I was wondering if you'd sleep all day."

"I'm getting up," I said.

She came in. "You okay?"

I said, "I'm achy." Swinging my legs off the bed, I put my head in my hands. It hurt, and I had cramps.

She placed her hand across my forehead. "Cel, you've got a fever. You should stay in bed. I'll get some Advil, and be right back."

"I'm sick?" I asked, fear gripping me.

Deb was already gone, but quickly returned with the pills and a glass of water, and put them on the nightstand. "Here you go, take these," she said.

"Okay. Okay," I said. My hand trembled a bit as I picked them up.

"Just take them. I can bring you toast or something," she said.

Standing, I washed the medicine down.

"Jesus, Celestine!" Deb said, pointing at the back of my thigh.

"What?" I asked, and then looked. There was a giant bruise on the back of my leg. My stomach clenched. *Holy shit, I'm sick. I'm sick. I'm going to die.* I said, "Deb! Deb! Oh my God!"

"I'll call the doctor! Get in bed!" she said.

"Get away from me!" I said. "Close the door!"

"Cel," she said, and started to cry.

"Close the door! Call them!" I said.

The door slammed and I looked at the bruise again. Remembering my mom's bruising, how it started small, but quickly grew. How she tried to cover it with makeup in the first hours, then how she scratched at the purple tissue as if it were something *on* her instead of *in* her. As the bruising spread, her strength left her.

Looking at my own bruise, I rubbed it, but I knew it wouldn't come off, and that it might never heal. I knew that the back of my leg might never return to normal flesh color. The fear was like someone stomping in the middle of my back, kicking the breath out of me, with each pound of my heart.

Closing my eyes, I recalled my mom taking her last breaths, and I began to cry. Even the whites of my mom's eyes had been bruised. Terrified, I fell to the bed; I sobbed and waited.

35

THEY CAME IN A RED minivan; the tires chirped as it stopped in front of the house. It was like any other grocery-getter you might see packed with kids and dogs, except three men and a woman stepped out of this one, dressed in button-down shirts without neckties, and each with a duffel bag. As I watched from my window, they sprinted into the house.

Once they were inside, I had no idea what to expect. I kept staring at the bruise and crying. So terribly scared, I wanted Nurse Norris and Dr. Kendall from the *Phaeacia*, and I needed my mom. Jackson. Oh my God, I wanted to see Jackson again. He was so close, right up the street. Please, God, let me see him again.

Even upstairs in my room, I could hear tense voices. One man shouted, "I'm hurrying!" and then I heard Deb calling, "Ray! Ray!"

Panicking, I paced from one side of my room to the other. This was all wrong. They weren't acting like doctors; they had run in like soldiers. For all I knew, Deb cried out when they beat Ray up. Or killed him.

Were they here to help? Or is that why other survivors had gone missing from the group sessions? They got sick, the red minivan appeared, and those survivors weren't seen again?

Hearing noise in the stairs next, approaching too quickly, I went to the door and listened, but then there was sudden silence. With my hands trembling, I reached for the door, and then leaned my ear against it. Breathing. I could hear them breathing on the other side. Slowly backing away, I climbed onto my bed, and pulled my pillows on top of me. With my knees bouncing uncontrollably, I looked over at my Cabbage Patch Kid, and wished my dad were there to save me.

A minute later, there was a pounding on the door. Jumping, I gripped my pillow and my crying intensified. I couldn't speak.

A slightly-accented voice came from the other side of the door. "Celestine, my name is Dr. Guy Thibodeau, and I am from the CDC. I know you must be frightened. We will not come in yet. Let's talk first. I do not want to alarm you further; I want you to be prepared. We are wearing protective suits, just in case, but we do not know anything yet. If you could please move to your bed, to make sure we do not strike you with the door, and to make sure everything goes as smoothly as possible, this would be helpful."

Already on the bed, I collected enough breath to ask, "What are you going to do?"

"Celestine, we're here to help. We don't even know what the situation is yet. I will tell you honestly, if you are actually sick with the syndrome, I would be very surprised. We only want to make sure," Dr. Thibodeau said.

"What the fuck are you going to do?" I shrieked.

There was only silence. It was so quiet; I could feel my pulse throbbing in my neck.

"We will take your temperature, blood pressure, we will swab your nose, and we will draw some blood. We will run a series of tests to look for the syndrome, and to also look for coronavirus. If you are confused or unsure, please continue to ask us questions. We are not here because of a disease; we are here for you, to help you, and to make sure those around you are safe," he said.

His voice sounded kind and confident, as if he was in control, and I really wanted someone to take charge. I hadn't been that scared since I was in space, but how could I trust him? They were always smooth talkers—doctors, shrinks, the people who put you in space... your parents.

Unable to raise my voice this time, as if I were physically shrinking, I whispered, "I can't do this."

The doorknob clicked, and he asked, "Celestine, may we come in now?"

Knowing they would come in even if I said that they couldn't, I was unable to do anything except focus on breathing.

The door opened slowly. They wore the same white hazmat suits I had seen when we landed; the feelings from that day came rushing back—the horror and disbelief. Extending my arm, my hand with palm out, I tried to push everything away. The doctors came in, slowly, and thoughtfully. One approached me directly while the other three fanned out.

My face was twisted, and while I was wracked with sobbing, I was silent. My eyes were squinted and filled with tears, I could hardly see, and I struggled to take the next breath.

"Celestine, I am Dr. Thibodeau," the closest one said. I could make out his eyes; they were as soft and kind as his voice. My crying finally took sound. Grief was back, and this time, ungoverned by the meds I'd stopped taking, it came out as screams.

"Shhhh, shh, it is okay, it is okay," he said, brushing my hair back with a gloved hand. My sobs subsided some, I tried to hear him, and I lay crying.

Another figure came over, this one the woman. "Hi, Celestine, I'm Dr. Sturgis," she said. She put a thermometer against my forehead, and said, "99.8." A cuff went on my arm, and when a beep sounded, she looked down and said, "180 over 110."

Dr. Thibodeau said, "Try to relax, Celestine. We're going to help."

I asked, "What about Deb and Ray?"

"They're here. They'll stay here," he said.

"But shouldn't you get them out?" I asked.

"No, we'll keep everything right here in this house until we know what we're dealing with. They are being taken care of," he said.

"They're not sick," I said.

"That is right. They have no symptoms of any kind," he said, and he smiled with his eyes.

The other two continued to work. They hung thick clear

plastic sheets over my bedroom door and windows. They were the same type of sheets that surrounded every one who died on the *Phaeacia*.

Dr. Sturgis said, "Now, Celestine, you're going to feel a little stick."

Looking down, I watched as she pushed the needle into my arm and then filled one vial after another, of different sizes and cap colors. Beginning to surrender to it all, I was still super scared, but I was coming to accept that I wasn't in charge, and then they swabbed inside my nose.

"What pain are you experiencing?" Dr. Sturgis asked.

"I have a headache and cramps. I thought the cramps were from my period," I said.

"Are you taking an oral contraceptive?" Dr. Sturgis asked.

"I'm not on the pill," I said.

Dr. Thibodeau said to Dr. Sturgis, "She has scripts for Celexa and Wellbutrin."

"I stopped taking them," I said.

"When?" Dr. Thibodeau asked.

"It's been a while. I'm not sure," I said.

"Has it been a day or a couple days or more like weeks?" he asked.

"Weeks," I said.

The doctors exchanged a glance without saying anything, and I wept softly. Knowing looks were terrifying; they were always signs of secrets, and on the ship, there had been no good secrets.

Dr. Thibodeau asked, "Celestine, would you like something to help you sleep? It would not make you unconscious; it would just help calm you. Would you like that?"

Nodding through the tears, I was frightened I might not wake up. On the *Phaeacia*, people took turns going in to say goodbye through the plastic sheets to loved ones. Hardly able to breathe, I asked, "If I'm dying, can Jackson come say 'goodbye' through the plastic? We did that in space; that'd be okay, right?" Despite the room being warm, I began to tremble all over, as if I was shivering in the freezing cold.

He turned to Dr. Sturgis and said, "Let's give her a little

Diazepam, let her sleep, and we'll set up in the kitchen."

Dr. Sturgis said nothing in return, but said to me, "One more little stick, Celestine."

The needle didn't really hurt, but I felt the drug burn. Dr. Sturgis rubbed the site; the medicine worked quickly and I felt my muscles begin to loosen and the shivering stopped. It was actually a nice feeling.

Left with sort of a hazy view through the meds, I watched as all but one of the doctors left my room. The one remaining sat in a chair across the way. Unable to see his eyes, and I didn't know his name, but I vaguely remember him saying, "If you need anything, just let me know."

•   •   •

When I woke next, a voice in the dark asked, "Do you need something?" It was Dr. Sturgis.

"Am I going to be okay?" I asked.

"I think so," she said.

Just those simple words, with the tone in her voice, made me feel a bit relieved.

"I need to go to the bathroom," I said.

She came over with a bedpan.

"Really?" I asked. "The bathroom is right across the hall."

"Really," she said. "I'm sorry, but we're collecting this too. Do you need to pee or?"

"Just pee," I said. *Gross.*

"Lift your bottom," she said, and she slid the cold bedpan beneath me, and then stood beside the bed.

"Are you going to watch?" I asked.

"Sorry," she said, and walked away. I peed in the pan, and it was embarrassingly loud. When I finished, she came back and pulled it out from under me.

"Is everyone else asleep?" I asked.

"Downstairs. We're the only ones up here," she said.

"Are Ray and Deb together?" I asked.

"Yes, and they still have no symptoms," she said.

"I feel better," I said.

"Your fever broke a couple of hours ago. We've seen no evidence that your bruising is increasing in size," she said. "How's your head?"

"Better I think," I said, blinking. "The cramps too. What was the fever?"

"Good," she said. "Seems like it was just a fever. People get them."

"So, this was all for nothing?" I asked.

"We have to wait for results on the samples we took, but I think you're going to be fine," she said.

"You're still wearing the suit, though," I said.

"We should know by late afternoon today," she said. "Want to try to go back to sleep?"

"I don't think so," I said. "What time is it?"

"A little past 3 o'clock in the morning," she said. "Want another shot to help you sleep?"

"No, thanks," I said. "Can I ask you something?"

"Go ahead," she said.

"The other survivors... have any of them had a scare like this?" I asked.

She said, "Well, you're all probably pretty close, but I can't reveal anything like that because of privacy laws."

"I know, but couldn't you give me a hint?" I asked, getting a bit frustrated.

"Sorry, but you can ask them yourself," she said. "Can I get you a drink of water or something?"

"I'm good," I said.

"Alright, I'll be sitting right over there if you need me," she said.

Lying quietly for a minute, I then asked, "What year were you born?"

She cleared her throat, and then said, "1969."

"The year after me," I said.

"That's right," she said.

"If I hadn't gone, I could be a doctor now," I said.

"You can still be a doctor," she said. "We've learned so much just in my lifetime, made so many advances. If you studied medicine, I can only imagine what breakthroughs you'd witness."

"If I live that long," I said.

"I think you'll be alright. Just waiting on the tests, as I said."

I paused, and then asked, "What advances have been made since I left?"

"Oh, so many. I can't even begin…"

"Try. Just tell me a few. I want to feel lucky," I said.

She didn't say anything for a while, but she said, "Well, just in the past few years there have been discoveries of ways to use viruses to carry poison to cancer cells. It seems to work on all kinds of cancers."

"How about something that is proven, on people," I said.

She paused, and then said, "Lung transplants. In the 1990s, we began to perform successful lung transplant surgeries, extending the lives of many people."

"For lung cancer?" I asked.

"Uh, no, if you have cancer, you usually can't get a transplant. But there are other diseases, the procedure has extended their lives, and increased the quality of living a great deal," she said.

Considering this, I imagined not being able to breath, slowly suffocating for years, feeling my lungs failing, and then suddenly getting new lungs. I said, "It would be like getting born again."

"Yes," she said.

Like me, I was reborn. "I'm a transplant." Feeling like I'd discovered something helpful, I almost smiled.

"I suppose you are," she said.

"With new lungs, you're cured? No worries after that?" I asked.

"Well, there is the serious threat of rejection, but the patient is prescribed immunosuppressant drugs, and they are closely monitored," she said.

"Rejection?"

"If the patient's body recognizes that the lungs are not the original lungs, the patient's immune system will attack the new lungs," she said.

"The patient's immune system will kill the patient?" I asked.

"In a sense," she said, softly.

Rejection. Rejection can kill. Trying to blend in, trying to act like it belongs.

"That sucks," I said.

"Well, very talented people are on the transplant teams to monitor and help," she said.

It must still be a lonely feeling, I thought. I didn't say anything else, and neither did she. Lying in the dark for a few minutes, I was sure I'd watch the sunrise, but I didn't. I fell asleep, and later woke to find three doctors in my room.

Dr. Thibodeau approached with the suit on, but the hood off. I could see his hair, but his mouth was covered with a surgical mask.

"Those masks didn't help much in preventing the spread of the illness on the *Phaeacia*," I said.

"They don't really protect the wearer in any situation. It's more about me not sneezing on you," he said.

Chuckling, I asked, "I'm going to be okay?"

"I think so; the final blood work results are coming," he said. "But the swab for coronavirus was negative, and nothing really seems to be growing as we'd expect by now if you were infected."

"What about the bruise?" I asked. It had not gotten any bigger, and was actually beginning to change color, but still…

"Seems it's just a bruise. It's healing, and not spreading. Before you flew, did you ever have a bruise and you couldn't remember where it came from?" he asked.

Thinking for a moment, I nodded.

"Given what you've been through, it probably looks twice as large to you as it does to the rest of us. It seems to be just a normal bruise. It should fade over the next week or so," he said.

"And Deb and Ray?" I asked, as the other doctors left my room, each carrying a piece of equipment.

"They're fine. No signs of symptoms. They check out okay," he said.

Licking my lips, I asked, "Could I get some water, please?"

"Of course," he said, and poured some.

The water was cool. I said, "I'm surprised the army didn't

surround the house, or that we weren't hustled off to a secret compound somewhere."

"We tried to keep a very low profile until we knew one way or the other. No reason to start a panic in the neighborhood until we know," he said. "In any event, you wouldn't be arrested, and you wouldn't be taken to a secret compound. You would simply have been taken to a major medical center, probably in Boston."

"How will you know for sure I'm not sick?" I asked.

"The blood work we're doing will tell us," he said.

"They did all kinds of blood work on the *Phaeacia*, and they couldn't always tell," I said.

"We're pretty confident that we'll know," he said.

"But how can you be sure?" I asked.

"You mean like 100 percent sure that you'll never become sick?" he asked.

"Right," I said.

"I guess for now we cannot be that sure, Celestine," he said.

"Well that's not good enough," I said.

"It might be the best we have for a while. We're still working very hard on understanding what Phaeacia Syndrome is all about," he said.

"When will you know?" I asked.

"There's no visible finish line. With this sort of work, we just keep digging, and the answers almost always come as surprises. At best, educated guesses get proven correct," he said.

I'd have to wait for a lucky accident to explain the deaths of my parents? I took a deep breath, and then asked, "Do you have kids?"

He seemed to hesitate, and then said, "I have one son."

"Do you ever worry about bringing something home to him, like a disease from something like this?" I asked.

"We're very cautious. We follow many safety protocols," he said.

"Do you drive straight from here and go give him a big hug?" I asked.

He just stared at me for a moment, and then said, "That wouldn't be following protocols."

"What if he was coming down the sidewalk as you left here? Would you hug him?" I asked.

"Why? What are you doing, Celestine?" he asked.

"I'm trying to find out if you would hug your son if he came by, just as you got out the front door," I said.

"I wouldn't," he said.

"Because you can't be sure that I'm not sick and contagious," I said.

"Because we have safety protocols for a reason. I wouldn't hug anyone just as I left this house. However, that is not because of fear. It is because I have a sense of responsibility," he said.

"Because I might be sick," I said.

"I don't think you're sick. We'll soon get results, and I believe they'll show you're fine," he said. "But I wouldn't hug someone as I left because it's irresponsible. Even if there was only one chance in a billion that I'd make someone sick, and a person did get sick because I didn't feel like following protocols, I couldn't live with myself."

"So, is there one chance in a billion that I'm sick?" I asked.

"I believe we'll find zero evidence that you are sick," he said.

"For now," I said.

"Best we can do," he said. "Celestine, doctors can't promise anyone that they won't eventually get sick. All we can do is take it one day at a time, one patient at a time."

"I know that. I just want to stop being afraid," I said.

"Most of us do," he said. He stood, and just before leaving the room, he said, "Maybe you should try to sleep. I'll be back in a little while."

Sleep. I felt like all I'd been doing was sleeping, but this time I couldn't. I just lay there, staring at the ceiling. I thought about Jackson.

36

BEFORE DR. THIBODEAU EVEN TOLD me the results, Dr. Sturgis and the other two were taking down the plastic sheeting.

When Dr. Thibodeau came in, he wasn't wearing any protective gear. "You're all clear," he said. "You still have the antibodies present, of course, as you were exposed on board the *Phaeacia*, but you are all set. We'll pack up and be out of here in no time. Thank you for being so brave, Celestine."

Not feeling brave, I was just exhausted. This time it was a false alarm, but I'd had enough time lying in the bed, the room wrapped in plastic as if I'd been placed inside a giant piece of Tupperware, to realize this nightmare might never end.

"Should you leave someone here? Just in case?" I asked.

"In case of what?" he asked.

"In case you're wrong," I said. "What if it flares up tonight?"

Dr. Sturgis came and sat on the edge of my bed. "Celestine, you're going to be fine."

Deb and Ray walked in then, and Deb came to me. She hugged me, and I gripped onto her.

"I'm so glad you're okay," she said.

Ray rubbed my head with one hand, smiling, but then they both backed away a bit.

I asked, "Do you think the whole town knows?"

"Nothing was publicized. It was kept quiet. The only sign the public might have had was our vehicle with out-of-state plates," Dr. Sturgis said.

"The neighbors must know then," I said.

"I was outside today, and talked to Jon Knauft over the hedge. He never asked, and he seemed relaxed," Ray said.

"Did anyone come by? Like Jackson?" I asked.

"His mother called, just to talk, and I told her we had guests," Deb said. "So, he probably just thinks we've kept you busy with that."

That sounded really lame. Jackson was going to have a million questions. "Do I tell him the truth?" I asked.

"You can do whatever you want," Dr. Thibodeau said. "The only secrets have been to protect your rights as a patient, but you have the right to tell anyone anything you like. I would keep in mind, however, that there is still some fear about Phaeacia Syndrome and coronavirus out there, so I might advise you to keep it a bit low key. Still, it is completely up to you."

I thought of the BlemBam messages and the protestors, and I nodded.

Dr. Sturgis turned to Deb and said, "You have our contact information. If you have any questions or concerns, just get in touch. It doesn't have to be anything scary; even if you have the simplest question, give us a call. Okay?"

"Thank you," Deb said.

We all went downstairs to see them out, and I winced when I saw all the equipment and plastic sheeting that needed to be carried to the van.

"Can't you wait until dark?" I asked.

Dr. Thibodeau said, "We'll be quick." He smiled.

I didn't feel much better about it; they were sure to be seen.

"Thank you for everything you did," Ray said.

Each of them grabbed a dolly loaded with gear, and headed for the minivan. Ray followed with an armload of his own. Watching out the window to see who might be seeing the CDC pack up, I spotted Lauren, just then, as she drove by in her car.

I looked at Deb, who said, "It's Lauren, I'm sure it's okay. Besides, you were probably going to tell her anyway."

"Was someone in the car with her?" I asked.

"I couldn't see," Deb said. "I don't think so. I'm sure it'll be fine."

The van was quickly loaded and drove away. Ray came back into the house.

"Was there someone else in the car with Lauren?" I asked.

"Did Lauren go by?" he asked.

"This sucks," I said.

"Cel, it's going to be okay," Deb said.

I wasn't so sure. "Where's my phone?" I asked.

"On top of the fridge," Deb said.

Wanting to message Jackson and Lauren, I also decided I was going to avoid BlemBam for a while. Turning on my phone, I saw there were many messages from Jackson.

"What's up? I haven't heard from you in a couple days. My mom said you had guests?"

Pausing, I took a deep breath, and messaged back.

"They're gone now. What's up with you?"

I didn't have to wait long. He messaged me right back.

"Did they take your phone?"

Ugh. He was pissed.

I wrote, *"Sorry, we just kept busy. Want to do something?"*

Waiting, I held my breath. His next message came a minute later.

"Sure. Mall?"

I wrote, *"Anything. I just want to get out of this house."*

"Be there in about an hour, Ok?"

I wrote, *"Ok."*

When my phone vibrated again, I thought it was Jackson again, but instead it was Lauren.

"Are you ok?" she wrote.

"Yeah, why?" I wrote.

"Those people coming out of your house…"

Oh no. Oh no. No no no.

I wrote, *"What about them?"*

My stomach was in knots.

"What was all the equipment and stuff? Like who were they?" she wrote.

"I'm not even sure. You'd have to ask Ray, but I don't know."

There was a pause. I closed my eyes until the phone vibrated again.

"You know, you can tell me anything," she wrote.

"Thanks. You too!" I wrote.

There was another pause.

"Ok. Love ya," she wrote.

"Me too."

Putting the phone down, I waited for Jackson. He showed up right on time. I never gave him a chance to come to the door. As I came out of the house, he was just getting out of the truck. He smiled as I approached, and I felt the warmth of it to my toes. Jogging to him, I threw my arms around him.

He chuckled, "Miss me?"

"So much, you have no idea," I said. A couple days before, I wasn't sure I'd ever see him again. We drove around, and went to Dunks instead of the mall. We spent the morning eating donuts, and drinking drinks more fattening than the pastries, and laughing about stupid stuff.

He was so cute, so sweet. He never mentioned the days I didn't message him. It was there, like an unopened box on the table, but we didn't discuss it. We were just being us.

37

THAT AFTERNOON, I NEEDED TO go for a walk. Alone. Goodwin had a set of hiking trails, with eighteen miles of loops, bridges over wet spots, and branches trimmed out of the way. Grabbing a small backpack, I put two water bottles in it, added a granola bar and an apple, and took off.

The trails themselves began about a mile from the house, and arriving there, I slipped into the forest. There were layers of green upon green, with shrubs scattered along the trail. Nothing was flowering now, but there were a few with berries. To be honest, I didn't trust myself to pick fruit that wouldn't poison me, so I didn't try any of it, although it did occur to me that maybe a handful of poison berries might solve a lot of problems.

The trees were filled with birds, although I could only see one for every five I could hear singing. Mostly robins and cardinals, but I heard the screeching of a blue jay off in the distance.

There weren't a lot of bugs. I had been worried about mosquitos or whatever, but it wasn't bad at all.

After walking for maybe an hour, up above me on a rise, deep in the underbrush, I thought I heard something. Maybe it was a rabbit or something, I thought, but then I realized it was too big when a branch snapped under its weight. I had a hard time imagining a deer walking that heavily. Maybe it was a bear? I heard it moving again.

Maybe it had cubs with it. Did they still have cubs with them this time of year? I had no idea. When it broke another branch, and it sounded closer, I decided I didn't want to surprise it and so I let it know I was there.

"Hey," I said, wishing I could've sounded more confident, but I wasn't sure a bear could tell these things. At that first word, however, all sounds of movement ceased.

"Hey," I said again. "Go away."

Silence. That was weird. Wouldn't a bear move away? Or maybe come investigate? Why would it freeze?

Then... it coughed. Heat flashed across my skin. It wasn't an animal cough; it sounded like a man. I was in the woods with a man who had heard me and froze.

"Hello?" I said. As soon as I said it, it sounded horror-movie stupid. Looking back the way I came, I knew that it had taken me almost an hour to get here. If I hurried back, and even doubled my pace, it would take thirty minutes to be clear of the woods. Looking ahead, I could see maybe that the trees thinned, but I had no idea where this loop went next. It could cross a street, maybe even pass within sight of a house, or just go deeper into the woods.

Deciding to go ahead, I walked quickly. After a few minutes, I heard movement behind me. It, or he, was following. Was it a random creeper? Was the government having me followed? My heart was pounding. Whoever it was might know the trails better than I did, but I did know the trails were a series of longer and longer loops, and most of them were off to my right. At least one was off to my left. I couldn't see it through the thick forest, but it was there. Not quite running at this point, I was moving fast enough that whoever was following me must have known I was trying to get away. My own footfalls were too loud for me to know if he was still coming. Watching to my left for any gap in the trees, I found one.

A narrow path led away from the prepared trail and into the woods. Maybe a game trail used by deer, but not a part of the trail system. I broke for it. Sprinting down the narrow trail, with branches whacking my arms, legs, and backpack as I went, I tried to put as much distance between me and the man as possible.

But then I could hear behind me that whoever was following

me was making no effort to hide it anymore. I was being chased. Sticks on the ground were cracking, and I heard a man grunt twice.

Running faster, with my arms outstretched, I was terrified, but I didn't scream. I just focused on the next set of branches, the next bit of the trail that I could see, and running as quickly as I could, until finally I broke out of the trees and onto the inner loop. Turning on this trail, I sprinted again. Sports had never been my thing, but I was flying down that path.

Listening, I couldn't hear him chasing me anymore. I slowed a bit, and looked over my shoulder. No one was there.

This inner loop was shorter than the path I had left, and within ten minutes I came out of the woods. When I got to the sidewalk and paved street, I stopped and looked back. Nothing. Putting my hands on my knees, I tried to catch my breath. Seeing the bruise on the back of my leg, fading now into greens and yellow, I checked myself over. There were the newer bruises on my arm from the medical blood draws. My hands and arms were scratched and scraped from running through the branches.

My heart and breathing slowing, I looked again toward the trails, and saw no sign of anyone. I took a couple more deep breaths and started walking back to the house. I began to cry softly.

Would the government really come and follow me? Dropping out of therapy, and then the scare with the sickness… was that enough of a reason for them to come monitor me, to chase me even? Why? To see who I was hanging out with, to keep a record maybe, contact tracing? Had those who had stopped coming to group therapy… had they disappeared after walks in the woods?

Walking into the house, I almost collided with Deb in the kitchen.

"What's the matter? You okay?" she asked.

"I was walking in the woods and, like, someone followed me," I said.

"You mean not just another walker?"

"Someone was in the trees, in the bushes, and then I ran and he was chasing me," I said.

"Did you see him?"

"I never saw him, but I heard him chasing me," I said.

Her face relaxed a bit.

"I know it sounds crazy, but it's true," I said.

"Why would someone chase you?"

"You don't believe me?" I asked.

"I'm just saying maybe your mind was playing tricks on you. It can happen to anyone," she said.

"You think I'm making it up?" I asked.

"I believe you believe it," she said.

"I'm not crazy, Deb!" I said.

She said, "Okay, okay, I believe you. Maybe you shouldn't walk alone in the woods anymore."

"No shit," I said, and went to my room. She was right; I wouldn't go into places like the woods alone. Falling onto my bed, I realized how exhausted I was. Lying there, replaying it all, I began to wonder if there actually had been someone following me, or if it had all been in my head.

• • •

Waking up late that afternoon, I went back into the kitchen and hoped there was still leftover lasagna in the fridge. As I looked for it, I heard shouting outside. Looking out, there were four people on the sidewalk with signs. Deb came into the room.

"Who are they?" I asked.

"I only know one of them, Mary Keilor, but I don't know the others," she said.

"Is that really about me?" I asked. One of the women had blue hair.

"There's a letter to the editor this morning," Deb said, pointing to the newspaper.

I moved to the table, and the paper was open to a letter with the headline, "Who Will Protect Us from Space Virus?" The letter named me, and said I was living in town, with relatives. I couldn't believe it.

"They can print stuff like this?" I asked. "How about, like, the privacy laws? Or isn't this harassment or something?"

"I called the police," Deb said. "I was told they have a First Amendment right to write those letters, and to be out there, as long as they stay off our property and don't physically prevent us from coming and going."

Glancing outside again, I saw the signs read, "Keep Our Kid's Safe" and "Quaranteen Celestine" and "Go Back to Space" and "Honk if She Should Go Away." I felt helpless, and they looked so angry. They hated me. I recognized one of them then; it was Thea Rand, Alicia's mother.

"They'll get tired eventually and go home," Deb said. "Are you hungry?"

I just stared at them. A car drove by and honked.

Something in my head just snapped then, and I went for the door.

"Cel, don't do it!" Deb called after me, but I was already crossing the lawn. I walked directly at Thea and said, "Why are you all doing this? I'm not sick."

They began chanting. "Keep our kids safe! Keep our kids safe!"

I shouted, "Stop it! I'm not sick! Stop it!"

Another car went by, honking. The protesters kept chanting.

I said, "Go away! Leave me alone!" I stepped toward them, and they moved back. Almost all of them stopped chanting, and I realized they were really scared of me. Taking two quick steps forward, I scattered them a few feet in every direction. It might have made someone else feel powerful, but to me, it was only more frustrating. Tears began to stream down my face. With my arms outstretched, my palms up, I pleaded, "I'm really not sick."

Deb suddenly had her arms around me.

Thea called out, "Yeah, get her away from us! Keep her in the house!"

As Deb guided me back inside, the protesters began clapping, and then they marched again. The next chant was different. "Lock her up! Lock her up!"

Deb moved with me to the table and we sat. She leaned over to me, holding me awkwardly as I cried. I said, "I'm really not sick."

"I know, Cel. I know," she said.

"No one believes me," I said.

She said, "That's not true. I believe you, and the doctors checked you over, head to toe, and they say you're not sick."

"Why are they doing this to me?" I asked.

"They're scared, the pandemic, but also they need a cause, something to be outraged about," she said.

"It's not fair," I said.

She waited for a minute before asking, "Could you eat? Can I get you something?"

No longer hungry for the lasagna, I shook my head. I missed my parents so much, and I wanted Jackson to come over and chase the protestors away.

My phone vibrated. It was Lauren.

"*My mom found out that those were doctors that time with the equipment. One of your neighbors says they were from the government or whatever. Is that true?*"

"Oh no," I said, sniffling. "Shit."

"What is it?" Deb asked.

"Lauren. She just messaged me. Her mom knows about the CDC doctors being here," I said.

Deb sighed. "I guess it was just a matter of time. Tell her you got a clean bill of health."

I wrote, "*Yeah, they came and checked me out, and they told me I was all good, so they left.*"

"*It took days to do that? Were you feeling sick?*"

I wrote, "*They said I don't have anything, that I'm healthy.*"

I waited, and finally she responded.

"*I believe you. But my mom is freaking out. She's like yelling at Jackson that you might have made us all sick and that you shouldn't be on the street and stuff.*"

I wrote, "*She said that?*"

"*Now she's saying that we can't see you, that you got to stay away. She's telling me to get off my phone. Don't worry. She'll calm down. GTG.*"

"Oh my God," I said, and I started crying hard again.

"Now what?" Deb asked.

"Jackson's mom is telling Lauren and Jackson to stay away from me," I said, feeling like I might throw up.

"Yeah, that'll work," Deb said. "Ever heard of a teenage boy who broke up with his girlfriend because his mommy told him to?"

"I don't want him to have to choose between me and his mom," I said, crying.

"That's sweet of you, but I think it'll be okay. She's probably just upset, you know, in the moment," Deb said. "She's scared. I'll talk to her." Deb pulled me into a hug again.

"Don't tell her that you found out because of Lauren telling me," I said.

"I won't," Deb said.

I said, "What if he does break up with me?"

"He won't," Deb said.

"What if he does?" I asked, and I wiped my nose on the back of my hand.

"If he broke up with you because his mom wants him to stop seeing you, then you'd be well rid of him. But I'm telling you, teenagers don't break up because of a mother's disapproval. Instead, they end up married and living together in North Carolina," she said, and smiled.

That made me feel a bit better, maybe there was hope. "You told your son to break up with his wife, like when they were just dating?"

"Well, not straight out, but I told him he shouldn't get tied to just one girl," Deb said. "I think she got ten times more interesting to him as soon as I said it."

She laughed, and I smiled through my tears.

"You really think you can calm her down? And this will all be nothing?" I asked.

"I think so," Deb said. "I'll talk to her. She's always been pretty reasonable."

I leaned my head into her shoulder. "Thanks, Debbie."

"No problem, sweetie," she said.

I let her hold me, and it felt good. Maybe it would all be okay.

38

I DIDN'T HEAR FROM JACKSON UNTIL the next afternoon, when he messaged that he'd swing by and pick me up after dinner. He showed up around 7:00 p.m. and never got out of the truck. I climbed in, and we drove off. It was immediately obvious that he was different and stressed out.

"So, what's up?" I asked, fidgeting with my hands.

He said, "I know Lauren told you."

"About your mom," I said.

"Yeah." He checked all three mirrors, and then looked over his shoulder.

"Yeah." My heart sank at what might be coming next.

We were quiet, and he turned left at the next stop sign. I had no idea where we were going. Taking a deep breath, I felt the anxiety in my chest. I asked, "So, are you breaking up with me?"

The truck suddenly stopped, with the tires barking.

Turning to me, he asked, "Are you crazy?"

"What?" I asked. "Well, with your mom and all." I rubbed my legs with my palms.

"I'm not breaking up with you. I love you," he said.

There it was. The first time he ever said that he loved me. We were parked in the middle of Cottage Road, with a horse paddock beyond the nearby fence.

"You love me?" It felt so good to hear.

"Yeah," he said, nodding.

The shift from wondering if he was about to break up with me, to him telling me he loved me was too much, and I started to cry. Leaning toward him, I hugged him hard.

"Me too, so much," I said.

"I wouldn't break up with you," he said.

"Deb said you wouldn't," I said.

"You told Deb?" he asked.

"Of course," I said.

"What did she say?" he asked.

We separated, and I wiped my face; my hands were trembling.

"That you wouldn't break up with me just because your mom told you to," I said.

He paused for a minute, and then said, "I'm not breaking up, but we're going to have to be cool about this. Like, you can't come over anymore, and I probably won't hang out with you at your place. You don't have to lie to Deb, but I wouldn't tell her everything. She's been friends with my mom a long time."

"I think we can trust her," I said.

"We probably can, but why?" he asked. "Let's not put her in that position."

"So, we'll be secret?" I asked. I didn't really like that either. I mean, it was better than losing Jackson, but I didn't like hiding, because it made us feel wrong somehow.

"I love you, and I'm not going to lose you, but I don't want to rub my mom's face in it either," he said, and then with a big sigh, he lay his head on the steering wheel. "It doesn't feel good, lying to my mom. I just don't know what else to do."

What he was saying made sense, and I knew it was going to be hard for him. It was too bad it had to be this way.

I asked, "But you told her, or Lauren told her, that I'm not sick, right?"

"Lauren told my mom that those doctors said you weren't sick," he said, and his tone was almost a question, asking for verification.

"That's right," I said.

Suddenly, a car honked behind us. We both jumped, and then laughed. Jackson drove away and waved back to the other driver.

"But she didn't believe it, obviously," I said, beginning to twist my fingers in my hair.

"She's just really afraid, Cel," he said, a bit defensively, so I decided not to press it.

I asked, "So, what's next? The mall?"

"How about we go down to Portsmouth?" he asked.

"New Hampshire?" I asked.

"It's only like an hour away," he said.

Things were going to be different; we were going to have to hide. "What do you want to do there?"

"We can go see a movie, or get a coffee at the bookstore, or whatever," he said, sounding like he needed me to accept the new reality, so I did.

"Sounds good, let's do it," I said.

He exhaled then, and visibly relaxed. "Let's do it."

We drove south. Once on the interstate, he put his arm around me. I tried to lay my head on his shoulder, but the thing between us made it uncomfortable, so I unbuckled my seatbelt. The car beeped at me for a bit, but then stopped, as I climbed up on the console and sort of hugged Jackson, kissed his cheek, and then leaned against him. He put his hand on my leg and rubbed near the knee, but inched higher each with each stroke. Kissing his ear, and then his neck, I rubbed his chest.

He said, "We're not going to make it to New Hampshire."

"No?" I whispered, and kissed his ear again.

We took the next exit, and headed for Old Orchard Beach. When I kissed his neck once more, we swerved a bit.

"Celly, you're gonna kill us both," he said.

I asked, "Want me to stop?" I sort of giggled and whispered, wanting to sound sexy, but it felt like I was trying too hard, and I was sure he could sense the tension, too.

"I didn't say that," he said, but he sounded more like he was playing along. With my arms around him, I put my head against his shoulder. My heart was pounding with excitement, but I also couldn't lose the worried feeling. Jackson quickly checked his mirrors, adjusting the rearview, and his shoulder pushed my head away.

As soon as we were parked, his hand slid all the way up my leg and I jumped.

"Let's go down on the beach," he said, kissing me.

Getting out of the truck and then walking down toward the pier, with the Ferris wheel standing high above, we held hands. Excited, I tried again and again to hold him as we went, but we kept walking into each other. He kept scanning the crowd in the distance. We finally reached the sand.

"The sun will be setting in about half an hour," he said.

"Let's stroll," I said, smiling, and we headed toward the pilings that supported the pier above. There were pubs and restaurants up there, and we could see and hear the tourists.

Passing into the shadows beneath the pier, he turned and kissed me passionately. We slowly lowered ourselves to the sand, and kissed again. Our hands moved over each other's bodies, and my skin was tingling with anticipation. He lay on top of me, my back in the sand, and I slid my hands under his shirt. He kissed my neck, working his way down, but he kept looking up and around.

"What's up?" I asked.

He looked at me, and I could tell he knew what I meant, but he said, "Nothing."

He kissed my neck again, and just as he got to my collarbone, someone yelled at us.

"Hey, you two there, this is a family beach! Go on and get out of there!"

We were startled, and scrambled to our feet, Jackson helping me up. About twenty feet away stood a skinny old man in khaki pants and a plaid shirt. He was clean-shaven, with close-cropped grey hair.

"Go on, now!" he said.

"Yes, sir," Jackson said, trying to sound serious, but we both started laughing. Embarrassed, I covered my mouth with my hand, until Jackson pulled me up the slope toward the Ferris wheel. Glancing back at the man, I saw him continue on his walk, disappearing beneath the pier.

We made our way up and off the sand onto the redbrick walkway, passing the restaurants and bars, past the Dairy Queen and pizza place, to Pier French Fries.

"Want some?" Jackson asked.

Still flushed by the excitement and the embarrassment, I said only, "Sure." I wasn't thinking about French fries though; I could still feel Jackson's hands on me. God, I so wanted a place to ourselves.

The sign atop the service window read, "The Original Pier French Fries. Serving fresh potatoes for over 80 years." It occurred to me that I'd missed thirty of those years.

"No ketchup," I heard him say to the person behind the counter, and I smiled. Looking out at the ocean, the sky was darkening as the last of the daylight was fading. Jackson turned with a box of fries, and offered them. Smiling, I tasted my first.

"These are delicious," I said.

"Right? I've always loved these. My Gramps used to take me down here just for these and a steamed hotdog," he said.

Wrinkling my nose, I said, "You and your hotdogs." I took another fry.

He popped three fries into his mouth, we sat on the curb, and he glanced around once more.

I asked, "So, in our secret romance, will you always be searching crowds for familiar faces?"

He stopped chewing.

"I mean, just asking," I said.

He said, "We'll just go with the flow, Celly. Let's promise to fight to stay together, and we'll just go with it. I just don't want to hurt my mom either."

"I get it," I said.

"We'll figure it out, how to make this work," he said.

"Okay," I said, but my stomach was in knots. The fries I'd eaten were not helping.

"Want to go for a ride?" he asked.

"Sure," I said. I wondered if he meant we'd go parking, and I sort of hoped he did.

But before we could stand, from behind us a voice said, "Hey, give me a fry."

We turned. It was Ken Apocino, the quarterback from Goodwin, smiling.

Jackson looked up, and his face blanched a bit. "Oh hey, man. Naw, buy your own."

Ken thumbed toward a short blonde standing beside him, and said, "She wanted fried dough."

The blonde smiled and quickly lifted and dropped a wave.

"It's good here," Jackson said.

"Yeah," Ken said.

An awkward silence followed.

"We gotta go," Jackson said.

"Yeah, whatever, see you," Ken said, and the blonde smiled.

As we walked to the truck, I asked, "Is it a problem that he saw us?"

"It's not like he'll call my mom, but it could've been someone else," Jackson said.

I said, "No matter where we go, word will get around that we're not supposed to be together, and we still are. There were protesters outside Deb's house yesterday. It's not like your mom is going to be alone on this. She will eventually find out."

Jackson didn't say anything. We climbed into the truck.

I asked, "What're we going to do when that happens?"

"I don't know. Let's not worry about it now," he said.

"How can we not worry?"

"Just don't think about it. Don't let it take the fun out of the time we have," he said.

"I can't just turn off the worry. I don't know how you can," I said.

"Because it doesn't do any good," he said. "Worrying today can't help with what might or might not happen tomorrow. It'll only stress us out."

"Do you not care?"

"Look, I care okay?" he said. "It's just that I can spend my time worrying, or I can just let it go for now, and deal with it when and if we have to."

Crossing my arms across my chest, I didn't say anything else.

"See? You see what worrying does?" he asked. "We were having a perfectly nice time, nothing has changed in the outside world, but we've got this new tension and stress, and that's it for the day. It's going be all screwed up now."

"It's not my fault," I said.

"I'm not blaming you," he said. "But don't tell me I don't care. I do."

"Well I can't help worrying. It's just who I am. I can't change it," I said. "I'm not worrying about getting grounded or whatever. I'm scared of losing you."

He didn't say anything, but he reached over and first gently rubbed and then patted my thigh, before pulling his hand back and putting it on the steering wheel. We drove back to Goodwin, without saying much. What we did say was polite and small talk.

I was still worried.

"Want to do something tomorrow?" he asked.

"Like what?"

"Let's hide right out in public somewhere," he said.

"So many people that we'll be anonymous?" I asked.

"Exactly," he said. "How about a baseball game?"

"I can't play baseball," I said, but then felt immediately stupid. "Oh, wait, you mean…"

"We'll go watch the Sea Dogs play," he said.

Ugh. "Okay, sounds good," I said. I was still worried, but it felt better to make plans in advance, and he was right. No one would notice us in a crowd like that.

"Good," he said.

"What time will you pick me up?" I asked.

"I'll pick you up at the corner at around 6:00 p.m.," he said.

I could tell he was intentionally not looking at me, waiting for my response. At the corner? Like, I'd be a girl standing on a street corner, and he'd pick me up? He didn't want to be seen picking me up in front of the house.

He asked, "You know the corner by the Harrisons?"

"I know the corner. That's fine," I said.

"It's just that…"

"I know, it's fine," I said.

He drove until he came to that corner and stopped, with this sort of sad look on his face. It was so stupid. Everyone in the neighborhood knew the truck, and me, and him. I rolled my eyes, and got out.

"See you tomorrow," he said.

Closing the door, I watched as he drove away. I mean, I understood why, but it sucked. I walked the 100 yards to the house and went inside.

•   •   •

The next night, after rushing through my dinner, I met Jackson on my street corner. He came by right on time, and I climbed in. To be honest, I was hoping I'd put feeling like a secret girlfriend behind me, and it would be like I was just on another date with Jackson, but it wouldn't go away. It was always in the back of my mind.

We got to Hadlock Field early, and went on in. The bleachers were the typical shiny metal, with blue seats and backs resembling long park benches. The first three innings went great. Jackson tried to impress me by trying to predict where a particular batter was going to hit a ball, based on his stance or whatever. I found myself loudly cheering hits and strike-outs along with him. We laughed a lot, and it was a lot fun. It reminded me of the laughing we did the night we watched *The Breakfast Club*, and then I missed his sister.

I asked, "Could we do something with Cole and Lauren?"

"I don't know, Cel. I haven't even told her that we're still hanging out," he said, and then he scanned the crowd.

"Do you think she'd be mad? Wouldn't she be like you? I mean, she'd pick friendship, right?" I asked.

"Lauren is really upset about the whole thing," Jackson said.

"I haven't even heard from her," I said.

"I know. She's trying to find a way. I mean, she's looking…"

"She's trying to find a way to tell me we can't hang out anymore," I said.

"Like I said, she's sick about it, Cel," he said, but then he winced.

"Well I'm not sick. I'm not. I guess you find out who your real friends are," I said.

"Blame my mother, not Lauren. Try to put yourself in her shoes," Jackson said.

I asked, "Is this impossible? Are we kidding ourselves?"

He straightened and said, "It's impossible. And like you said, she's eventually going to find out and all hell will break loose. It's going to be a right fucking mess."

I looked down at the bleachers, but he reached out and lifted my chin, and he said, "But I decided you're worth it. This time is worth the rough times ahead."

Taking a deep breath, I said, "Jackson, I…"

Never hearing the crack of the bat, I did hear all the shouted warnings, and Jackson suddenly pulled me over, and covered my head with his hand. A foul ball landed maybe a dozen feet from us, and fans scrambled for it.

"We're missing the game," he said, letting me go.

Pulling him back, I held him. His arms wrapped around me.

"I'm just scared. I'm scared of losing you," I said.

"I know," he said. "You won't."

We kissed, briefly, and then I sat against him, with his arm around me. We watched the rest of the game. We weren't cheering as much, or laughing as much, but I was more present than I had been.

"What should we do tomorrow?" he asked. "How about the art walk?"

"What is it?"

He said, "On the first Friday of each month, Portland opens its sidewalks to artists who sell their work to the public there. I never buy anything really, but you walk and people have paintings and photos, and there are musicians and dancers. It's cool."

"Will it be too public?" I asked.

"It's mostly young people. It's not as if my mom will be there," he said, but he didn't sound convinced.

"Okay, sounds fun," I said.

Not talking much after that, we just watched the game.

• • •

The next day, the sidewalks were filled with pedestrians, all of them walking without a destination, at a pace that gave them a chance to look over the art along Congress Street. I held Jackson's hand as we walked. He frequently stopped to look at paintings, while I was more interested in jewelry and pottery.

"You like art?" I asked.

"I used to oil paint. I took lessons," he said.

"Really?"

"Yeah, I just haven't in a long time," he said.

"Maybe you should get back into it," I said.

We came to what looked like a rack of butterfly wings.

"Cool," I said, lifting a pair of monarch wings from where they hung. I turned to Jackson to show him and said, "Earrings."

"Did she pluck butterflies?" he asked.

"Oh no." A woman appeared from behind the display. "I didn't hurt any butterflies. These are from photos of the wings. I shrink them down and then I coat them with epoxy, and turn them into earrings."

"They're beautiful," I said, but I put them back.

"Thank you," she said, and smiled.

Turning to leave, we almost ran into another woman. It was a full second before I realized it was Thea, and right behind her was Alicia. My heart sank. When Thea realized who I was, she immediately looked us both over, Jackson and me, as we stood there shocked and holding hands.

"What are you doing here?" Alicia asked.

"What are *you* doing here?" Jackson asked.

"You shouldn't be out in public," Thea said.

"Just leave her alone," Jackson said.

"It's not right," Thea said.

"She's not sick," Jackson said.

More than anxious, I was really afraid. "Please just leave me alone," I said, my voice cracking.

"You and the others are a threat to everyone," Thea said, and she said it loud enough for people around us to hear. Heads were turning our way.

"Please," I said.

"They've been checked out, and they're all clear," Jackson said, his face turning red, he squeezed my hand.

"She, and everyone else that was on that spaceship, needs to be quarantined until they are ready to announce exactly what it was that made them sick, and how exactly they can assure us that no one on Earth can get that disease from them," Thea said.

"You want everyone's parents to die, like yours?" Alicia asked.

"Shut up!" I said.

"It's a fair question," Thea said.

People were stopping now, staring. I heard at least one person say the word, "*Phaeacia*." Looking around, I began to panic.

"Go home. Stay inside. Stop risking all of our lives. It's very selfish of you," Thea said.

"You're that kid," an obese man said. "Celestine, from the *Phaeacia*."

"Wait, they're sick?" asked a woman with orange hair.

"I thought they were okay," said a young woman with tattoos and dreadlocks.

"They should be locked up," Thea said. "Go home and stay there."

Terrified and furious, I started to say something else, but Jackson led me away. I heard Alicia say, "Space freak."

After a few steps, I said, "Oh God. Thea will tell everyone. Your mom will find out we were together."

"Probably, yeah," Jackson said.

Stopping, I said, "Actually, I need you to tell me it's going to be okay." I was trembling.

Jackson put his hands on my shoulders, looked me in the eyes, and said, "I can't. I think things are about to get hard. I can't promise; it's not all up to me."

"That's not good enough," I said.

"Cel," he said.

"No. That's not good enough," I said again.

"You're right, she's going to tell everyone and my mother will find out," he said.

"So is that it?" I asked.

"What do you mean?"

I asked, "I mean are we done? Picking me up at the corner isn't going to help anymore."

He pulled me close, and put his arms around me. "I can't promise everything is going to be okay. I'm caught between you and my mom, it sucks, and I don't really know what's going to happen."

I had wanted him to reassure me, but instead I was more afraid. This wasn't some corny YA romance book or movie; this was real. I said, "Don't let me wonder. Whatever happens, let's make sure to keep talking. Things might get hard, but not knowing what the hell is going on would be worse."

"I promise," he said.

We drove home, and when he dropped me off, he drove right up to the house.

"Goodnight, Celly," he said.

"Good luck at home."

He sighed, and looked up the street. "I'm sure she's waiting."

He leaned my way, we kissed quickly, and I climbed out. I watched him drive off, and then I went inside.

• • •

The next afternoon, a dozen of the protesters were back. Thea was out there holding a sign high above her head that read, "Were Not Safe." Just then, a sheriff's deputy pulled up in his cruiser.

For a moment, I was hopeful that he was there to ask the protesters to leave, but instead he walked past them without a word. He came to the door and rang the bell.

"Deb!" I said.

"What is it? Who's here?" she asked, coming into the room.

"The cops," I said.

She went to the door, and opened it, and the deputy stepped in.

"Hey Joe, what's going on?" Deb asked.

"Hi Deb. Is Celestine here?" he said.

She looked my way, and I suddenly felt a sense of dread. I asked, "Is Jackson okay?"

"Can we sit down?" he asked, motioning both of us to the kitchen table.

We did, and he lay a small stack of paperwork down. Near the top of the page, I noticed that the paperwork read, "Celestine Tolland."

He said, "Jackson's mother, Mrs. Silva, has filed a complaint for a protection order against Celestine."

Deb asked, "To keep Celestine away?"

He said, "That's right. There will be a hearing; the date isn't set yet. A judge will hear the complaint. Celestine, you'll have to go. Deb, because she's a minor, you'll have to appear as well."

"Can she really do this?" I asked, looking at Deb, and then at the deputy.

"They won't be able to have any contact with each other at all?" Deb asked.

"Neither direct nor indirect," he said. "Direct would mean face to face, a phone call, an email, a text message, a note or letter. Indirect would mean having someone act as a go-between. Celestine cannot even ask someone to tell Jackson something."

Wait, this can't be. I asked, "You mean, if we lose at the hearing. After the hearing this would take effect?"

He sighed. "I'm afraid that it starts now. This here is a temporary protection order, put in place until the hearing," he said, and slid the paperwork in front of Deb and me. "It means that you are to have no contact, neither direct nor indirect, with Jackson, any member of his family, or go within 100 feet of his house, until the hearing. Then, after the hearing, you'll know what the new conditions are, if any."

"What about school? How can she go to the same school?" Deb asked.

"Schools deal with these things. They'll make sure the two of them share no classes and have minimal contact," he said.

"There's no way to fight this?" I asked, tears in my eyes.

"You can file for a hearing on dissolution of the temporary order. If the judge agrees to a hearing on dissolving the temporary order, he will schedule one. He may even hold the hearing on the temporary order simultaneously with the hearing on the permanent order. You will be able to hire a lawyer, call witnesses, etc. However, the judge must give notice to the plaintiff at least forty-eight hours prior to the hearing on dissolving the temporary order," he said.

My head was spinning. *Lawyers and witnesses?*

"On what grounds, Joe? On what grounds is she doing this?" Deb asked.

"She's claiming Celestine is harassing her son, her daughter, and the family," he said.

"I haven't even been over there in weeks. I haven't seen Lauren, my best friend, in forever. And Jackson, I love him, and he loves me. He's my boyfriend. I'm not harassing anyone," I said.

"It's not up to me. I just deliver the bad news," he said.

"I know, Joe," Deb said. "How quickly could a hearing to dissolve the temporary order be set up?"

"I've seen them go as quickly as a week after the defendant filed," he said.

He looked at me when he said "defendant," and I felt sick. Crying now, openly but softly, I wondered if this was it. Was this how I would lose Jackson? I couldn't imagine not seeing him, talking to him, or not even a text for a week.

"Joe, I've known Barb Silva a while… think it would help to just call her and see if we can work this out?" Deb asked.

"I wouldn't advise calling. Once it gets this serious, it's best to just leave it to the judge," he said.

We were all silent for a moment, and the only sound was my heavy breathing and sniffling. He softly tapped the papers, and said, "I'll ask you to both sign this. You too, Deb, since she's a minor in your care."

Looking at it, the words were blurry through the tears, but I could see "no direct or indirect contact."

"What if I don't sign it?" I asked.

"It won't matter, really, you've been served now," he said. "I'll just note you refused."

"It's so fucking unfair. She's scared I'm sick. Well, I'm not sick. Why can't that bitch get that through her fucking head? I hate her. I hate her so much," I said.

His tone became much more official then. "Just so we're clear, Celestine, you are not to violate the conditions of this temporary protection order in any way. Don't even look for a loophole. Just pretend he's on a vacation far away; he's not even there. It'll be easier that way, on everyone. If he does love you, like you say, he'll be hurting too, and probably angry with his mother," he said.

I hadn't considered that Jackson would be hurting in that moment too. Was he shattered? Was he resigned? I needed to talk to him.

"If you violate this protection order, and see or talk to Jackson, things can get ugly very quickly. Besides, to the judge, you might look like you are out of control and unreasonable, maybe obsessed. At the very least, you'll seem like you have no respect for the court and its orders. You understand? What you want to look like, is that you are mature, responsible, and under control. If you seem calm, rational, and you can address her complaint at the hearing with reasonable explanations, you might get the whole thing thrown out."

Beginning to sob, I reached for the pile of papers, but then didn't touch them. Deb hugged me, and she whispered in my ear, "Hon, why don't you go lie down in bed? I'll be in in a bit."

Nodding, I stood, walked into my room, fell on the bed, and cried into my pillow. I could still hear them talking in the other room.

Deb said, "She's just a kid, Joe. She lost her parents. Now this is happening to her."

"A lot of people are scared of getting sick, Deb," he said.

Deb asked, "If she does violate the order, will you slap her in cuffs, drag her to jail?"

"Deb," he said.

"Seriously, will she get arrested?" Deb asked.

His tone a bit angry, he said, "You know what? We hate these things. When it's a battered wife, I encourage a protection order, but these protection orders—when a mother wants to keep a boyfriend or girlfriend away—we all hate it. You won't find a law enforcement officer who likes them."

"But will she be arrested?" Deb asked.

"Deb, between us, it's unlikely if they're caught together that a deputy or town cop will even respond. But you'll likely end up in court, with a judge that wants to know why his order wasn't followed," he said.

"It's just cruel, Joe," Deb said.

"I know it," he said. "Like I said, I'm just the messenger." I heard his heavy footsteps. "Okay, we'll see ya, Deb."

Hearing the door close, I soon felt Deb's weight move my bed as she sat.

"I'm really sorry, Cel. I honestly don't know what to say," she said.

"What do you think I should do?" I asked.

"I don't think you have any choice," she said. "Follow the rules. We can go down and file about the temporary order. Hopefully, in a week, this is all behind us. You haven't harassed anyone, and I think a fair judge will see that."

"I know it's not that long, but that feels so bad," I said. "A week of no contact? It seems like forever."

She rubbed my back. "I know, I know it does. I think it would be best though."

My heart was shattered, and a wave of hopelessness surged over me.

Deb asked, "You going to take a nap?"

Shrugging, I wasn't sure. I was weary, but I didn't think I'd sleep. Rubbing my eyes, I could feel my pillow was cool and wet on my cheek.

"Okay, I'll leave you alone," Deb said, and stood. "Let me know if you need anything."

"Okay," I said. The sadness I felt was indescribable.

"I'll wake you for supper," Deb said, and she left.

Although I didn't think I'd sleep, my eyes closed, and when they opened it was dark outside. She hadn't wakened me to eat. Picking up my phone to check the time, I saw there were four messages from Jackson.

"Pack some clothes, I'll pick you up at 10pm."

"You there?"

"Did they take your phone?"

"Pls msg me if you get these."

I wrote, *"Jackson?"*

He immediately wrote back, *"Thank God."*

"Where are we going?"

"I don't want to say on here. Meet me at your corner."

Checking the time, I saw it was just after 9:00 p.m., and I wrote, *"At 10pm."*

"Can you sneak out?"

Looking out my door toward the kitchen, I saw no sign of anyone, but I still thought the window would be the best way out.

"I'll be there."

My heart was racing.

He wrote, *"See you soon."*

Getting up, I quickly but quietly began packing. Having no idea what to bring, I just took the practical stuff. Jeans, sneakers, T-shirts, a hat, PJs, toothbrush, and hairbrush. When I was done, I went to the window and carefully removed the screen. I lowered my backpack to the ground outside. Stashing the screen in the closet, and then making my bed, I stood there for a minute. I wrote a quick note to Deb that read only, "Don't worry. I love you," and left it on the nightstand.

I checked the time again. 9:40 p.m. Climbing out the window, I closed it, picked up my pack, and made my way to the corner. My chest was pounding as he pulled up. Jumping in, I kissed him, and we pulled away. Unable to help myself, partly from happiness and partly from nerves, I began giggling. Leaning over and hugging him, I bumped into him hard enough that we swerved into the other lane. We both laughed.

"Sit down," he said. "Buckle up."

"Where are we going?" I asked.

"You'll see. Oh, but turn off your phone. Power it right off and you can't turn it back on. They can track it," he said.

"We're really running away?" I asked, smiling, excited, and scared.

"We're really being together," he said, smiling back.

Powering my phone off, I dropped it into my backpack.

We drove out of town, and got onto the highway, and headed north.

•   •   •

Leaving the highway less than an hour later, we drove into farmland. I could see him smiling by the glow of the dashboard lights.

"Can you tell me now?" I asked.

"Where we're going?" he asked.

"It'd be nice," I said.

"You won't know it."

"Try me," I said.

"Sand Pond," he said.

I didn't know it. "We're going to a pond?"

"Mike Lepen's parents have a camp on Sand Pond. When I told him what my mom did to us, he told me where to find the key. He said we can hang out there," he said.

"That's really cool of him. He won't say anything?" I asked.

"Not in a million years," he said. "Mike is rock solid."

"Won't the neighbors wonder?"

"It's pretty secluded. Besides, a lot of people on a lake are from out of town," he said.

"We can't stay there forever," I said.

Looking my way, he said, "What did I tell you about missing the present by worrying about the future?"

Even though I wanted to start working on the plan for after the camp, instead, I let it go. It was after 11:00 p.m. when I first saw the moonlight reflecting off Sand Pond, and soon we were driving down the dark driveway.

Amidst the pine trees, I could just make out the silhouette of the small cabin, until the drive turned that way and it was fully illuminated by the headlights. It was clad in cedar shingles and a small deck looked out over the water. He stopped the engine, and turned off the headlights. As our eyes adjusted, details were slowly revealed once more.

Climbing out, I grabbed my backpack, and walked toward the cabin. Jackson came around, took my hand, and led me onto the deck. Reaching down, he moved a watering can, and picked up the key. He unlocked the door, and we went in.

"Are the lights electric?" I asked, a split second before Jackson turned on a lamp.

It was cute in there, with a small couch draped with an afghan, a wingback chair, a wicker chair, and a coffee table all within twelve feet of a woodstove. Beyond was a small kitchen with a little circular table.

Jackson said, "Want the bathroom?"

"All yours," I said.

He went in and closed the door behind him, and I walked past and down the hallway. Moving first into one room that had two unmade bunk beds, and then into the room across the hall. This bed too was unmade. I had a flutter in my stomach. That's the bed we'd be sleeping in. I mean, I assumed. Turning on a lamp, I found some bedding. Making up the bed, I heard the toilet flush in the other room, and was putting pillows in cases when Jackson came in.

"Hey. Whoa. Like, we've never spent the night together, in a bed," Jackson said.

I smiled. "I thought the same thing."

Looking around, he said, "We get to be just normal people, huh? Like a normal couple?"

I walked over to him, and put my head on his chest. Holding me tight, he stroked my hair. Looking up into his eyes, although he was handsome, he also seemed tired.

He asked, "Want to go to bed? Like, not go to bed, but like go to bed?"

I didn't really know which he meant, but I said, "I have to go brush my teeth and stuff." Retrieving my backpack, I took it into the bathroom. I brushed my teeth, brushed my hair, and changed into pajamas, and then put lotion on my face and hands. I peed, and washed my hands, and then put lotion on my hands again. While checking my teeth, I froze, and I looked deep into my own eyes.

With worry creeping back in, I was starting to have doubts, but stopped myself. I whispered, "Live for now. You might have one night together. Live for now." Fixing my hair a bit more, I went to the bedroom. Jackson was in the bed, and was clearly already sleeping. Moving around to the other side of the bed, I climbed into the sheets. He was shirtless, but wearing boxer-briefs. By moving closer to him, I woke him for a second, and maybe only half-awake, he put one arm beneath my head, and I cuddled up to him. He fell right back to sleep, and I was awake only a few minutes longer than he was.

39

WAKING UP ALONE IN THE bed, I could smell coffee. Jackson walked in just then, dressed in jeans and a T-shirt, but barefoot.

"There's no food," he said, and grinned. He came over and kissed my forehead, and then we kissed on the lips, but I kept my mouth closed. He pulled away.

"Sorry, morning breath," I said.

"No problem," he said, smiling still. "Be right back."

Hearing him drive away, I pulled the blankets up to my chin, and snuggled in. It was nice, but when I heard a loon cry out on the lake, I decided to get up. Pulling a blanket off a chair in the room, I wrapped it around my shoulders, and went out on the deck. It wasn't really cold, just the morning cool. The loon cried again.

Looking left, down the shore, and then right, I couldn't see the neighboring cabins. We did have some privacy here. Thinking of Deb, I knew she must be worried, but that was really the only downside. I had Jackson to myself. The loon cried again, and I searched the water's surface for the bird until I spotted two of them, out past a small island. This place was perfect. Taking a deep breath, I looked up at the morning sky, and spotted robins chasing each other across the space between the pines.

I went inside and poured myself a cup of coffee, threw some sugar in it, and went back out. Slowly sipping, I felt myself relaxing, really coming down for the first time in a long time. He had called it, "Sand Pond," but it was a decent-sized lake. I spotted my loons again.

It wasn't long before Jackson returned with a small bag and a grin. "How about bacon and eggs?" he asked.

"That would be amazing," I said.

Left alone with the lake again while he cooked, I took my cup down to the water's edge, and then I walked out onto the short dock. The water got deep surprisingly quickly; I guessed it was well over my head at the end of the dock. I wondered if it were like this all the way around the lake. The loons were closer now, and singing a duet, as they cruised by.

It wasn't long before Jackson called me to breakfast.

"It's going to get cold quick," he said.

"Coming," I said. Back onto the deck, my eggs were peppered and the bacon was crispy.

"It's nice out here, huh?" he asked.

"So pretty," I said.

We ate and talked like we'd been there all summer.

"Supposed to be nice all day. There are a couple kayaks around the other side of the house. Wanna take them out?" he asked.

I smiled. "Want to go find an island?"

"We have a bed now," he said, and smiled.

"We could do both," I said. He stopped chewing, and I laughed. We both ate quickly, and I dressed, while he took the kayaks to the shore.

•   •   •

Out on the water, we saw many more loons. Paddling around the first little island, across the pond, we then passed beneath a bridge where a road separated Sand Pond from the next.

"Do you know where we're going?" I asked.

"I don't know this area very well," he said.

"It'd be a nice place to get lost," I said.

There were other cabins, and full-sized houses, too. Some looked like they had been there since the 1950s, and others looked like they were brand new. Jackson came alongside me, and we both stopped paddling.

"This is cool, right?" he asked.

"So cool," I said.

He smiled. "Would you and your friends have called it 'groovy'?"

Laughing, I said, "'Groovy'? I wasn't a member of the Brady Bunch."

"I don't get it," he said.

"That's more like the 1960s, not the '80s," I said.

He just kept smiling. "Other than friends and family, what do you miss most from the 1980s?"

"I was talking about this with people at the mall a while back. In the 1980s, we were more optimistic somehow," I said.

"Do you think I'm a negative person?" he asked.

"You aren't, and Lauren isn't either. Maybe that's why I like you so much," I said, and winked. Mentioning Lauren was a mistake though. It made me miss her, and think of Deb worrying, and miss my mom, and it reminded me that all of this would end soon, because we obviously couldn't live out our lives here in a stolen cabin, and it…

"Stop it," he said. His smile was gone, and he said, "Stop it. You were beginning to worry again. Live in the moment."

"I'm trying to live in the present. I really am," I said.

He seemed to consider this, as if trying to decide if I really was trying. "Okay," he said finally, and paddled and pulled away.

I didn't follow for a moment. Was it really that easy for him not to worry? Or was he just putting up a front in order to make sure that we had as good a time as possible? I really didn't know. Wondering if I was ruining his day, I considered turning around and paddling back to the cabin, but I decided he'd take that as pouting, so I followed.

He paddled into a little cove, and pointed to some Canada geese. They were on the water, and then with a few flaps of their wings, they would reach high into some bushes without actually taking flight, and then fall back into the water.

"What are they doing?" I asked.

"It's a mother, teaching her babies to pick blueberries," he said.

"Which one is the mother?" I asked. They all looked the same to me.

"There's one that's a bit bigger than the others. There she is, she's up right now," he said.

"That's really cool," I said. "Do they do this a lot?"

"Actually, I've never seen geese do this before," he said, looking at me and smiling.

We paddled in closer, and the geese paid no attention to us. They ate their fill, and then turned and followed their mother as she headed straight at us.

"Oh my God," I said, smiling.

"Shhh," Jackson said, and smiled back.

The geese swam between our two kayaks, just out of arms' reach of either of us, and kept on going without so much as a backward glance.

"That was a moment," he said, softly.

"That totally freaked me out. That was awesome to the max," I said.

He chuckled. "Let's go back to the cabin."

I nodded, and we started back. We passed beneath the road once more, and when we had the cabin in sight, we noticed a man walking on the shore near the dock.

As we neared, I thought maybe we should keep paddling, as if we weren't putting in there. Jackson chose another way.

With a wave and a confident voice, he said, "Hi there!"

The man waved back, and said, "Mornin'."

Our kayaks beached, and we climbed out.

"You folks staying here?" he asked.

"We sure are," Jackson said, with a broad smile. The man, maybe in his 70s, had a lined face and tired eyes.

"Name is Tom Jelders," he said.

"I'm Jack, this is Megan," Jackson said.

Megan? "Hi," I said.

"You friends of Mike?" Tom asked.

"No, Will," Jackson said. I was thoroughly confused, and focused on dragging the boats up onto the grass.

"Ah, Will. How's he doing?" Tom asked.

"He's loving it, loves college. He was always going to end up in the city," Jackson said.

Tom smiled. "Oh, yup, that boy was never one for the country."

"No, sir," Jackson said.

Tom seemed satisfied, as if a secret password had been given, and said, "You folks have a nice day, there."

"We will, you too," Jackson said.

Tom ambled off down the shore. As Jackson and I walked back up to the cabin, I asked, "Will he be a problem?"

Jackson looked at me, but didn't say anything.

"Okay, okay, I'm not worrying," I said.

He smiled, put his arm around my shoulders, and pulled me close. As we walked, though, he looked back in the direction old Tom had gone.

"Who is Will?" I asked.

"Mike's older brother. He's at BU," Jackson said. "I didn't want him thinking we were high school friends of Mike, but instead college-aged friends of Will."

"Smart," I said.

"I have my moments," he said.

We went into the cabin, and Jackson asked, "Are you hungry?"

"We just ate breakfast!" I said.

"But then we went out on the lake," he said.

"Pond," I said.

"Pretty big pond."

We spent the rest of the day playing chess, reading, talking. No stress. I didn't even worry, much.

Well after dark, he went to bed and I began my tooth and hair brushing once more. This time, when I went into the bedroom, he was not sleeping. He was standing. The bed was turned down. Candles were burning and even a few flowers, clearly picked from the flowerbed outside, were standing in a vase.

Jackson was standing in only his boxer briefs. He walked to me, and I didn't move. He kissed me, a deep and passionate kiss. He lifted my arms, and pulled my shirt up and off. We had made love before, but I was still nervous. And excited. We kissed again, our arms around each other. He picked me up and carried me the three steps to the bed. He climbed in, and we undressed each other. It seemed that part would always be clumsy, and we laughed a bit. We kissed again. The kissing was more passionate.

Neither of us were as shy with the other this time. We were not as gentle or cautious, and we were not as patient either. We made love.

It wasn't like in the movies, all perfect and melodramatic. At one point, our teeth clacked together, pinching my lip, and he burned his fingers moving a candle away from the edge of a nightstand. Still, it was amazing, and when we finished, we rested, and then started again. I felt happy, safe, and loved.

We eventually fell into a deep sleep, holding each other until the loons woke us early the next morning.

40

WEARING ONLY JACKSON'S T-SHIRT, I made breakfast for us before he got out of bed. I boiled four eggs, made toast, and cut up an apple. "Dig in," I said.

He went for the apple first, and then bit off a piece of toast, and then apple again. Finally, he bit an egg in half, and immediately washed it down with juice.

"You don't like hard-boiled eggs, do you?" I asked.

"What, no, it's great," he said, and popped the remaining half of the egg into his mouth. After two chews, he chased it down with juice again.

We grinned.

"I hate them," he said.

We both laughed, and I said, "Well, don't eat something you don't like! What do you want to do today?"

He pulled me close, I felt his lips on my ear, and he whispered, "Guess."

Pulling away, laughing, I said, "Besides that. Want to take the kayaks out again?"

He said, "Actually, I found something, if you want to try it."

"What is it?" I asked.

"Wait here," he said. He disappeared into another room, it sounded like the bedroom with the bunk beds, and then he returned with a box, an easel, and some small white canvases.

"Painting?" I asked.

"Want to try it?"

"I don't have a clue how to do that. I can barely draw stick figures," I said.

"Then we won't draw those," he said.

"You could paint, I could watch," I said.

"C'mon, you have to try it. I'll get you started. Everyone is born an artist; some got encouraged and, you know, stuck with it. Others decided they weren't good at it and stopped," he said.

"You stopped," I said.

"Well, you got me thinking about it, and when I found these... What do you think?"

He sounded like he really wanted me to try it, as if he would be disappointed if I didn't, so I gave in. "Sure. I'll try it. But don't make fun of me."

"I wouldn't," he said.

Looking into his kind eyes, I believed him.

We took the paints out onto the deck. He set me up with a brush, tubes of color, and a canvas. He took a sketchpad for himself.

"Just play around with it," he said.

Nervous and smiling, I began slapping green paint in a sort of childish tree shape, while he sketched.

Pausing, I said, "I know I'm supposed to only think about the present, and live in the moment. But you know what? That doesn't allow for wishing."

He stopped sketching, and turned to face me.

"I wish, for us," I said.

Smiling, he said, "I wish for us, too." He leaned toward me, and I kissed him.

I went back to painting. "I like this."

"Looks good," he said.

"No peeking," I said, but then I asked, "It's okay?"

"Yeah, Cel, it's good," he said.

He sketched the cabin, but never painted that day. We sat out there until early afternoon, the sun on us, mostly quiet with the occasional loon cry from the lake.

"Are you hungry?" he asked.

"I'm not," I said. "Are you?"

"Why don't we pick up, and take a paddle around the lake again?"

Looking at my painting, I wasn't thrilled, but it wasn't horrible. I sort of liked it, and asked, "Any advice on this?"

"The only advice I have is the more you do it, the more tricks you'll learn. I think your first painting, though, is a huge win," he said.

We put everything away, but we left my painting to dry on the easel, standing near the woodstove.

Pushing out into the lake, this time we took the canoe. Hardly paddling, I just relaxed and let him take us around the lake. It was wonderful.

He had scarcely said a word until he said, "I really love you, Celestine."

Although I immediately felt guilty for it, I thought he said, "I love you" too often. I asked, "Why?"

"Why do I love you?" he asked.

"Yeah. You say it a lot. Why me?"

"Because you're amazing. You're smart and interesting, you're beautiful, and you have a way about you that is… kind of mysterious. I don't know. Now I sound stupid."

"No, you don't," I said softly, my scalp and face were tingling. "You just need glasses."

When I heard him chuckle behind me, I smiled. We spent the afternoon that way, lazy and in love. Back on shore, we strolled hand in hand, slowly up to the cabin where we talked about football, painting, loons, cake, the ocean, and Paris.

When we went to bed, we were exhausted, and he fell asleep first. I lay there and tried not to be anxious, but it was almost as if, because the day had been so perfect, it only reminded me that the time we had together, like the cottage itself and the paints, was stolen.

•   •   •

That night, when I finally fell asleep, I dreamt of the *Phaeacia* and of my father, sitting beside him, talking about breakfast, and he said my name. I looked at him and he had fear in his eyes. He began to wither, like a plant, his body seemed to shrink beneath his skin; it wrinkled, became loose, and his eyes sank out of sight into their sockets. I was shrieking.

He wilted right before my eyes, and was left a pile of loose flesh and clothing on the seat. I bolted awake, still shrieking.

"Shit! What is it?" Jackson asked, sitting up beside me.

Unable to stop screaming, I tried to jump out of bed, but Jackson grabbed my arm and held me there, wrapping his arms around me.

"It's okay, you're okay," he kept whispering.

My screams became sobs, and I let him hold me and rock me.

"It was just a dream," he said, stroking my hair.

"I miss them so much," I said, tears flowing.

"I know. I'm so sorry, Cel," he said.

Holding me until I calmed, he asked, "Can I get you anything? A drink?"

Trying to joke, I asked, "Vodka?"

Rubbing my back, he asked, "Want to try to lie down again? Get some rest?"

Lying down, we curled up against each other, and once again, he quickly fell asleep, but until the sun rose, I lay there awake, missing my parents.

41

GETTING OUT OF BED, I pulled on Jackson's T-shirt again, and pulled the afghan off the couch as I went by. Wrapping it around my shoulders, I stepped out onto the deck. The sky and lake were grey, and I couldn't see any of my loons. Down at the shore, over past the dock, old Tom appeared. I waved and, although I'm sure he saw me, he didn't wave back. He turned and walked out of sight behind some trees.

Jackson came out onto the deck and asked, "You okay?"

Turning, I put my head against his chest, and we held each other.

"Did you ever fall asleep after your bad dream?" he asked.

"I couldn't," I said.

He held me tighter. "Do you want to talk about it?"

"I don't really," I said.

Before either of us could say anything more, we heard gravel crunching beneath tires. A lot of tires. Someone had driven into the driveway on the other side of the cabin. We quickly moved inside and looked out the window. In the first car was Jackson's mother, and in the next, there was a couple I didn't recognize. In the third car were Deb and Ray, and behind them was a Kennebec County Sheriff's Deputy's cruiser. Old Tom wandered into the driveway from next door, pointing at the cabin, saying something I couldn't hear. The deputy stepped out, and joined the other adults.

My stomach fell hard, and I was filled with dread. "Oh shit!" I said.

"Calm down, it'll be okay," Jackson said.

"It's not going to be okay!" I said.

He said, "No matter what, Cel, I…"

"They're going to pull us apart," I said, starting to cry.

"Calm down, Cel," he said.

"No, I won't calm down. You're all I've got and they're going to take you away. I always lose everyone I love," I said.

The man I didn't recognize had a key to the front door. They came in and stopped in a speechless group in the doorway. Jackson and I held each other.

"How could you do this?" his mother asked.

"You brought a cop?" he asked. "For what, to arrest Cel because of a bullshit protection order?"

"I am not here for that," the deputy said, stepping forward. "I'm here because the two of you are trespassing."

"Mike gave me the key," Jackson said.

The man I didn't recognize said, "This isn't my son's cabin, its mine. It belongs to me and my wife, and we really don't appreciate you two coming here, and using it for whatever it is you've been doing here."

"We just want to be together," I said, still crying.

"You both have to leave," the deputy said. "Mr. Lepen agreed not to press charges, if there is no damage."

"We didn't damage anything," Jackson said.

"We just want to be alone," I said.

"You can't be alone here," the deputy said.

"You can't be alone anywhere," Jackson's mother said. "The protection order says you have to stay away from my family. I'll be going to court on Tuesday. You may not listen to me, but we'll see what the judge has to say about you ignoring his order. You won't be coming anywhere near him again. Just stay out of our lives."

"I love her, mom," Jackson said. "Please don't do this."

Mr. Lepen said, "Look, I really don't care about all this teen mess, but remember the Lord said to honor your mother and father, and you are not honoring her right now, young man."

"Sir, I appreciate you not pressing charges, and I really do apologize for coming here; I know we shouldn't have. But we really are in love, and we were desperate," Jackson said.

The deputy stepped toward us, and I moved behind Jackson. Shaking all over, I felt like it was the end of the world. The deputy said, "Let's get your things and get out of here. Come on."

Jackson began walking to the bedroom, and I hung onto him tightly. His mother suddenly came at me, and said, "Let him go! Get off of him!"

Deb shouted, "Barb!" and she came rushing forward, too.

Jackson's mother was pulling at me, we were both screaming; I was clawing into Jackson, trying to hold on. Deb was shouting and pulling on Jackson's mom, the deputy stepped in and separated everyone, except for me and Jackson.

"Enough!" the deputy said. "I want everyone out of here, except for the Lepens and the kids. Now!"

"But they aren't supposed to be together!" Jackson's mom said.

"Ma'am, I'm going to take care of that, but right now I need you to get out of here before I arrest you for assault, on a minor no less. Clear out, everyone, right now," the deputy said.

There was grumbling, and in Jackson's mother's eyes, I saw hate. They all went out the door, except for the Lepens.

"Mr. and Mrs. Lepen, if you could check to make sure nothing is damaged, I'll make sure these two are out of your hair as quickly as possible," the deputy said.

The Lepens moved off toward the kitchen. Mrs. Lepen stopped to look at my painting, and then looked back at me. She looked sad.

"Alright, kids, get dressed, get your stuff, and let's go," the deputy said.

Jackson and I went into the bedroom, holding each other. Crying so hard, I couldn't talk, while he stroked my hair and held me.

"It'll be okay," he said.

I could only shake my head.

"It'll be okay," he said again.

I wished I could've believed him; my heart was shattered. It was more than just that moment. It was everything I'd lost on the *Phaeacia* compounded with losing him, and even Lauren. It was losing my childhood, and the familiar world. It was the high of yesterday only to be followed by this catastrophe. The world was done. The world was shit.

"Let's go," the deputy said.

Jackson's grip loosened. Mine didn't. I forced him to push me away, which must have killed him. "Cel, let's just pack and go. We'll figure it out," he said, but I could barely hear him. Nauseated and trembling, I could feel something in my mind coming loose. He packed, was soon done, and I sat on the bed, unable to breathe. He kissed the top of my head.

"C'mon," the deputy said, and he stepped over and guided Jackson out.

Jackson said only, "Celestine," as he went out of the room. Unable to even look at him, I knew I was breaking.

When the deputy returned, I was on the floor in a fetal position. I had had enough. All I could do was silently sob, my mouth wide open. He tried to pull me to my feet, but then Mrs. Lepen came into the room. She said, "You stop that. Go get her mother."

The deputy seemed to hesitate, and then he left the room. She knelt beside me, and stroked my shoulder. My sobs took some sound, at least some gasping. Deb appeared, with the deputy right behind her. I heard a car pull away, spitting gravel, and I knew Jackson was gone. The women pulled me up to the bed, and I curled into Deb. She hugged and rocked me, as I cried some more.

Ray appeared. "Jesus."

Mr. Lepen, behind him, did not say a word.

"Ray, take her to the car, I'll get her things," Deb said.

"I'll help you," Mrs. Lepen said.

Ray came over, and while gentle, he was firm as he guided me to my feet. My crying began to slow, as numbness started to settle in. I felt something clicking over, as a new indifference and hopelessness took hold. *The hell with it. Why was I fighting? Jackson was gone. Just like mom and dad. Just like everyone. I don't belong here anyway.*

Ray's hands were on my shoulders, just guiding me, no real pressure, and I looked out at the lake.

"Let me go," I said softly.

"We should just get in the car," Ray said.

Turning, I faced him and said, "Please, just let me go." He did.

Walking away, slowly, I made my way toward the lake. The gravel beneath my feet became grass as I crossed the lawn. Ray didn't follow. He couldn't have followed where I was going anyway. When I was almost to the water, I bent down and picked up a large smooth rock. It was so heavy, about the size of a soccer ball, that I could barely hold it. Walking out onto the dock, I didn't feel like I wanted to die; I just wanted to be with my mom. It wasn't an accident, though. I knew what I was doing. I was all set with this life, and wherever I was going after drowning, it'd have to be easier than this had been. Even if it were nothingness. Peaceful nothingness. But I hoped I'd be with my parents.

Just before I stepped off the dock, I heard Ray shout, "Celestine!"

Not only did I sink, but holding that rock to my chest, I raced downward and landed flat on my back. I hit the bottom hard enough to hurt, and the rock on my breastbone hurt, too. Holding my breath for the first few seconds, I then exhaled. Just before things went black, someone entered the water. It was the last thing I remembered.

42

THE INTERIOR WAS PAINTED IN soft yellow and tan, with burnt-orange colored carpeting, and not the wide tiles I had expected. Carpet absorbed sound and, in a place like that, there were a lot of sounds you wanted absorbed. It smelled faintly of urine and strong disinfectant.

When I first arrived, mere hours after being pulled from the bottom of the lake, I was numb; I didn't speak or resist.

The ward had books and I had hours and hours to kill. They tested me three times to see if I was pregnant. Three times in the first three days. They said they wanted to be sure. Every single morning, they drew blood; I'm not even sure why. It wasn't about the sickness on the *Phaeacia*; they did it to everyone. I spent the first two days in my bed because the cocktail of meds they put me on made me so sick. The last time I woke up in a hospital I tried to bite the arm off a nurse, but this time, I was just chill. Maybe it was a combination of the drugs, and being exhausted and still sort of numb.

On this particular day, my fifth day at Winter Harbor Hospital, a nurse came in and brought me the usual breakfast.

"Remember, Celestine, I'm going to weigh it after to make sure you're eating," she said.

I only nodded and she left. In no time, there was nothing left to weigh.

"Sick. You ate that?"

Standing in my door was another patient; I'd seen her come in the day before. She hadn't looked as scared or confused as people usually looked on their first day.

"She would've known if I didn't," I said.

"So, let her know," she said.

"Who are you?" I asked.

"I'm Tee," she said, and leaned up against my doorframe.

"Tee? We're not allowed nicknames in here," I said.

"Dude, I know the rules. It's my third time in here," she said.

"Third time?" I asked.

"No-yeah, if I even look at a sharp object or take an extra ibuprofen, they throw my ass in here again," she said.

The nurse appeared behind her, and said, "Excuse me, Taylor. I need to collect her plate."

Tee didn't move. The nurse said, "Come on, now, move aside."

"I don't know who you're talking to," Tee said.

"Taylor, move over or you'll lose movie privileges tonight," the nurse said.

"Gasp. And miss another Lifetime movie about drug addiction? Please no, I'll be good," Tee said, but she still didn't step aside.

"There's always the chill room," the nurse said.

Tee stepped aside. "I'm chill enough."

"Thank you, Taylor," the nurse said.

"My name is Tee," she said.

"Not here it isn't," the nurse said. "Oh good! You ate all your food. Good for you." She smiled. I stood and she patted the pockets on my pajama pants to make sure I hadn't stuffed some of the food in them. My pants fell a bit. They had cut the drawstring out of them. The nurse took the tray and left.

"Have you been in the chill room?" I asked.

"That white room they showed you, during orientation," Tee said.

"I know what it is; I was asking if you've been in there," I said.

"You haven't?" she asked. "How long have you been here?"

"A few days," I said.

"You don't have a roommate. Lucky," she said.

"You have a roommate?" I asked.

"No," she said.

I thought she might say something more, but she didn't. She just smiled broadly and shrugged her shoulders. I chuckled and she giggled back.

"You going to group?" she asked.

"I'm going to shower instead," I said.

"They'll get mad at you," she said.

"I miss a lot of group," I said. I felt like I'd had enough group therapy sessions for a while, and this place had four per day. Some of the nurses seemed to hate me for skipping them.

"You'll never 'level up' that way," Tee said, faking a stern voice and furrowing her brow.

To "level up" meant that if you attended all of your group sessions and personal therapy in a day, you would move one level up on the reward list. At the first level, you got to have a second dessert, which I found a bit odd since at least one girl there had, in addition to other things, an eating disorder. The second level gave you the privilege of choosing which Hallmark or Lifetime movie, featuring self-harm, that the kids in the ward would watch that night. At the third level of rewards, you got your bedtime extended and you could even have a radio in your room. The highest level, the fourth level, granted a coffee from Dunks and you got to go out for a few hours with a parent. You could do all these right things, but then be prevented from leveling up simply by refusing to let the staff read a letter you received, or any number of other things. "Leveling up" was one of their primary methods of control. To be honest, at first, I hadn't taken the idea of four days of following the rules that seriously because I hadn't really believed I would be in here for that many days. I was wrong.

Still, a reward like picking among the stupid television choices and a punishment like the padded chill room all seemed a little silly compared to the *Phaeacia*. I mean, what were they going to do? Put me in a tin can with my dead parents? I wasn't going to outright fight and kick and bite, but I really didn't care if I ever got to go out with a parental-type person and buy new socks like the kid across the hall. I sure as shit wasn't going to go to sixteen group sessions in four days in order to earn a cup of coffee from Dunkin' Donuts.

"Whatever. I don't need two desserts," I said.

Tee came and sat on my bed. "So, your name is Celestine?"

I reflexively backed away a bit, but I was starting to like her. "Yeah," I said. I braced myself for all kinds of questions about space and the sickness.

"Did your parents hate you or something?" she asked.

She didn't know? She hadn't heard of me? "People just call me 'Cel'," I said.

"Cool," she said. "How'd you end up here? You cut or pills or something?"

"Nothing like that," I said.

"You must have done something. At least ideation," she said.

Ideation. Suicide ideation. Even thinking about suicide could get you in there. Well, not just thinking about it. You had to tell someone you were thinking about it. No one knew about your ideation until you shared it. Of course, even being a teenager who used the word "ideation" revealed a lot about you.

"I walked into the lake," I said.

"Whoa, intense," she said. "Did you, like, sew rocks into your clothes and shit?"

"What, no, I just grabbed a big rock," I said.

"So, you lived," she said.

"You sound disappointed," I said.

"It just doesn't sound like a real attempt," she said. "Sounds more like trying to get attention."

"I didn't plan it," I said. "I just wanted it all to be over. I just walked off the dock."

She looked dissatisfied.

"Sorry my story isn't more dramatic," I said. "How about you?"

"Pills this time," she said. "I tried bleach once."

"Holy shit," I said.

"Naw, actually, you can drink a lot of bleach and it won't kill you. It might burn your throat or whatever. It's not an effective way out," she said. When she brushed hair from her face, I spotted a tattoo on her wrist.

"What's that?"

"It's a butterfly," she said, and showed me. "I used to cut, and I had this tattooed over the scar tissue. You know, a sign of rebirth."

"But you're in here," I said, thinking of the butterfly earrings, that day in Portland, at the First Friday Art Walk with Jackson.

"Rebirth is no guarantee," she said.

"How old are you?" I asked. A person had to be eighteen years old to get a tattoo, and this one was nice so I knew she hadn't gotten it at some party.

"I was in New Brunswick," she said. "You know, Canada."

"What's the legal age there?" I asked.

She shrugged. "No idea." She smiled broadly again, got closer, and I moved away. She noticed and asked, "So, what's up with that? With you backing up? You still scared of COVID?"

"Look, I don't really know you yet. You don't believe in, like, personal space?" I asked.

"That's horseshit," Tee said.

"Personal space?" I asked.

"I think you have problems with people. Probably can't get close to anyone. Separation anxiety and trust issues, or whatever," she said.

"You think I'm mentally ill?"

"I'm going to go with the majority on this one," she said. "The staff here… they seem to think you need some time here, right?"

"So?" I asked.

"You don't think you have some shit to work out?" she asked.

"I had it worked out," I said.

"They disagreed with your solution. They must think there's a reason you should stick around," she said.

"What if they're wrong?" I asked.

"See, that's what this place is about, Cel. When you think that everyone in the world is wrong, and that you are right, you get to come to a place like this and realize that maybe you're the one who stepped off," she said.

"You think I'm crazy," I said.

She looked around and said, "You're not on the firmest ground for making an argument that you're perfectly okay. You're in a psych ward, Cel. You know, the loony bin, the nut house, all those weird ways of saying it when you're little? You're there.

You're not here by mistake. So, maybe you should take a look at what you're sure about, because that's what got you here."

We sat quietly for a moment until she said, "Anyway, going to be late for group."

"I'm going to take a shower," I said.

"Cool. See ya," she said, and she walked out of my room.

I grabbed my shower stuff and a towel and went to the bathroom. Closing the door behind me, there was no way to lock it. A patient could shower as often as she wanted. Looking in the plastic mirror, my image was a bit distorted. On the bottom corner, someone had scratched in the words, "Help me" but I couldn't imagine how; obviously, we weren't allowed anything sharp.

After showering, I toweled off, dressed in the same pajamas and went back to my room. I lay on my bed and read. It wasn't more than an hour later when two members of the staff came in and asked me to stand near the door.

"Again?" I asked. I moved to the door.

They began at the far wall and searched the room—in the curtains, behind the dresser, in each drawer, under the mattress, and under the bed. They pulled the bed apart and then loosely remade it. Then they thanked me and left.

Lying back on my bed, I read again. What else was there to do?

"Did you get searched?"

Looking up, there was Tee. "D-bags," I said, and I went back to my book.

She stayed anyway. Sitting up, I asked, "Why do you keep leaving the ward and then coming back? Why not just stay here until you're ready?"

"They won't let me stay. They ask me in therapy if I'm ready to leave, and I tell them I'm not, and they send me home anyway," she said.

I had asked to leave three times, and they told me I wasn't ready. Was I really crazier than Tee? "How old are you?" I asked.

"I just turned sixteen," she said. "How 'bout you?"

"I'm seventeen," I said.

"You're the oldest then," she said. "Marie is nine."

"I know," I said. "How could a nine-year-old need a place like this?"

"Her parents dumped her here," Tee said.

"It's awful," I said.

"At least we outnumber the boys, like 6-4," she said.

All of the boys were teenagers, but none of them were especially menacing. Only Christopher kind of freaked me out. He wasn't big or scary or anything, but he was weird, and he showered all the time.

Tee said, "Come to group session with me after lunch."

"I hate those," I said, not wanting to share why. With a little luck, I thought, I wouldn't have to explain the *Phaeacia* to anyone. I mean, I knew that the staff knew, but if any of the others knew they hadn't said anything in the couple of group sessions I'd been to. None of them had come into my room the way Tee had. I hadn't socialized with anyone; I just kept to myself and read. I had individual therapy too, which I went to, but we hadn't even had a real conversation, let alone made any progress.

"Nobody likes group, but I don't like any of the other people, and I want you to come," Tee said.

"Aw, you like me," I said, teasing.

"I just dislike you less," Tee said, smiling back.

"That's my life goal. To suck less than other people," I said.

"You're succeeding, but just barely," she said. "Come to group after lunch."

"Alright, alright," I said. "Friggin' nag."

Tee smiled with her entire face and she clapped, but didn't say anything. She sat so quickly on the end of my bed that I had to pull my feet back to keep her from landing on them.

"So, what's up?" she asked.

Really? "Um, as you pointed out, I'm in a psych ward. You?"

"Same," she said.

There was a moment of silence, and then I said, "You're so weird."

43

AFTER LUNCH, I WENT TO the group session as promised. The furniture in the multipurpose room included a television, a cabinet that held board games that could be played only with visiting family members, and a few incredibly heavy wooden couches with cushions. It was these couches, turned to form a loose circle, that we sat on.

All of us were there. I sat with Tee on my left and Christopher on my right. On Tee's left was little Marie, and Tee was holding her hand. Directly across from me was the session facilitator, Mitch. He was soft-spoken, and gave off an air of such kindness that it was hard to imagine that he'd ever been angry in his life.

"Who would like to start?" asked Mitch, scanning our faces.

"I will," said a girl a few seats off to my right. I'd seen her, but hadn't spoken with her. She had long, straight, blonde hair, and every pair of her pants appeared to be hospital scrubs. After a few days, they allowed family members to bring you jeans and T-shirts, but she seemed to wear nothing but scrub pants. She also had a slight accent that I didn't immediately identify.

"Fine, Valeria, go ahead," Mitch said.

She cleared her throat and we all shifted in our seats. She said, "My name is Val, well, Valeria. I was having a lot of stress at school."

Mitch interrupted. "I'm sorry, Valeria." He pointed at Taylor's and Marie's hands, and they let each other go. Physical contact, even holding a little girl's hand, was forbidden. Kind as he might be, rules were rules. Mitch then said, "Go ahead, Valeria."

"So, I had stress at school. Like, everyone there is so annoying," Val said. "I mean, how many adults use stuff they learned in Chemistry anyway?"

"Or Algebra," Christopher said, but Mitch waved him off.

Val said, "And people make you feel like every test will impact your future. None of that stuff will matter. Not really. And people trying to be in the right clique with the right clothes. You know. High school is a nightmare; it's just hell. There has to be a better way."

Softly, Mitch said, "Tell the group how you came to be here."

Val hesitated, then she said, "I tried to catch a bus." She giggled a bit, but no one else did.

"Valeria," Mitch said, and tilted his head. He was nice and everything, but he was getting on my nerves.

Val said, "One morning, I was standing at the side of the road, waiting for the bus, wishing I had my license so I didn't have to ride with all the losers. And the bus smells."

"Valeria," Mitch urged.

I said, "Just let her tell it."

Mitch looked at me, and his mouth went a bit hard, but he sat back and remained quiet. Val looked at me, a bit surprised maybe, and then continued.

"So, there's a bus that comes by without stopping and then my bus comes. And the dick that drives that first bus always drives like a maniac, so I waited for him and at the last second I stepped in front of him," Val said. Her eyes went glassy in the telling.

Marie said, "He missed you."

Val rolled her eyes back into focus. "Yeah, he missed me. He swerved. I thought he might crash into the ditch on the other side. If there had been oncoming traffic, he would've had to choose between hitting me and a head-on collision. So, I should've thought of that."

"Tell us about your episodes," Mitch said.

Val paused again, and she looked at me as if I could help, but I hadn't even known her name before this session. I just looked back at her until she said, "I had these episodes, I guess. I freaked out. They'd tell me after that I was, like, crazy, but I don't remember them that good."

"Let's try to avoid words like 'crazy' and maybe you can tell us what leads up to your episodes as best as you can remember," Mitch said.

"Okay, I won't use the word 'crazy.' I guess when the stress builds and builds, eventually I kinda just blow off all that steam at once and go completely bat-shit," Val said. Everyone laughed, except for Mitch, who frowned, but didn't take the bait.

We each took turns explaining what led up to the big event that landed us in the ward. When I explained what happened to me, Val was the first to speak.

She asked, "Did you put rocks in your pockets?"

I quickly looked at Tee, who smiled and shrugged.

Val asked, "You know, like Virginia Woolf?"

"It's like a how-to class in here," I said. "No, I didn't. I just had one big rock."

"Are you still mad at Jackson's mom?" asked Christopher.

"Not really," I said.

"I don't get it," Val said. "Why would she be so worried that you were sick? Did you go somewhere where people are sick? Coronavirus or something?"

"There were sick people, but I never got it," I said.

"How long have you been back?" Val asked.

"A few months," I said.

"So, you're sure you're not contagious?" Val asked. Christopher shifted in his seat next to me. I'm not sure why, probably just frustration, but I burst into tears.

"I'm not sick," I said. "I lost my parents, but didn't get it. It killed my parents but somehow it spared me." The tears flowed freely, and Tee put her hand on my leg. My first thought was of pulling away, but I fought it. Her hand felt really good.

"No physical contact," Mitch said softly.

Marie got off her chair, came around Tee, and hugged me. It felt wonderful. I hesitated, but then I hugged her back and saw Tee flip Mitch off, forcefully and dramatically. I collected myself, not wanting to cause an all-out rebellion in group.

"I'm okay," I said, and Marie went back to her seat.

"Taylor, you need to control yourself," Mitch said, with that chill room tone in his voice.

"They say I'm not contagious, that I'm not sick, and that you guys don't need to worry. I'm not sick," I said.

Mitch said, "Taylor, your turn."

Apparently, she was no longer in the mood for group. "So, yeah, I was, like, hearing voices. You know, telling me to collect all the newts in the neighborhood, and then at breakfast, out of nowhere, the Loch Ness monster spoke to me from my cereal bowl and told me to build a device out of coat hangers and duct tape to communicate with aliens, but my heroin addiction and nymphomania got in the way, and anyway, you know, newts are harder to catch than you would think," Tee said.

Again, everyone laughed, except for Mitch. Giggling, my face was still wet with tears.

"Taylor," Mitch said.

"Mitchell," Tee said back.

"Alright, if you don't want to work... but I'm afraid this session won't count toward leveling up," Mitch said.

"Dammit. I guess I'll have to sleep with someone to get a second dessert then," Tee said.

Everyone laughed again, especially Marie, who was leaning against Tee now.

"Okay, that's enough for today folks," Mitch said and stood. What had been chuckling and giggling turned into outright laughter as Mitch walked away.

Christopher said to Tee, "I'll trade you my dessert."

"Don't even think about it, dude," Tee said.

We all went back to our rooms. Rubbing my eyes, I lay down with a book, and dozed off.

•   •   •

In the middle of the night, I woke to screaming I couldn't understand. I walked to my door and Tee came running by.

"What's going on?" I asked.

She stopped and spoke with both hands flailing. "It's Val, she's flipping out."

"I can't understand a word of it," I said.

"Yeah-no, it's Russian. She's having an episode," Tee said, and then turned to leave.

Grabbing her by the sleeve, I asked, "Where are you going?"

"To get her stuffy, her duck," Tee said. "I think she left it in the multipurpose room."

"Where's Val?" I asked, as Tee broke away.

"Her room," she called back.

A nurse went jogging that way as the hallway lights came on, and I followed. Someone passed me on the way and, although I'd never seen him before, he was recognizable as a therapist by his khakis. Regardless of gender, the nurses and doctors wore scrubs, and therapists wore khakis.

Val was still screaming in Russian when I got to her door. Speaking to her in English, a nurse held Val down. The khaki-therapist asked about sedating her. Suddenly, Tee pushed me into the room and brought the stuffy-duck to Val, but the nurse pulled it away. Tee put it back against Val's arm.

"Taylor, will you please wait with that?" the nurse asked.

Val was shrieking in Russian now.

"No, she needs it!" Tee yelled at the nurse.

"Taylor, back up!" the nurse yelled, and then she pushed Val back down.

"Tee, maybe…" I said.

"Get off her, you bitch!" Tee said, shoving the nurse, who then grabbed Tee's arm.

Without thinking, I shouted, "Let her go!" and jumped forward, crashing into the nurse. Meanwhile, Val was still screaming.

"That's it, clear the room!" the therapist said. He wrapped both arms around Tee from behind. I clawed his forearms, and Tee bit down on his bicep. He cried out, but didn't let go. The nurse grabbed me from behind, and I struggled, but she was a big rugged yeti-woman. Another nurse and a doctor arrived.

The nurse said, "Holy cow, what's going on?"

The doctor rushed passed us, and began speaking to Val in Russian, who said only a few more words and then fell silent. We stood motionless, watching. The doctor repeated something, again and again, in Russian, in a soothing voice. Val's entire body relaxed.

Tee said, "Okay, let me go."

"Oh no, young lady, you're coming with me," the therapist said. He let her out of the bear hug, but a nurse and he each had an arm, and they walked Tee down the hallway toward the chill room.

The nurse who had me, led me to my room, and pushed me inside. Turning around, I tried to get past her to go to the chill room with Tee, but the nurse stopped me.

"You just calm down in there. You stay in there a while and cool it," she said. Standing with my fists clenched, and looking her in the eye for a moment, I turned and walked to my bed. I wanted to throw something at her, but there was really nothing to throw. I just sat, cross-legged on the bed, back against the wall, and folded my arms.

44

TEE WAS OUT OF THE chill room before lunch so we ate together in the multipurpose room. She didn't eat much of hers, and I ate all of mine. I would've devoured all of the rest of hers too, but I wasn't allowed. It would throw off the weighing and record keeping.

"How are you not 300 pounds?" she asked.

"I probably will be someday," I said.

She paused, as if she were considering whether or not to, but then asked, "So Jackson was pretty cool?"

"He was," I said.

"Did you guys have sex?" she asked.

Hesitating initially, I said, "He was my first."

"That's rugged," she said.

"Who was your first?" I asked.

She grinned broadly. I thought she was going to say something about there being too many to remember, but instead she said, "I'm a virgin."

"You are not," I said.

"Ouch," she said, and she smiled. "What are you trying to say?"

"But in group you, like, joked about sex, like it was no big deal," I said.

"I like to keep Mitch on his toes," she said.

We laughed. I looked around and then snuck a grape off her tray.

"Ooh, you rebel," she said.

Smiling, briefly, I then said, "I miss Lauren, too."

"Jackson's sister, right?"

"She was cool," I said.

"You'll see her again. You'll be buds again," she said.

I looked at her, and then our eyes met. She was pretty; I had never been attracted to another girl before. It freaked me out a little. People seemed way more relaxed about it in 2022. Just then, our eyes still locked, she reached out to touch my cheek, and I pulled away. She smiled, and dropped her hand. I suck, I thought, and I dropped my gaze.

I said, "When you get out next, don't hurt yourself or even think about it, ok?"

"Sure," she said.

"Tee, I mean it," I said.

We locked eyes again, and she said, "I'll try."

"Promise?" I asked.

"I pinky-swear, dude," she said, and then smiled that broad smile of hers. "I'll drop by this little town of yours and straighten everyone out. Give myself a purpose and all."

"That'd be awesome," I said.

"Jackson's mother was behind it all?"

"Yeah," I said, but then felt immediately uneasy about it. Tee was in a psych ward, after all. I worried for a second if I had just put out a hit on his mom, but then I was okay with it.

I was about to say something else, when there was a shout. A nurse stepped out of the bathroom and asked, "Can I get a hand over here?"

Another nurse immediately responded. Tee and I went to see, and Val met us there. Within a couple minutes, the nurses led Christopher out, with only a towel around his waist. He seemed to be in a daze, he was not making a sound, and he sort of stumbled as he walked past. On his back, blisters were forming on the crimson skin. Large, irregularly shaped bubbles were strung together across his shoulders and down his spine, disappearing beneath the towel.

"He's so burned," I said.

A nurse said, "Everyone go to your rooms."

Another nurse asked, "Isn't the temperature governor set? How did the water get this hot?"

Christopher stumbled, but kept his feet.

"How do you let water that hot run down your back?" Tee asked.

"I said, back to your rooms," the first nurse repeated. They led Christopher away toward the double doors, through which I had never been.

We didn't see much of Christopher after that. He was back from the regular hospital for maybe a day when they, during a search, discovered a sharp stick. One of the nurses, not knowing Tee and I were listening, said it was like a stake for a vampire. After that, he went away. I assumed it was to another facility.

In addition to comments about vampires, I overheard something else later that day. Walking by the office, I overheard a therapist named Lewis talking on the phone. Well, I heard him but couldn't understand much of it. For a therapist, he was a terrible mumbler, and he was sitting far from the door. Had the door been completely closed, I wouldn't have heard a word of it. It hadn't latched and was open, just a couple inches, but just enough for me to hear Lewis say, "Yes, Dr. Caledon."

I froze. I had privacy rights, like they had me sign a form that said I knew I had those rights, like hippo or something. They had to be discussing me, but why would Dr. Caledon have any right to know anything about me? It made me mad, and I wanted to storm in there and demand to know what they were talking about, but I was also afraid. Like, what if I disappeared and they gave me like a lobotomy or something? I saw part of that movie, *Cuckoo's Nest*, they erased this guy's brain and his Native American friend, like, smothered him with a pillow to put him out of his misery. Deciding I wouldn't barge in, I also decided to let Lewis know that I knew. Standing straight in front of that door, staring in through the door's window, hands at my sides, I was so nervous. After he hung up, he swiveled around in his chair, and he visibly jumped at seeing me. His eyes got wide. Actually, it scared me as badly as it scared him. Walking away, I hoped I looked like a bad-ass, but I was trembling all over.

• • •

I went to early morning therapy with Lewis. He was okay. Neither of us mentioned the phone call. He seemed nice enough and appeared to actually care, but he was clearly exhausted. I wondered how many more of the ten of us he would speak with that day.

"How are you feeling?" he asked. This reminded me of Dr. Caledon, but Lewis seemed to be holding nothing back. No guile here; there was none of the unease I felt when asked that.

"I feel okay. The ward has been a bit crazy the past few days," I said.

"It's a rollercoaster around here sometimes," he said. "Do you feel safe?"

"I feel perfectly safe," I said. Despite Christopher's blisters, I felt sheltered in the ward.

"Do you think you'd be safe on your own?"

"You mean like getting out?" I asked. I hadn't asked about leaving. Was I afraid to? Was I afraid I'd walk into the first lake I came to? I decided I wasn't.

"Do you think you'd be safe? Have you had any more thoughts of harming yourself?" Lewis asked.

"I feel safe," I said.

"Would you like to go home?"

"I would," I said, but I knew I couldn't. Home was lost, back in 1984.

"Well, we'll talk some more, but I think you've made great progress," Lewis said.

This was our first official meeting. I had been to therapy, but with other therapists. Did he think I was someone else? Or was he looking at their notes?

I asked, "Do people usually get better, and go home, this quickly?"

"Usually a week, maybe two at the most. We feel it's best to get young people back on their feet and back out into their regular lives as quickly as possible. As long as it's safe, of course," Lewis said.

I said, "Well, I feel like I have made progress."

We wrapped up the session without promises, and with few additional questions. When I arrived back in my room, there was someone else in there.

"Hey," I said.

"Hey," she said.

"What's up?"

"Not much."

I was getting annoyed. "Who are you?"

"I'm Julie, who are you?" she asked.

"I'm Cel."

"Cel?"

"Short for Celestine," I said. "What are you doing in here?"

"It's my room; I just got here."

Shit. I wanted to run back to Lewis and tell him I felt safe to leave right now, but instead I said, "I guess we're roomies."

Julie didn't say anything. She brushed back some of her long, stringy hair.

"How'd you get here?" I asked.

"My parents put me in here," she said.

"That's what most people say on their first day," I said.

"Didn't your parents put you in here?" she asked.

I wished they had, because then I have them to go home to. "It's almost lunch," I said.

"I'm not that hungry," she said.

"Meals are pretty much how we mark time passing around here," I said.

Tee came into my room, stopped, and looked Julie up and down. "Who is this?"

"Tee, this is Julie," I said.

"Tee?" she asked. "I thought nicknames weren't allowed."

"That's why we use them," Tee said. "Do you have a nickname?"

Julie didn't say anything and just shook her head.

"Kay," Tee said. "So, going to group today?"

I said, "One of the khakis asked me if I'm ready to go home yet. I'm thinking if I play nice at group and level up a bit, I'll get to leave."

Tee looked a bit sad, and said, "Probably."

"Level up?" Julie asked.

"Didn't they tell you?" Tee asked.

"I don't remember," Julie said.

"You'll figure it out," Tee said. "Come with us to lunch. We're going to eat in the multipurpose room."

After lunch, we turned the couches in anticipation of the group session, and people began to appear. When Mitch arrived, he smiled at Julie, but she did not smile back. She only looked at the floor.

"Everyone, let's welcome Julie," he said.

Several people did and she nodded in response.

"Do you want to share right away? What brought you here?" Mitch asked.

"No, thanks," she said. "Actually, I don't know why I'm here. I didn't do anything."

"You must've done something," little Marie said.

"I didn't do a thing," Julie said.

Mitch said, "Well, maybe we'll come back to you."

"You don't just end up in here," Val said. "It's not like you took a wrong turn looking for the bathroom at Burger King. You're in a psych ward."

"That's enough, Valeria," Mitch said.

"I didn't do anything; I shouldn't be here," Julie said.

Tee leaned into my ear and said, "She's going to cry. Watch, she's going to pop."

I pushed her away.

Val said, "You keep saying that you didn't do anything."

"I didn't," Julie said.

"Did you think something?" Val asked. "Because thinking the wrong thing can get you in here too. The thought police will throw you in here too."

Julie was quiet. Mitchell said, "Look, I don't want to end the session before it really gets started, but we can't badger Julie. She'll share when she wants to."

"It was my thinking," she said softly. "My thoughts got me put in here."

"Suicide ideation?" Tee asked.

"Taylor," Mitchell said.

"A steak knife," Julie said, stone-faced. "I was thinking about a steak knife."

"Julie, you don't have to share this fast. There's no pressure," Mitchell said.

Leaning into Tee, I whispered, "She's not going to cry. Look at her, she's like Spock."

Tee asked, "That's *Star Trek* or something right?"

Mitch said, "Ladies."

Tee and I separated, and I looked back at Julie. She was staring at me and Tee.

"It was a steak knife," she said.

Suddenly feeling incredibly uneasy, I sensed Tee must have felt it too. My reaction was to withdraw, but Tee was more like a fearful dog. She tended to bark when afraid.

"What the hell are you looking at?" Tee said.

"Taylor! Enough!" Mitchell said.

Julie never blinked, and said, "It was a steak knife, and my thoughts. I couldn't think of anything but pushing that steak knife into this one bitch at school. I dreamt about it." Julie smiled.

The group fell absolutely silent.

Tee looked at me, and said, "Nice roomie you got there."

Closing my mouth, I looked at Mitchell, who was staring at Julie. I scanned all the faces. Everyone was looking at either Julie or at me. I needed to go tell Lewis I was ready to go home right now.

Later that night, I lay awake listening to Julie breathe. It was so quiet; I felt like I could hear the dark.

"I'm not going to hurt you," Julie said.

"Thank you," I said. It seemed she drifted off to sleep; her breathing changed and she didn't say anything else that night. It occurred to me that I was in Winter Harbor because I had lost my grip on wanting to live, and laying in the dark with a potential murderer that night, I realized that while I was not especially hopeful, I was at least a bit curious about what life would bring next.

45

JULIE DIDN'T KILL ME, AND I met with Lewis again.

Lewis asked, "Do you feel safe with yourself? If you went home, would you be okay?"

Figuring we'd be playing this game for at least another week, I said, "Sure, I would."

"Great," he said, "because you're being discharged today."

"Today?" I asked.

"Isn't that great news?" he said, still grinning.

"Like, I'm not going to sleep here tonight?" I asked.

His smile fell. "You're okay with that, right? You feel safe, right?"

I asked, "What about... am I in trouble when I go back?"

"What do you mean?" he asked.

"I violated the protection order. Will I be arrested or something?" I asked.

He smiled again and shook his head. "Honestly, that never happens. Dr. Jelinkova told me once in all the years she's been working with at-risk youth, no teenaged patient has ever actually gotten in trouble for violating a protection order. Judges never impose a penalty, except for another verbal warning."

So, we hadn't needed to run away. All that drama for nothing. Still, I remembered the sun on my face on the lake, the painting, and the weight of Jackson on me.

He asked again, "So, you feel safe going home, right?"

"I totally do," I said, and forced a smile, but I wondered what that would look like. Would Debbie be waiting with a big hug?

How soon was school? I didn't even know what day of the week it was. Deciding I shouldn't ask Lewis, I then thought of Tee and how much it was going to suck to tell her.

"Well, we have some paperwork to do, but your guardian has already been told. You'll be home for supper," Lewis said.

"That's awesome," I said.

Lewis said, "You seem a bit unsure."

I said, "It's Taylor. I'm just a bit worried, and I'll miss her."

Lewis seemed relieved. "We'll take good care of everyone here," Lewis said. "You take care of you." He pointed at me emphatically with a finger-gun, and smiled again.

Standing, I said, "Thanks so much," and he gave me a big cheesy thumbs-up.

I immediately went to look for Tee, and found her sitting in Val's room.

"How'd therapy go?" Val asked.

"I'm getting out today," I said. Tee's faced tightened.

"Lucky," Val said.

"Like this afternoon?" Tee asked.

"Yeah, I guess Debbie has been told and she's coming to get me. So I just found out and came to tell you guys," I said.

"That new roommate of yours scared you right out of this place, huh?" Tee asked.

"I had no idea I was leaving. Lewis just dropped it on me," I said.

"Seriously, that's awesome, Cel," Val said. She came over and gave me a big hug. Tee watched us, and then stormed out. I followed her into her room.

"What do you want me to do?" I asked.

"Nothing. I'm good," she said.

"Seriously, how can I help?"

"There's nothing to do. Go home," Tee said, and she lay down on her bed.

"Want to hang out before I go?" I asked.

"Nah. Just want to chill by myself for a while."

Standing there feeling like an idiot for a minute, I didn't know what to do. Then, Tee got up, walked silently over to me, took my face in her hands, and gently kissed me. I froze for a moment, and then kissed her back. Her mouth was warm, soft, and lovely. I had butterflies, but when I reached out to put my arms around her, she stepped slowly backwards with one hand on my chest. She climbed back onto her bed, and waved me out of her room.

My heart was pounding as I took a step toward her and the bed. She didn't say anything; she showed me the palm of her hand, shook her head, and then once again waved me out, so I turned and left. At first, I was really confused, and then I was simultaneously happy and sad. Wrestling with whether or not to barge back into Tee's room, I thought of nothing else until Deb arrived, and I didn't see Tee again before I checked out.

After all the paperwork was squared away, we simply left. No big group goodbye. No big hello, either. The drive back was pretty uneventful and quiet. I mean, we actually talked about the weather.

Ray wasn't home when we got back. I went to my room, and lay down on the bed. Looking around at the walls, the desk, and the window, I realized that while life still sucked, I cared less than I had.

• • •

The first five days back in Goodwin, I spent all my time in my room. I came out to eat, shower, go to the bathroom, and that's it. Actually, I only showered once. I kept thinking about Christopher's blistered back, and Tee, and the kiss. I hoped she was okay. I mean, I knew I was into guys; what Jackson and I had was real, and my body and heart definitely responded to him, but could I fall in love with women too?

Having no idea, I tried looking up stuff online, but I just kept getting gross porn sites. Or crazy religious people wanting to fix me if it turned out I was gay or whatever.

Spending those days in my room, and in my head, I knew I wasn't suicidal. I just didn't want to look at Deb or Ray and have them look at me as if trying to decide if I was a danger to myself. They had even taken the tweezers out of my room. I mean, just the uni-brow I was growing was going to make me want to kill myself.

The saddest part was that I didn't hear from Jackson or Lauren. No welcome home. I assumed it was because of the restraining order and everything that happened at the lake, and the trouble he probably got in. After two days, I stopped checking my phone for messages from them, and I didn't message him.

To be honest, I was sort of pharmaceutically numb. I tried reading, but I struggled to focus. Wanting to escape and hide at the same time, I wanted to forget. The meds helped, but I wanted to be somewhere else, or someone else. Anonymous. Alone, but not.

•   •   •

Sitting in my room, I received a message. Strangely, it was from Emily. I wondered if she still had a purple streak in her hair. Her message read:

"What's up?"

"Not much. You?" I answered.

"There's a party at the pit tonight. Wanna go?"

She was inviting me? Other than the conversation at Dunkins long ago, we hadn't talked much.

"I dunno," I wrote.

"There's someone who is hoping you'll be there."

Who? Maybe it was Jackson? I wondered if people would make a thing about me being back, and pictured protesters at the party. To be honest, because of the new meds, I cared less about it than I had. Group session members disappearing, creepy Dr. Caledon, my scare with being sick, and the protestors just didn't seem to matter as much. I wasn't quite apathetic, but I certainly felt... less.

Still, I had a deep ache about Jackson. It was there, muted, but there. Like a painful echo. During the day, it felt pushed down, but he came to me while I slept and I often woke up crying.

"Who is hoping I'll be there?" I wrote.

"I'll pick you up tonight. You'll see."

Maybe it *was* Jackson. Would he even talk to me?

"Will I be happy?" I wrote.

"I think so. See you then."

"Ok"

I thought it would be nice to be happy. Whoever it was, it was better than sitting around the house. That evening, I didn't put on any makeup. A pair of jeans, a T-shirt, with a hoodie over that. Emily showed up and we went to the party. We didn't talk much. She didn't seem that interested, which was weird since she invited me. When we arrived at the pit, I scanned quickly for Jackson, but he wasn't there. Neither was Lauren, or almost any of that crowd.

Instead, it was a smaller gathering, and the music was more rock than dance. The atmosphere was not one of celebration. And then, I saw him. He walked directly toward me, took a long sip from a bottle of cheap vodka, and smiled.

"Hey," he said.

"Hey Dylan," I said.

Emily didn't say another word to me; she simply walked off and stood with Arielle and a few others. Dylan offered me the bottle, and I scanned the crowd again. These were not the people I had called friends before. These were the misfits. The angry. I had a flash of disappointment, but then I realized that this was perfect. Looking at Dylan, I took the bottle. If I did start to really feel again, I wanted to be angry, instead of scared and sad. Angry would feel good by comparison. Angry like these people who felt life was stacked against them, like they never had a fair shot, so why give a shit. Gulping down some of the vodka, it tasted terrible, but I felt it rush to my fingertips and face. I took another swig. So, maybe these were my people now. I mean, if others thought I was too contagious or psychotic to talk to, but Dylan was willing to share a bottle with me, why not? Whatever.

He took the bottle back, and took a sip of his own. He said, "C'mon."

Following him, we soon stood in a circle of people. No one said anything for a minute, and then Dylan said, "Why's everyone so quiet?"

A guy I didn't recognize said, "I heard you were in the psych hospital."

"Dude," Dylan said. "Really?"

"I was," I said.

"What's that like? Was it weird?" a blonde girl to my left asked.

Grabbing Dylan's vodka bottle and taking a swig, I then handed it back. "Yup, it was."

"Are you better now?" the blonde asked.

"Nope. Still fucking crazy," I said.

There was a second of silence before everyone laughed, and then the guy said, "Yeah, me too."

After that, they moved on to other topics. They spoke about nothing, gossip about this person, a story about that party, a complaint about the summer weather. Mostly they were just filling the time in between drinks of cheap alcohol. It was perfect, and I was soon too drunk to stand still. It was then that Dylan asked me to go for a walk, and I agreed.

As we walked, I think we held each other up. We laughed a lot, we didn't say much, I vaguely remember him kissing me, but we never left our feet. A flash of sadness about Jackson moved through me, but then it was gone, and we were soon back at the pit. A girl I didn't know dropped me off at a house three doors down from Debbie and Ray's, and I went in as quietly as I could. Falling onto my bed, I woke up the next morning on top of the blankets, fully dressed.

Getting up, I went to the kitchen, and poured myself some water. I went into the cupboard, took down my meds, washed them down, and leaned against the counter. Debbie came into the kitchen.

"Came in late last night," she said.

"Yep," I said.

She asked, "That's it?"

"What do you want me to say? Want me to lie?" I asked.

"Cel, what's going on with you?" she asked. "I'm worried about you."

"Don't be. I'm all set," I said.

"You're just getting on your feet, Cel," she said.

"Let it go Deb," I said, and I walked away, back to my room. Just one school year and I'd be out of there, not that I really thought I'd go to school.

My phone vibrated; it was a message from Dylan.

"You up?"

"What's up?" I wrote.

"Go to the mall?"

Remembering kissing him, I wasn't sure what he thought we had going on.

"Why?" I wrote.

"Just to hang."

Debbie came back into the kitchen. She asked, "Are you going to lie around here all day?"

Whatever. I'll go to the mall then.

"Come get me," I wrote.

"Cool."

We went to the mall, but never sat. Seeing the table where Jackson and I had fries made me vaguely sad. I half-heartedly looked around for him, but he wasn't there. I couldn't bring myself to text him. Some part of me was ashamed, or felt undeserving, but all those feelings were quiet; they were buried under the meds.

"Hey, there's a party at Benny's tonight," Dylan said. "Want to go?"

"I don't know who that is," I said.

"Who cares?" Dylan asked. "I barely know him. But it's a place to party."

"Sounds good," I said. I didn't care, honestly. I mean, I had a flash of anxiety, but it was more fun than lying around in my room, and I wouldn't have to pay for the drinks.

Later, at the party, I just walked around, drank, smoked, took molly, and kissed a random guy. The memory of that night gets hazier as it goes. I remember throwing up in the yard, and going in to get another drink.

In fact, the days and nights began to sort of blur together. I partied at night, or lay around in my room watching Netflix and

YouTube, and slept all day. Sometimes feeling a bit gross about my behavior, or nervous, I'd think that I should clean myself up and get a grip, but then I just let one party blend into the next.

It's not like I suddenly became a "bad kid." To be honest I just wanted to be a numb kid. It beats suicide. Besides, who was I trying to be "good" for? Jackson? Lauren? The memory of my parents? It's not that I radically changed. My entire universe had collapsed, and the meds were messing with my head. Honestly, I simply didn't give a shit anymore.

Eating a single meal per day, and sometimes just a snack, I was like a virtual, online monk, except, you know, like a girl. When I did think of what I'd lost, first my family and then Lauren and Jackson, the thoughts were fleeting and sad, and only made me want to drink more. Trying to stay on chemical autopilot, I only waited for the messages letting me know where the next party would be.

Coming home one night, I was more drunk than high, and Deb was waiting for me. As I stepped inside, she was standing there, and said, "Celestine, this has to stop."

Unsteady on my feet as I stepped out of my shoes, I said, "Not tonight. I just want to go to bed."

"This has gone on too long. This behavior is self-destructive. You have to stop. Look at you," she said.

Blocking the door to the living room, she prevented me from walking away this time. It made me mad, but I was also vaguely embarrassed. "Get out of the way, Deb," I said.

"No. Talk to me. I want to help you," she said.

"I don't want your fucking help. I just want to go to bed," I said. "Can't we just not do this?"

"You're not going out for a while," she said.

"What did you say?"

"You're not going out. You can stay in for a few nights," she said.

The was a heavy pause, and then I said, "Who do you think you are? What do you think this is all about right now?"

"You need limits," Deb said.

"Are you fucking kidding right now?" I asked. "I'm an adult, not to mention I watched my parents die horrible deaths; I spent more than a year scared, every day, that I'd die the same way or in the cold of space or at the hands of another crew member; I've attempted suicide twice… yeah, that's right, twice… I lost my best friend and my boyfriend, and, what… you think you can ground me? Fuck that," I said.

Deb's mouth dropped open, and then she said, "While you're under my roof…"

"Want me gone?" I asked. "I can do that."

"Cel, I only…" she said.

"No. Just stop. I don't need you to mother me. I appreciate everything you've done for me, Deb, but I don't need you to parent me," I said. "Just back off."

Turning, I walked away from her, and she neither said anything more nor followed me. Entering my room, I went straight to the bed, and fell forward onto it.

46

ONE MORNING, DEBBIE AND RAY were mercifully out, and I was in the bathroom. My face was pale, and my hair was a mess. I looked like shit, really, but I didn't care. There was a party at Emily's that night; I had tried to hydrate so I could drink without suffering quite so much the next morning. As I drank a cup of tap water, my hand trembled a bit. I wasn't nervous or anything; I just had the shakes.

The doorbell rang, and I was wearing only a long T-shirt. I went out into the kitchen and looked out a window to see who was at the door. At the street, there were five people carrying signs saying I should be sent away or locked up.

At the door, however, was Dr. Jane Kendall, who I hadn't seen since that support group session that Lauren had walked in on. My heart sank. Why would she come here? Was someone sick? Could I really care anymore? I let her in.

She seemed a bit taken aback at my appearance, but then hugged me tightly, while my arms hung limp.

"Oh Celestine, it's been too long," she said. "Are you never coming back to the group sessions?"

"Well, I just didn't want to be the last one logging on," I said.

"No, Dana has come back," she said.

"Is that why you came here? To ask me back?" I asked.

Dr. Kendall looked around and then pointed at the dining room table. "May we sit?" she asked.

We moved there, and I asked, "So Dana wasn't sick?"

"No one is," she said. "There was nothing nefarious in their absences. They simply didn't want to participate in the group for a while. They left, just as you have."

Wondering if she were part of a conspiracy, I asked again, "She was never sick?"

"We can't be," she said. "At least not like our families were on board the *Phaeacia*."

"Why not?" I asked.

"The doctors, the researchers, they've determined the exact nature of the virus. While all of us were carrying it at some point aboard, just as many people on Earth are too, it can only make a person sick if that person is traveling in interstellar space," she said. She brushed some hair from my forehead.

"So, I had it? And didn't know it?" I asked.

"We all had it, probably still had it when we landed, but then our immune systems developed antibodies and killed it within a day of our arrival. Some of us probably had it before we left Earth," she said.

"Flying in space made the virus worse?" I asked.

"Being in space exposed us to radiation, our entire bodies were exposed to gamma radiation, and that suppressed a very specific part of our immune systems mediated by T-cells and…"

"So the virus didn't get stronger, we got weaker?" I asked.

"Our immune systems got weaker," she said.

"Why did some of us survive, and some of us didn't?" I asked.

"Those of us with the strongest immune systems had the most time to get back. Eventually, we would've all succumbed, I believe," she said.

"So, the virus could still kill someone on Earth if their immune system were weak?"

"Perhaps if they were going through chemo or something, yes, but they would be under the care of doctors," she said. "But we have nothing to fear, and neither do normally healthy members of the public," Dr. Kendall said. She took my hand.

"Why didn't scientists know this before we flew? If they can figure it out after we get back within a few months, why didn't we know this before we lost all those people?" I asked.

"It was a long time ago. Everyone did the best they could. We went as explorers, and we expected risks. We came back with crucial information about long-term deep space flight," she said.

I paused, and then quietly said, "The price was too high."

She nodded. "It was." She leaned forward in her chair and hugged me. I hugged her back, and it felt good.

"Will the public be told?" I asked. It wouldn't put all their minds at ease, but maybe strangers wouldn't treat me like a walking plague anymore. She and I separated, and she wiped her eyes. She looked back at the door, as if she could see the protestors through the wall.

"There's a press conference tomorrow, at Brigham and Women's Hospital in Boston. Researchers there were the ones who figured it out. We've all been invited. We called your foster mother, but we haven't heard from you," she said. "It would be like a reunion. You should come."

"I'm not going," I said, without any particular tone to my voice; I simply knew I wasn't going to go.

She didn't urge me to go; she smiled a half-smile and stood. We hugged again, but this time, only politely, and said, "You should come back to group. I'd like to see you once in a while; see how you're doing."

"I probably won't," I said.

She nodded and turned to leave without saying anything more.

I said, "But we could Zoom, just me and you."

Turning back, she hugged me tightly. "I'd love that." After she left, I stood there absorbing it all. My parents, all those people, were actually killed by radiation exposure. The next day, the world would learn that we weren't carrying some exotic virus that we caught in space, but instead the virus was always all around us here on Earth. Even though the tragedy was still back there in the foggy compartment I'd learned to leave it in, the weight of wondering if I might make people sick, or get sick myself, was lifted. It was gone. It had been perhaps a bit lost in a haze of drugs, and alcohol, but the fear had still been there, and it was suddenly gone.

Dylan messaged, *"Hey, what's up?"*

I smiled.

"I feel like celebrating," I wrote.

"Party tonight at Emily's."

"I know. Let's do it."

"I'll pick you up."

. . .

At Emily's party, I felt free because of a mixture of good news, my meds, and the alcohol. I was drunk within the first hour.

"Here, have a mojito," a guy said, handing me a plastic tumbler.

"What's in it?" I asked.

"I think it's gin," he said.

"Ed, mojitos are made from rum, dumbass," Emily said to him.

"We don't have rum. We have gin and I found mint growing in your yard," he said.

"Yeah, there's mint out there. There's also catnip. Damn, you're dumb. Cel, don't drink it. I mean, catnip isn't poisonous or whatever, but you could get sick," Emily said.

I didn't care; I was celebrating. I drank that drink, as well as the many more to come, and smoked a little weed as it was passed around. I think I took only one molly, but I'm not sure. It was just another party with a bunch of free stuff floating around.

The drunker I got, and the higher I got, the more I drank, until my memory of that night shifted from a linear sort of video into more of a slideshow of still photos and mini-clips of movement and sounds. I remember dancing and laughing, and I kissed at least two of the guys I danced with, hardly thinking of Jackson at all.

I was sitting on a couch, when Dylan came and sat beside me and started kissing my neck, but I wasn't into it. I wanted to be free, not have Dylan kissing on me again. I told him to stop, and he didn't. Pushing him, I said it louder. Some guy I didn't know told Dylan to stop. They stared at each other for a minute and said something I couldn't understand, and then Dylan left. The guy sat beside me.

"What's up?" he said.

"Just getting buzzed. Just being me," I said, trying to focus. He was kind of cute.

"I hear you," he said. "I'm Brendan."

"You from Goodwin?" I asked.

"Shit, no," he said. He took a couple gulps from his beer, and I took another sip of my drink. I had no idea what this one was. It was strong enough and that's all I cared about.

"And you are?" he asked.

"Cel," I said.

"Interesting name," he said.

Shrugging, I said, "Yeah." Drinking again, I looked up, and across the room, Dylan was staring.

"Are you with that guy or something?" Brendan asked.

"I'm not with anyone," I said.

"Let's get out of here," he said.

Turning my head to look at him, it felt heavy and wobbly. "And go where?" I wasn't going home with him, or anyone else.

"There's another party. Not as lame as this one," he said, and smiled. "C'mon, it'll be fun."

Looking at Dylan, and then back at Brendan, "Sure. Let's go." Still, I did have some anxiety, like a warning voice calling from far off. As if leaving this party was one step too far.

We started walking to the door, when I was suddenly spun around. It was Dylan.

"Where are you going?" he asked.

"Another party," I said, raising my glass.

"You don't even know him," Dylan said.

"That's Brendan," I said.

Brendan stepped in. "Hey, man, fuck off."

"She's wasted, leave her here," Dylan said.

"So you can keep climbing on her?" Brendan said. "Let her have some fun, dude."

"Cel, you don't know this guy, don't go. It's like 3 o'clock in the morning," Dylan said.

Brendan stepped forward and shoved Dylan, who almost fell. "I said, back off."

I almost stayed. There was something in Dylan's face, in

his eyes, that almost caused me to not go with Brendan. All the time we'd been partying and even making out, he'd never actually looked worried about me before, that combined with that nagging inner voice made me pause. But in the end, I left.

As we drove, I got sleepier. It seemed to take forever to get to the next party. We drove through the woods and past the pond, and we clearly weren't in Goodwin anymore, but I had no real idea of where we were.

"Are we almost there?" I asked, my anxiety level rising.

"Yeah, it's right up here," Brendan said.

We pulled up to a farmhouse, but there were only three cars in the driveway.

"There's no one here," I said.

"There is, they're inside. Let's check it out," Brendan said.

When we entered, it was smoky, and there was a blue light coming from the living room, where half a dozen people were lying around watching a movie or something. There were bottles everywhere and the smell of weed was heavy.

"Hey, what's up," Brendan said. Two people looked up and then looked away; one of them said, "Hey."

"Want something to drink?" Brendan asked me.

Actually, I wanted to leave. He made me a drink for me anyway, and he grabbed another beer from the fridge. We went into the living room and sat on the floor amidst everyone else. The movie was weird, and the volume was too low for me to really hear it. Especially with all the noise from the chip bags and the whispering.

Another girl came into the room and sat on the other side of Brendan and before I was done my drink, they were making out. The guy on my left suddenly leaned in and kissed me on the mouth. I had no idea who he was, and my inner voice was shouting, but I robotically kissed him back. I can't explain why. He lay on top of me, and we kissed. We were making out. The images were broken and out of sequence. Fear started to build; I felt clumsy and weak, and then he started unbuttoning my shirt. I pulled my mouth away. He kissed my neck and then my collarbone.

"Wait," I said. I felt fear rising fast, a panicked feeling just sweeping through me, but he didn't say anything.

"Wait," I said again. When he unbuttoned the button between my breasts, I pushed at him. He stopped, but then kissed my chest.

"No, get off me," I said. I was so afraid, but my arms were heavy. Like fighting someone off through a heavy blanket. He didn't stop, and he put his hand on my breast. Glancing around, I saw no one was watching. No one cared and there was no help. Starting to cry, I thought of my mom, and I thought of Jackson. I felt trapped. I was trapped again, like on the *Phaeacia*; I felt like I was going to suffocate. I began to freak out. I felt it building and then it just exploded out of me, and I was slapping and screaming and kicking. I don't know what parts of him I hit, or with what parts of me, but he was suddenly off, and I was up and out. I ran out of the house and into the woods.

It was cold, the leaves were damp, but I didn't care. Catching a branch across my forehead, I went down. Listening for a moment, I could hear no one chasing me, or even calling after me. No one in the house knew me, or cared. Lying on the cold, wet ground and listening to my breathing, I could smell the rich soil beneath me, and I could see moonlight on the leaves, but not the moon itself. Just wanting to sleep, I heard my dad's voice tell me to get up. I swear it was his, and so I did. Walking with my hands outstretched until I came out of the trees, and into tall grass. I walked in the easier direction, downhill, and fell into a ditch I didn't know was there. Coming out the other side onto a dirt road, I spotted the moon, and decided to follow it.

Eventually, it led me to a paved way. Walking for a long time, I felt the alcohol slowly losing its grip. My head was slowly clearing, but I was so tired. Covered in mud and scratches, I walked as the sky lightened a bit.

The first car that came along, stopped. Opening the door, I didn't immediately climb in. It was a woman in jeans, with wellies on her feet, and a well-worn T-shirt that said "Eat Local" across her chest.

"Are you okay?" she asked.

"I just need a ride," I said. "To Goodwin."

"Sweetie, are you okay?" she asked.

Hesitating, I started to cry with the realization that I was almost raped. I felt like it anyway; I was definitely attacked. How did I get here? How did it come to this? Was I no better than this?

"Get in. I'm taking you to the hospital," she said.

"Just take me home," I said. "I just want to go home."

"Are you sure?" she asked.

"Please take me home," I said, and climbed in.

She reached into the backseat and pulled a jacket up to the front. She laid it in my lap, and I slowly warmed under it. Once we were in town, I guided her.

When we pulled up in front of the house, she asked, "Are you sure you'll be alright? Is there someone home?"

"Thanks. I'm okay. Really. Thanks so much," I said, and got out.

She nodded and drove away. Debbie's car was gone, but Ray's pickup was in the driveway. Hoping he was out back, or in the basement, I just wanted a hot shower and to go to bed.

47

HE WAS IN THE KITCHEN. Ray sat at the table eating a big helping of the Fruity Splash Sponge Bob cereal.

Looking at his bowl, I asked, "Is it good?"

Looking up, his mouth fell open. "Cel, are you hurt?" He stood, and pulled a chair for me to sit, but I didn't.

"I'm alright. I'm just a mess. Scrapes and bruises," I said.

"Were you beaten up or something?" he asked.

"I'm really okay. I just need a shower," I said.

Sitting back down, he took another bite of the cereal and asked, "Would you sit with me a minute?"

I just looked at him; my head hurt.

Swallowing, he asked, "Please?"

Rolling my eyes, I dropped into the chair. I felt gross and so tired.

"I don't have a speech for you," he said. "I raised my own, and I'm done."

"Good," I said.

"I think it's possible that you don't know something that I do," he said.

Oh great. "What?"

"I think you're amazing," he said.

Except for what? I waited for him to say the rest.

"That's it. You're amazing. That's what I know that you don't. I don't mean unique because you've been to space. I mean you have such strength. To survive the trip, to attempt to adapt back here, to allow yourself to fall in love, to trust enough to have a best friend, and then to lose those two important people and ultimately survive. I think any of those challenges would've either killed a normal person or at least driven them to a point where they tried nothing new," he said.

"What choice did I have?" I asked.

"You could have hidden. You could've hidden from all of it. From new friends, new family, new boyfriend, new love, new school. You could've simply refused and hidden. But you never did. Until now," he said.

"What do you mean?" I asked.

"With the drugs and the drinking. You're hiding under a blanket of chemicals," he said. "You're hiding by staying only with the people you don't care about. You're hiding by pushing away people you do care about, like Deb."

"I am not hiding," I said.

His voice was soft. "Cel, look at you. Right now, you look like you feel. You've been hiding in a deep, scary hole. But you're amazing; you're better than that."

My nose burned, and I could feel tears welling up. I didn't want to cry, but I was just so tired that I couldn't keep my guard up.

"You've been hiding from a disease you may or may not have," he said.

He didn't know, because the press conference hadn't happened yet. Still, it was true; I had been so afraid of the virus.

"You're not just a piece of meat that guys should try to get drunk and use," he said.

That felt like he went too far, and I wanted to be angry, but instead the tears came. The shame I felt. Looking at myself, I was gross. Not because of mud or blood or the smell of alcohol. I was gross. I asked, "What can I do? How do I fix this?"

"There's not that much to fix. I told you. You're amazing. We just have to get you to remember how special you are. We just have to get you to believe that you are too valuable a person to throw yourself away on getting drunk, and not caring about others or yourself," he said.

"What do I have to do?" I asked.

"I've found you a psychiatrist."

"Aw, shit, not that again," I said.

"This one's different," he said. "She is different. Talk to her one time. Just once, as a favor."

"What?" I asked. "A favor to you?"

He leaned forward. "To your parents. To the others that didn't make it back. To the other survivors. Just try talking to her once, as a favor to them."

Oh my God. It was so corny, so cliché, and so true. Saying nothing, I lay my head on the table. He stroked my hair, and let me cry. Feeling my defenses coming down, so exhausted, after what had happened... that guy at the house... his thick fingers working at my shirt, his breath heavy with gin and weed, my head hurt. Feeling beaten, I had no fight left in me. With heaving, silent sobs, I felt the world shift, and I surrendered. It felt good.

He said, "I'll take you to see her tomorrow."

Never lifting my head, I nodded.

48

WHEN I WALKED INTO HER office, I thought worst case it would be like Muriel's bullying or best case it would be like playing along with Lewis in the hospital. She was wearing a black knee-length dress, with black heels on her feet, but the big clunky kind. Her glasses had thick, black frames. Her hair was shoulder length, light brown, and straight. She smiled a professional smile, shook my hand, and waved to a big leather chair.

"Hi, Celestine, my name is Dr. Nora Kalinova. I'm very glad to meet you," she said.

So far, this was achingly familiar. "You can call me Cel."

"Fine," she said. "You can call me Nora, if you're comfortable with that?"

"Okay," I said.

"So, Ray tells me you've had a rough stretch," she said.

A rough stretch? Going back to what? The death of my parents? "It hasn't been much fun," I said. I still had my scratches and bruises, but I was all cleaned up, and wearing leggings with a sweater. I felt clean and comfy.

"You want to tell me something about yourself?" she asked.

"Like what?"

She said, "Whatever you'd like to share."

"I once took a rock for a swim," I said.

"I heard about that," she said, and smiled.

That's it? "Look, I'm only here as a favor. I had a therapist once; she was awful."

"How were you?"

"What do you mean?"

"What kind of a patient were you? Did you go in there hoping to heal? To find answers? To examine yourself?" she asked.

"Are you blaming me for it not working out with her?" I asked.

"I'm not. I was just asking," she said.

Pausing, I then asked, "Okay, which answers should we look for first?"

She smiled again. "Cel, let's slow down." Her voice was soft, soothing.

"How could we go any slower?"

"Let me ask you to do something for me," she said. "I want you to tell me why you came here today."

"I told Ray I would," I said.

"Besides that. You don't even really know Ray," she said.

"He asked me to do it as a favor," I said.

"Yes, to your parents and yourself," she said. "I know. I wish he hadn't said that."

"Why not?" I asked.

"Do you feel like you owe your parents any favors?" she asked.

I sat quietly for a minute. "I loved my parents."

"Of course you did," she said. "I know you did. That's not what I asked you."

"Of course I owe them, they were my parents," I said.

"You feel like you owe them a favor?" she asked.

"They raised me. They took care of me," I said.

"I know they did, and I know you loved them," she said. "And you miss them. And I'm sure you've been told about survivor's guilt and you probably feel like you have that too."

"Don't I?" I asked.

"I have no idea yet," Nora said. "But that's a huge question. Let's start with a really small one."

"Which one?" I asked.

She paused, and then asked, "Why would anyone owe someone a favor?"

Thinking for a moment, I said, "You owe someone a favor when they do something for you."

"Every parent is supposed to feed and house and protect their children, right? It's expected, don't you think?" she asked.

I didn't like where this was going. "Not every parent is a good parent. Not every parent does those things."

"Very true, I've seen the hard end of that right here in this office. But it's expected of every parent, just to be counted among decent parents, that the kids should come first. That parents might even go without in order to provide kids with a good home and upbringing. To the best of their ability," she said.

"My parents were good parents," I said.

"I'm sure they made sure you had enough to eat and a dry place to sleep, and you guys had laughs, hugs and that they loved you," she said.

"That's right," I said.

"That's right. They loved you so much, they had to bring you with them," she said.

Not saying anything, I felt like I was being pulled in a direction I didn't want to go, like being pulled around blind corners not knowing what was coming next.

"They had to bring you with them, because they loved you so much," she said.

"So?" I asked.

"Did they love you enough to not go?" she asked.

"What?" I asked.

"Why didn't they decline the opportunity to go into space?" she asked. "They had a young daughter."

"It was an amazing opportunity," I said.

"So is raising a kid," she said.

"Besides, I wanted to go," I said.

"Cel, you were so young," she said. "The decision to go along, was it ever really yours?"

"They asked me if I wanted to go with them," I said, feeling something in my chest, like bubbles. It grossed me out.

"They asked you if you wanted to go with them," she said. "They were going to go anyway, weren't they? Where were you going to live if you didn't go?"

"I don't want to talk about this," I said.

"Where?" she asked. Her voice was still soft, but it was insistent in a strange, gentle way. I felt like I wanted to answer her, in spite of my best efforts not to. It made me angry.

"Don't you think I can tell that you're fucking with my head right now?" I said.

"Cel, there's nothing wrong with your head. We're just taking an honest look. Turning on the light doesn't make the room messier," she said.

"What the hell is that supposed to mean?" I asked. "Don't play games. Don't mess with me."

"Celestine, just answer the question," she said.

"What's the fucking question?" I asked.

"Where were you going to stay if you hadn't gone with your parents into space?" she asked.

Staring at her, I felt my heart pounding, and my face was hot. I wanted to jump at her and slap her. Standing up, I stormed out of the office. I walked through the outer room without even glancing at Ray, passing him before he even put the magazine down. I went to the elevator, and waited for it.

"Cel, what's going on?" Ray asked, coming into the lobby.

"Fuck this," I said, and headed for the stairs. He followed me. I was going faster and faster until I was running down the flights, and I could hear him huffing and puffing behind me, trying to catch up, and then I heard him fall. Turning, I saw he was sprawled out on the landing behind me.

"Ray!" I said. Running back up the stairs, I knelt beside him. "Are you okay?"

"I'm okay, I just slipped. It sucks being fat and old," he said.

He started to sit up, but my eyes welled up with tears and I fell onto his chest.

"I'm okay," he said, stroking my hair again.

I didn't say anything. My face was against him, tears streaming. Not sobbing or anything, it was just tears. People soon appeared, an older woman in scrubs came into the stairs, and then a man in jeans.

"Hey, mister, you okay?" he asked.

Ray said, "We're okay. I slipped; I'm not hurt. She's going

to be okay."

"You sure?" the woman said.

Looking up, face wet, I nodded. The people slowly turned and walked away, and soon it was just Ray and I again.

"Want to go home?" he asked.

"Can you get up?" I asked.

"Of course. This was all just a ploy to get you to slow down," he said.

Smiling through the tears, I said, "Liar."

"Yeah, well, it worked," he said, sitting up.

We started down the stairs together, his arm around my shoulders.

"Don't tell Deb I fell," he said.

Laughing a bit, I rubbed my eyes.

His voice grew much quieter. "What happened in there, Cel? With Nora?" he asked.

Stopping, I looked up at him. His face was still red, and his eyes looked worried.

"Do you think she'd let me come back?" I asked.

"I'll call her and ask," he said.

We went home, and I went straight to my room, leaving him to tell the story any way he wanted to Debbie. I hit "play" on my cassette player, and listened to Journey as I dozed off on my bed.

• • •

The next time I sat with Nora, I was scared. I was drawn to being there, but I couldn't explain why. I knew it was going to hurt, that the path she wanted to help me walk would be painful, and that I couldn't come back from it. I sensed it would change everything. I was scared, and yet I wanted to be there. Not really trusting her yet, but I felt there was something different about her.

"You were asking where I would've stayed if I had chosen not to go with my parents," I said.

"That's right," she said.

Pausing, I then said, "We never discussed a specific place."

"Why not?"

"I'm not sure," I said.

"Think about it," she said. "Why do you think you and your parents never explored what that alternative would look like?"

Thinking back to before the flight and even the flight prep, I tried to remember back to a time when the decision that I would go along with them had not yet been made, but I couldn't. I remembered them talking about being happy that we would all go together, but I couldn't recall the discussions that led to my agreeing to go. In fact, I was struggling to place when I actually consented. Nora must have seen the effort on my face.

"Did they ask you, Cel?" she asked.

I vaguely remembered it. The scene, but not the words, that represented my parents asking me if I wanted to go with them, my agreement, and then the hugging, but I couldn't remember the specific words.

"I remember we were near the dining room table, and they were so happy that I decided to go," I said.

"Did they ask you? How did they ask you?" she asked.

Trying to remember the words, I could only remember the smiles and the hugs, and then my mom hugging my dad.

"They seemed relieved that I agreed to go," I said.

"Were they relieved that you were going, or that you were going without a fight?" she asked.

"Are you going to attack my parents?" I asked. "Because I'm not sure that will help. I want to remember them as loving, good people."

"They were. I'd never question that," she said.

"What's your point then?" I asked.

"Try to remember how it went. I think it's part of what we really need to work on. How did you truly feel about going on the *Phaeacia*? How did you really feel about your parents bringing you with them?"

"I agreed to it. I mean, in hindsight, it was obviously a tragedy, so it's hard to remember it in a positive way," I said.

"Think about when you decided you were going. Tell me what you see, explain it in detail, not generalities," she said.

Digging deep into the memory, I said, "My father had papers out in front of him, on the table. He was happy. My mom beside him was smiling, but nervously. We were all standing."

"So, he was happy. Smiling. Did he seem concerned?" she asked.

"Just happy," I said.

"So, think about just before you said you'd go," she said. "Was he happy then too?"

I tried hard to remember.

"Just before you said, 'Yes,' did he seem nervous then? Concerned?" she asked. "Try thinking about the minute before you agreed to go."

"I can't remember it," I said, and I really couldn't.

"Okay, think about before you were standing at the table," she said. "Were you in your room?"

"I was watching TV," I said.

"And they called you into the dining room," she said.

"I guess so," I said.

"Don't fill in the memory with guesses," she said. "What do you actually remember?"

"They called me into the dining room," I said.

"Your father, your mother, both?"

"My father called us both into the dining room, I think," I said. It was foggy.

"And you all stood together and he said he had a question for you?" she asked.

"No. He was smiling when I got to him; I got to the dining room before my mom did. My dad was very excited."

"So, did he ask you? Or did he tell you something?" she asked.

In that moment, I realized he hadn't asked me if I wanted to go. "He told me, he didn't ask me." Tears welled up, but didn't flow; they fell one at a time.

"Told you that you were going?" she asked.

The words were coming back suddenly, or maybe just the feelings. "No, he told me that he and my mom had been accepted for an amazing opportunity. He told me that it was a secret. He told me there was a spaceship and another planet."

"So, he never asked you anything?" she asked.

The memories were coming in rush now. "He asked me…"

"What did he ask you?"

"He asked me, 'Isn't that great?'" I looked up at Nora. "That's all he asked me."

There was a pause, and then she asked, "And you agreed that it was great."

"And I agreed," I said. That was it. That was me agreeing to go along. That was all the consent I'd given, and my life was ripped apart after that.

"And your mom was by his side when he asked you?" she asked.

Oh my God. My mom wasn't. I said, "She wasn't there. She was coming from the kitchen, and I was alone with my father when he told me."

"She was coming from the kitchen?" Nora asked.

"Yes, he told me and then she arrived from the kitchen," I said, the picture was getting clearer all the while.

"If he called you both to him, why did you beat her to the dining room?"

"I was faster," I said.

"Wasn't the kitchen closer to the dining room than the living room was?"

"Yeah, but I was faster," I said.

"Tell me about your mom arriving in the dining room," she asked.

"My mom arrived right when I agreed it was great news," I said.

"Did you think she was happy? Did you immediately hug you?"

"She didn't," I said. Why didn't she?

"She was happy?"

"Yes, she was smiling. She was so pretty," I said.

"So, why no hug?" she asked.

"Her hands were full," I said. Her hands were full. They were, that's right.

"What was she carrying?"

The image was coming into focus like an old movie flashback. It was like reeling in something much too heavy for the line it was on, and then I saw it.

"What did she have in her hands?" Nora asked.

"Champagne," I said.

There was a pause, and then Nora said, "She brought Champagne."

"She was carrying a bottle and three glasses. The bottle was open," I said. "They started pouring, and we drank some."

"Why?" she asked.

"To celebrate," I said.

"To celebrate that you agreed to go," she said.

"Right, that we'd be together on this adventure. We had no idea it would turn into a nightmare, we had no idea that they might get sick and die. So we were celebrating," I said.

"Cel," she said.

"What?"

"Your mom had the bottle open, and on the way, before you even agreed to anything?" she asked.

I thought the order of events through again. Dad called us to the dining room, and I beat my mom to there. Why? Because she was busy in the kitchen with the Champagne. Why? Because no matter what, they were going. So, did I ever really have a choice? Maybe not. But regardless of how I felt about it, they were celebrating.

"They were always going to go. With or without me," I said. Tears fell, but no sobbing, no twisting of the face.

Nora just gave me a moment, and said nothing until she said, "Cel, you can let go. You can really cry here, I won't judge you."

"Crying feels different somehow with these meds," I said.

"Your scripts? Wellbutrin and…" she checked a pad in front of her, "Celexa?"

I nodded.

"Those shouldn't have you unable to cry," she said. "How much are you taking?"

"The Wellbutrin is 300mg in the morning, the Celexa is 60mg per day," I said.

"60? Are you sure?" she asked.

"Yeah," I said.

She didn't seem to believe me. "How many pills do you take?"

"Celexa?"

"Yeah, just the Celexa," she said.

"I take three," I said.

That seemed to do it. She said, "So you are taking three 20mg pills of Celexa each day."

"Is that a lot?"

"FDA recommended the max daily dosage be lowered to 40mg years ago. That combined with Wellbutrin… it's a lot," she said.

"Am I taking too much Wellbutrin?"

"It's generally the target dosage, but it might also be more than you need. What would you think about lowering the Celexa to 40mg per day? And maybe down the road we'll try to ease the Wellbutrin back to 150mg?" she asked.

How would I know? "If you think I should," I said.

"Would you like to feel a bit more, without walking completely away from the meds?"

"I think I would," I said. "The Celexa is for anxiety, right?"

"Yes, but the Wellbutrin has been shown to help with that too, so you might even be double-dipping as it is, without the huge Celexa dosages," she wrote something down. "Going forward, let's have you take only two of the Celexa each day, and not three, ok?"

I shrugged. "Okay."

"Don't change the Wellbutrin. We'll do this slowly," she said.

"Okay."

"Now, back to your parents," she said.

I took a deep breath. "They were going to go with or without me. They opened the Champagne to celebrate before they even told me."

"They were excited and happy. They thought this was a great thing. I'm not sure we can know if they would've let you stay behind. Maybe they hadn't considered that," she said.

"I know they loved me," I said.

"They loved you. They might have been sure you would want to go," she said.

"But they never asked if I wanted to go," I said.

"It appears not," she said.

I wasn't sure how to feel about it. "Why not ask?"

She paused and then said, "Cel, if your parents had been moving to California because your dad was offered an incredible job out there, do you think they, or most other parents, would check first with their child to see if the move would be acceptable? Or would they simply get the family together and announce the new position, the move, and that's it?"

"They probably would do the second one; they would just announce it," I said. I knew where she was going with this.

"I think you're right," she said. "Do you think most kids would think this was unfair?"

"Probably," I said.

"What if a kid was moving to California from Maine, and out in Kansas, their car was hit and the parents were killed," she said. "Do you think that kid would, in addition to be very sad, have some anger and resentment toward the parents?"

I leaned back in my chair. "Probably."

"So, do you think your parents were obliged to ask you if they could go?"

"No, I guess not," I said.

"Do you think your parents should have offered you the chance to stay here?" she asked.

Thinking for a moment, I said, "Yes, they should."

"Would you have gone with them?"

"Probably, but they should have offered me the chance to stay," I said.

"And they didn't, but any chance they were protecting you there too? Is it possible they didn't want you to be responsible for any part of this risky undertaking?" she asked.

I hadn't thought of that. If they dragged me along, I wouldn't own any of the blame for our going if things went wrong, and they certainly had. Maybe my parents were keeping the blame for going on the *Phaeacia* all for themselves.

"Does that sound like them?" Nora asked.

My eyes were wet again. I said, "It sounds just like them."

49

SITTING IN MY ROOM WATCHING Netflix, I was a bit startled when Deb came in. "Let's go for a ride."

"I don't know, Deb," I said. We had been just ignoring each other really, although it had become less tense since I started working with Nora. It was polite, but I had spoken with Ray more than I had with Deb. Maybe we just never knew where to start to rebuild our relationship, and it was so fraught with landmines, we decided it was better to have a relatively quiet truce than risk a new round of fighting. I understood that she was trying to connect, but I wasn't sure it was worth it.

"Come on, Cel, I want to show you something," she said.

"What is it?"

"Something pretty cool. For old times sake, like remember when we were kids. Do this for me, please. I promise you won't regret it," she said. Her tone was almost tender, vulnerable. She wasn't being bossy; she was taking a risk, as if we were two little girls again.

Closing my laptop, I said, "Okay."

"Come on," she said.

Heading out to the car, I saw that in front of the house, there was still a lone protester. Since the press conference, their numbers had quickly dwindled until there remained only one.

"Hi Thea," Debbie called.

Thea just stood there, motionless, with her sign raised high. It read, "Honk if you feel unsafe." Two cars passed while I watched, without honking, and I almost felt sorry for her.

We got in the car and drove out past the middle school, past the town's recycling center, and we drove past the marshes.

"I'm wearing sneakers," I said.

She turned off the paved road and onto a much rougher secondary one.

"Where the hell are we going?" I asked.

"You don't remember this road?" she asked.

Looking around, it was vaguely familiar, but I couldn't place it until we came around a sweeping corner and up on the hill I saw the old farmhouse. Dark, boarded up, weathered cedar shingles, and surrounded by a broken fence.

"Gram's old house?" I asked.

"Gramp lived there too," she said and smiled.

Looking back up the hill as we turned up the drive, I remembered how the house appeared when I was a kid, back when I thought it seemed old. It appeared as if it were right out of an old horror movie now. I hadn't been to that house in a long time. Our grandparents had sold it the summer that I turned seven years old. There was some mud, but for the most part, we had no trouble driving nearly the whole way to the house.

"Why are we here, Deb?" I asked.

"Let's go for a walk," she said.

Heading out, I stumbled a couple times when I didn't pick up my feet on the rough path. We went past the house and the trail snaked into the woods.

"It's beautiful out here," I said.

"Isn't it?"

"Thanks for bringing me out," I said. The trees, mostly spruce, were thick, and there were birds singing; I saw the bright red of a cardinal flash by. The breeze was nice, and the trail got easier. After almost half an hour, I saw something up ahead.

"What is that?" I asked.

"That's what I wanted to show you," she said.

As we got closer, I asked, "A bench?"

It was, with wooden boards set into granite. I asked, "What kind of wood is this?" It wasn't finished, but was an even grey, smooth and solid.

"It's teak," she said. "Look on this end."

I went around the stone end and saw a plaque. It read, "To honor our cherished pioneers to the stars. Peter, Mary, and Celestine Tolland. We love you."

I asked, "Gramp did this?"

Deb nodded. "He came back to the land where your mom and my dad grew up, and asked permission to put this here. No one was living in the house, the Maguires had died, and their kids were fine with it. He missed you all, and talked about you all the time."

"When did he put this here?" I asked.

"About ten years ago, so almost thirty years after you left. He was in his eighties then. He died a couple years later," Deb said.

Touching the plaque, I thought it was a beautiful bench, and in a wonderful spot.

"I know your parents don't have headstones anywhere. I thought this might do. And maybe, when we get them back, maybe we could have them laid to rest here, and we could come visit them," Deb said.

Standing, I turned to her, and took her in a big hug.

"I loved them too, you know?" she said.

"I love you Deb. I'm so sorry," I said.

Hugging me back, she said, "I know, I'm sorry too."

With one arm still around each other we looked down at the plaque again, and I said, "Thank you. For everything. Thanks, Debbie."

"You're welcome, Cel," she said. We tried to walk with our arms around each other, but we made clumsy progress so, laughing, we separated and headed back to the car. As we drove away, I was smiling, and so was she. It was a quiet drive, but a nice one, and I felt like I had my Debbie back.

50

A FEW DAYS LATER, I CAME out of the Goodwin School District central office and was walking to Deb's car when Jackson pulled up. My stomach fluttered, and as he rolled down his window, all I could think was, *Be cool.*

"Hey Cel," he said.

"Hey," was all I said. *God, I miss him.*

"How are you? I mean, how are you feeling?"

"I'm okay, doing better," I said. "How about you?"

"I'm okay," he said.

There was an awkward pause.

Nodding toward the building, he asked, "Are you going to go to school?"

Shaking my head, I said, "I'm going to get my GED, or whatever they call it now, instead. Maybe take a gap year after that, and then see if I can find a college that will take me."

"Sounds like you have a plan," he said.

"A loose one anyway," I said, and then, looking both ways, I asked, "Should you be talking to me right now?"

He paused, and then said, "The protection order doesn't apply to me anymore."

"Your birthday," I said, realizing. "You're eighteen." My heart began pounding at the possibilities.

"Yeah, a couple weeks ago," he said.

"I'm sorry, I forgot," I said.

"You've had a lot to deal with," he said. "I mean, the order is still in force for my family, but I had my name taken off. But, like, it still applies to my mom's house, so don't just drop by." He smiled, apparently trying to be cute, which he was, but it was too soon to be funny.

"You had your name taken out of the order?"

"Yeah," he said. "I mean, it seemed the least I could do. With everything you've been through."

Smiling, I said, "Thanks."

There was another pause, and I wondered if I should ask if he wanted to do something, but I was also waiting to see if he'd ask me first. Maybe he was doing the same. Or maybe he only took his name off the order because he felt sorry for me.

"Well, I've gotta go," he said.

Ugh. "Okay," I said.

"Okay. Bye," he said, and drove away.

Watching him go, I thought I should've asked him to go to Dunkins or whatever. Anywhere. I watched him drive away until he went around a corner, and then I climbed into the car.

Deb asked, "That was Jackson, right?"

"Yeah," I said.

"You okay?" she asked.

"It hurts," I said.

"It'll get easier. It'll get better," she said.

I hoped it wouldn't.

51

DURING MY NEXT APPOINTMENT WITH Nora after the visit to the memorial bench, and after seeing Jackson, I was in a decent mood, feeling like I was making progress.

"Let's talk about drinking," she said.

I shifted in my seat. "I haven't been drinking since that night."

"The night you were assaulted," she said.

"That's right," I said.

"Have you decided you'll never drink again?" she asked.

"I haven't made myself any promises, I just didn't like where I ended up that night, so now I don't want to, I guess," I said.

"What if you had a glass of wine with dinner?" she asked.

Thinking for a moment, it sounded so good, just one glass, but then I realized how happy I was at just the thought of a glass of wine. "I don't think so, not yet. It's too soon."

"What does alcohol represent to you, you think?" she asked.

"Represent?"

"Yeah, like what role does it play in the world," she asked.

"Like other people, I guess. It's a way to feel good, relax," I said.

"But now it scares you," she said. "Why do you think that is?"

I said, "I think I like it too much."

"And you're scared of it," she said.

That was almost it. "I'm scared of myself. I'm not sure I could have only one glass. At parties, drinks seemed to go 1-2-6. Like, I'd remember the first two drinks and the next thing I knew, I'd finished off half a dozen. When I'm drinking, when I get buzzed, I also can't seem to pass on weed, or even molly, and that just makes things worse, and I drink more, and smoke more weed…" My anxiety level was rising, but at the same time I longed for the escape I was describing.

"Cel, this might be a lifelong effort for you. I'm not saying you'll always have to deny yourself a glass of wine or a beer, but I think you'll have to be careful," she said. "Have you gone to parties where there was alcohol?"

"I haven't, but it isn't just because of the alcohol. The friendships I had, they haven't reestablished yet. I mean, I haven't really tried, either. I saw Jackson. I missed his birthday. But the protection order is gone now, for him anyway," I said.

"Because he's turned eighteen, and can decide for himself," she said.

"That's right. As far as other friends, I don't know how to send that first message. Like, can you imagine? 'Hey, I got out of the psych ward, and almost got raped, so I'm done partying, what's new with you?'" I said.

"Will you contact Jackson?" she asked.

"Do you think I should?"

"That's up to you. I just want you to feel safe," she said.

"I think I'd like to," I said.

"Are you lonely here in town?"

"I am, but I was also thinking that maybe Goodwin is not in my future anyway," I said.

"Will you leave?"

Suddenly becoming aware that leaving Goodwin might mean losing these appointments with Nora, I said, "If I did, when I was back in town, could we still get together?"

"I'd like that," she said. "As long as you think it would help. And you continued to pay me."

We laughed. "I think I have insurance until I'm twenty-six," I said.

"Actually, NASA pays me," she said, and smiled.

It got quiet for a moment, and then I asked, "Am I an alcoholic? Or an addict?"

"You're you. You're Celestine. We don't need any more labels than that. I don't think one more diagnosis for you will help anything. Use your best judgment, forgive yourself if you fall, and then get up and try again," she said.

Thinking back to the party, and remembering that guy unbuttoning my shirt, I said, "I think I'll hold off drinking."

"That's probably a good idea," she said. "Maybe you could even wait until you're legally old enough to have it."

I smiled, nodded, and wanted a drink in the worst way.

52

AS I WALKED THROUGH THE mall, I recognized many faces. No one was being mean. They all smiled, some waved, but no one approached, and no one stopped to talk. I was not hanging out anyway; I had come to find some sneakers.

On the way to Olympia Sports, I saw the Spencer's where Jackson and I had kissed, and I impulsively went in. Finding the pin art, I pushed my hand into the back of it. Clearing the pins, I then pushed my face into it. I looked at the 3D representation of my face, and smiled, but I was sad. I missed him.

Leaving Spencer's, I turned into Olympia. I was looking at the shoes when Lauren walked in with Cole; they didn't see me, and went over to the men's hoodies. Missing her almost as much as I missed her brother, I remembered when she gave me advice on what to wear when we first met.

Cole walked over to the hats and left Lauren at the rack. Taking a deep breath, I headed over to her.

"Hey," I said.

She looked up with a small smile, and then that smile fell from her face when she saw it was me.

"Hey," she said, and then she looked at the hoodies.

This was not starting well. I asked, "How's it going?"

"Fine," she said.

Taking another deep breath, I said, "Listen, I was wondering if you would want to…"

She looked up and interrupted. "No, Celestine, I wouldn't."

"What?"

"First, forgetting there is still a protection order in place, do you have any idea what you did to my brother, or my parents?" she asked. "I mean, you two running off, no one knew if you two were alive or dead. Then you pull that stunt in the lake. You really screwed him up. I actually hadn't heard my brother cry like that since he was a little boy, until you came along. Even when you got out, he couldn't bring himself to call or go see you. He blamed himself."

"I was sick, but not like your mom thought. I mean, it wasn't a stunt. I was in a hospital, Lauren," I said.

"You were sick alright," she said. "Not the virus, maybe, but you're still sick. So, no, I wouldn't want anything to do with you."

I was stunned that she was being so harsh. Couldn't she understand how I felt? I asked, "So there's no way for us to start over?"

"With what you did?" she asked. "I'm all set."

"Lauren, I'm sorry," I said.

"Apology accepted," she said. "But leave me alone, and stay away from my brother. One flirty word from you and he'd probably turn his life upside down again."

"I'm not like that. You have to know that," I said.

"Cel, I don't think I ever knew you," she said. "Now, are you going to leave me alone, or do I have to shop later?"

Not knowing what to say, I held my hands up, and softly said, "I'm really sorry." I left without looking back. Beginning to cry in the food court, my walk turned into a jog. By the time I was in the parking lot, I was running, and then I realized someone was running behind me. I slowed and turned, and saw it was Cole.

"Hey," he said, as we stopped.

Wiping my eyes, I asked, "Yeah?"

"So, she's just pissed and hurt. You know?"

"I know," I said. "Still, she didn't have to be that cold."

"She'll feel bad about it later," Cole said.

"Good," I said.

"C'mon, Cel. You two will figure it out. She's hurting and you're hurting. Just give it a little while."

I shrugged, and wiped more tears.

"I know what it's like," Cole said.

"What?"

"To be that alone. To be the only one," Cole said.

"Because you're Black, you mean?" I asked.

He raised one eyebrow. "Yeah, that," he said.

"How's it the same at all?" I asked.

"I didn't lose my parents, I know, but I know how lonely it is to be different," Cole said.

"People don't act racist with you. People are nice to you," I said.

"Imagine if you went to a restaurant or even the mall," he said, gesturing to the building, "and every single person inside was Black. Even if they were all nice to you."

That would be weird, I thought. "Awkward," I said.

"Life," Cole said. "So I get what it's like to be different, and for people to be afraid of you for no real reason."

I nodded and sniffled.

"Okay. I just wanted to say hey. I've gotta go back and find Lauren. I hope I'll see you around soon," he said.

He turned and jogged back into the mall. I walked a few steps and stopped near the cart corral, and through some fresh tears, I texted Deb that I was done and needed her to come get me.

She replied, *"Already?"*

I wrote, *"Please just come get me."*

I think she sensed something was wrong, because she didn't argue.

She replied, *"Be right there."*

Crossing the parking lot, I quietly cried as I walked down the road I knew I'd meet Deb on.

53

RAY AND I SAT IN the living room. He was lightly snoozing and I was shopping for clothes online, while *Family Feud* played on the television with the sound muted. Deb was out.

My phone vibrated; it was a message from Jackson.

"Hey, how about I buy you some fries at the mall. :)"

I felt warmth, grinned, and immediately began to respond that I'd love to go, but then I deleted my response without sending it. Smiling, I remembered the last time he bought me fries, his smile, and the way we'd laughed. Still, I put the phone down on the coffee table.

Just then, the doorbell rang, and I honestly wondered if Jackson was on the front step. Ray woke and slowly stood up. "I'll get it," he said.

When he opened the door, I could see Ray, but I couldn't see who it was.

A female voice said only, "Whoa."

"Can I help you?" Ray asked.

"Can you help me?" the female voice asked, mockingly. "What are you, like the butler or something?" I knew the voice.

Running to the door, I pushed Ray to one side. "Get outta the way!" I said.

There, on the porch, was none other than Tee.

"Hey!" I said.

"Hey yourself, let me in. I'm freezing my adorable ass off out here," Tee said.

"It's not that cold," I said, stepping aside so she could enter.

"Who's this?" Ray asked.

"Ray, this is Tee," I said.

"Hi Ray," said Tee. "You're kinda cute for an old guy, you know that?"

Ray's mouth fell open, and I hit her, open-handed, in the head.

"Ow, bitch," she said, rubbing her ear. "That hurt." She grinned.

"Don't be weird," I said.

"He's cute," Tee said, looking at Ray again.

Ray recovered, and said, "You're the crazy friend from the hospital that Cel was talking about."

"He's quick," Tee said. "And I'd point out that I wasn't the only crazy one in there."

"What are you doing here?" I asked, closing the door. I wanted to talk about the kiss Tee and I had shared my last day at Winter Harbor, but not in front of Ray.

"Well, I didn't escape from Winter Harbor, if that's what you mean," Tee said.

"No, I mean…" I said.

"I just thought it was time to see if I could find you. Well, first, I had to find Goodwin, Maine. It's not the easiest to find, you know, and then I got stuck on the stupid drawbridge. Then, I found my way here," Tee said.

Ray said, "You know, they've got GPS now."

She looked around me. "Yeah-no, you're not cute enough that you can start being a pain in the ass," Tee said.

I couldn't help but laugh. Ray shook his head and went to the couch.

"Have a seat," I said.

We all sat in the living room and caught up. Actually, anytime Ray tried to talk, Tee interrupted him… so Tee and I caught up. We laughed a lot, and even Ray laughed now and then.

"So, what have you been doing here?" she asked.

"Getting cleaned up. I have a great new shrink," I said.

"Is he hot?" Tee asked.

"Jesus, no, she's a she," I said.

"Is she hot?" Tee asked, and winked.

Grinning, I didn't answer, but I did feel a rush. Nora was pretty and all, but it was Tee that was hot. I mean, her personality alone was just so kick-ass.

"Okay, okay, so what's good about her?" Tee asked.

Shrugging, I said, "I don't know, she just gets me. I think part of it is I know she's smarter than I am."

"Whoa. You lucky shit," Tee said.

"I know, right?"

Ray said, "I don't get it."

Tee said, "I don't doubt it."

Laughing again, I said, "Tee, stop picking on Ray. He found my therapist for me."

Tee laughed, leaned forward toward Ray, bit her tongue between clenched teeth, stood up, and said, "Okay, let's go to dinner. On him. Let's go."

"But it's like 4 o'clock," Ray said. Tee shot him a look, and he said, "Okay, I'll get our jackets."

Tee and I moved to the rug at the door, and put on our shoes. Ray brought me my jacket, and before Ray had his on, she was out the door.

"Let's go!" she said.

Looking at Ray, I grinned, and asked, "Isn't she fun?"

His eyebrows went up, and he looked out at her on the sidewalk. He grinned, and said, "Yeah, she's something alright."

We stepped onto the porch.

"Should we give Deb a call? Maybe she could join us," Ray said.

"I don't think we should inflict Tee on Deb yet, do you?" I asked.

Ray laughed. "Probably not."

Tee pointed at her wrist and shouted, "C'mon! Pick up the pace!"

"Shut up, Tee! You don't even wear a watch!" I said.

Ray said, "I'll drive."

"Let's walk," Tee said.

"Well, there's really no place to eat around here," I said.

"Except for like hotdogs at the convenience store."

"Is there a microwave in there? And frozen burritos?" Tee asked.

"I don't know," I said.

"Yeah, there is," Ray said, with a huge smile on his face.

"Oh man, I could use a convenience store frozen burrito right now. Let's do it," Tee said. She moved between Ray and me, hooked arms with us, and we headed out.

"You're nuts," I said.

Tee laughed, drew a deep breath, and said, "So, Cel, where you going to go to school?"

"I'm going to get my GED instead," I said.

"I mean, like, college," Tee said. "My hometown is like two hours from here, and it has a great little university," she said.

Another rush of excitement. *Had she just invited me to…? To what? And why was I so happy about it?*

"Is that where you're going to go, Tee?" Ray asked.

"I'm not going to waste my money on college," Tee said. "But I thought maybe smarty-pants might."

Ray said, "Hey, you might save some money that way, Cel. You two could be roommates or something."

My face flushed hot. Tee leaned in hard, and in my ear breathed, "Or something." My knees almost buckled. Pulling me along, she giggled.

54

I T WAS FRIDAY AFTERNOON, AND a beautiful day. The air was cool and dry, and the leaves were beginning to hint at autumn color. The sky was so blue, and I could feel the sun's warmth on my shoulders. Reaching out toward the blue with both hands as I walked, I grinned.

I felt better, in every way. I'd had a dozen sessions with Nora, and they were helping. My drinking had slowed to a few beers on the weekends. I really didn't do drugs anymore. Some of my self-confidence had come back, and most important of all, I was beginning to make peace with myself.

When I entered Nora's office on that day, she had an extra computer monitor on a stand beside her desk.

"Are we going to watch *Good Will Hunting* or something? Make a breakthrough?" I asked. I wasn't being a bitch; we'd gotten to the point where we could tease each other.

"Have a seat, Cel," she said. She sat behind her desk and typed a few keystrokes. I watched the screen, and a single grey panel appeared, like in my old group sessions, but instead of a name beneath the panel, it read only, "Guest."

"Who is it?" I asked.

The face appeared. It was the astrobiologist who served as team leader while aboard the *Phaeacia*.

Instantly nervous, I smiled in spite of myself. "Hi, Dr. Stenhouse."

"Good afternoon, Celestine," he said.

Looking to Nora, I asked, "What's up?"

Nora said, "Talk to him, not me. But if at any point you've had enough, let me know."

She was smart, letting me talk to Stenhouse in the comfort of the trust I had for her. Nora had my back.

"Celestine, how are you?" Dr. Stenhouse asked.

"I'm doing pretty good," I said. "How are you doing?"

"Well, thank you," he said.

It was quiet for a moment, and so I asked, "Is there something I can do for you? Did you want to ask me something?"

"Ask you something?" he asked.

"Cel, he's here to answer your questions," Nora said. "Anything you want to ask. I feel like you've made some progress. You can begin to ask questions so you can continue to try to make sense of the most consequential part of your life so far."

"My questions?" I asked. "I don't know what to ask."

"You may ask me anything," Dr. Stenhouse said.

I glanced at Nora, and she nodded.

"What do you think I should know?" I asked. "Let's start with whatever you most want to tell me."

Dr. Stenhouse smiled, and he visibly relaxed. He said, "Alright then, let me tell you who your parents really were. Let me tell you about my friends, Peter and Mary Tolland, and how they—and you—came to sign up for a very special mission."

I leaned forward, with my elbows on my knees. Nora leaned way back in her chair, and put her feet up on her desk. Dr. Stenhouse took a deep breath and began to tell the story.

Epilogue

THE FIRST DRAFT OF THIS novel was completed in May 2015, years before the coronavirus pandemic. In October 2020, with the novel under contract, I made some updates to acknowledge the reality through which we have all been living. As a student and teacher of history, I find it is truly remarkable how world events can suddenly change how we judge a person's words and actions. A character who once seemed unduly worried about something becomes suddenly reasonable, and the opposite is true as well. History, once read, can certainly be reaffirming and/or humbling. I hope the core story I tried to tell in *Celestine* ages well.

I'd love to know what you thought of this novel, and honest reviews help other readers find the right book. Please feel invited and appreciated for any review you leave for all of us to read.

Acknowledgments

TO ALL MY CHILDREN—WHO PROVIDED inspiration and great ideas.

Eddie Vincent, Cynthia Brackett-Vincent, and the entire Encircle team, thank you so much for so much.

Deirdre Wait, whose cover art for my novels, and her positive energy, are always a terrific part of the process.

Taylor Connell, who, throughout the first half of the manuscript, was what Stephen King called an "IR" or ideal reader, and who was usually first to see the newest drafts of chapters and provided crucial help.

Nylah Lyman, who read the entire first draft of the manuscript, and gave some of the first comprehensive feedback.

Victoria Sanders, who believed in this novel in ways no one else did. She did so much to help it become what it is, and her friendship is treasured.

Lauren Stetson Dezileau, without whom a huge part of this novel could not have been written.

Shelley Burbank, Emma Cost, Emily Marquis, Caroline Murphy, Madeline Bauman, Ashley Bomba, and Olivia Bradley who all provided great feedback.

Joyce Nadeau, whose professional advice and wonderful sense of humor helped me through the crazy parts. C'etait bien fun.

Dr. Sara Zwart, who works for NASA, and who was generous with her time and help.

Arabica Coffee Shop on Free Street in Portland, Maine. Good coffee and cool places really help. A lot of this novel was written in the back, on the raised portion, at a corner table, which has since been removed.

Café Younes Beirut, Lebanon. It's the one around the corner from AUB. A great space, with good coffee and food. It was lovely writing there.

La Muse Artists & Writers Retreat in Labastide Esparbairenque, just outside of Carcassonne, France. This lovely centuries-old manor in the mountains, with its wonderful community of artists, was the perfect place to get away and work. Ask for the Calliope suite.

About the Author

KEVIN ST. JARRE is the author of *Aliens, Drywall, and a Unicycle*, his first novel with Encircle Publications. He previously penned three original thriller novels for Berkley Books, the Night Stalkers series, under a pseudonym. He's a published poet, his pedagogical essays have run in *English Journal* and thrice in *Phi Delta Kappan*, and his short fiction has appeared in journals such as *Story*.

He has worked as a teacher and professor, a newspaper reporter, an international corporate consultant, and he led a combat intelligence team in the first Gulf War. Kevin is a polyglot, and he earned an MFA in Creative Writing with a concentration in Popular Fiction from University of Southern Maine's Stonecoast program. Twice awarded scholarships, he studied at the Norman Mailer Writers Center on Cape Cod, MA, with Sigrid Nunez and David Black, and wrote in southern France at La Muse Artists & Writers Retreat.

He is a member of MWPA and the International Thriller Writers. Born in Pittsfield, Massachusetts, Kevin grew up in

Maine's northernmost town, Madawaska. He now lives on the Maine coast, and is always working on the next novel. Follow Kevin at www.facebook.com/kstjarre and on Twitter @kstjarre.

If you enjoyed reading this book,
please consider writing your honest review
and sharing it with other readers.

Many of our Authors are happy to participate in
Book Club and Reader Group discussions.
For more information, contact us at info@encirclepub.com.

Thank you,
Encircle Publications

For news about more exciting new fiction, join us at:

Facebook: www.facebook.com/encirclepub

Twitter: twitter.com/encirclepub

Instagram: www.instagram.com/encirclepublications

Sign up for Encircle Publications newsletter and specials:
eepurl.com/cs8taP

CPSIA information can be obtained
at www.ICGtesting.com
Printed in the USA
BVHW072334110521
607042BV00003B/229